"Would yo[...] ten her lips, and [...] tongue sensually caressing her lips made him feel like begging indeed. "Would you see them all snicker at me over your obvious cut? Regardless of what they say about you, surely not even you are that cruel."

"What do they say about me?" he challenged.

"I know that you are Armond Wulf—one of the wild Wulfs of London. The oldest of four. Feared by men. Forbidden to women. A man no decent young debutante would associate with."

Armond blinked down at her. "And you want to dance with me?"

She straightened her shoulders and thrust out her breasts, he supposed in a show of courage. His gaze lowered to those twin mounds on the verge of spilling forth, and his hands itched to catch them.

"I more than want to dance with you, Lord Wulf," she announced. "I'd be most grateful if you'd ruin my reputation."

~

"This story hooked me from page one and never let me go. I can't wait for the next one!"
—Amanda Ashley

The Dark One

Book One in the
Wild Wulfs of London series

Ronda Thompson

St. Martin's Paperbacks

THE DARK ONE

Copyright © 2005 by Ronda Thompson.

Cover photo © Herman Estevez

ISBN: 0-312-93573-0
EAN: 9780312-93573-3

Printed in the United States of America

St. Martin's Paperbacks edition / November 2005

St. Martin's Paperbacks are published by St. Martin's Press, 175 Fifth Avenue, New York, NY 10010.

10 9 8 7 6 5 4 3

This book is dedicated to my fellow cubbies: Marilynn Byerly, Barbara Cary, Susanne Marie Knight, Diane Drew, Delores Fossen, Debbie Gafford, Liz George, Katherine Greyle, Anita Lynn, Kathy Ishcomer, Katriena Knights, Gael Morrison, Norah-Jean Perkin, Laura Renken, Catherine Sellers, Patricia White, and Karen Woods. Your support over the years, your willingness to share your knowledge and expertise, but most of all your friendship, have meant more to me than you will ever know. Rock on, Ladies!

Special Acknowledgments

To Linda Kruger for being there for me, sharing in my dreams and believing in my talent. You were a great agent, but you're an even greater mom.

To Monique Patterson, my editor, for seeing something special in me. You're the best!

Damn the witch who cursed me.
I thought her heart was pure.
Alas, no woman understands duty,
be it to family, name, or war.
I found no way to break it,
no potion, chant, or deed.
From the day she cast the spell,
it will pass from seed to seed.

Betrayed by love, my own false tongue,
she bade the moon transform me.
The family name, once my pride,
becomes the beast that haunts me.
And in the witch's passing hour
she called me to her side.
Forgiveness lost, of mercy none,
she spoke before she died:

"Seek you and find your worst enemy,
stand brave and do not flee.
Love is the curse that binds you,
but 'tis also the key to set you free."

Her curse and riddle my bane,
this witch I loved yet could not wed.
Battles I have fought and won,
and still defeat I leave in my stead.
To the Wulfs who suffer my sins,
the sons who are neither man nor beast,
solve the conundrum I could not
and be from this curse released.

Ivan Wulf,
In the year of our Lord seventeen hundred and fifteen

Chapter One

His heart was the deepest, darkest chasm of hell. A cold, bitter place where dreams and hopes had long since been laid to rest. And without dreams, without hope, why did he bother? Armond Wulf, the Marquess of Wulfglen, Earl of Bumont, moved freely among society, but only as a ghost—a dark presence who haunted the shadows of the living—waiting, always waiting, for the sins of the past to catch up with him.

Although titled and wealthy, the Wulf family was cursed, their futures bleak. Men were born to take chances, to test the limits of their strengths and their weaknesses. He could do neither. A normal existence for him was out of the question. Survival alone kept him shuffling along. One foot in front of the other. Trudging mindlessly forward to no particular destination. Oh, to hell with it, even he was not in the mood for his dark thoughts.

Nor was he enthused to find himself standing alone at the Greenleys' first ball of the season, forced out among society by boredom—no, not boredom, he admitted, but a simple need to feel life teeming around him. No one dared approach him. He was a man cloaked in mystery, murder, and madness. But still only a man . . . at least for the time being.

The sound of feminine giggles reached Armond's over-sensitive ears. That he was the object of several women's attention did not go unnoticed by him. He couldn't ignore the scent of their attraction, the earthy smell of woman's musk hidden from most by a liberal dousing of rose water.

If he closed his eyes and concentrated, he could hear the excited flutter of their hearts, the blood that rushed through their veins. But Armond did not torture himself with his strange gifts. He'd accepted his lot in life, his position among society, or, rather, his lack of it.

Regardless of his dark appeal to the ladies, none were brave enough to approach him. He supposed it was another curse he must suffer . . . or perhaps simply a consequence of the one that already rested upon his head. The family curse. A Wulf's curse.

"Lord Wulf, good to see you, my boy. But why are you here alone sulking about? You should be chasing young women or at least in one of the back rooms playing cards with the older gentlemen."

A rare smile shaped Armond's lips. He glanced down into the Dowager Duchess of Brayberry's faded eyes. The lady was an old family friend and the only blue-blooded woman in London who wasn't too leery to approach him. She enjoyed causing a stir among society by refusing to shun him as everyone else did. And for that he was grateful.

"The trouble with chasing young women these days, Your Grace, is that they simply refuse to run," he teased. "The old men in the back rooms are even less sport. They might as well hand me their money and be done with it."

Her cackling laugh rose above the din of conversation, and she swatted him with her fan. "You are the devil, Armond, my boy. Even if you do look like an angel. It's the contrast, I think," she added, running her faded eyes over him, "that the ladies find fascinating."

It was his indifference, and Armond well knew it. All he had to do was act truly interested in a society miss and she'd run for the hills. His family background, the rumors, the mystery, the intrigue of it all, was what drew women to him like a moth to flame—but also kept them at a safe distance.

"Have you met your new neighbor?" the dowager cut into his thoughts. Her hair was thinning, he noticed from his superior height above her. He saw her scalp beneath the thin gray strands scraped back from her face.

Armond wasn't aware that he had a new neighbor. He didn't even know the last one. Chapman, he believed his name was, and neither had spoken one word to each other since the man and his mother first took up residence at the townhome ten years prior.

"Has Chapman sold the house?"

She shook her balding head. "It isn't his to sell. His mother, the duchess, was given the house by her late husband, the Duke of Montrose. During your absence, Chapman's stepsister has come to live with him. The girl's been hidden away in the country for most of her life. Now that her father has passed, she must take her place among society. She's an heiress. Sure to be plain if she has money. But you might have a chance with her."

"A chance to do what?" he asked drily. "If it's not something indecent, as you well know, given my dark reputation, I'm not interested."

Her thin lips twitched even as she pretended to find his response shocking. "Naughty boy. I'm speaking of a possible match. You still retain titles, estates, and wealth. I don't care what society has decided; a girl could do worse. If you were to sweep down upon her and steal her heart with those wasted good looks of yours before she's been here long enough to hear the rumors about your poor family, you might have a chance with her."

In the same dry tone, he asked, "And what makes you believe they are only rumors? Perhaps we Wulfs are all as mad as toads."

She swatted him again, but a little too hard to be counted as playful. "Rubbish. You and your wild brothers are not the least bit insane. What a perfect scheme to remain bachelors and keep the women falling at your feet at the same time."

Women hardly fell at his feet . . . unless they were dying. And it was not that one brother in particular had decided upon their current course of action, but it was an agreement made by all of them. All save Sterling, the youngest, and he'd fled London shortly after the curse first visited the Wulf household. The remaining brothers, Armond, Gabriel, and Jackson, had made a pact—none of them would ever give his heart to a woman.

Love was supposedly the curse and the key. Whatever the hell that meant. All they'd found of any reference to the curse upon their family was a faded poem tucked away inside of a book once belonging to their father. There was a riddle there, Armond supposed, although none of them had been able to decipher the message.

The dowager needed reminding that he and his brothers had more to deal with in society's eyes. "And what of the other matter?" he asked. "The one that took place only eight months ago? The one involving murder?"

The twinkle in the dowager's eyes dimmed. She glanced around as if afraid their conversation would be overheard. "You do yourself no good stirring that dark pot again, Lord Wulf. It was your misfortune to find the poor girl. No one could prove a thing. You and your brothers all had alibis. What you need is a wife. A nice society girl who will disprove these dark rumors about your family. Your parents, God have mercy upon their souls, might have been insane, but I see nothing but intelligence in your eyes. Why invite their sins upon yourself? Let the past die. Get on with your life. Prove the snobs wrong."

But that was the problem. Society wasn't wrong about Armond. True, he didn't murder the poor woman he'd found dying in his stable eight months ago, but he wasn't positive that her blood didn't stain his family name. What if one of his brothers had been lying? And what if the woman had been planted there purposely, to bring even darker sins upon the Wulf brothers?

Armond had spent the past few months trying to prove his family's innocence regarding the matter, but the trail to find the woman's murderer had grown cold. Society was right about their parents, however. They had both gone insane; society just didn't know what had pushed them over the edge to madness. Armond knew. All of his brothers knew.

"Lord Wulf?"

The sound of his name being spoken interrupted Armond's conversation with the dowager. The lady who'd spoken stood behind him and her voice raised hackles on the back of his neck. Something in her tone, the softness of it, the slightly husky texture of it, flowed over and around him, inside of him, and touched a nerve. He turned slowly and came face-to-face with ruin.

Whoever the vision in white before him was, she was pure sin packaged deceitfully in the guise of innocence. If ever a woman existed who could make a man forget his principles, his pledges, his dark promises, this was one. Armond's blood turned to fire, his groin tightened, and heaven help the lady, she managed to do what none before her had accomplished. In the space of a heartbeat, she totally captivated him.

"I hate to be forward," the young woman said. "But I

cannot find anyone to provide me with a proper introduction to you. I fear I am forced to take matters into my own hands."

Armond had something he'd like for her to take into her hands . . . and her mouth and the deepest, sweetest part of her. Words failed him. He could only stare . . . mesmerized.

Her hair was the color of midnight. Her lips, full, red, ripe, inviting, would tempt a saint. Eyes the purest shade of violet, and slightly slanted, stared up at him from thick, dark lashes. Her skin was pale, soft and smooth— creamy as the froth on the top of a bucket of milk. He wanted her immediately. Not a reaction a man who prided himself on control cared to admit.

"You are forward, dear," the dowager said, since Armond's voice seemed to have deserted him. "I daresay whatever finishing school you've spent time in has failed you miserably."

Still staring boldly up at him, the young woman replied, "I've resided in the country for most of my life. Forgive my rude manners, but time is of importance. I require Lord Wulf's assistance in a matter of urgency."

With his blood on fire, his senses reeling, Armond momentarily forgot his vows, his pacts, his pledges. This was a woman who could have the world at her feet if she but crooked her little finger, and she needed his assistance? What could he possibly do for her that her flawless complexion, her lustrous dark hair, and her sinful mouth could not?

He managed, with difficulty, to slow his racing heart and present a false facade of control. "How may I assist you, Miss . . . ?"

"Rutherford," she provided, her voice a tad breathless. "Lady Rosalind Rutherford."

"Ah, your new neighbor," the dowager interrupted,

reminding Armond that the old woman still stood a party to their conversation. "The young heiress I was just telling you about, Armond."

"The breeding stock," Lady Rosalind corrected, and then blushed as if she realized she'd revealed her resentment. She quickly recovered. "Since we are indeed neighbors, Lord Wulf, I don't feel that it would be inappropriate if we danced together."

His complete attention focused upon the young lady, Armond hadn't noticed that the music had begun. His thoughts ran rampant with all the things he'd like to do to and with Rosalind Rutherford, but dancing did not top his list.

Armond never danced. There didn't seem to be a point. Men only danced to please women or to woo or seduce them. He had no intention of doing any of those things. Or he hadn't up until tonight.

He couldn't keep his eyes from roaming her generous curves, curves displayed a bit scandalously by the low cut of her neckline. She noticed his interest and possibly the lust he felt certain was stamped across his face and took an involuntary step back, which proved she had a measure of common sense. Then she straightened her shoulders and stepped forward again, which was the worst thing she could have done.

His infatuation grew, if indeed, infatuation could be likened to the reaction taking place in the front of his trousers, which in this instance seemed to be the case. What was she doing to him? Whatever it was, he had to put a stop to it.

"I'm sorry, Lady Rosalind, but I do not dance, and I am not the neighborly sort." He thought to rudely turn away from her, but she touched his arm.

The slight contact sent a jolt through him. His senses sharpened to a painful point. Armond was aware of everything about her—even the fast pulse beating at the base of her throat. Especially the fast pulse beating at the base of her throat. She was frightened but determined, and again, the combination intrigued him.

Armond allowed the young woman to pull him a short distance from the dowager, who pouted over being denied further witness to the conversation.

"Would you make me beg?" She paused to moisten her lips, and the sight of her small pink tongue sensually caressing her lips made him feel like begging indeed. "Would you see them all snicker at me over your obvious cut? Regardless of what they say about you, surely not even you are that cruel."

"What do they say about me?" he challenged. If she knew much, she knew that according to rumor, Lord Wulf had no qualms about making women beg, and that a suspected murderer, a man cursed by insanity, could hardly be expected to possess a trait like compassion.

"I know that you are Armond Wulf, the Marquess of Wulfglen—one of the wild Wulfs of London. The oldest of four. Feared by men. Forbidden to women. A man no decent young debutante would associate with."

Armond blinked down at her. "And you want to dance with me?"

She straightened her shoulders and thrust out her breasts, he supposed in a show of courage. His gaze lowered to those twin mounds on the verge of spilling forth, and his hands itched to catch them.

"I more than want to dance with you, Lord Wulf," she announced. "I'd be most grateful if you'd ruin my reputation."

Armond struggled to maintain his bored expression, although he felt as if one of his spirited horses had just kicked him in the gut. "Here?" he asked.

The lady tilted her dimpled chin up to him. "Now," she insisted. "This very night. In this very room in front of all these people."

Was this some bizarre dream? Armond was almost tempted to pinch himself. Women didn't proposition him, at least not *this* kind of woman. Lady Rosalind Rutherford, tempting morsel that she was, was either as insane as his family was rumored to be, or up to something. He glanced away from her sinful mouth and tried to gain control of himself. It was something he did well . . . control.

He didn't lose his head over dark-haired angels. Losing one's head could go hand in hand with losing one's heart, and Armond couldn't afford to do that . . . ever.

"Did you hear me, Lord Wulf?"

Since it seemed as if everyone in the grand ballroom had ceased their own business and now stared at them, Armond took her arm and steered her toward the dance floor. Her waist was incredibly small beneath his hand. He swept her into the dance.

People were shocked, as they should be, to see a Wulf dancing, but Armond tried to concentrate on the steps so long ago taught to him. He was surprised that he remembered, but he did, and together, he and the young lady twirled, their bodies in perfect accord, almost as if one were an extension of the other.

"You dance very well," his new neighbor commented, nibbling at her full lower lip. "But I had hoped for more."

"More?" He suddenly felt like an idiot who couldn't string an intelligent sentence together in her presence.

"You're holding me quite properly," she pointed out. "Given your reputation, I assumed you'd be less formal. There's not much to find shocking about your manners."

Armond felt it was his duty to enlighten her upon the subject. "The fact alone that you are dancing with me, I as-

sure you, is shock enough for those present this evening."
When his comment didn't seem to satisfy her, he asked,
"Would you have me ravish you?"

Her raven brows, perfectly set upon her forehead, furrowed. She pressed her lips together as if in consideration. "I had hoped to avoid such drastic measures but now
realize that might indeed become necessary. Could you? I
mean, would you mind terribly?"

He nearly missed a step. *Would he mind?* Was the young
lady daft? No, she wasn't daft; her lovely eyes sparkled
with intelligence.

"What game are you playing, Lady Rosalind?"

Rather than answer, she scanned the crowd. He naturally did likewise, his gaze falling upon a group of young
debutantes staring at them, their faces flushed with obvious excitement over seeing him dance. Was her earlier
approach some sort of bet among friends? A dare? Had
she decided to make her debut into society on a grand
scale?

Perhaps she simply wanted notice—a night that would
set her apart from every other beautiful, eligible young
lady who'd come for a season in London.

"My wishes are most sincere, Lord Wulf," she said, her
gaze returning to him. "I am very disappointed in your
good manners thus far this evening. Your reputation falls
short of my expectations. If you have no desire to assist
me, perhaps I should find someone who will."

His infatuation diminished somewhat. Armond had
spent the past ten years being the brunt of society's jokes.
He didn't mind being feared or whispered about, but
he wouldn't be made to look the fool. When the lady
started to pull away, as if she meant to leave him standing alone like a throwaway, he jerked her up flush against
him.

"If it's compromised you want, you've come to the

right man," he assured her. "And I promise that you won't be disappointed. There's nothing short about me, Lady Rosalind."

He steered her toward the edge of the dance floor, plans of where they could find privacy uppermost on his mind. Lady Rosalind had foolishly fired his ardor. She had thrown down a gauntlet, and if she wanted something to giggle about with her silly friends, he'd damn sure give it to her.

right men," he argued. "And I do hate that you won't be disappointed. There's nothing short about me, Lady Rosalind."

He settled her toward the edge of the cushioned seat, and she felt almost bereft as the warmth of his body left her. The carriage door opened, and the light of the moon bathed her in a silver glow. She had rarely known gumption, and it had proved worth its weight in gold. There, no more than inches from her face,

Chapter Two

Lord Wulf led her through two side doors left open to allow the night air into the stuffy ballroom. Dazed by her own daring, Rosalind followed him past a small garden and out to the street, where carriages sat lined and waiting for their occupants to return from the ball. Her heart pounded so loud and fast she thought it might leap from her chest. Despite her bold actions, her knees shook. She was desperate, and desperation could often be disguised as bravery.

When Rosalind had first spotted Armond Wulf among the guests at the Greenleys' ball, she imagined her mouth might have dropped open and drool might have dribbled down her chin. She'd never seen a more handsome man. He was tall but lean, like a great hunting cat. His hair brushed the shoulders of his finely cut coat and was a rich golden color, reminding her of her home in the country, of wheat ripening in the fields. His eyes were blue—dark, turbulent like the sky during a thunderstorm.

His face was finely etched, his jaw strong and square. His mouth could only be described as disturbing, his lips neither too full nor too thin but sensually shaped. His brows and lashes were surprisingly dark for a man with his blond coloring, and his skin was tawny colored, as if he spent a great deal of time out-of-doors. When

he'd arrived at the Greenleys', every woman in the ballroom had turned to admire him. . . . Then the whispers
began.

Once she'd learned his name, Rosalind realized he was
the neighbor her stepbrother, Franklin, had warned to stay
clear of. Wulf had been missing since her arrival in London, but his return tonight couldn't have worked out better for her. Rosalind had formed a plan. A plan to ruin her
stepbrother's schemes for her and, she hoped, to find herself banished back to her late father's country estate, where
she longed to return.

"Thomas, jump down and find something to do," Wulf
called to the driver upon reaching his carriage.

Rosalind's cheeks blazed. What must the driver think?
She couldn't worry about that. Not at this point.

"For how long, Your Lordship?" the man asked.

Wulf ran his stormy blue gaze the length of Rosalind
and back again. "For a while."

Nervous, Rosalind glanced behind them toward the
house. Franklin might come looking for her and spoil
everything. "Could we drive during, that is, while we . . ."
She couldn't complete the question.

"Interesting," he said. "Change of plans, Thomas. Take
us around a few times; then bring us back when you hear
me rap upon the ceiling."

Thomas nodded. "Briggs is off sharing a pint with a
few of the other footmen. Should I get the door for you,
My Lord?"

"No." Wulf opened the carriage door and, rather than
assist Rosalind up, lifted her in a no-nonsense manner
and deposited her inside. He climbed in and slammed the
door.

The moment grew awkward. Rosalind had no idea
what to expect. She sensed that Lord Wulf was angry, but
angry about what? She'd offered herself to him. Wasn't

that what all men wanted? To climb beneath a woman's skirts given the first opportunity?

According to her stepbrother, that was exactly what men wanted. The carriage lurched forward. Rosalind glanced at the door. They weren't moving fast enough to cause her serious injury were she to jump.

"You have made your bed now. You'll have to lie in it."

She looked at him. The interior of the carriage was dark, the lamps unlit, and she couldn't see his expression. "My offer was sincere. I will see my end of the bargain fulfilled."

Lord Wulf sighed. "We are no longer within eyesight of anyone at the Greenleys'. No need to keep up the pretense."

Pretense? Had he mistaken her invitation? Rosalind needed him to perform a service and thought he understood the exchange. He'd looked at her as if he was willing enough earlier. Everywhere his eyes had touched she'd burned, not with the heat of embarrassment but with something else. Something her sheltered existence had not prepared her for. Something wicked.

"But you should learn that not all men are to be toyed with. Me being one of them."

So, he didn't believe the offer she'd made was a serious one? Of course he wouldn't. Rosalind supposed it was a rare occasion for a lady of good breeding to approach a man and request that he ruin her reputation. Perhaps there was still a chance to rescue herself from the path she'd taken.

"Maybe I should have given the matter more thought," she admitted. In the darkness, she cut her eyes toward him. "If we return in all haste, our absence might go unnoticed."

He laughed, but the response did not sound sincere. "No chance of that happening now. You wanted to create a scandal, Lady Rosalind, and you did. And you used me for whatever gain it is you hope to secure yourself. Although for the life of me, I can't figure out what that might be. Perhaps you will enlighten me upon the matter?"

Rosalind couldn't. It was none of his business really. She'd only given him one task to perform; after that, she need never see him again. But she had approached him with her own gain in mind. The return of her freedom. Escape from her stepbrother and his foul plans for her. Escape from Franklin at any cost.

Her courage renewed, Rosalind said, "I'm surprised that you'd demand explanations, Lord Wulf. I doubt that another man would." She felt rather than saw him turn to look at her. Even though she knew he could not see her, she raised her chin. "I thought that I could count upon you. You—"

His mouth suddenly found hers in the darkness. She'd been speaking, so her lips were parted. Rosalind tried to clamp them shut, but he captured her chin, holding her in a way that didn't allow her to shut him out. He tasted like champagne and fresh strawberries.

The kiss was punishing, as if to teach her the lesson he'd claimed she needed to learn. Rosalind's natural instinct was to struggle. A small whimper of fear escaped into his open mouth. Suddenly he pulled back, staring down at her.

"You're hurting me," she whispered.

He released his firm hold upon her chin. His fingertips grazed her cheek, as soft as the flutter of a butterfly's wings. Slowly, his face bent toward her again. The brush of his lips against hers this time was gentle. She found the sudden contrast more disturbing than she had his brute force. Rosalind was accustomed to abuse. She was not schooled in seduction. But he obviously was.

His tongue traced the line of her bottom lip, warm,

moist, seeking. Some instinct uncurled within her and she opened wider to him. His tongue slipped into her mouth, teasing, exploring, evoking shocking sensations that she had never felt before.

"God, you're sweet," he said against her lips, and the husky timbre of his voice sent heat racing to her most private places.

When he captured her lips again, she let him guide her, followed his example, and reveled in the way their lips merged perfectly together. Rosalind had only been kissed once—the gardener's son when she was twelve. Her first kiss had been awkward and unimpressive. This was nothing like that. This was like nothing she'd ever experienced or even imagined.

He slanted his mouth across hers and deepened the kiss, and her arms crept up around his neck, her fingers twining in his long, silky hair. She had trouble catching a normal breath, as did he, for the sound of their ragged breathing filled the silent carriage. She was suddenly hot all over and she didn't mind what he did to her. She didn't mind it at all.

The carriage hit a rut and bounced them apart. Rosalind landed against the seat on her back, but he was there a second later, nearly on top of her. She couldn't say why the sight of him looming over her, his face hidden by shadows, excited her. Only that it did. He'd unleashed something that had been slumbering inside of her for years, and she had no idea how to call sanity back. He bent toward her.

His teeth grazed her neck, sending shivers down her spine. He paused against the strong pulse beating at the base of her throat. That he should do so momentarily alarmed her; she didn't know why. Then he captured her mouth again, and all thoughts of fear fled.

When he suddenly cupped her breasts, Rosalind regained a little of the good sense he'd stolen from her. She nearly jerked away from him. A foolish response, she admitted a moment later. If she couldn't allow him to touch her intimately, how in heaven's name could she allow him to despoil her?

Determined to see her reputation ruined, she kept still. He kissed her again—a long, languid kiss that almost made her forget where his hands rested . . . almost. His thumb dipped inside of her low-cut gown and grazed her nipple. She jerked automatically, but the response did not deter him. Slowly, his thumb circled her nipple until the crest hardened into a tight pebble. The sensation drew a soft moan from her lips. Her back arched, as if she could force herself more firmly against his hand.

Her mind fogged by passion, she didn't realize that he slid the straps of her gown off her shoulders until the night air caressed her fevered flesh. She immediately tried to raise her arms and cover her exposed breasts. He anticipated her reaction and captured her wrists, pulling them up over her head.

"Are you afraid of me?" he asked.

"Yes," Rosalind wanted to answer, but then no, that wasn't entirely the truth. "I'm afraid of what you make me feel," she answered.

"Do you want me to stop?"

Again, her first response was to answer, "Yes." His voice, naturally deep, had lowered an octave. The sound of it skittered along her nerve endings and brought a desperate longing. She had longed before, for home, for family, but never for a man. She should tell him to stop, but she had to fight the morals taught to her. Rosalind couldn't stop him if she truly wanted to foil her chances of making a suitable match. What man in his right mind would have her once it became common knowledge that she'd been ruined?

"No. Please don't stop."

He hesitated long enough to worry her. What if he refused? What would she do then? And how humiliating to offer herself to a man who didn't want her. When he didn't continue, she worried that the problem might not be with her but with him. She'd heard of such things.

"Do you have a problem with your . . ." She wasn't sure what to call it.

"Conscience?" he asked.

She felt exposed, lying half-naked beneath him. The issue needed to be resolved, and quickly. There was no point in barking up the wrong tree.

"Can you not perform?"

He pressed against her. "No. I don't have a problem."

Armond Wulf might not have a problem, but she suddenly did. His had not been an idle boast earlier. There was nothing short about him. She swallowed down her sudden trepidation.

"Please continue then," she urged him.

Slowly, he lowered his head to her breasts. He took her hard nipple into the warm, wet recesses of his mouth and sucked. She nearly came up off the coach seat. He held her down and sampled one breast, then the other. His tongue did indecently sensual things to her nipples, circling, swirling, then again, drawing her deep into his mouth to suck.

Her stomach muscles tightened, as if his mouth drawing against her breasts was somehow connected to the response. Even lower, she felt wet, hot between her legs. She arched up against him and would have tangled her fingers in his hair had her arms not been pinned at her sides. He moved back up to kiss her again. As his tongue moved deeper into her mouth, his hips pressed against hers, creating a sensual rhythm that left her breathless, shaken, desperate for something more.

She throbbed for him—ached, lusted, fell into a deep abyss of sensation, aware only of him, of her, of their heated responses to each other. He tugged at her gown, settling it farther down her waist.

In the darkness, he left her, sitting to struggle with his stock, then tugging his fine lawn shirt from his snug trousers. All the while he tugged, he stared at her. Rosalind couldn't see his features clearly in the carriage's dark interior, but oddly enough, she saw his eyes.

They glowed . . . like the night eyes of an animal. Gooseflesh rose on her arms. Her hand snaked up to shield her throat, perhaps in an unconscious gesture.

The light from a street lamp suddenly threw the carriage's dim interior into stark brightness. She saw him clearly in the flash. He was still breathtakingly handsome, his shirt gaping open to reveal smooth, tawny flesh, but his eyes, they had not changed. They were filled with a radiant blue light. She gasped at the strange sight. Abruptly he looked away from her; then he took his cane and rapped sharply upon the ceiling.

"Cover yourself."

He practically growled the words at her. Rosalind scrambled up, embarrassed that the street lamp had revealed her half-naked state to him a moment earlier. She pulled her gown up over her breasts, dazed by what had just happened between them . . . and by what had not happened.

"When we return, you are to go directly to your carriage and ask your driver to see you home," he instructed. "You are to speak to no one. I will have a message sent to your stepbrother. You became ill, understand? You had your driver take you home as soon as I saw you safely to your carriage."

She paused in her flustered attempts to right her appearance. He gave her an alibi she didn't want. "Are you saying that I should lie about where I've been and what I've been doing?"

Straightening his own clothing, he responded, "Only to those of importance. By all means, share your experiences with your young friends in secret. I hope I gave you what you wanted."

He had not. She was still as chaste as when she'd left the Greenleys' ball with him. Chaste if not untouched. And Rosalind had no friends to share her secrets with. What did he imply, and worse, why wouldn't he finish what he started?

"You don't want me," she suddenly understood. Something about her had repulsed him. Perhaps her boldness with him.

Wulf turned to look at her, but she couldn't see his eyes this time in the darkness. She wondered if she'd seen them glowing oddly to begin with. Maybe it had been a trick of the moonlight.

"The game is up, Lady Rosalind." His tone was cold, though she still felt his body heat curling around her. "I played along. I've given you gossip to tell your spineless little friends. I've made your debut into society a memorable one. Be glad that I didn't give you more than you bargained for."

The carriage came to a halt. He jumped out and held the door for her. Rosalind let him assist her down, too confused to do anything but follow his lead. Her knees were weak, a reaction from either the passion they had shared or dread of facing the consequences of her actions. Armond steered her along the line of waiting carriages.

"Which one is it?"

Still dazed, Rosalind merely nodded to a coach directly ahead. He escorted her to the vehicle, opened the door, and helped her inside. She thought he would simply slam the door in her face and leave, but he paused, looking up at her from the ground outside.

"Good night, Lady Rosalind. The pleasure was . . . well, mostly mine anyway."

He slammed the door. Rosalind heard him instruct her driver to take her home. The carriage lumbered forward. She scrambled toward the window, threw back the drapes, and stuck her head outside. Armond still stood where she'd left him, watching the coach depart.

Their gazes locked. She saw the fading embers of desire still burning in his eyes, the rapid rise and fall of his chest, as if he still battled with himself. She might be innocent, but her innocence was fast fading. He wanted her. Then why had he stopped when he did? Why hadn't he taken what she had offered him?

Despite the rumors about him, did he indeed have a sense of decency? Had he stopped because he still followed a code of ethics a society that had all but deserted him had laid down? If so, she'd chosen wrongly tonight. If so, he had been fooling the ton for a good long while. Anger replaced her confusion and the passion still burning beneath her skin.

He had toyed with her. Worse, he had ruined her plans and she would face serious consequences for her actions tonight. But not serious enough to see her sent back to the country in shame, as she had hoped.

"There was one rumor that I didn't hear about you tonight, Lord Wulf," she said to herself. "No one told me that you were a coward."

Chapter Three

The force of the slap made her stumble backward. Rosalind brought a hand to her stinging cheek. Tears of pain and humiliation burned her eyes.

"How dare you behave as you did this evening!" Franklin Chapman thundered. "You were supposed to be securing yourself a rich and titled husband, not creating a scandal with the likes of Armond Wulf!"

"It was only a dance," Rosalind whispered. What would Franklin do if he knew the whole of what had taken place between her and Lord Wulf? Despite the consequences, she would tell Franklin if she had for a fact been successful in her plans, but she had not been and saw no reason to suffer her stepbrother's wrath without good cause.

Franklin had been banished from her life when Rosalind was a child. He'd been a nasty young man; he was a nastier adult. Now her father was no longer alive to protect her from Franklin. Her stepbrother considered it Rosalind's duty to restore a family fortune that he had recklessly squandered . . . her own inheritance.

Marrying her off to a wealthy man for a high bride's price was the easiest solution . . . at least in her stepbrother's eyes. Rosalind didn't mind the thought of marriage so much, but she did mind being forced into it, and all because Franklin had accumulated enough gambling debts during the past few years to see him in debtor's prison.

"Only a dance?" he repeated. A pulse throbbed in his smooth forehead and he took a menacing step toward her. "You left with him! Everyone saw it! I told you to stay away from him. Any affiliation you have with the damned man will greatly jeopardize your reputation. Besides, he'd eat you up and spit you out. Armond Wulf is dangerous!"

Rosalind suspected a man could hardly be more dangerous than Franklin Chapman. Her childhood recollections of Franklin were vague, but even then, he'd been a bully. She'd thought he had changed when he visited her in the country three months prior, but he had fooled her.

He'd told her that his mother was on her deathbed and wanted to see Rosalind one last time. In the short period that the Duchess of Montrose had lived beneath the same roof with Rosalind's father, the lady had been kind to her, almost like a mother, in truth. Rosalind had left the country estate and traveled to London with Franklin. His mother, true to his word, was in a room upstairs, dying a slow death, too weak to even converse with Rosalind. But what Franklin had lied about was his reason for wanting Rosalind beneath his roof.

"Your foolish actions tonight have caused gossip. You leave me little choice but to end your season early and accept an offer for you that I've received from the Viscount Penmore. You recall him? We met him in town last week when we visited the milliner's."

Recalling the viscount wasn't difficult. Franklin had allowed Rosalind to socialize little until he'd presented her at court; then tonight, the Greenleys' ball had launched the season. Lord Penmore was a short, fat, balding man who drooled all over her hand and eyed her in a way that made her skin crawl.

"He's old enough to be my father," she pointed out. "If you force me to marry, I had hoped I at least might be allowed to choose my husband."

Franklin reached out and pinched her chin between his cold fingers. "And what would a country mouse like you know about choosing a husband? Big brother knows what's best for you. I'll handle your life until I see fit to turn it over to another man for his handling." His fingers pinched harder. "Unless you've spoiled even your chances with Penmore by your bold behavior this evening."

"I told you, it was innocent," she lied. "I became ill on the dance floor and Lord Wulf merely escorted me to the carriage before I embarrassed myself."

What had she been thinking? She knew that Franklin was capable of violence against her. He had slapped her when she'd at first refused to wear the indecently low-cut gown he'd had made for her this evening. She hadn't seen him this enraged, however, and if she had in fact let Armond Wulf ruin her, she wasn't positive that Franklin wouldn't have killed her.

Franklin released her chin, but his eyes remained cold, dead, like the eyes of a snake. "You'd better not be lying to me. Your virginity is an important asset in securing yourself a suitable husband. Stay away from Armond Wulf. If you escaped ravishment by him tonight, count yourself one of the fortunate few women who go off with him in the night and return with their virtue . . . or return even at all."

She couldn't help her curiosity, even though she'd as soon put an end to the conversation and flee to the safety of her room. "What are you saying?"

Her stepbrother smiled his snake smile. "I should have told you more than I did about Lord Wulf. He murdered a woman a few months ago in his very stable. Murdered her and was never called to account for the crime."

A chill raced up Rosalind's back. "Murder," she whispered. "But he and I—that is, he seemed like a perfect gentleman when he escorted me to the carriage." The "perfect gentleman" claim was a lie to be sure, but she'd been alone with Armond Wulf and had never felt as if her life was in danger . . . her virtue yes, but not her life. A flash of memory came to her. The feel of Armond's teeth against the pulse at the base of her neck. She'd felt a moment of alarm, as if he meant to bite her.

"Everyone saw you leave together," Franklin reminded her. "He wouldn't be so brave as to think he could possibly get away with the crime a second time, not when he was seen escorting you from the ball. Which brings me back to Penmore. He will be at Lady Pratt's tea day after tomorrow. Be nice to him."

Still thinking about Lord Wulf, she replied, "I will be civil. Provided that he has better manners than he did when last we met."

Franklin reached out and dug his fingers into the soft skin of her shoulders, recapturing Rosalind's complete attention. "You will be charming regardless of how he treats you. Penmore and I have a business arrangement of sorts. I owe him a considerable amount in gambling debts. Among other things . . ." he added, as if to himself. "I had no idea that he would be so taken with you. He likes pretty things."

To Franklin, Rosalind was only a "thing." Not a person with dreams or hopes or feelings. He'd always been a bully. And even as a child she had felt frightened around him. She suspected Franklin was the reason her father and her stepmother had not lived beneath the same roof for long. But as wonderful as the duchess had been to Rosalind, the woman had doted upon her mean-spirited son.

"Perhaps I should look in on your mother," Rosalind

said, moving toward the stairs. "I'm sure Mary could use a rest from her vigil over the poor woman."

"My mother doesn't even know who you are," Franklin snorted. "Instead, I shall come to your room and help you choose what you will wear to Lady Pratt's tea. You must look your best, Rosalind. Appearances are everything."

She could very well understand why Franklin would hold a person's outer appearance more important than what rested on the inside. Her stepbrother could be quite charming in the presence of others. Only she knew what sort of man he really was. Rosalind and, she supposed, her father, since he'd sent Franklin and his mother away. Rosalind didn't want Franklin in her room. It was the only place in the house where she felt safe from his abuse.

"I can certainly choose my own clothing," Rosalind said. "No need to bother yourself with such trifling matters."

"No bother," Franklin countered smoothly. "The creditors will come circling soon enough to collect the considerable sum I've paid to have your wardrobe updated. Your modest taste was a bit juvenile. You must put your assets on display, Rosalind. Who better to tell you which gowns suit you for that purpose than a man?"

When Franklin moved ahead of her, as if he expected she'd follow like a docile pet, Rosalind put her foot down. "I will not have you in my room, Franklin. My father paid for this house, even if it by right belongs to your mother. He would have never left my future in her hands had he known she would become so ill shortly after his death."

Her stepbrother stood poised in front of the stairway, his back to her. "Yes, a pity about the duchess. But her lawyers quite agreed that she is in no condition to handle your future, or your inheritance. They were all too happy to pass that responsibility on to me."

When he turned to face her, his face was red and the

vein still throbbed in his forehead. "I have control of you, Rosalind. Your doting papa is no longer alive to order me out of his house. You will do exactly what I tell you to do, or you will suffer the consequences. Consequences I don't think you will enjoy . . . but maybe you will; care to find out?"

As brave as Rosalind wanted to be, she backed down, and lowered her gaze. What he said was true. Her guardianship had been given to Franklin. He had control of her money, which was how it had come to be recklessly lost to her. Franklin had a gambling addiction. It was the reason she was able to slip away with Armond Wulf at the Greenleys' ball. Franklin had been in the back rooms playing cards instead of chaperoning her as he should have been doing. Not a mistake she imagined he'd make again.

Her stepbrother turned back and started up the stairs. "Are you coming, little sister?"

Rosalind's gaze drifted toward the foyer, and for a moment, she was tempted to run. But she had no money of her own, nowhere to go except back to the country, and no way to pay her passage there. For the time being, she was at Franklin's mercy. But she hadn't given up on her idea to foil his plans for her. How she would do so without making him angry enough to beat her she hadn't figured out as of yet. But she would.

"Rosalind," he called, his tone more demanding. "Come along as I've told you to do."

Shoulders slumped, she followed, very much dreading her destined meeting with Lord Penmore in two days' time and still feeling the sting of Franklin's slap upon her cheek.

"He's all that you said he is; I'll grant you that. Not an unsound bone in his body. The animal is magnificent," Lord Pratt said.

Armond brushed imaginary lint from his dark riding coat. He wondered why, with his reputation for breeding horses, people still seemed surprised by his integrity. If he didn't deal fairly with the silly people, he wouldn't have gained the reputation he had as a breeder.

He'd recently returned from his country estate, Wulf-glen, where he'd taken special care to choose the horses he brought back to London with him to sell. The Wulfs might be rumored to be murderers or worse, but they were unrivaled as horse breeders.

"Let's go inside," the earl said. "We'll have a brandy in the study and I'll pay you for the animal."

"It's barely teatime," Armond reminded the man. "I care little for spirits. Just payment and then I'll be on my way."

The earl nodded, probably happy to be granted a civil reprieve from his duties as a proper host. Armond followed his client down a brick path to the house. The moment they stepped inside, the murmur of voices could be heard coming from the front parlor.

"My wife is hosting a tea," the earl said. "She's introducing the late Duke of Montrose's daughter to proper society. Oh, but I've forgotten: you met the young woman at the Greenleys' ball."

Judging by the sly gleam that entered the earl's eyes, the man more than knew Armond and Rosalind had already met. He was spoiling for gossip.

"Yes, a lovely young woman," Armond found himself replying. "A pity the roast duck served at supper that evening did not agree with her. I was forced to help Lady Rosalind to her coach in all haste lest she embarrass herself on the dance floor."

"Oh." The earl sighed. "Well, so I've heard. She was a bit brazen, though," he added. "Dancing with a man she hadn't been properly introduced to."

"Dancing with me, you mean," Armond drawled. "The lady is my neighbor. She's been kept to the country and didn't realize I was an unsuitable dance partner. I should have spared her the embarrassment she has no doubt suffered since regarding the matter, but then, no one expected better of me."

"Of course not," the earl agreed, then realized what he'd said and flushed. "This way to the study, then."

The fine carpets in the hallway muffled their footsteps. They had to pass the parlor, and, doors thrown wide in welcome, Armond fought himself not to glance inside the room.

"William!"

The earl skidded to a halt, forcing Armond to pause in their progress, as well.

"You promised me that you'd attend my tea and said the matter of the horse wouldn't make you late."

Lady Pratt, the earl's aging wife, drew up short at the sight of Armond darkening her hallway. She placed a hand against her heart. "Oh, I didn't realize that you were still conducting business with Lord Wulf. Please pardon my interruption."

Armond smiled at the flustered woman. He knew it would unnerve her even more. "And I beg your pardon for keeping your husband from his obligations."

She nodded acceptance of the apology, but her hand still rested against her heart, as if she'd received a fright and hadn't yet recovered.

"I offered Lord Wulf a brandy and he wisely pointed out that it is too early for spirits. It would only be proper, my dear, to offer the man tea while I tend to the bill of purchase for the horse."

The earl obviously sought to punish his wife over some earlier transgression. Armond cared little to be the tool of her chastisement.

"Certainly Lord Wulf is welcome to take tea with us," Lady Pratt croaked. Her frightened gaze landed upon Armond. "I would be honored if you would join my party."

She would be beside herself, and Armond knew it. He also suspected that the lady knew he never attended anything as boring as a social tea. "I would be honored to join you."

Armond couldn't believe he'd said those words. The way the lady's eyes rounded, she couldn't believe he'd said them, either. Armond wanted to snatch back his acceptance, but his cursed pride would not allow him. The truth of the matter was that he wanted to see Lady Rosalind Rutherford again and, by God, he would.

Chapter Four

Armond followed the lady into the parlor. Conversation went from a roar to a whisper in a heartbeat. He wasn't dressed for a social visit, but even had he been, he doubted those in attendance would be any less shocked to see him.

"Lord Wulf," the lady announced. "The gentleman will join us for tea while my husband concludes business over a horse."

Lady Pratt had to spell out the reason Armond was there or find herself the object of gossip for having poor taste in tea guests. For years the title attached to the family estate, Wulfglen, had been shortened to Wulf, the family surname. Thus the reason society referred to Armond as Lord Wulf rather than Lord Wulfglen. He seated himself apart from the other guests, accepting a dainty teacup that looked odd in his large hands.

Once the whispers about him quieted, he searched the room over the rim of his cup. He recognized Lady Rosalind immediately, although her back was turned toward him. She held herself well, her spine straight. A cascade of glossy curls hung down her back, set off nicely by a small blue hat with a short veil attached. A pity, he thought, to hide that face.

Her skin looked paler due to the dark veil, her high

cheekbones and large expressive eyes blurred behind the thin obstruction, but her mouth—God, hiding away half of her face made his gaze automatically focus upon her full red lips. He remembered the taste of them. They were sweet, like sun-ripened berries.

As if she felt his scrutiny, Lady Rosalind glanced toward him. Their gazes locked, although the veil blotted any reaction he might discern in her lovely eyes. She quickly turned back to the conversation, dismissing him. She'd obviously learned her lesson about playing false with dangerous men. A pity, he thought. He'd enjoy another lesson with her.

When she broke from the group and walked across the room to study the paintings that fairly littered one wall, Armond couldn't help but notice her figure. She wasn't tall, but neither was she short. Her waist was small, her hips slightly flared beneath her gown.

Although she was dressed modestly, the curve of her breasts pronounced delectably beneath her bodice only made a man sit and wistfully contemplate removing all that taffeta in order to get down to her bare bones. Armond had gotten more than a glimpse of her bountiful charms already. He'd gotten a handful and a mouthful. He wanted more.

He stood and placed his teacup aside, but rather than quit the room as he intended to do, he found himself moving toward her. She drew him. Whether he wanted to be drawn or not.

"I see that you have recovered from the Greenleys' ball," he said once he stood beside her. "And obviously none the worse for your daring escapade or you would not be here this afternoon."

Her head snapped in his direction. "Please do not speak to me," she said, then turned her attention back to the paintings.

Normally, Armond had no trouble avoiding women. It was simple, really. A man just had to walk away. He stepped closer to her, pretending to find the garish painting she studied of interest.

"Two nights ago you asked me to compromise you. Would have possibly allowed me to fully ruin your reputation. Today you ask me to act as if we've never met. Women. Fickle to a fault."

"Approaching you was obviously a mistake on my part," she said through tight lips. "If you have any manners at all, do as I ask and leave me alone."

He scratched his chin and considered. "I'm sorry. I have no manners. I thought you knew that."

She stepped away from him and paused before another painting. "I beg to disagree. You do have manners, although you'd rather allow society to think otherwise."

So, she'd given the matter at least a moment of her thought. Obviously only a moment. "I don't give a damn what society thinks," he said. "Do you honestly believe that I don't know what you were about at the Greenleys' ball? You approached me on a dare. You dangled yourself like bait in order to win favor among your friends. You were lucky that I didn't take the game farther than you intended."

"Lucky?" As if she realized she'd spoken too loudly, she took another step away from him. "Luck had nothing to do with it. Regardless of your dark reputation, I knew I was not in any serious danger. No man is ignorant enough to think he can seduce an innocent and not face repercussions from society. Not even you."

"And I am a coward."

Her head snapped in his direction again. "What did you say?"

Armond leaned closer. "You think I'm a coward," he repeated. "You believe I didn't take full advantage of the situation due to some fear of reprisal. You're right. But the reprisal I fear is not what you think. I'm very tempted to ask for another chance, just to prove you wrong."

Pink crept up her neck. "There will be no second chances," she said. "I made a mistake. One that I don't intend to repeat."

When she walked away, Armond didn't follow. He still had a measure of sense, although it seemed to desert him in Rosalind's company. From the corner of his eye he watched her. She spoke softly to the earl's wife, received directions, and left the room. She'd retreated to the safety of the water closet, he imagined.

Armond needed to leave as well. He had business to conclude, and the sooner the better. He wanted out of the house, away from Lady Rosalind and the spell she'd cast over him. He knew all too well about spells and curses and to take them seriously.

He nearly ran over Rosalind in the hallway. They tried to sidestep each other, each making a move to the same side, then back to the other side. It was rather comical.

"Shall we dance again?" he teased.

She did not smile. "Please let me pass."

His playful mood vanished. "You are not nearly as friendly as you were the last time we met," Armond said. "Do you make it a habit to go around propositioning men you don't know? If you do, I feel that I must warn you that the next time might not bode as well for you."

"I've told you, there won't be a next time, Lord Wulf," she responded, her tone still cold. "Our last meeting was a misstep on my part, one greatly aided, I suspect, by a bad reaction to champagne. I have since been advised to refrain from spirits, and also, to refrain from being seen in your company. Neither, it is now clear to me, is beneficial to a lady's health."

The lighting in the hallway was dim, but Armond had unusually good eyesight in the dark. Now that they were face-to-face, rather than trying to appear as if they were not conversing as they had done in the parlor, he thought he saw something beneath her veil that disturbed him. When he reached for the thin obstruction, she flinched. Despite her response, he lifted the veil. What he saw made his blood run cold.

"What happened to your face?"

She batted his hand away and quickly lowered the veil. "That is none of your business, Lord Wulf. Again, I ask you to allow me to pass."

When she tried to step around him, Armond blocked her path. "I didn't do that to you, did I?" He knew he'd been impassioned, but he prayed he would never have raised a rough hand to her.

Her eyes, barely visible through the veil, softened. "No," she assured him. "I'm terribly clumsy. I tripped once I got home from the Greenleys' ball. I fell and hit my cheek on a chair. It's nothing really."

Armond lifted her veil again. He gently touched the small, round bruise. "I've never seen a woman move more gracefully than you do when you walk across a room. You look like a princess, holding court."

Her lashes lowered. "Do you often insult women, Lord Wulf, and then spout poetry to them in the next breath?"

"No," he answered honestly. "Never. And you may call me Armond. Formality with one another seems a bit odd considering what we've done together."

She glanced up. Something sparked in her eyes. He wasn't certain if it was anger . . . or desire. "I've asked you more than once to forget about that."

"I've tried," he admitted. "A hundred times."

Her hand crept to her collar. "Then you must try harder. You don't understand. I didn't fully realize the danger—"

"I see," Armond interrupted, and he did, and he felt like a fool to believe that for one moment she might cast the rumors aside and judge him fairly. "But you've no doubt since been filled in about just what sort of man you were playing with at the Greenleys' ball."

He was surprised when she cocked her head to one side and regarded him intently through her veil. "Are you a murderer, Lord Wulf?"

Armond was used to whispers behind his back. Rarely was anyone brave enough to confront him face-to-face. "What do you think?" It bothered him to honestly want her answer. It bothered him to suddenly care what someone thought of him.

"I think if you were a murderer, perhaps we would not be having this conversation."

He smiled at her witty answer.

She surprised him again by saying, "You should do that more often. You don't look at all scary when you smile."

Armond sobered. She might not believe the rumors about him being a murderer, but she didn't know the whole truth. She didn't know about the curse on his head. She didn't know that it was ludicrous for him to be even carrying on a conversation with her. She was forbidden to him. Just as he was forbidden to her.

"Promise me that from this day forward, you'll watch who you climb into coaches with, Lady Rosalind."

Rosalind's face suddenly flamed beneath her veil. She realized she had been flirting with him, although she didn't have much practice in that area. She was flirting, and she was remembering.

Remembering the feel of his hands on her skin, of his

mouth moving against hers. He was dangerous, but Lord
Wulf didn't understand that Rosalind had been referring
to the danger from Franklin earlier. When she'd spotted
Lord Wulf at the Greenleys' ball, she'd been too enthralled
by his handsome face to pay much attention to the whispers. She'd heard only enough to realize that he was perfect for ruining her reputation. But Franklin had warned
her to stay away from the man, and if he caught them together . . .

"Lord Wulf." She tried to regain her composure and
put a quick end to the conversation. "I do owe you my
gratitude. It was good that one of us had some sense. I
mean, that you didn't take the game farther than you did.
I suppose I am lucky that you are, are . . ."

"A coward?"

A shiver raced up her spine. How did he know she'd
said that about him? He couldn't have possibly heard her.
"I was going to say 'an honorable man.' But then, that isn't
entirely true, either."

"You asked," he reminded. "I merely obliged."

He had not obliged, but she wouldn't bring the matter
up again. Rosalind needed to return to the tea. She couldn't
look at Armond's mouth without remembering his kisses.
She couldn't look at his hands without remembering the
way they felt on her bare skin. And she thought she must
have imagined how handsome he was, but she was wrong.
He was sinfully good-looking.

"When you look at me that way, I have regrets about
our first meeting."

She quickly lowered her gaze. "I am also ashamed
of my behavior. We must both try to forget what happened."

"I meant, I have regrets that more didn't happen than
did."

Rosalind glanced back up at him. He had the wrong

impression about her. What man wouldn't? She wasn't even certain what to think herself. She'd never reacted so brazenly to a man before. She had thought the affair would be a cold, impersonal matter, but now she knew differently.

"You are no gentleman, Lord Wulf."

He lifted her hand, bringing it to his lips. "That is something you already knew," he said, then turned her palm facing up to him and kissed her wrist. Her pulses leaped. She snatched her hand away as if she'd been scorched.

"Is there a problem, Rosalind?"

Rosalind tensed. She glanced past Armond. Exactly what she'd been worried might happen, had. Franklin stood staring at her, his expression calm enough, though she saw the tattletale vein that throbbed in his forehead.

"No, Franklin," she answered. "I was just returning to the tea."

Armond turned and looked at her stepbrother. He recognized the man from the clubs, though they'd never spoken to each other. "You must forgive me for keeping Lady Rosalind from the party. We accidentally ran into one another here in the hallway. Since I danced with her at the Greenleys', and she soon became ill, I wanted to inquire about her health."

"Her health is fine," Chapman said coldly. His gaze moved to Rosalind, and Armond saw a flare of anger ignite within his dark eyes. "At the moment, anyway."

An intuitive man, Armond immediately sensed a disturbing undercurrent between Rosalind and her stepbrother.

"Return to the social, Rosalind," Chapman ordered. "I'll join you there shortly."

Rosalind's gaze traveled from one man to the other. "I thought you might escort me back, Franklin."

"Go along as I've asked you to do," Chapman said, his tone clipped.

Armond watched Rosalind move past them and down the hall. His gaze lowered to the slight sway of her hips. It was an unconscious act, but he realized what he was doing and quickly glanced back up at Chapman.

"She's lovely, isn't she?" he asked.

"Very," Armond agreed.

The man steadied him with a dark look. "Stay away from her."

Although Armond could hardly fault the man for being protective of his stepsister, something about Chapman immediately rubbed him the wrong way. He was used to insults, rather less accustomed to threats. It was easy to avoid confrontation. A man simply had to walk away. Armond steadied the man with his own cold stare.

"Lady Rosalind has nothing to fear from me . . . and I hope she has nothing to fear from you." He didn't know why he'd added the last. Again, instinct.

Chapman's face flushed. "I don't know what you're implying, but my sister is my business."

"Stepsister, isn't she?" Armond continued to goad.

Chapman switched tactics and smiled, although his expression never reached his dark eyes. "Yes. And while it may be true that we share no blood bonds, I can assure you that I feel deeply for Rosalind. I wish to see her make a good match this season. You know that any attention you pay her will cause gossip and jeopardize her reputation. I doubt that you have any honor, but would ask that you take her future well-being into consideration and avoid attending any social functions this season."

The man's audacity surprised even Armond. The fact that the eldest Wulf brother rarely attended social functions anyway was beside the point. In the past, the choice had been his to make.

"Of course you're right," Armond said, then smiled in return, the same emotionless expression Chapman had given to him. "I have no honor."

Armond turned and continued down the hallway, where he hoped he'd come upon the earl's study. He felt Chapman's gaze cutting into his back. He had one other thing to say to the man and turned back.

"In the future, keep your hands off of your 'dear sister' or you will deal with me. And I promise, that is not something you would wish upon your worst enemy."

Franklin Chapman didn't respond, but then, Armond didn't expect him to. As much as he prided himself upon accepting his lot in life, remaining in the shadows where society was concerned, he wasn't the type of man to stand by and see a woman abused. Perhaps Rosalind had in fact caused herself the injury, but Armond suspected that was not the case.

He would watch the situation, judge his first gut reaction, and see if, as usual, he was correct when it came to his intuitive feelings. And if Chapman laid another hand upon Rosalind, he'd be the sorry one.

Armond had to suddenly rein in his thoughts. He might have laughed at the absurdity of his notions. Him, protect Lady Rosalind? And again, he wasn't positive that she even needed his protection.

He should be more concerned about who would protect her from him. He'd nearly lost all control with her at the Greenleys' ball. He'd never been more attracted physically to a woman in his life. Already he was thinking about the short jaunt across the lawn that separated them. A pathetic boundary really—of little consequence to a man of his athletic ability.

Lady Rosalind had been considerably cooler in her manner toward him today. He wanted to feel her heat again, to watch her eyes fill with desire, see her lips part in invitation. He wanted all they had shared the first night they met . . . and more. And he would go to her. He knew it as surely as he knew his future was damned. God help him, he could not resist.

Chapter Five

Rosalind couldn't have been more relieved when Franklin returned to Lady Pratt's social tea and Armond Wulf did not. Something about Lord Wulf was irresistible. Well, she had to mentally correct, everything about him was irresistible. But she had to avoid him.

No sense in making Franklin angry over the matter. Although she couldn't help but wonder, as Lord Penmore approached her from across the room, why Armond Wulf couldn't be considered a good catch on the marriage market, instead of the disgusting man Franklin might force her into accepting.

"Lady Rosalind," the viscount gushed, taking her hand and then proceeding to slobber all over it. "I am so pleased I didn't miss you in passing. I'm deplorably late."

Deplorable stuck in her head, but she managed to smile. "Nice to see you again, Lord Penmore." Rosalind wrestled her hand from him and wiped it on her gown.

"Good afternoon, Penmore." Franklin joined them. "I see that you are fashionably late," he said drily. "Too bad you weren't here a moment earlier to chase the Wulf away."

Penmore lifted a busy brow. "What wolf would that be?"

"Lord Armond Wulf," Franklin drawled. "It seems he's taken an interest in my poor little sister."

Rosalind was shocked that Franklin would so freely discuss the matter in front of the viscount. The shorter man huffed up like a toad.

"The cursed man has never shown an interest in one of our own before. Prostitutes are more to his liking." He winked at Rosalind. She failed to see the humor in his statement.

"The woman found murdered on his property," Franklin explained to her. "She was a prostitute."

Rosalind still failed to see the humor. She fiddled with the folds of her gown. "I don't believe that either Lord Wulf or . . . women of that ilk is a proper topic for discussion between gentlemen and ladies."

Both men cast her a dirty look, as if she had no right to an opinion. Finally Lord Penmore shrugged.

"Forgive our rude manners," he said. "We can surely find a topic of discussion more pleasing than the Wulf brothers. You know about the curse that haunts them?"

Despite the fact that the subject had not changed, Rosalind was curious about the man. "Curse?"

"Insanity," Lord Penmore said. "The father killed himself. The mother followed him to the grave shortly afterward, and she was crazy as a loon before she went. The sons, four of them, although I don't know what's become of the youngest one, are tainted with the same blood, and with it coming from both sides, well, there will be no escaping it. No decent woman would tie herself to a family with those faults. They have vowed, I believe, to never marry. A wise decision."

"Perhaps we should indeed discuss something else," Franklin cut in. "Will you visit the clubs once we leave this stuffy affair?"

Penmore nodded. "An excellent idea. You must join me, Chapman. Perhaps you can manage to win back even a little of the fortune you already owe me."

Rosalind didn't miss Lord Penmore's reminder that Franklin was indebted to him, but she wasn't interested in the conversation. She was thinking about Armond Wulf. How horrible for him. To be cursed by insanity. Was he insane even now? She didn't think so. But surely if it ran in the blood of both his mother and his father, it would strike him down one day as well. Had he truly made a vow to remain unmarried? And was that even his decision? Perhaps society had decided the matter for him.

"Will you accompany us tomorrow?"

She realized that Lord Penmore had asked her a question. "Beg your pardon?"

"I don't think it would be a good idea, all things considered," Franklin answered for her.

"Oh, come now, Chapman, we'll be along with her. I'd like for Wulf to try something out of line. We could beat him to a bloody pulp."

Franklin smiled obviously over the possibility, but Rosalind still wasn't certain what the men were discussing. "I'm sorry, I didn't hear where it is you'd like me to accompany you to, Viscount."

"I'm thinking of purchasing a matched pair of horses for my carriage," the man explained. "Wulf may be a murderer, and soon to be as insane as his cursed parents, but he does know how to breed horses. I thought you might come along with me and your stepbrother on the venture."

Now Rosalind understood Lady Pratt's remark about the business of a horse. She could see Armond's residence from the balcony of her bedroom and had wondered why he had such a large stable for a townhome.

She'd rather not. "Horse business is better left up to men," she said, although Rosalind didn't believe that for a moment. She was an accomplished horsewoman and knew how to judge an animal's quality.

"But I want you there." Penmore pouted. He turned a more serious expression upon Franklin. "I want her there, Chapman."

Her stepbrother stared the other man down for a moment, then shrugged. "I see no harm in taking her along with us. As you said, she will be protected."

Rosalind understood that she had no further say in the matter when the two men went back to discussing the clubs and which they would visit after the tea ended. She tried to picture Franklin and Penmore getting the better of Armond Wulf in a fight. Regardless that she'd thought him a coward the night of the Greenleys' ball, she couldn't imagine Lord Wulf coming out the loser in a battle of fisticuffs. She would see him tomorrow. Her pulses raced with the thought.

"I'll have our driver take you home after the affair ends," Franklin was saying to her. "I'll see you after I've enjoyed a few rounds of cards. We can talk about the incident in the hallway then."

She'd been foolish to think that her stepbrother would let the matter drop. Would he strike her for simply having the misfortune of running into Lord Wulf in the hallway? Her stomach twisted at the thought. The afternoon promised to be a long one while she waited for Franklin's return—waited to see just what form of punishment he had in mind.

Pacing seemed to calm her nerves. Rosalind did so while Lydia, her personal maid, went about the business of changing her bed linens. Her opinion had not changed about

Lord Penmore. The man was as disgusting as she'd first found him. Her opinion had changed somewhat about Armond Wulf. She no longer thought he was a coward. She shouldn't think of him at all. And even as Rosalind told herself so, she moved to her balcony doors and stared outside toward the property next door.

"What am I going to do?"

"You should do what your stepbrother wants and find yourself a husband," Lydia, the maid, answered, as if the question had been directed to her when, in fact, it had only been a thought that had escaped Rosalind's lips. "I've seen the way he looks at you when your head is turned the other direction. Won't be long until he'll be creeping in here during the night and climbing into your bed."

"Lydia!" Rosalind was shocked. "You mustn't say such things." The maid mostly shouldn't say such things because Rosalind didn't want to face the possibility that Franklin might lust after her. It was bad enough that he abused her. She'd allowed the maid too many liberties or Lydia would never have been brave enough to say as much to Rosalind. But the young woman was the only friend Rosalind had made, or was likely to make since Franklin had tricked her into traveling to London with him—since he'd trapped her in this house. Rosalind valued their friendship, even if the rest of society would frown upon such an affiliation.

Undaunted by the warning, Lydia shrugged. "Do you think I don't know about the master's appetites?" The maid visibly shuddered. "Takes what he wants, that one. Last time he ordered me to his bed, thought he'd kill me with his rough ways. Bled for a week, I did."

Rosalind supposed her mouth dropped open. Her life in the country had been fairly sheltered. She'd certainly heard her share of vulgar talk exchanged between the maids, but nothing like what Lydia had just insinuated.

"Lydia, are you telling me that Franklin . . . that he forced himself upon you?"

"Thinks no woman would say no to that handsome face of his." Lydia looked up at Rosalind from plumping one of her pillows. "But we know he isn't so handsome on the inside, don't we, Lady Rosalind?"

Rosalind walked across the room to join the maid. "Why didn't you tell someone, Lydia? Why did you stay here if you were subjected to acts against your will?"

The maid shrugged again. "Don't have any family; you know that. And I need this job. The master said if I didn't do as I was told, he'd make sure I got no good reference from him. He may not be as upper-crust as you are, Lady Rosalind, but he can make my life harder than it already is."

Rosalind brought a trembling hand to her temple and rubbed. "This is unacceptable behavior. He can't get away with treating you as if you had no say regarding an intimate decision. As if you are only an object put on God's green earth to do his bidding, no matter how foul you find your duties."

Lydia placed a hand upon Rosalind's shoulder. "He has gotten away with it. And I fear for you beneath his roof. Do as he asks and save yourself while you still can. If he calls me to his bed again, I swear I'll jump from yonder balcony before I let him tear me up like he did the last time. No woman should be forced to suffer that humiliation."

Rosalind's gaze strayed toward her balcony, as she wondered if she wouldn't rather jump than live in fear over what Franklin might do to her next or marry Lord Penmore. Like poor Lydia, she had no family. No doting uncle to come to her rescue, no cousins whom she might seek shelter with. She was alone in the world, the same as the maid.

"I'm sorry, Lydia," she said softly. "Sorry for your shame and your suffering. I will speak about it to Franklin, you can be sure."

"No, milady," Lydia whispered. "If he knows I've been telling tales, he'll only hurt me worse. Don't go against him. Not for the likes of me."

Rosalind opened her mouth to argue, but a short knock sounded upon her door, and speak of the devil, he entered. Lydia quickly lowered her gaze and slunk toward the door. Rosalind was left to face Franklin alone.

"We must talk, little sister."

Still battling her outrage about Lydia's confession, and debating whether to call him to account over the matter regardless of Lydia's request, she keep silent, Rosalind instead found herself immediately on the defensive.

"It was by accident that I ran into Lord Wulf in the hallway at Lady Pratt's tea," she said. "I would have certainly never purposely sought him out after the warning you issued."

Franklin lifted a brow. She knew that even if he didn't show it on the outside, he was secretly pleased to walk into a room and immediately have her babbling about her innocence like a spineless ninny. Fear had turned her into a coward. But Rosalind couldn't keep silent regarding the maid.

"And . . . and you mustn't touch Lydia again."

Her demand wiped the smug expression from her stepbrother's face. "What has that little whore been telling you?"

Rosalind unconsciously took a step back when he approached. "She—I—that is . . ." She forced herself to stand still. "She accidentally let it slip that you had demanded rights from her that are not yours to demand, Franklin. She said that she was unwilling and that you forced her."

He reached out and grabbed her shoulders, digging his strong fingers into her flesh. Rosalind winced, but she refused to cower.

"The servants in this house are none of your affair," he bit out. "Are you going to take the word of a maid, a whore, over my word? I can tell you now that she came sneaking into my bed, hoping to earn a few more coins. I took nothing that she wasn't willing to give. How dare you confront me on such an issue! You have no say here, Rosalind, not beneath my roof!"

The harder his fingers dug into her skin, the harder it was for Rosalind to remain strong in the face of her enemy. And Franklin was her enemy. She had no doubts about that. His fingers dug deeper, and Rosalind couldn't stop the moan that escaped her lips. "I understand," she whispered. "Please, Franklin, you're hurting me."

As if it took almost more will than he possessed, Franklin released her and turned his back. "You sorely try my temper. You keep forgetting that you are in a circumstance far different from the one you once knew. Your father threw me out, you know? I rather like the idea of being able to throw you out, or to the dogs, or to do anything I damn well please."

"That was a long time ago," Rosalind reminded him, rubbing the stinging places on her shoulders. "I was a child; you were a young man barely out of short pants. I had nothing to do with you and your mother leaving. In fact, I cried when the duchess told me she had to go. I've held a fondness for your mother all these years. That's why I came with you, remember, to see her?"

"Of course I know you were fond of her, and she of you. That's why I knew you would come. You walked right into my trap. Little idiot," he insulted her. "Now, back to more urgent matters. Tomorrow morning you will accompany me and Penmore next door to Lord Wulf's pride and joy. His stable. I hope we don't have any more problems between you and Lord Wulf. I'd hate to have to thrash him. As I told Penmore, Wulf was quite frightened of me when I warned him off."

Rosalind held her tongue, but she seriously doubted that her stepbrother could frighten Armond Wulf. At the moment, she would say anything to have Franklin leave her alone. Rarely did they spend time together that she didn't manage to enrage him.

"If you wish me to be there, I will," she said. "May I see your mother this afternoon? I've been lax in my visits and wish to make amends."

Franklin shrugged. "I suppose if you must. I've just had tea fixed and taken up to her. A special blend she was always fond of. Do give her my best."

The way he said the parting remark was sarcastic, but Rosalind was too happy to see him leave to care. She walked to her mirror, applied powder to help cover the small bruise on her cheek, grabbed her sewing basket, and went up to the third floor.

The duchess dozed in a chair by the window. The remnants of her morning tea sat on a small table to her left. Mary, the housekeeper, was busy cleaning the dreary room.

"Is she any better today?" Rosalind asked the housekeeper.

The woman shook her head. "I haven't managed to get a peep out of her for two days now. Her mind has gone somewhere else. She's so terribly tired it's almost more than I can manage to get her up and at least to a chair so the bedsores don't come."

Rosalind knelt before her stepmother and took the woman's cold hand in hers. "Good afternoon, Your Grace. I'm sorry I haven't visited more often of late. I promise to be better about it." She turned to Mary. "I will stay with my stepmother for a while. I'm sure you have other duties to attend."

"Bless you, but I do," the housekeeper admitted. "Runs a tight ship, Master Franklin does. Hardly enough of us in the house to keep up with what needs to be done."

The dwindling servants were obviously a result of Franklin's now limited funds, along with the dwindling furnishings downstairs. Rosalind was certain her stepbrother had sold off anything in the house of value to feed his gambling addictions and pay his pitiful staff.

After Mary left the room, Rosalind tried to think of something cheerful to chatter on about in her stepmother's company. She didn't expect the lady to converse with her. The duchess's eyes always had a glazed look, as if she no longer lived in this world but had escaped to another. Rosalind wished at the moment that she could do the same. She tried to hold her emotions at bay, but her still stinging shoulders and the prospect of continuing to live in a house where abuse had become a fast companion got the better of her. She bent her head and allowed herself the weakness of weeping. A moment later, her stepmother's hand touched her hair.

The woman's gentle touch, in a world that had become violent, only brought more tears. Rosalind continued to weep as the lady, her eyes still glazed and staring straight ahead, continued to gently stroke her hair.

They stayed that way for a time; then the lady's hand fell limply by her side and Rosalind realized the woman had fallen asleep. Rosalind rose, took a comforter from the bed, and covered the duchess. She worked on her needlepoint until Mary returned to take up her vigilance with the poor woman.

In the evening, Mary sent Rosalind up a warm bath and she allowed the scented water to soothe her outward aches. Nothing could soothe her inward turmoil. She needed a savior.

A vision of Armond Wulf's handsome face surfaced. Maybe because he had the look of an angel with his golden mane of hair. But no, she shook her head to dislodge the thought. He was no angel. But was he a murderer? Was he insane?

Rosalind slipped into bed with those questions tumbling through her mind. Sleep had almost claimed her when she felt a presence inside of her room. Her first thought was that Lydia had been right about Franklin's unnatural affections toward her and he had managed to make it past the lock on her door. She sat, her gaze scanning the shadow-filled room. A darker shadow stood next to the balcony doors.

"Franklin?" she whispered, fear tripping her heart.

He stepped into a moonlit swath left by her open balcony doors and she saw that the man was not her stepbrother. Perhaps Rosalind should have been more frightened by his identity, but she was oddly relieved.

"What are you doing here, and how did you get in?"

Armond Wulf, dressed in a white lawn shirt open at the neck, and snug black trousers, took a step closer. "You shouldn't sleep with your doors open," he said. "And the trellis outside isn't so difficult to climb, not if a man is determined."

Rosalind pulled the covers up higher around her neck. "Determined to do what?"

He stared at her for a moment, long enough for tension as thick as fog to fill the air between them, then said, "To speak with you privately."

"Speak with me?" Had she detected a note of disappointment in her voice? "Speak with me about what?"

Armond moved toward her. "About the bruise on your cheek. It's been bothering me."

Her nostrils flared slightly as he drew nearer. Lord Wulf had a distinctive scent. Not unpleasant by any means. Not the result of any tonic, but a natural one. She couldn't identify it exactly, but it reminded her of danger. Of maleness. Of something wild.

"I told you about my clumsiness," she reminded him. "You should not be here. And you are not so far removed from manners that you don't understand that."

"Should your stepbrother be here?" he questioned. "In your room at this time of night? You thought I was him for a moment."

She hoped the darkness hid the embarrassed flush she felt creep up her neck. "Why wouldn't I?" she responded. "He's the man of the household. It makes perfect sense that I would assume you were Franklin, perhaps come to check on me."

"Is that a habit of his?"

Rosalind gasped when the man had the daring to sit upon the edge of her bed. She scooted as far from him as her mattress would allow. "No, it is not, and if it was, it is none of your business. You must leave at once. It isn't proper for you to be here."

"Did I mention that besides being a coward, lacking in honor and manners, I don't give a damn about being proper?"

"I am quite able to figure that out on my own," she assured him. Rosalind supposed she should scream. But Franklin would be the only man who'd come to her rescue. She had a strong feeling that Armond Wulf was the lesser of those two evils. Still, she couldn't let the man believe it was acceptable to slip into her bedroom in the middle of the night. "If you don't leave immediately, I will call out for my stepbrother. He said you were quite terrified of him."

Armond's teeth flashed white in the darkness when he laughed. "And do you believe him?"

The sarcastic tone of his voice confirmed her earlier suspicions in that regard. Armond Wulf made her uneasy, but Rosalind wasn't positive that the fluttering in her stomach and her inability to catch a normal breath resulted in any way from fear of him.

"What do you want?" she demanded.

His gaze ran a slow study of her. "You know what I want."

Chapter Six

Armond had told himself that he'd only come to question her about the bruise on her cheek. That it was some heroic duty of his to make certain the lady was not being abused. He had lied to himself. What he really wanted was to touch her again. To kiss her. To feel the heat spring up between them the way it had the night of the Greenleys' ball. She drew emotions from him that he thought he'd long ago gained control over. She made him feel. She made him want. She made him behave foolishly.

"I have misled you," she said, and tried to scoot farther away from him. "Regardless of my behavior at the Greenleys' ball, I am not the sort of woman who would allow a man who came into my room uninvited to also easily slip into my bed. This matter must be set straight between us once and for all."

He knew what sort of woman she was. Her kisses, although they had affected him far more than those of any experienced woman he'd spent private time with, had been innocent the night of the ball. Her responses to him had been too honest not to be new to her. She had been an innocent playing the part of brazen. But why had she carried the game so far? He still didn't understand that. For attention? Well, she had gotten that, and he should remind her that attention wasn't always a good thing when dealing with the ton or with a man like him.

"This formality with me does not suit you," he said to her. "Not when I know beneath the ice a fire rages. Aren't you even a little tempted to get burned again?"

Her hand crept up to pull her gown's modest neckline closed. Her small pink tongue wet her lips, an unconscious gesture, but one that drew his gaze to her sinful mouth.

"If I could possibly go back and change what happened between us at the Greenleys' ball, I would. I understand now how silly it was of me to leave with you. I understand that I wasn't thinking clearly, that I had not realized all the ramifications of doing something so daring. I used you for my own purposes, and I have apologized. What more would you ask of me?"

A lot more, he was thinking, but despite her sinful mouth, an air of innocence still clung to her and made conscience rear its ugly head. Her dark hair hung around her shoulders in wild disarray. Her curves were clearly visible beneath her modest nightgown. How could she call to something both decent and yet wild inside of him? What more would he ask of her? Not as much as he wanted to ask, but more than he should. He leaned closer to her.

"Another kiss."

"A kiss?" she whispered breathlessly, then held up her hand as if to stop him. "A kiss and nothing more? Then you'll leave me alone?"

"If that is your wish." Truth be told, Armond had to leave her alone. She was dangerous to him. He wouldn't try to fool himself into believing she wasn't. He supposed he liked playing with fire as well, because that was exactly what he was doing.

Slowly, she lowered her hand. Permission granted, he understood. Yet, now that Armond had permission, he wasn't certain that he shouldn't turn tail and run. Could he kiss her and want nothing more? Could he kiss her and leave her alone from this night forward? Not bloody likely. But he did anyway.

How could Rosalind not be curious to know if the night in his carriage was some strange magical occurrence that would never happen to her again? Or if Armond Wulf had unearthed something inside of her that had been asleep all these years? Rosalind sensed that she could trust his word, perhaps because he hadn't taken full advantage of her that night and he could have. She thought she was relatively safe with him . . . until he kissed her again.

His lips were firm against hers, his open mouth moist, his tongue seeking. She opened to him like a flower starved for rain. It was a slow burn, the buildup between the first tentative touch of their lips and the way he took complete possession of her. The fire within her roared to life, creeping into her bones, licking at her flesh, sending the flame dancing through her until she burned everywhere.

"Rosalind," he spoke her name. "How can I promise you that I won't ask for more, when everything about you makes me want more? More heat, more skin, more than my cursed life can give me?"

She remembered, then, about the curse upon his family. Although his kisses threatened to make her forget everything. Was he a madman? If he was, he spread his disease. She was surely just as mad to allow him into her room, into her bed, into a part of her that she had not known existed. Even though she should push him away, her hands curled into the collar of his shirt and pulled him closer.

"This is madness," she managed to whisper between kisses. "It's wrong to feel this way. I don't even know you."

He pulled back from her suddenly. She saw his face in

the glow from the fading embers of her night fire—saw his eyes. For a brief moment, they sparked and filled with an iridescent blue light; then, as quickly as it had come, the glow was gone.

"No, you don't know me," he agreed.

Armond disentangled her hands from his collar. He rose and without a word moved across the room, out of her open balcony doors, and disappeared. Rosalind wondered for a moment if she was dreaming. If he'd been in her room at all. She touched her swollen lips. They burned. She burned. Beneath the cotton of her proper nightgown, very improper things were happening to her body.

Her breasts were swollen and aching. She felt warm and moist between her legs. She was hungry for more than what he'd given her. And she felt confused that he could elicit such feelings from her. And perhaps even a little angry that he could always so easily walk away. What would it take to shatter his seemingly inhuman control? And what possessed her to want to find out? She had enough problems in her life. Armond Wulf wasn't a problem she needed.

It occurred to her in that instant that nothing about Armond Wulf appealed to a woman's needs, but everything about him appealed to a woman's wants. He had warned her the first night she met him about the danger of playing false with men like him. Men like him? She wasn't even certain what kind of man he was, but she sensed there were few, if any, like him.

Chapter Seven

Rosalind was exhausted. Last night was much too eventful, and once Armond had left, she'd had trouble falling asleep. Later, she'd had nightmares. Nightmares that had her screaming in her sleep, or she supposed she had been the one screaming. She couldn't recall what the dreams had been about, only that Armond Wulf had been part of them.

This morning, she'd begged Franklin to allow her to stay home, but he had refused. Now here she was, on Armond's property. Forced into the company of two men whom she despised with close to equal fervor, and in Lord Wulf's stable no less. A place where a woman had died.

Rosalind wasn't certain if it was those dark thoughts that made her uneasy or if it was simply being forced to share Lord Penmore's company that set her nerves on edge. The viscount wasn't any less subtle in his ogling of her today than he'd been on the previous two occasions she'd been in his company. Franklin was acting even stranger than usual this morning. Her stepbrother had scratches on his face. Rosalind hadn't seen Lydia that morning. She had a bad feeling about that . . . a very bad feeling.

"Ah, there you are, Lord Wulf."

Rosalind glanced away from the horse she'd been admiring. Armond stood facing the two men. He had his back to her. His coat hugged his broad shoulders, tailored to display his impressive frame to its best advantage. He wore snug trousers tucked into tall black boots, both calling attention to the length of his muscular legs. Armond Wulf was a man who looked impressive, either coming or going.

A spark of heat flared up in her belly and spread to her lower regions. Curse the man, how could he affect her when he wasn't even looking at her? And how should she act with him, considering that he'd slipped into her bedroom and kissed her last night?

"What are you doing here, Chapman?"

Hardly the way a businessman greeted potential clients, Rosalind thought. It didn't take a great deal of intellect to understand that Armond didn't care for her stepbrother, and vice versa.

"I came as Penmore's guest," Franklin answered. "Me and my sister."

Since Franklin nodded in her direction, Rosalind fully expected Armond to glance at her. What she did not anticipate was the sudden heat that flared in his eyes when their gazes met and locked. They stood staring at each other for an uncomfortably long time.

"I've had the grays hitched to my carriage, Penmore," Armond said, finally glancing away from her. "I'm assuming you want to try them out before making a final decision."

The disgusting man nodded, his jowls flapping with the motion. "Jolly good idea, Wulf. Maybe the young lady and I can jostle about together." He grinned lewdly at Rosalind.

"I don't allow women to ride along when testing out the horses," Armond intervened, casting the viscount a dark look. "Too dangerous. I'm assuming you want them full-out, to see what they can do?"

Penmore formed his fish lips into an obvious pout; then he nodded. He turned to Franklin. "But you'll come along, won't you, Chapman? I did want another opinion and see no point in having you accompany me if you're not inclined to provide one."

"It wouldn't be proper to leave Rosalind alone," Franklin said. "I'll wait here for your return."

"I don't mind staying here alone," Rosalind spoke up. She longed for even a few minutes without Franklin breathing down her neck. And despite grisly thoughts of murder that kept entering her mind, she loved the smell of the stable and rubbing the horses' velvet noses. It reminded her of the country and brought pangs of homesickness.

"I'm sure Lady Rosalind will be fine," Armond said to the men. "But if you'd rather come another day, Penmore, I understand. Perhaps the animals will still be available."

Penmore pouted his lips again. He turned to Franklin. "Come on, Chapman. She'll be fine here while the rest of us have a short jaunt. I'll tear up your markers from last eve if you'll do me this favor."

The viscount had obviously made the offer too sweet for Franklin to refuse. He nodded. "Very well then. Let's be off so we can get back."

When the men left the stable, Rosalind wanted to shout with joy. Finally, time alone when she wasn't shut up in her room. She could breathe again; she could twirl in wild abandonment. Perhaps she could steal one of Armond's fine horses and escape. She entertained the idea for only a moment. She had nowhere to run. She had no money with her, no food, no extra clothing. If she truly meant to escape, she would have to plan better.

She returned to the horse she'd been petting, drawn to the Arabian's sleek lines, her silky mane and soulful brown eyes. Rosalind wished she had her horse with her in London. She'd loved to ride when she lived in the country and missed her daily outings.

"You have good taste in horses."

Startled, she wheeled around. Armond stood watching her. "I thought you were driving the carriage," she said. "I mean, I assumed . . ."

"So did Penmore and your stepbrother," he countered with a half smile. "My driver is well equipped to show off my animals to their best advantage. I saw no reason to accompany two men whose company fast frays upon my nerves."

"Oh," she said. Oh, like an idiot who couldn't string an intelligent sentence together. But what could she say? Nothing about last night. And now that the fog that seemed to cloud her brain when Lord Wulf was in smelling distance had cleared, at least somewhat, Rosalind realized she shouldn't be caught alone in his company. Franklin would be angry.

"Don't let me keep you from your duties," she said. "I'll be fine here alone."

"Are you afraid?"

"Afraid?"

He sauntered toward her and leaned against the stall next to the mare. A fine chestnut stallion arched his head over the gate and nuzzled Armond's neck. Rosalind had the strangest urge to do the same.

"To be alone with me?" he specified.

"Should I be?" she challenged.

His smile was devilish. He sobered a moment later. "I mean here. Where a woman died."

A sudden chill seemed to penetrate the air. Rosalind shivered. "Where did you find her?"

Armond nodded toward the end of the stable where it was darker. "Down there. I can't stall the horses on that end now. They seem to smell the blood."

She shivered again. "Did you know her?"

Turning to face the stall he leaned against, Lord Wulf stroked the chestnut's muzzle. "Her name was Bess O'Conner, and no, I didn't know her. She was a prostitute, no one of consequence, or I'm sure more would have been done in the search to find her killer."

"How did she get here?" Rosalind walked to the center of the stable and stared down the long row of stalls.

"I don't know. I came home from an evening out. I had dismissed the stable hands for a wedding. One of the grooms got married that night. I went to put my horse up and I heard a moan. That's when I found her."

Rosalind rubbed her arms. "Did she say anything to you?"

When he didn't respond, she glanced at him. He seemed lost in thought. As if he felt her regard, he straightened and turned away from the chestnut.

"No. The woman had been beaten. I tried to learn more about her shortly after it happened. I wanted very much to find the man responsible for her suffering. I wanted very much to make him suffer in turn."

The passion in his voice made Rosalind believe him. She thought at that moment it was very fortunate for the man responsible for Bess O'Conner's death that Armond Wulf hadn't found him.

"Rosalind!"

She jumped and then wheeled around to see Franklin and Penmore standing inside the stable door. Her heart slammed against her chest, and she imagined the color drained from her face. Her stepbrother looked livid.

"Back already?" Armond asked. He walked to the middle of the stable, placing himself directly between

Rosalind and the two men. "I was just showing Lady Rosalind the horses. She has taken a liking to the Arabian filly. Perhaps you'd like me to have her saddled for your stepsister to try?"

Marcus's face turned a darker shade of purple. "You purposely misled us," he accused. "We thought you were driving the carriage. Had I known you wouldn't be going along, I would have never allowed Rosalind to stay behind, and you know it."

Armond didn't flinch at Franklin's angry tone, not the way Rosalind did. But then, Armond had never been on the back side of his hand.

"Lady Rosalind is no worse for wear for a few moments spent alone in my company, as you can plainly see."

"That isn't the point," Franklin bit out.

Armond lifted a brow. "Isn't it? Then what is, Chapman?"

Her stepbrother took a menacing step toward Armond. "Had anyone seen the two of you here alone together, it would have caused gossip. Penmore plans to offer for her. He won't want a woman whose name has been dragged through the mud."

Obviously not in the least intimidated by Franklin, Armond glanced toward the viscount. "Is that right, Penmore? Do you plan to make an offer for Lady Rosalind? The same as you'll make an offer for the horses?"

Penmore had worn a rather amused expression during the confrontation. Now he sobered. "Watch your step, Wulf. What I plan to do as far as Lady Rosalind is concerned is between me and her stepbrother." The man lifted a bushy brow. "You don't plan to offer for the lady, do you?"

Rosalind's gaze traveled back and forth from one man to the other during the exchange. Now her gaze landed on

Armond, and for a brief moment she willed him to say, "Yes." Why she would was not anything immediately clear to her. Well, besides the obvious. A tall, blond god of a man pitted against a short, plump, balding viscount. But Rosalind knew in her heart more than desperation must drive her to make such a decision. Respect? Armond glanced away from the viscount, and even that option was taken from her.

"That is what I thought," Penmore snorted. "You know better than to go sniffing around a lady of quality's skirts. No woman wants a madman for a husband, or to pass on his bad traits to her children. Shall we see to the sale of the horses, then?"

It nearly broke her heart to see that Penmore's words had taken some of the arrogance from Armond's stance. He looked as if he was ashamed for a moment. He quickly covered any weakness he might have displayed by schooling his handsome features into a mask of indifference.

"If you'll all come to the house, I'll have tea served for Chapman and Lady Rosalind while we tend to the bill of sale," Armond said.

Franklin stepped forward. "I hardly think your home would be a fitting place for my stepsister. We'll wait in the carriage for you, Penmore. We could walk the short distance home if not for Rosalind. The heavy dew would ruin her slippers."

Armond turned to look at Rosalind. "And is that a suitable arrangement, Lady Rosalind? The air has gone damp. I assume you'd be more comfortable inside my parlor, sipping a cup of hot tea."

Damn him. Rosalind had the distinct feeling he had purposely pitted her against Franklin. Perhaps in retaliation for having her witness his weakness. Now she was forced to display her own.

"I'll be fine in the carriage," she said, refusing to meet his gaze.

"Nonsense," Penmore finally said. "Chapman, sheathe your dislike of Wulf for the time being, and the both of you come into the house. I don't want to feel rushed in my offer because I'm worried your sister will catch her death waiting for me. I had hoped to speak with her about a matter after I've finished here and have another engagement that I must attend to shortly."

Rosalind glanced up at Franklin. Her stepbrother frowned at the viscount but after a moment nodded his permission. Rosalind thought that was odd. She knew Franklin owed the man a great deal of money, but even so, she didn't believe her stepbrother could be bullied by anyone. He was the bully. And she suddenly felt as if she was the thorn they all used to prick at one another's male egos.

She would have flat out refused Armond's offer of tea, simply because she refused to become a further source of friction between the men present, but she was curious about his home. She was far too curious about everything to do with Armond Wulf, she realized. Penmore approached her and offered his pudgy arm.

"Shall we?"

Although she'd rather not touch the man, Rosalind was too schooled in manners to refuse. She didn't miss Armond's look of disgust when she took Penmore's arm. She also didn't miss the fact that Armond hadn't been the one to come forward and offer her escort to his home.

"The path to the house is rocky." Armond suddenly stood before them. "I should escort Lady Rosalind, since I am familiar with the terrain. I would see her secure in her footing."

He left no time for arguments but took her hand from

Penmore's arm, placed it on his, and started from the stable. "This way."

Rosalind felt Franklin's fuming gaze cutting into her
back as they all moved toward the house. She was surprised she could feel anything except Armond's muscled
arm beneath her hand. Surprised she could even think
clearly with his scent stroking her awareness of him. Sandalwood. She deciphered that much, but that was all she
could identify that wasn't Armond's own scent.

When they reached the front of the house, a manservant immediately opened the door, as if he'd been poised
there simply waiting on Armond to return. He showed no
surprise upon seeing that Armond had guests. He showed
no emotion whatsoever. Armond led them all into the
house.

The decor wasn't what Rosalind expected. For a man
whispered about and steeped in mystery, there were no
black cats roaming the hallways, no cobwebs hanging from
the ceiling, no skeletons waiting to pop from the closets,
at least none that she could see.

"Hawkins, settle my guests in the front parlor," Armond said to his steward. "I'll take Penmore ahead to the
study."

Hawkins answered with a nod. Armond moved down
the hallway with Penmore, and Rosalind and Franklin were
ushered into a front parlor. A cheery fire blazed in the
hearth. The parlor was decorated tastefully. The couches
were plush and comfortable, the carpets immaculate, and
the artwork stunning. Particularly one portrait that hung
above the large fireplace. Rosalind was drawn to the
painting.

That it was the Wulf family there could be no mistake.
She recognized Armond immediately, a boy, fast approaching manhood. There were four boys, in fact, each more
breathtakingly handsome than the last.

"Odd, how they all look perfectly normal." Franklin had come to stand beside her.

"Maybe they *are* perfectly normal," Rosalind said. "Just because the parents, I mean, perhaps the brothers will not be affected."

"I seriously doubt that will be the case, and obviously they feel the same. You heard Penmore; they've all sworn off marriage. Why else would they unless they wanted to be certain the curse ended with them? Then again, who knows? Maybe it was those innocent-looking lads who drove their parents insane."

It was hard to believe that the blond angels staring down at her could be guilty of anything. They looked perfect . . . maybe too perfect. "Where are the other brothers?" she found herself asking.

"Gone."

She wheeled around to see Armond standing behind them, looking out of place holding a silver tea service.

"Lord Gabriel and Lord Jackson are both in residence at the country estate. Keeps them both out of trouble. Please, let me serve you." He indicated a velvet settee. "Penmore is going over the papers. Hawkins isn't used to serving guests, so I took the matter upon myself."

When Franklin kept his stance, snubbing Armond's offer of generosity, Rosalind seated herself. There was something particularly fetching about a man taking on the role of servant. Although Armond's hands were big, his fingers long and slender, he handled the dainty china cups with gentle ease.

"That is only two," she said. "Don't you have three brothers?"

For a moment, pain flashed in his eyes. "Sterling, the youngest, left home years ago."

"He's the sensible one, if you ask me," Franklin said.

"With all that you have hanging over your heads, I don't know why the rest of you don't disappear from society as well. It's not as if you'll be missed."

Armond glanced up from pouring a second cup of tea. "I didn't ask you." He further insulted Franklin by taking a sip of the tea he'd just poured rather than offering it to his other guest.

Franklin sputtered, then marched toward the door leading from the parlor. "Come along, Rosalind. I won't stand here and be insulted by the likes of him. We'll wait for Penmore in the carriage as I originally suggested."

Setting her cup aside, Rosalind rose. She knew better than to argue with Franklin. "Thank you for your hospitality," she said to Armond.

He took her hand and bravely brought it to his lips, planting a warm kiss against her wrist.

"While your stepbrother is not welcome here, you are invited to visit any time you wish."

His eyes scorched her. She realized that he wasn't being polite but reminding her of the kiss they had shared last night. The kiss neither of them was supposed to think about today. It angered her that he would remind her of their intimacy together, but earlier he would not rise to Penmore's bait about courting her seriously.

Rosalind jerked her hand from his grasp. "I wouldn't count on it," she said stiffly, then moved past him.

"Oh, but I do," she heard him say, so soft and low that she knew his words were meant only for her ears.

A shudder raced up her back, one that had nothing to do with the chill in the air. She hurried past Franklin into the hallway, where Hawkins, as if appearing out of thin air, held the door for them.

Franklin immediately began to interrogate her once

they'd climbed inside the carriage. "What happened when you were alone in the stable with Wulf?"

"Nothing," she answered. "We were just looking at the horses."

"You were talking about something when I arrived. The murder that took place there. What did he say about it?"

Rosalind shrugged. "Nothing much. He didn't know the woman. He had no idea how she came to be there. He did claim to be searching for the killer."

Franklin scrubbed a hand across his face. "For all we know, he was the one who murdered her. In fact, I'm willing to wager that he is guilty. Either him or one of his wild brothers. Again, I must insist that you keep your distance from him, Rosalind. An affiliation with him of any kind could damage your reputation. Penmore may act as if he doesn't care what society thinks of him, but believe me, he does."

Rosalind glanced outside the coach window at the drizzly day. She didn't see any sign of Penmore. "About Penmore," she said. "I don't care for him, Franklin. I don't like the way he looks at me. As if I'm a fat pig up for sale at the butcher's market."

Her stepbrother sighed. "I've told you, your opinion of him is of no concern to me. Penmore is interested, and as long as he's interested, you will pretend to be interested in him. He may seem like a jolly fellow, but he is not. He's a man used to getting whatever he wants, and uncaring of who he must destroy in the bargain. I am indebted heavily to him. As much as it sickens me, I must dance to his tune."

If it wasn't Penmore who had Franklin under his thumb, Rosalind could enjoy the irony. Now her stepbrother knew how it felt to be at someone else's mercy. But she could not be happy about the situation. Although she didn't know Penmore that well, she already despised what she did know of him.

The object of their discussion suddenly wrenched the coach door open. "Arrogant bastard," Penmore grumbled, settling his ample girth beside Rosalind. "I have my horses, but at a much higher price than I had hoped to pay for them. Wulf just laughed at my offer and rose and left the room. I had to chase him down the hall to conclude our business."

"The man should be run out of London," Franklin concurred. "He has no business here among the ton, rubbing elbows with everyone as if he had no black marks against his name. They've certainly ousted men of more importance for less than the dark stories floating around about the Wulf brothers."

"Knows horses, though," the viscount grudgingly admitted. "Not a better breeder in the country. Hell to finagle a sale with. Do you know he said if he ever heard of my driver abusing those horses, he'd come and take them back? The nerve of the man."

As much as she supposed she shouldn't, Rosalind admired Armond Wulf in that instant. Defender of the poor beasts left at the mercy of perhaps the cruelest of predators . . . man.

"Will I see you at Lady LeGrande's soiree in two nights' time, my sweet?"

It took her a moment to realize that Penmore had addressed her and that he was drooling down his chin as he eyed her up and down.

"You shall," her stepbrother answered for her. "In fact, you may have the honor of escorting Rosalind, with me along as a chaperone of course."

Rosalind bit her tongue to keep from objecting.

Penmore pulled his usual pout. "I had hoped to spend some private time with Lady Rosalind," he said. "I'd like to get to know her much better."

"You know as well as I do, a young unmarried woman is not seen in public without some type of chaperone," Franklin said. "You'll have her to yourself in due time. First, you must court her. No sampling the pie before you pay your coin to the vendor."

"Must you speak of me as if I am not sitting here?" Rosalind couldn't remain silent any longer. "And must you speak in a manner that insults me? I—"

That was all she managed before Franklin reached across the coach and slapped her. Rosalind gasped and brought a hand to her stinging cheek. She immediately looked at Penmore, embarrassed, humiliated, and wondering if he'd come to her defense.

The man frowned. "If you must discipline your stepsister, Chapman, do not hit her in the face. She's much too pretty to go around with bruises, at least bruises that show. Control yourself, although I know it is not your strong suit."

Both men exchanged a glance. Rosalind was too horrified that Penmore seemed accepting of Franklin's abuse to decipher any hidden meaning there. Was this the kind of husband she wanted? One who would sit by and watch another man humiliate her? One who indicated that hitting a woman was all right, as long as the bruises didn't show? She glanced away from both men.

Her eyes stung and her heart ached. Whatever Armond Wulf was, he was not a man who would stand for that. She knew because he'd questioned her about the bruise she'd tried to pass off as a result of her own clumsiness.

What if he'd been the man sitting beside her when Franklin struck her? She couldn't see Armond remaining indifferent, as Penmore had done. Perhaps she should have told Armond the truth when he'd questioned her about the bruise on her cheek. But what could he have done? He was not a relative, not even a proper suitor. Still, she wasn't certain if given a second chance, she wouldn't tell him, just to see what he was really made of.

Chapter Eight

Lydia had not come to help Rosalind prepare for the LeGrandes' soiree earlier. Mary had told her that Franklin had dismissed the maid. Rosalind felt horrible. She knew confronting her stepbrother about his treatment of the maid had led to his decision. She hoped Lydia would find a position elsewhere, one where her employer would be kind to her.

Rosalind also wished she'd at least been given the opportunity to tell the young woman good-bye before she'd left. If Rosalind had any funds of her own, she would have given Lydia what she had until the woman could secure herself another position. Rosalind had stewed about it all evening up until Penmore had arrived to escort her to the LeGrandes' affair.

Now Rosalind fidgeted with the skirt of her silk gown and tried to pretend an interest in the conversations taking place around her. The LeGrandes' soiree seemed to be a success and most seemed to be enjoying the festivities, but she was not one of them. It was odd to her that her arrival upon Penmore's arm had garnered her acceptance among the tonnish set when the foul man wasn't by half as acceptable to her as the man they all shunned, Armond Wulf.

"What was it like?" Lady Amelia Sinclair, a young

socialite Rosalind had been introduced to earlier, whispered the question to her.

"Beg your pardon?" Rosalind wondered if she'd somehow lost the boring thread of conversation.

"Dancing with Lord Wulf," the young lady clarified, her voice so low Rosalind could barely hear her. "Leaving with him."

Society had obviously not forgotten her faux pas the first night she was introduced to the tonnish set. "A mistake," she muttered, and then tried to pretend interest in another conversation taking place.

"You didn't do anything most of us haven't dreamed of doing before," the young lady admitted. She surprised Rosalind by taking her arm and steering her away from the small cluster of people conversing. "Once you were alone together, what happened?"

Rosalind felt nervous given the line of questioning. She had to answer correctly or give the young lady further gossip to spread about her. "Nothing. He was a perfect gentleman," she lied.

Lady Amelia frowned. Her eyes sparkled mischievously when she said, "How disappointing. Don't you think it's tragic? That the most handsome man in London is forbidden to us?"

Stunned by the young lady's forwardness, Rosalind could only nod. She recovered a moment later, worried that the young lady was attempting to trick information from her. Damning information. "I think his reputation for being dangerous is highly exaggerated. I certainly don't believe the notice I sought to gain by dancing with him was worth the bother."

Glancing around, the young woman argued, "But that is where you're wrong. Everyone noticed you. I for one was simpering with jealousy over your bravery. Imagine, having the courage to dance with the devil himself? No one will forget you, Lady Rosalind, of that you can be certain."

Rosalind suspected the young lady's assurances should not be counted as a compliment. It didn't matter much anyway what society thought of her. If Franklin had his way, she would soon be engaged to Penmore. Her reputation would no longer be an issue.

"I found your daring admirable," Lady Amelia continued. "And refreshing. At least you're not like the other pasty-faced debutantes whose circles I am forced to run in, never daring to do anything that would raise a brow or cause gossip. I find them terribly boring."

Rosalind laughed. "You are quite shocking yourself to have that view."

Lady Amelia shrugged. "I suppose I am. My mother says often enough that a young woman with my improper attitude can only come to ruin. I hope she's right."

Again Rosalind laughed. She found to her utter surprise she was actually enjoying herself in Lady Amelia's company. Rosalind had few friends. She'd grown up in the country beneath her father's sometimes overprotective attention. Franklin had forbidden her to have interaction with young ladies her own age. She supposed he was worried she might somehow enlist aid in helping her to escape from him. And if Rosalind thought she could, she certainly would.

"Your stepbrother seems to keep a tight rein on you," Lady Amelia commented. "I see him heading this way, and he doesn't look pleased that we have become fast friends."

Rosalind glanced in the direction in which she'd last seen Franklin and Penmore engaged in conversation. Neither man, it was obvious, was popular, even if Penmore seemed to be accepted. No doubt because of his title and his wealth.

"Are we friends?" she asked the pretty blonde. It embarrassed Rosalind to realize how hopeful she sounded. She needed a friend now that even Lydia was lost to her. She needed one badly.

The young woman clasped Rosalind's hand and squeezed. "Only if you promise not to become boring like the others. Who knows, if the handsome Lord Wulf shows his face at another social function this season, perhaps I will ask him to dance."

When Lady Amelia glanced over her shoulder toward a rather stern-faced woman standing a few feet away and received a frown indicating displeasure over her choice of current companion, Lady Amelia squeezed Rosalind's hand again. "My mother doesn't approve of you," she said candidly. "But you're not to take it personally. My mother doesn't approve of anything or hardly anyone. She says I'm to marry Lord Collingsworth. She says he's appropriate for me."

Casting another nervous glance toward Franklin, who was bearing down upon them, Rosalind asked, "And what do you say?"

The young woman frowned. "I probably will marry him. I'm like you, a duke's daughter. I must marry well."

The two were nothing alike. Lady Amelia had a mother to watch over her. A father to make wise decisions on her behalf. Rosalind knew that if her father were alive, he'd never approve of Penmore for a husband. He would have at least tried to find someone closer to her age, and he wouldn't have condoned a man who turned a blind eye to another man abusing her.

"Excuse my stepsister; her escort for the evening was called away on an urgent matter and I am ordered to make certain that Rosalind enjoys the dancing." Franklin was suddenly there, taking her arm in his cruel grip.

Lady Amelia turned away and hurried toward her

mother, like a brave chick who'd wandered too far from the nest and now sought cover from a fox.

"Penmore pointed out to me that I am lax in my position as chaperone again," Franklin explained. "Since he was called away, we will have a dance before I escort you home."

Rosalind wasn't disappointed that Penmore would not escort her home, but she was upset that her conversation with Lady Amelia Sinclair had been cut short. "I was fine," Rosalind assured him. "In fact, I made a friend."

"You have no need for friends," Franklin said in a clipped voice. "If you do, Penmore will choose them for you once you are married."

Feeling brave in the company of so many, Rosalind said, "I have not agreed to marry him, Franklin. What if I chose someone else? Someone who is willing to settle your debts and willing to accept me without a dowry?"

They had reached the edge of the dance floor and Franklin swept her into the sea of ladies and gentlemen. He crushed her hand in his. "You count too much upon your pretty face and your pedigree, Rosalind. Besides, you do not have that option. I thought you did until Penmore caught sight of you, but now that he has, your future is decided. He made that quite clear to me earlier this evening."

Again Rosalind was surprised that any man could hold Franklin under his thumb. But then, if he owed the man a great deal in gambling debts, debts that could be called in at a moment's notice, debts that could land Franklin in prison, she supposed even Franklin wouldn't thwart the man. Her spirits sank with the realization.

"I can't say that I'm sad he was called away," she bravely admitted. "He's disgusting to me. If he were at least kind—"

"Stop your complaining," Franklin interrupted. He

squeezed her hand painfully again. "Your wishes, as I've told you time and time again, do not matter to me. If it will give you a measure of comfort, I know a little secret about our viscount."

She glanced up at Franklin, who was taller than her but not as dashingly tall as Armond Wulf. "A secret?"

He smiled down at her, and for any who might be watching, it was the doting smile of a stepbrother, only, as always, his eyes remained flat and dead. "Our viscount has problems with his manly parts. I doubt that he can get it up long enough to consummate your marriage. Although he talks a good game, likes to pretend that he's as randy as a young stud still full of lead."

Rosalind wasn't innocent enough to misunderstand what Franklin told her. While it made marriage to the man only a little less intolerable, he still sickened her with his lewd grins and fondling hands. She did wonder then why her reputation was so important to a man who couldn't do his husbandly duty anyway.

"I know what you're thinking," Franklin drawled. "Penmore has been a bachelor for so long that it is for some reason important to marry a young lady of good reputation, and good bloodlines, although I'll warn you that any children you may have with him will no doubt be fathered by a man of his choosing."

Her stomach rolled at the thought, and for a moment she feared she might become ill on the dance floor, which would be ironic, since that was the ruse Armond had made up to spare her reputation the first night they met.

As if merely thinking of Armond Wulf summoned him, she caught sight of a tall blond figure moving along the outer edges of the dance floor. Her eyes were drawn to him, as she suspected were everyone's present. He commanded attention, though he did not demand it.

He wore black as usual, which contrasted sharply to

his blond hair and tawny skin. His long hair was tied back, drawing attention to the chiseled lines of his face. His eyes were centered directly on her as he moved—but no, he didn't move; he stalked her, like an animal that had caught sight of his prey. That she was the object of Armond's regard would be impossible to miss if anyone was paying attention. And everyone was.

"Don't look at him," Franklin hissed down at her. "The two of you are making a spectacle."

How she could possibly be making a spectacle when a good ten paces separated her and Armond? But Rosalind supposed she had managed, since the very air around her seemed suddenly charged with speculation. She didn't care, she realized. And she couldn't seem to look away, as if she were indeed a rabbit mesmerized by the steady gaze of an animal about to gobble her up.

Her blood started to tingle, her face to flush. She forgot everything. Her good upbringing, the fact that she was dancing with a man who had made her life a living hell and would continue to do so for as long as she was at his mercy. Franklin brought her back to reality. He squeezed her hand so hard she almost cried out.

"Time to make our excuses and leave," he growled down at her. "That man makes you lose your head. I won't have him ruining everything! Do you hear me, Rosalind? He will learn that I am not a man to be taken lightly. And neither is Penmore."

He nearly dragged her from the dance floor. "Franklin," she breathed, suddenly regaining her wits and hurrying to keep up with him. "If you whisk me away from the soiree right now, it will be you who is making a spectacle. Everyone will be talking about how you ran from Lord Wulf. Please, allow me to have a little dignity and rethink your decision on the matter."

Rosalind was afraid to leave with Franklin. Better for

her if he had time to cool his temper and she had time to appease him by pretending she had no interest in Armond Wulf whatsoever. If she could pretend, that was. Recalling the way he'd avoided Penmore's taunt in the stable helped in that regard.

Franklin slowed his steps. "I do think you have a brain in that pretty little head of yours, after all," he said. "Wulf is no doubt using you to anger me. The man enjoys taunting me, but he will soon learn that is a mistake. We will rejoin the guests and pretend we are having a conversation until a suitable amount of time has passed; then we will make our excuses and leave."

Although she would rather allow herself to be swallowed by the crowd and avoid Franklin, better to be in his company, where he wouldn't dare strike her, than alone with him. No matter how tempted Rosalind was to look in Armond's direction, she would control the impulse. Or so she hoped.

"You are a wicked man, Armond Wulf," the dowager duchess scolded. "Here I thought you were innocent and wrongly accused of the gossip that constantly floats around your angelic head like a tarnished halo, and you are proving everyone right."

Armond forced his eyes from Rosalind to meet the dowager's frown. He lifted a brow in inquiry over his sins. She nodded in the direction he'd been staring since he first arrived at Lady LeGrande's soiree.

"You're causing the worst kind of speculation with the heated looks you constantly throw across the room at Lady Rosalind."

He frowned. "Have I been staring at her?" He knew he had been but seemed helpless to stop. She looked beautiful in a rose silk gown that set off her pale skin and dark hair. He couldn't take his eyes from her.

"My, my," the dowager clucked. "Armond Wulf has finally lost his heart. And about time, too. I told you the young woman would make a good match for you."

Her speculations snapped his head in the woman's direction. "My heart isn't what's speaking to me when I look at Lady Rosalind; I can assure you of that."

The dowager gave him a good swat with her fan. "Naughty boy. Love very often begins with a strong attraction to the physical. You should try to control your lust in public, though. The way you're staring at the young woman you might as well strip her bare and have your way with her in front of the whole social set. Do you do everything so . . . intensely?"

He thought about the question for a moment. "Yes," he finally answered.

The dowager laughed. "Her stepbrother is growing more livid by the moment. You should tone it down at bit, Armond. You know she arrived on the rather pudgy arm of the disgusting Lord Penmore? I do hope the young heiress can do better than him. It would be a pity to see her wasted on such a scoundrel."

Rosalind had allowed the foul man to escort her to the soiree? She was the most beautiful woman he'd ever set eyes on. Why would she settle for Penmore? She could have any man in London. Any man but Armond.

He forced his gaze from her. "Do not think to bait me into behaving foolishly where the young woman is concerned," he warned the dowager. "You know that I have vowed to never marry."

"You're behaving foolishly enough on your own," the woman said smoothly. "Why are you here, Armond? To see me? I hardly think so. You came to see her; admit that much."

He would not admit it to the dowager, even if it was the truth. Armond had suspected Rosalind would attend the soiree. He had no business being here. He hadn't been invited, though that usually proved no problem for him. People were afraid to turn him away. But he'd come anyway, again as if he couldn't resist his pull toward her.

"I did come to see you." He turned his charm and his attention on the woman who had been a friend to his parents and hadn't forsaken their children when the curse had come upon his family. "I adore you, and if there is a woman in all of London who could tempt me to break my vow to remain a bachelor for life, it would be you."

The dowager, long past her prime, blushed like a young girl. She quickly swatted him with her fan again. "Naughty boy."

Rosalind's resolve had weakened by the time she realized Armond had left the soiree. Obviously, the same as every other woman present, she found it nearly impossible not to glance in his direction. He was sinfully handsome, and as he spoke with the old dowager, his face relaxed and his smile, when he flashed it upon the woman, was enough to take Rosalind's breath away.

Franklin had insisted they leave shortly after Armond had disappeared. Now they rode home in silence, though her stepbrother still brooded across from her. Rosalind closed her eyes and leaned her head back against the seat, reliving the night's events.

Armond had ignored her once he'd joined the dowager. Although Rosalind should have been grateful his attention didn't further enrage Franklin, she admitted to feeling a bit stung by Armond's indifference toward her. Perhaps because she found it impossible to remain indifferent toward him.

They did her no good, these feelings that leaped to life every time she was in close proximity to Armond Wulf. Franklin had made up his mind about her future, and even

if he hadn't, Armond Wulf would be the last man he'd allow her to court seriously. And obviously, Armond had no
desire to court her properly. He instead had chosen to
pursue her very improperly.

The clip-clop of the horses lulled Rosalind. She remembered another night, another carriage ride. Another man.
There in the darkness behind her eyelids, Armond came to
her again. She felt his lips against hers, soft but commanding. Her breasts swelled, ached with the remembered feel
of his hands . . . his tongue . . . his mouth. She remembered exactly how she had felt in his arms, how he had felt
pressed against her. The heat that had sprung up between
them, the hunger. The sound of her own soft moan startled
her, and she abruptly opened her eyes.

Franklin stared at her, his expression much like that of
a cat watching a sleeping mouse. "What were you dreaming about just now?" he asked softly. "Or maybe I should
ask who?"

Rosalind straightened. "I must have dozed off. Are we
home?" She made a great show of pulling back the carriage drapes to peek out into the dark night. Only a few
lights burned in the townhouse. "Oh, I see that we are.
Well, good. I'm exhausted."

"Don't think that you'll simply scamper up to your
room and avoid punishment for your behavior this evening," Franklin said. "I've been thinking about what
would be appropriate."

Rosalind had never suspected that mere words could
make her blood freeze in her veins, make her heart rise in
her throat, but she was wrong. In spite of her sudden terror, she would make a stand.

"I'm a grown woman, Franklin," she said. "I won't be
punished like a child. Not by you, not by any man."

He lifted a brow over her daring, and his calm expression was more frightening than if he'd flown into a rage.

"We will see," he said. He leaned forward and opened the coach door, then bounded outside. When he extended his hand to help Rosalind alight, she refused to take it.

"You will not beat me," she said sternly. "I will no longer stand for your abuse."

His calm facade cracked, and for a moment his eyes flared with barely suppressed rage. "You dare tell me what you will or will not tolerate beneath my roof?"

The coachman appeared to help them alight, saw that Franklin had already done so, and went around in front of the horses to take their reins and lead them to the carriage house. Franklin reached forward, grabbed Rosalind's arm, and nearly wrenched it from the socket when he pulled her outside. She gasped with the pain.

As the coach moved from their path, she wanted to call out to the driver, beg him for help, but the rattle and sway of the carriage would have drowned her out, and Franklin would have only become more enraged.

Panic overtook her and Rosalind tried to bolt. Where she would go, she didn't know, only that she turned toward the house next door and managed to make it a few feet before Franklin caught her.

"You think he can help you?" he hissed in her ear. He squeezed her already aching arm and she whimpered. "No one can help you, Rosalind."

Desperation made her whisper Penmore's name as Franklin hauled her toward the house. Her stepbrother only laughed.

"He doesn't care, as long as the bruises don't show." His gaze ran the length of her. "Of course we'll have to get you out of that gown. It cost a fortune and I won't see it ripped and stained."

Rosalind tried to dig in the dainty heels of her slippers, but it did no good. Franklin was too strong. If Mary answered the door for them, she'd appeal to her for help, although Rosalind wasn't sure what the woman could do. No one got the door, and Rosalind realized at this late hour, Mary would be upstairs with the duchess.

Franklin dragged Rosalind inside, headed toward the stairs and the bedchambers upstairs. Both of them drew up short at the sight that greeted them.

There along the rafters that ran the length of the tall ceiling hung a rope, on which a body swung slowly back and forth. The corpse was that of a woman. Rosalind might not have recognized her; the woman's face was blue from suffocation, not to mention the bruises that blackened her sightless eyes and distorted her features. But Rosalind did know her. It was Lydia.

Chapter Nine

Armond had just come in from a few rounds of cards and removed his coat when the sound drifted to him. He turned an ear toward his open window. Again he heard it. The distant sound of weeping. Always he had been aware of his keen sense of hearing, his even keener sense of smell.

He had never really thought much of it, not until he learned of the curse. Now he knew why his senses were more adept than those of normal men. It was the animal in him . . . the animal waiting to be set free.

Why did she weep? That it was Rosalind, he had no doubt. Should he rush to her aid? Or did she simply weep over something insignificant? A slight barb someone had delivered to her at the LeGrandes' soiree? But no, she cried with her heart, with her soul. Something was horribly wrong, and he would go and find out what it was.

Without bothering with his coat, he left his bedchamber. There were few servants at his townhome. All men. Women were too frightened to work for him. He saw no one as he descended the stairs, then went out the front door.

The grass was damp. Fog hung heavy in the air. A light drizzle fell. He'd be soaked through by the time he reached Rosalind's room. The closer he came to her residence, the easier it was to hear her tearful sobs. He hurried.

He climbed the trellis to her balcony without incident, half-worried that she had taken to bolting her doors. The doors were closed against the chilly night air, but they were not locked. He let himself in. His eyes easily adjusted to the darkness. He saw her huddled beneath her covers.

"Rosalind?"

With a start, she threw back the heavy covers and sat up.

"Armond?"

"What's wrong?"

"Oh, Armond." She was out of the bed, racing across the carpet. He couldn't have been more surprised when she threw herself into his arms. "It was horrible."

His hand automatically strayed to her loose hair. It felt like the finest silk beneath his fingers. "What was horrible? Why are you crying?"

"Lydia," she managed between sobs. "She hung herself."

Armond steered Rosalind toward the bed. He helped her to sit before settling beside her. "Lydia? Was she a friend of yours?"

"My abigail," she answered. "She had been dismissed earlier in the week, but tonight when I came home from the LeGrandes', there she was, hanging from the rafters."

When Rosalind covered her face with her hands and another sob escaped her, he placed an arm around her shoulders.

"It's my fault," she whispered. "I'm the reason Franklin dismissed her. I can only assume that she couldn't find other employment and then, well, something must have happened to her and she decided death was an easier escape than facing her bleak tomorrows."

Rosalind's deep distress over a servant surprised him. True, what she must have seen would affect anyone, but most young socialites, he imagined, would have spent a few tears over the incident and then simply gone on, quickly forgetting the matter. Of course, she must have discovered the maid only a few short hours earlier.

"Did she leave a note? Any explanation as to why she would feel moved to take her own life?" he asked.

Rosalind shook her head. "No. Not that anyone has found anyway. She . . ."

"She what?"

"She had bruises on her."

An alarm sounded in Armond's head. "Bruises?"

"On her face," Rosalind continued. "It looked as if she'd been recently beaten, and beaten badly. Franklin said she ran with a rough crowd. I heard him tell the constable that one of her men, drunk on ale, had probably beaten her up. Maybe he ended their relationship. Maybe that along with being dismissed was why she hung herself."

"Chapman was with you at the LeGrandes' all evening, correct?"

She nodded. "Yes. Why do you ask?"

Armond might suspect her stepbrother of foul play, but the man had been at the soiree with Rosalind all evening. He couldn't have possibly been responsible for the maid's death. At least not the hanging part.

"Were you close to this woman?"

Rosalind hiccupped softly. Her eyes were bright with tears when she looked up at him. "I thought we were friends. We were closer, I suspect, than most of different classes. But she never really talked much of her personal life."

"Why was she dismissed?"

Suddenly Rosalind looked away from him. She wouldn't

answer. Armond started to turn her toward him, but the moment he touched her arm, she flinched.

"What happened to your arm?"

"I hurt it," she answered softly, but still refused to look at him.

"How?"

"I don't recall."

A suspicion surfaced, one that had surfaced before. He had to know this time. Armond had to know for certain. He reached out, took the sleeve of her cotton gown, and tore it from the shoulder. Rosalind gasped and tried to scramble away, but he would not let her escape. In the soft glow from her night fire he saw the ugly bruise, the imprint of fingers against her skin. His blood began to boil.

"Who did this to you, Rosalind?"

Her eyes filled with tears again. For a moment, he thought she wouldn't tell him. She drew in a deep breath and answered, "Franklin. He's hurt me before. He has a horrible temper."

Armond cursed, rose, and moved toward her bedroom door. "We'll see how well he fares against another man."

Rosalind bounded up from the bed, rushed ahead of him, and pressed herself against the door before he reached it. "No, Armond, you mustn't. He's not even home. After the constable left and Lydia's body was taken away, he went to the clubs."

Undeterred, Armond turned toward the balcony doors. His rage grew by the second. "Then I'll find him."

"Please don't leave me."

Her choked request stopped him in his tracks. He turned to look at her, so delicate, so frightened. She stood shaking in the middle of the room, her torn gown hanging off of one creamy shoulder. He'd left the doors open and the night chill had crept into the room. Armond walked over and closed them, then joined her.

"Get into bed," he ordered softly. "You'll catch your death."

She moved toward the bed and climbed beneath her covers. Armond joined her, sitting on the edge. His shirt was damp with drizzle, and now the chill penetrated his rage and made him aware of the cold.

"You didn't really trip and fall against a chair that night after the Greenleys' ball, did you?"

"No," she answered. "Franklin slapped me for . . . for leaving with you."

"And you didn't leave with me to impress your friends, either, did you?"

"I have no friends," she admitted. "Franklin will force me into marriage because he needs money. I thought if you ruined me, no man would have me and he'd let me go back to the country."

Armond sighed. He raked his fingers through his damp hair to push it back from his face. "Rosalind, you must have people who will help you. Family—"

"I have no one." She suddenly sat. "My father is dead. He left my future up to my stepmother because he knew that she loved me and would look after me, but now she's terribly ill, and her lawyers have given Franklin my guardianship. He's squandered my inheritance. Now he thinks to use me further."

His suspicions were mild compared to her admissions. Good Lord, how had she managed to survive under such deplorable conditions? She'd been little more than a prisoner in this house, at the mercy of a man who would use her for his gain and abuse her in the bargain. Armond wanted to kill Chapman. He more than wanted to kill him. He wanted to rip his throat out with his teeth.

"Why didn't you tell me the truth from the beginning?"

Rosalind glanced down at her hands. "I don't know you. I couldn't see where telling you would do me any good." She glanced up. "I still can't."

She was right. What could he do for her except perhaps kill the man who would dare treat her in this manner? The social set would jump on an opportunity to prove that he was, in fact, a murderer. How could he offer her his protection without offering her his name? And he could not offer her his name. He could not offer her a bright future, children, any of the things that she deserved.

"You're trembling again," he noted. Armond pulled the covers up around her, but her teeth began to chatter. She needed more warmth than the fire could give her. He removed his damp shirt before he stretched out beside her, pulling her into his arms. She tensed. "Don't be afraid of me," he said against her hair. "I mean only to give you my warmth."

After a moment of being held by him, she relaxed against him. He wanted more information on Chapman. "You didn't tell me why the maid was dismissed," he reminded her. "Or why you believe her dismissal was your fault."

Rosalind's head was tucked beneath his chin. Her hair smelled of lavender and brushed against his chest. "She told me that Franklin had forced himself on her. I called him to account for it, and he flew into a rage. The next thing I knew, Mary, the housekeeper, said that Franklin had dismissed Lydia."

A rapist and a man who would beat a woman with his fists? The more Armond learned of Chapman, the more he thought about Bess O'Conner. He couldn't figure out how she'd come to be in his stable, but if she was trying to escape, say from this house, she could have very well run across the lawn to hide on his property. Chapman hadn't been under suspicion, not when the murder could be pinned on a man who already had a questionable reputation among society.

"Will you stay with me for a while?" Rosalind asked. "Just until I fall asleep?"

He was itching to find Chapman—beat the man senseless at the very least. Threaten him perhaps that if he ever raised a hand to Rosalind again, he'd get worse. But she still trembled in Armond's arms, and if his presence made her feel safe, even for a little while, he would give her that. It was all that he could give her.

"Yes, I'll stay," he answered, stroking her silken hair. A question suddenly popped into his mind. "How does Penmore figure into all of this?"

She shivered against him, but he didn't know if it was from the chill or from the mention of the man's name. "Franklin owes him a great deal of money in gambling debts. He wants me in exchange."

"So your stepbrother will trade you, like a used carpetbag?"

She didn't answer. He knew she was humiliated, having Armond discover her secrets. It angered him even more, if that were possible. He had to get Rosalind away from this situation, and away quickly.

"The dowager," it suddenly occurred to him. "I could get you sanctuary with her. She's old, and she's frail, but she's as mean as an old hen when someone she's taken beneath her wing is threatened."

"I don't think Franklin will let me go," Rosalind said. "Not without a fight."

Armond pulled her closer. Protective instincts rose inside of him. "If he wants a fight, I'll bloody well give it to him."

• • •

Rosalind had wondered what Armond would do if she was given a second chance to tell him the truth about her stepbrother. Now she knew. She felt safe in Armond's arms, safe for the first time in months. Safe and yet not safe. Even in her state of mind, she was aware of the steady beat of his heart beneath her ear. Aware of the smooth, warm texture of his skin. Aware of his scent that awakened her senses.

She wondered at times if she hadn't put her daring plan into play that night at the Greenleys' ball, she would still be as attracted to him? But then she knew she would. She'd been attracted to him on sight, before she'd learned his name. Before she heard the dark whispers about him. Who would have thought then that Armond Wulf would come to a woman's defense? That he was perhaps more honorable than those who snubbed him?

Exhaustion claimed her. She'd sobbed out her strength for poor Lydia, and now Rosalind closed her eyes and allowed Armond to hold her. He gently stroked her hair, and the action lulled her into closing her eyes. She didn't want to think about tomorrow. About the battle that would soon rage when Armond tried to take her from beneath Franklin's roof and from his cruel control. Tomorrow would come soon enough.

Chapter Ten

Dawn had just begun to streak the sky when Armond crept from Rosalind's bed and pulled his still damp shirt over his head. He stared at her as he dressed. She slept on her side, her hands beneath her cheek. Her hair was a riotous tangle of dark curls, her full lips slightly parted. He couldn't believe he'd spent the whole night just holding her when what he really wanted to do was make love to her.

He'd heard Chapman come in at some ridiculous hour and would have gone to confront the man if gossip wouldn't put him in the man's home at an unusual hour, coming from the man's stepsister's room, no less. Rosalind had been through enough.

Armond wouldn't ruin her reputation, though that had been her exact plan the night she approached him at the Greenleys' ball. He realized now how desperate she must have felt to do something so out of her character. He hated Chapman all the more for forcing her into taking drastic measures.

Armond's plan was to clean up once he arrived home, then, as soon as the hour was suitable, pay the dowager a call and enlist her aid in seeing Rosalind removed from Chapman's guardianship. Dressed, he started toward the balcony doors.

Rosalind stirred. He walked back to the bed and waited until she'd settled back to sleep. Something inside of him twisted while he stood over her. Something unfamiliar. Protectiveness he had never felt for any woman. He bent down and lightly kissed her on the cheek, then forced himself away from her.

Once on the balcony, he glanced around and, seeing no one had yet begun to stir outside the townhome or in the carriage house, climbed down the trellis. He'd almost made it to his stable when he noticed something odd. His grooms all stood outside talking, their breaths steaming on the early morning air. Henry, a lad who'd been with Armond for a good year or so, saw him before he reached the stable. The lad's eyes rounded, and he motioned Armond to stay back.

Armond drew up. Two men emerged from the stable. Armond recognized them immediately. They were the inspectors who'd questioned him the night Bess O'Conner had died in his stable. The hair rose on the back of his neck. One man glanced in his direction.

"There he is!" he shouted. "Do not try to run, Lord Wulf!"

Why would he run? But he knew the answer. He smelled the blood. He didn't run. Instead, he moved toward the men.

"Lord Wulf," the inspector said once he reached the group. "You are under arrest for murder."

Armond walked past the man and into the stable. There on the ground lay a woman, bruised, dead. The paint on her cheeks and lips and her manner of dress told him she was a prostitute, the same as Bess O'Conner had been.

"I see his shirt's damp," one inspector said to the other. "Tried to wash the blood out of it, I'm guessing."

"Lord Wulf, do you have anyone who can say where you've been all night this time?"

The second man's question was sarcastic. He'd never felt that either inspector had believed he wasn't responsible for the last murder. Either him or one of his brothers. Armond did have someone who could say where he'd been all night. But of course he couldn't name her. Not without totally ruining her.

"No," he answered.

"Then you'll want to come along with us."

A man appeared on either side of him and forcefully took his arms.

"Henry, have Hawkins bring me a fresh change of clothing to the inspector's home," Armond said. "The rest of you see to the horses once . . . once the lady has been removed."

He left with the inspectors, wondering if he'd ever see his home again, or anything besides a hangman's noose or the gray walls of Newgate.

Rosalind was surprised to see Franklin at late breakfast. He usually slept most of the day due to the hours he kept. Mary could hardly serve without breaking down to weep, and on several occasions Rosalind had joined her. Franklin, she noted, did not even look as if anything untoward had happened in his home the previous night. In fact, he looked uncharacteristically cheerful.

"I have news of our neighbor," he said, methodically buttering a scone. "It seems Lord Wulf was arrested this morning for murder. They found another dead woman in his stable."

At first, Franklin's words would not register. Rosalind stared across the table at him, a fork poised halfway to her lips.

"Seems he had no one to help him cover his crime this time. No one saw him in the clubs last night, myself included. The stable hands all said nothing was amiss up until around midnight, when they finished a round of cards and went home. Seems the one left in charge for the night had drunken himself into a stupor and heard nothing."

"He's not guilty," Rosalind whispered.

Franklin paused while buttering to glance across the table at her. "How could you possibly know that? Because he's handsome? Because you fancy him? Because you wish it to be true?" He laughed before he finally took a bite of his breakfast. "All the wishes in the world won't save his neck this time. I can't say I'm sorry to see him go. Perhaps I can fetch a higher price for the house now, should I decide to sell . . . that is, after my dear mother is gone."

Rosalind was glad she hadn't eaten anything yet, for she felt certain it would come back up. Another murder had taken place. Another dead woman found in Armond's stable. Rosalind tried to remember when he'd left her bed and was certain it was early this morning. He couldn't have killed the woman. He'd been with her all night. Only he had not said he'd been with her, she realized.

"Excuse me," she said, then placed her napkin on the table and rose. "I'm going back up to my room. I'm still terribly upset about poor Lydia."

"You know . . ." Franklin paused again before he took a bite of his scone. "I'm not positive that he couldn't have had something to do with her death as well. We both dislike one another. Wouldn't put it past him to leave her dangling there among the rafters as a cruel joke."

"God save us," Mary muttered.

Rosalind hurried from the room. She rushed up the stairs, entered her bedroom, and automatically threw the bolt home. Then she sank to the floor, too stunned to move. Why hadn't Armond told the authorities where he'd been all night? To save her reputation? Good lord, the man had more honor than all the ton gentlemen put together. She was sick.

Sick that he would sacrifice himself for her reputation. A reputation she would have ruined herself at the Greenleys' ball if he hadn't proved so damned honorable that night, as well.

She could not let it stand. She would not. She also couldn't go to Franklin with the truth. He'd never allow her to ruin herself for Armond Wulf. He'd probably beat her half to death for admitting she'd allowed Armond into her bedroom, not once but twice now. But what could she do? Franklin had never given her free rein to go gallivanting around London on her own.

Rosalind gathered her strength. For the past three months her stepbrother had controlled her, had weakened her will with threats and abuse, and had stolen most of her spirit. She would not allow him to continue. Armond had given her hope last night. Hope of escape. Now she must do the same for him.

Rising, Rosalind walked to her balcony, opened the doors, and went outside. She eyed the vine-covered trellis that stood next to the balcony. Armond had told her it was not so difficult to climb, not if a man was determined. Not if a woman was determined as well, she decided. Rosalind went to the railing, hiked up her skirts, and carefully placed one leg over, then reached for the trellis.

Her arm still ached where Franklin had been rough with her, but she bit her lip and grabbed onto the trellis. She eased herself off the balcony. Then she started the climb down. It was no easy task, despite what Armond had told her. But then, Armond hadn't had to manage it in a gown and two petticoats.

Once she reached the ground, Rosalind flattened herself against the house and glanced around. No one was

about. Franklin would still be eating his breakfast. She
didn't believe that she could march into the carriage house
and order his meager staff about. She must enlist aid elsewhere. She glanced across the yard toward Armond's
property. Hawkins, his manservant, might help her. Surely
he would if she said she had information that would free
Armond. At least she prayed that he would.

Armond had been questioned by the inspectors for several hours. He'd been asked the same questions over and
over, to which he gave the same answers. He was alone
last night, and no, he wasn't guilty of the woman's death,
and again no, he had no witnesses to attest to the fact. He
was surprised he hadn't already been hauled off to Newgate, but it seemed that even a Wulf, because of his titles
and wealth, received special treatment concerning the
matter of murder.

A soft rap sounded upon the door, and one of the inspectors rose and answered it. Her scent found him before
she actually entered. Armond sat up straight in the chair
he'd been slumping in. What in the hell was Rosalind doing here?

Words were exchanged and he could have easily deciphered them with his abnormal hearing, but he was too
stunned that she'd come to try. She swept into the room a
moment later.

"This lady has information regarding Lord Wulf," one
inspector said to the other. "Seems she knows about his
whereabouts last evening."

"Don't, Rosalind," Armond commanded quietly.

She straightened her shoulders and ignored him.

"And you are?" the seated inspector questioned.

"Lady Rosalind Rutherford, the late Duke of Montrose's daughter and Lord Wulf's neighbor."

The inspector's brows lifted. "So, you might have seen something last night, say from one of your windows?"

"No," Rosalind admitted. "I saw nothing, but I do know where Lord Wulf was for the entire night."

"Rosalind," Armond warned again, "think about what you are doing."

"Please keep quiet while Lady Rosalind is speaking," one of the inspectors said to Armond. "Otherwise we'll have you removed until the lady has left."

"She's lying," he informed the inspectors.

Each cast him a dark look. "How do you know she's lying when she hasn't even told us anything yet?" one of the men asked.

"I have a feeling I know what she's going to say," Armond answered. "I hope I'm wrong," he stressed, staring at Rosalind.

She wouldn't look at him in turn.

"Lady Rosalind, you say you know where Lord Wulf was last evening," the inspector prompted. "If you did not see him from your window, or your property, how do you know where he was?"

Her gaze slid toward Armond, then quickly back to the inspector. "I know because he was with me," she answered. Her cheeks flushed a pretty shade of pink. "In my bedroom," she specified. "In my bed."

Armond might have enjoyed watching both men's mouths drop open if not for the seriousness of the situation. She would ruin herself with her admissions. Ruin herself beyond even his help.

"You are willing to swear to that, Lady Rosalind?" one man finally recovered. "Even though by your doing so the admission will undoubtedly, well, it will cause talk among society that your character is, well—"

"I'll be ruined," Rosalind provided for the man. "Yes,

I am aware of the consequences, Inspector. But I cannot allow an innocent man to be charged with a crime he did not commit. It is my duty to come forward, is it not?"

"Might I have a word with the lady, alone?" Armond asked. He had to make Rosalind withdraw her admission. He had to make her understand that if she so publicly ruined herself, even the dowager couldn't help her. That would leave her at the mercy of her stepbrother and, no doubt, his raging temper over what she had done.

"Lord Wulf, until we get this matter settled it would be very foolish on our part to leave a suspected woman-killer alone with Lady Rosalind," one man said with a snort.

"I would be perfectly safe," Rosalind assured the man. "Because Lord Wulf is not a killer. He has . . . he has been to my room on more than one occasion."

"Then you are, ah, lovers, Lady Rosalind?"

Again her cheeks turned pink. "So it would seem," she answered.

Armond felt like howling. No, he didn't want to pay, and probably pay with his life, for murdering two women whom he'd never met, but he knew where this was leading, saw the only choices Rosalind had left him, and he wasn't sure Newgate and swinging from a rope by the neck weren't safer options. He had made a vow. Rosalind had just forced him to break it.

"And you will swear to this in writing?" the inspector pressed.

She raised her chin. "Yes, I will."

The inspector who was seated puffed up his cheeks and blew air out of them. He steadied a cold look upon Armond. "Lord Wulf, it seems women keep showing up dead on your property, and you keep having alibis that allow you to go free of the crimes."

"Someone is obviously trying to incriminate me," he remarked calmly, although he did not feel calm inside.

"When I leave here, it will become my greatest passion to discover who, and why."

"Ours, as well," the man assured him before turning back to Rosalind. "Which house do you occupy, Lady Rosalind? And you will be required to write out a sworn statement that Lord Wulf was with you all night on the evening of the murder."

"I live with my stepmother and stepbrother," Rosalind answered. "Franklin Chapman."

The inspector had been gathering paper and ink but glanced up abruptly. "Chapman? Seems another woman died last night, and at your very residence. The constable is obligated to inform us of these matters, although he said it appeared as if the woman had hung herself."

Tears gathered in Rosalind's eyes. "Yes, a maid, Lydia. She had been dismissed and I assume that was why she took her life. It's one of the reasons Armond came to me. To comfort me."

Both men exchanged a glance. Armond suspected they were making mental pictures in their heads about the kind of comforting Rosalind had received from him.

"Your stepbrother let him in the front door, did he?" one man asked suspiciously.

Rosalind shook her head. "No. There is a trellis next to the balcony leading into my bedroom. When Lord Wulf visits me, he climbs up it. My stepbrother is unaware of his visits."

"I see." The inspector shoved a piece of paper, a quill, and an inkwell toward her. "You are aware that Mr. Chapman will soon learn the truth about Lord Wulf 's late night visits?"

"Yes, Rosalind, you are aware of that?" Armond added for good measure. "It's not too late to withdraw your admission."

She finally glanced at Armond. Her eyes softened.

"I could never live with myself if I forced you to sacrifice your freedom, perhaps your very life, only to save my reputation. I want you to know that about me."

Damn her goodness! She had backed him into a corner, and he could see only one way out, at least for her. "And I want you to know this about me. If you sign that paper, Rosalind, you are also agreeing to become my wife."

Her face paled. "What?"

"You know that I would not so completely ruin you, then leave you to fare as you will among society. Or in your stepbrother's house," he added meaningfully. "Think long and hard before you commit yourself to me. I do not love you." Even though her stricken look reached inside of him and tore at his heart, he felt he had to add, "I will never love you."

Rosalind's hands began to tremble. The inspector seated across from her muttered, "Bastard," under his breath. This was not an Armond Wulf she had seen before, but wait, it was. The Armond Wulf who had nearly seduced her inside his carriage the night of the Greenleys' ball. A man who could turn his heat on and off in a heartbeat. She thought since that night she'd come to know him better. He had comforted her last night. He had held her in his arms and been enraged on her behalf. He had offered a solution to her problems. Now he offered her another one.

But unlike the other solution, this one came with a condition. He did not love her; she supposed she could only count him as truthful to give her such an admission. He would never love her. That was cruel. But then, love had seemed too much to hope for in a marriage when Franklin held her future in his hands. At least Armond wouldn't beat her or stand still for another doing her harm. At least she was attracted to him.

Society would shun her for becoming his wife, but her rational mind told her she had no other choice. Better to be shunned as a married woman than to be shunned and single and still living beneath her stepbrother's roof.

She tried to control the shaking when she wrote out the statement saying she knew Armond to be innocent of the crime of murder, and that he had spent the entire night with her. She swore to her statement upon her father's good name. Once she finished, she laid the quill down and straightened.

"You may go, Lord Wulf," the inspector said. "But know that we will be watching you, and let us pray that no more dead women are found upon your property."

Armond rose and walked to the door. Rosalind turned to follow him.

"God have mercy upon your soul, Lady Rosalind," the inspector said quietly. "I hope you know what you are doing."

She had no idea what she was doing. Her mind had gone numb. Once, in his stable, Rosalind had wanted Armond to at least pretend as if he might offer for her. Now she had agreed to marry him over something that had nothing to do with love. Before her very eyes, he seemed to have retreated from her. She had lain in the warmth of his arms the night before; now she only felt coldness from him.

They left the inspector's home. Outside, Armond's carriage sat. When she'd reached Armond's home, Hawkins had been in the process of sending Armond a change of clothing and some personal items he thought he might need. Rosalind had implored the man to allow her to go along in the coach, saying she had evidence that would clear Armond of the murder. The man had only given his usual expressionless nod and had the driver assist her inside.

"Where do we go now?" she asked Armond as they neared his coach.

"To see the archbishop of Canterbury," he answered. "I'll get a special license and we'll be married today."

"Today?" Rosalind croaked.

Armond glanced at her. "You don't think your step-brother is going to allow us to post banns or plan a wedding, do you?"

"No," she agreed, and the thought of Franklin's rage when he found out she had married Lord Wulf and ruined all of his plans made her feel sick. In fact, it terrified her.

"The archbishop only grants a special license at his discretion," she informed Armond. "Do you really think he'll give us one?"

"His discretion, or so I've heard, can be greatly influenced by how much one is willing to pay for the license. I'll make certain he agrees." Armond opened the coach door and helped Rosalind inside. He joined her after giving instructions to the driver. Well, here she was, inside Armond's coach again. Only this time, she didn't imagine he would try to seduce her.

"You don't have to do this, Armond," she said once the coach lurched forward. "I didn't come to force you into a marriage with me. I came to help you, the same as you wanted to help me last night, remember?"

He ran a hand through his hair. It hung loose, brushing the tops of his shoulders, the way she liked it. "I am not trying to be cruel to you, Rosalind. I had vowed to never marry. I planned to keep that vow. There is a reason why I made that pledge to myself."

She thought she knew why. "Because of your family? Because of the curse?"

"Yes," he answered.

"Perhaps you and your brothers will be spared from the insanity your parents suffered," she offered.

He surprised her by laughing. It was the same kind of laugh she'd heard from him the night of the Greenleys' ball. One without true humor. He sobered a moment later. "All of society thinks the Wulf brothers are cursed by insanity. That isn't the curse at all."

Rosalind was confused. "Then what is?"

He glanced away from her. "Pray you never have reason to find out."

That was all he said, and from the way he stared outside the coach window at the congested traffic in the streets of London, that was all he intended to say. Now that the numbness had started to fade, Rosalind had to wonder if she'd just made the biggest mistake of her life or if somewhere in the detached man sitting across from her lived the same Armond Wulf she was just beginning to know before fate had tossed them into this stormy sea together. She supposed she would soon find out.

Chapter Eleven

It was the dead of night when Armond's coach lumbered up before his residence. Rosalind came awake with a start. The day had been eventful, to say the least, and she'd fallen asleep once they'd left a small parish not two hours' drive from London. They'd been married there by the parish priest, had their wedding witnessed by a blacksmith and his young son. Now her stomach began to twist into knots. Would Franklin be waiting for them? What would happen? And what exactly did Armond expect from her now that she was his wife?

She hardly remembered the ceremony that had forever tied her life to Armond Wulf. She'd been in shock, she realized. Too stunned to do anything but answer "yes" to the questions that made her a stranger's wife. And he was a stranger. She realized she'd known her husband for less than one week.

Armond helped her down from the carriage. He held her hand as they approached the door, which swung open immediately, the expressionless Hawkins forever at his post.

"Ready the bedchamber next to mine for Lady—Lady Wulf," Armond said to Hawkins.

The man's bored expression never wavered. "Very well, My Lord. I've left a cold supper spread for you in the dining room in case you returned home tonight. I thought you might be hungry."

"Good man, Hawkins," Armond responded, then led Rosalind through the darkened house.

The dining room was lit by a candelabra placed in the center of the table. Only one place had been set, she noted. Armond led her to the seat next to his at the head of the long table.

"We'll share, since Hawkins wasn't expecting you," he said. "Are you hungry, Rosalind?"

She was famished. "Yes," she answered.

Armond took assorted slices of ham and cold chicken from a plate, slices of thick cheese and soft bread, and put them upon his plate. He lifted a goblet and took a drink, then offered the goblet to her.

The setting was intimate. Rosalind took the goblet and drank. The sweet wine nearly immediately went to her head because of her empty stomach.

"There are matters we should discuss," Armond said.

Indeed, Rosalind thought. Such as what he expected of her, what they planned to do about Franklin, and then there was the issue of her stepmother. Rosalind had almost forgotten her duty to the woman.

"I must continue to see to my stepmother," she said. "I must visit her regularly. I don't expect she'll live much longer."

Armond took a bite of ham as he reached for the wine goblet again. "You are never to visit the house next door unless I am with you or you know for certain that your stepbrother is not at home," Armond specified.

"Yes," Rosalind agreed. "I don't want to be alone with him. Not ever again."

"Likewise when you wish to go out, or you wish to attend a social event, which unfortunately, now that you have become my wife, will probably be seldom, if at all,

I will escort you, or Hawkins will escort you when you wish to shop. I do not want you to feel as if you are now my prisoner, Rosalind. I only want to protect you, as I have sworn to do."

He sounded far more formal with her than he'd ever sounded before. Formal but gallant. "And what of our marriage?" she bravely asked. "What sort of marriage will it be?"

The candlelight was reflected in his eyes when he lifted his long lashes and looked at her. "Are you asking if I expect you to share my bed?"

She knew by the heat flooding her face that she was blushing. Well, she did want to know. "Yes," she answered.

He ran his finger slowly around the rim of the wine goblet as he stared at her. "No."

Mesmerized by the seductive way in which he handled the goblet, she glanced up at him. "No?"

He smiled slightly, and she realized she'd sounded almost disappointed.

"No, not tonight, or no, not ever?" she asked.

"I suppose that will be up to you," he answered. "Would I demand husbandly rights from you when you feel as if I am still a stranger? No. Will I play unfairly to get them? Most assuredly."

"And what of children?" she asked, unnerved by his last statement. She had a feeling that he could play very unfairly if he wished.

"Out of the question," he answered. Armond glanced away from her and muttered, "And from the day she cast the spell, it will pass from seed to seed."

She barely heard his words. "What did you say?"

His gaze returned to her. He took another sip of wine, staring at her over the rim. "Do you think Chapman is capable of murder?"

Rosalind nearly choked on the piece of chicken she'd

put into her mouth. She swallowed it with a gulp. "Murder?"

Armond handed her the wine. "I think he killed Bess O'Conner, or rather he inflicted the injuries that led to her death. I think he planted the woman found this morning on my property to get back at me, perhaps to get me out of the way."

"But what would he hold against you that would cause him to do something so horrible?"

He shrugged. "You. Perhaps he thought you might at some point turn to me for help. Perhaps I am simply an easy target for the game he plays. The only way I find it plausible that Bess O'Conner could have ended up in my stable was if she had been trying to escape from the house next door."

Taking another sip of wine, she considered his suspicions. They rang true. Franklin was cruel, abusive, but was he a killer? Rosalind shivered at the thought. "I don't know," she answered. "I know I was afraid of him. I know he has a temper that at times he cannot control. Still, I would hate to think he would be capable of . . . of killing a woman."

"Perhaps I'm wrong," Armond said. "But I don't think so. If I prove that your stepbrother is responsible for the murders that I have been implicated in, how will you feel about it?"

Rosalind wasn't sure. She'd feel awful for her stepmother's sake, but then, the lady hardly seemed to know what took place around her. Rosalind supposed it would damage her own reputation somewhat, guilt by association, but then, she'd forgotten, her reputation was no longer an issue. She was surprised that didn't bother her more than it did. She supposed someone like Lady Amelia Sinclair would be devastated to be shunned by society, no matter how brave the young woman pretended to be.

"How do you intend to prove Franklin is guilty?" she wanted to know. "And when do we face him with the announcement of our marriage? By now, I am certain he knows that I am missing."

Armond nibbled on a piece of bread. "We will face him in the morning. I am surprised he wasn't already waiting for us. As for proving his guilt, I plan to follow him, catch him in the act."

Her heart skipped a beat. Rosalind hated the prospect of facing Franklin, but knew it must be done. She was also worried about Armond's plan to follow her stepbrother. "Following Franklin could be dangerous," she said. "If my stepbrother could stoop so low as to kill a woman, I don't imagine he would have qualms about killing a man."

"I am aware of that," he assured her. "Regardless of your first opinion of me, I am not a coward."

Recalling that first night together, she felt her cheeks flush. She supposed she had misjudged him, after all. "I see now that you were only being sensible, whereas I was not," she admitted.

He reached out and traced his thumb along the line of her wine-wet lips. "I didn't want to be," he admitted, then brought his thumb to his own lips and stuck it inside of his mouth.

Suddenly she knew that he would not play fair. His seduction had already begun. . . . It began the first night she met him. She was attracted to him physically—it would be pointless to tell herself otherwise—but she needed more. She wanted more. She deserved more, and so did he. But how to make him realize that?

"Excuse me, Lord Wulf, but Lord Gabriel has just arrived."

Startled, Rosalind glanced away from Armond and toward Hawkins, who'd entered without her hearing him.

"Gabriel?" Armond also looked surprised, she noted. "What's my brother doing here?"

"I took the liberty of sending for your brothers this morning after you had been taken away," Hawkins answered. "I thought you might want them here."

From his expression, Rosalind thought Armond felt the opposite. He sighed. "Send him in."

Armond took the goblet and drank. Rosalind sat staring at the doorway. She heard the soft tread of boots; then a man, a blond giant of a man, one as tall as Armond but built like a peasant field hand, walked into the room.

Rosalind couldn't help but stare. Gabriel Wulf immediately struck her as a man less refined than his oldest brother, but what he lacked in polish, he more than made up for in blatant rugged attractiveness. He had a bit of scruff on his face, the dark whiskers shadowing a strong jaw that looked etched from granite. His hair was darker than Armond's. More sandy-colored than blond, but with a few streaks so pale they nearly appeared white in the candlelight. He quite took her breath away with the sheer strength of his presence.

"What the bloody hell happened this morning and how—"

The man stopped speaking in mid-sentence when he caught sight of Rosalind.

"Gabriel," Armond acknowledged drily. "This is Lady Rosalind, my wife. Rosalind, this is Lord Gabriel."

"Wife?" the man asked, barely giving Rosalind a glance. "Are you bloody mad?"

"Meet me in my study," Armond instructed his brother. "I will join you in a moment."

"But when did you marry this woman? And why in God's name would you do such a thing? We agreed—"

"Gabriel," Armond cautioned. "Greet my wife properly and take your leave."

That Armond was the oldest immediately became clear. His brother seemed to remember himself. He straightened and walked farther into the room.

"Lady Wulf. . . ." he clipped, bowing stiffly.

"You may call me Rosalind," she offered, smiling at her new brother-in-law.

He did not smile back. "If that is your wish," he said, his tone still void of warmth. He cast Armond a dark look and quit the room.

"My brother has bad manners," Armond said to her. "He spends too much time in the country. The estate is his one true love. He'd work himself to death if Jackson wasn't around to drag him in for meals and an occasional game of cards."

Rosalind didn't feel as if the marriage was off to a good start. "I'd like to retire," she said, and now that the wine had time to sink into her bones, she found she was exhausted.

"Hawkins will show you to your room." Armond rose and pulled out her chair, took her hand, and helped her stand. When she swayed slightly, he pulled her closer. Rosalind looked up at him. His eyes had taken on that strange glow again. Perhaps it was simply the way the candlelight fell upon him.

"Good night, Rosalind."

He'd bent his head and his lips almost brushed hers when he spoke. Her lashes drifted downward and she leaned into him, a little startled to realize she'd just instigated a kiss. Even more surprised to part her lips beneath his in invitation. The wine, she assumed, coupled with exhaustion, had lowered her defenses against him.

His lips nuzzled and teased hers for a moment before he finally kissed her. The wine was nothing compared to the potency of his mouth moving against hers, the warm intrusion of his tongue, the feel of his hands moving down her back to press her hips against his.

She knew that he was aroused, for she felt him hard against her. Rather than alarm her, Rosalind found that her ability to so easily excite him, in turn, excited her. Her body melted into his, her hands traveling up his chest to curl around his neck and twine her fingers in his hair.

"I remember," he said against her lips. "I remember what you feel like, what you taste like. You haunt my dreams."

She remembered as well. The feel of his hot mouth against her breasts. The way her nipples had hardened and she had ached between her legs. She wanted to feel his hands upon her skin again, his mouth at her breasts. She wanted all they had shared that first night together and more.

A loud clearing of a throat made them separate abruptly. Hawkins stood in the doorway. "Lord Gabriel is growing impatient and asked me to see why you have not yet joined him. I have the lady's room prepared and wondered if I should escort her upstairs."

Good heavens, Rosalind assumed she must be drunk to have instigated intimacy between her and Armond when she'd just been earlier thinking she needed more than physical pleasure from him. She wondered if her body had failed to receive the message. Or if he was simply that skilled at seduction. It took little effort on his part. All he had to do was be in the same room with her, kiss her, and she forgot herself.

"I think I should come along with you, Hawkins," she said, and started toward the man. "Good night, Armond," she added, but didn't turn back to look at him.

She felt his gaze boring into her back, not sharp, like a knife, but warm, like a caress. He did not respond and she hurried after Hawkins like a coward running from a foe she'd picked a fight with, but soon realized she could not defeat. The trek up the stairs to the second story helped clear her head somewhat, in that it stole the languid heat Armond had spread to her bones and brought her mind back into focus.

Hawkins opened a door and she followed him inside of a large room, tastefully decorated, though the furnishings were outdated. The adjoining door into the next room suggested these had once been Armond's parents' bedchambers. If, indeed, the house had once belonged to them. She would have to ask Armond.

A fire struggled to catch in the grate and Rosalind rubbed her arms due to the chill. One of Armond's shirts had been laid out upon the bed. She glanced at Hawkins in question as to what it was doing there.

"I see that you have no luggage, Lady Wulf. My Lord's shirt is the best that I can provide for you in the way of sleeping attire. I hope it will suffice, at least for tonight."

"It will be fine," Rosalind said to him. "Thank you for your thoughtfulness."

"There is no lady's maid in service," Hawkins informed her. "If you wish, I will assist you."

He looked perfectly serious, as always, and even managed to maintain his air of boredom. Rosalind couldn't see the stuffy man playing the part of maid.

"I can manage," she assured him.

"Will that be all then, Lady Wulf?"

"Yes, thank you, Hawkins."

He inclined his head and moved toward the door. "I can have a bath drawn and sent up to you in the morning. Would that please you, Your Ladyship?"

"Immensely," she answered, and wished she could have one tonight, but she wouldn't put such a burden on the man at this late hour. "Good night, Hawkins."

Again he inclined his head; then he left the room. Only after he'd gone did the enormity of her situation strike Rosalind. She was married. Married to Armond Wulf. Living in his home now. She moved to the fire and held her hands toward the warmth. Her gaze strayed to the adjoining door. There were no locks. She couldn't lock him out even if there were. He was her husband. On the bright side, better Armond Wulf than the disgusting Viscount Penmore.

The thought brought home the realities of her situation. Franklin would be furious she had managed to foil his plans for her after all. And Penmore. She suspected he would be angry that he would not have her as his wife, simply because the man was used to getting what he wanted. Would he call in Franklin's debts and see her stepbrother put in prison? It was a pleasant possibility. Then she and Armond wouldn't be forced to deal with Franklin.

Rosalind wondered how her husband fared with his own brother. Lord Gabriel hadn't looked at all pleased to learn that Armond had married.

Chapter Twelve

"I will ask you again. Are you mad?"

Armond poured his brother a glass of warm brandy. He walked across the study and handed it to Gabriel, who was seated in a plush leather chair in front of Armond's mahogany desk. Armond took the chair next to him.

"Well, that is the rumor, isn't it?" he asked drily. He sighed and leaned his elbows upon his knees, scrubbing a hand over his face. "It's complicated. Rosalind lives next door, or she did. I have visited her bedchamber on a couple of occasions, last night being one of them. I spent the night, but only to comfort her," he added. "Then this morning when I arrived home, two inspectors were in my stable with another woman's dead body."

"Ah," Gabriel said. "So your neighbor was your alibi?"

"She came forward without me asking," Armond told him. "She completely ruined herself regardless that the lady and I have not been intimate . . . at least not *that* intimate together. What could I do but marry her?"

Gabriel snorted. "Still playing the gentleman, Armond? What for? It makes no difference to society. Those our parents once rubbed elbows with are all too happy to now stab us in the back. Every flock must have their black sheep. It's what keeps their insignificant little lives from boring them to death."

And Armond thought he was the cynical one. He straightened and rubbed the back of his neck. "There is more about Rosalind. I strongly suspect that her stepbrother is guilty of Bess O'Conner's death, and of the death of the woman he left as a surprise for me this morning. He's been abusive to Rosalind, has in fact tried to force her into a marriage with a foul man by the name of Penmore. She needs my protection."

Gabriel shook his head. "You cannot afford to play the gallant, Armond. None of us can be the gentlemen our parents raised us to be, because we are no longer who we once were. You are half in love with her already; I can tell that. Who will protect your wife from you, Armond?"

His brother's question struck to Armond's core. What made him believe for even a moment that he was a better solution for Rosalind than the one she had? He would not beat her. He would not force himself upon her. But if he fell, he might kill her. He couldn't fall; that was all there was to it. He couldn't love her. Not ever.

"What's done is done," he said to Gabriel. "It cannot be undone. I will give Rosalind sanctuary, and I will hunt her stepbrother as the wolf in me wants to hunt him. I will at least disprove one false rumor about us."

Gabriel rose, walked to the liquor cabinet, and replaced his empty glass. "We have another problem. Jackson has gone missing."

Armond assumed that his younger brother had simply been too anxious to visit the brothels of London to stop and inquire if Armond might have been hanged by the neck for murder first. "Missing since when?"

"Right after you left. I thought he'd decided to catch up with you and assumed he was here, but Hawkins informed me that was not the case, and that he hasn't seen Jackson since you returned home."

"No, neither have I," Armond said. Jackson worried

him. His little brother was the reason the Wulf brothers had a bad reputation. He was vain, a womanizer, and sadly, he'd become much too fond of spirits since his return from abroad eight months prior. He had no interest in the estate, no interest, it seemed, in anything but liquor and willing women.

"I didn't want to say anything to you, not unless I had proof, which I do not, but I think something happened to Jackson while he was abroad. Something that has forever changed him," Gabriel said.

Armond's blood froze. "You think he fell?"

Gabriel joined him again, seating himself across from Armond. "He seems to spend a lot of time in the woods behind the estate. Especially when the moon is full."

A thought occurred to Armond. One he'd as soon he hadn't thought of. Jackson was here in their townhome when the first woman had been discovered. Now another one had shown up, and Jackson was missing, probably running amok in London. Armond didn't like what he was thinking. He didn't like it at all.

"We need to find him," he said. "We'll begin our search for Jackson in the morning."

Gabriel nodded. His gaze turned toward the ceiling. "And what about your wife, up there, alone in your room? Waiting for her bridegroom? What kind of a marriage can you have with this woman, Armond? What kind of a marriage could any of us have?"

"It is a marriage of convenience," he decided. "Nothing more."

Gabriel laughed sarcastically. "She's convenient all right. Pretty, too, I noticed."

"Maybe you shouldn't notice too much about her." Armond's voice almost resembled a growl. He glanced away from the surprise on his brother's face. "Rosalind is *my* problem. I'll deal with her."

"Just remember what happened to our father when a marriage of convenience turned into something more, even after all those years of living with our mother. You were there the same as the rest of us. Do you want to turn into that?"

Armond remembered all too well. And no, he did not want to turn into that. "When we find Jackson, I want both of you to return to the estate. I will fight my own battles."

"Maybe this is the one," Gabriel said quietly. "The one battle that may save us all."

Armond hadn't thought of that—the riddle in a poem left by the first cursed Wulf. He hadn't gone in search of the enemy, but perhaps the enemy had decided to come to him.

"Good night, Brother." Gabriel rose. "It would be nice if I could carry you up the stairs on my shoulders and deliver you to your bride with well wishes. But I cannot. We are not normal men, Armond. See that she doesn't make you forget that with her ripe red lips and her deep violet eyes."

Armond didn't respond and Gabriel obviously didn't expect him to. His brother left the study. Armond glanced toward the ceiling as his brother had done earlier. He'd told Rosalind the choice of sleeping arrangements in their marriage would be up to her, but he wondered if he could stay on his side of a door that joined their rooms. He wondered if he could manage to resist her, even for tonight.

The bath was wonderful, but lacking in that Rosalind had none of her perfumed soaps along with her. Hawkins had given her a bar of something that smelled like Armond. A hint of sandalwood. Well, she supposed it would have to do until she was able to retrieve her things from the house next door. She shivered at the thought of confronting Franklin. She wouldn't take the clothing he'd had made for her when she first arrived in London. None of the gowns were to her taste anyway. They were meant to show her figure. They were meant to entice a man—to trap him into marriage.

She felt as if she'd trapped a man after all. And she wasn't certain Armond Wulf was the type of man a woman wanted to ensnare. His voice had been cold when he'd said that he did not love her—would never love her—and yet when he kissed her, or touched her, there was nothing but heat between them. Last night she'd awoken at some point, feeling as if someone was standing over her, staring down at her.

Now the memory seemed hazy to her, as if she might have been dreaming, for she remembered opening her eyes in the darkness and seeing only the shape of a man and, in place of his eyes, two glowing coals of blue fire. Again she shivered, and realized her bath had grown cold. Rosalind reached for the towel Hawkins had provided. She stood and wrapped it around her and had only stepped from the water when the adjoining door suddenly swung open.

Her gaze locked with her husband's. He did not blush upon realizing he'd intruded upon her bath, nor did he look away. "Forgive the interruption, Rosalind," he said. His gaze ran the length of her, settled upon her exposed legs, then finally lifted to her face. "It is time to go next door and retrieve your belongings. Afterward I have business to attend to."

For a moment, Rosalind forgot about her state of undress. "Next door? Already?"

He moved farther into the room. "I told you last night it would be our first order of business. You need your belongings."

"Perhaps I could just wear the same gown for the rest of my life," she said. "Sleep in your shirts."

Armond walked to the bed where she'd shed his shirt, picked it up, held it to his face for a moment, then laid it back down. "I am not poor, Rosalind. I can have everything ordered new for you if you wish. I assumed you'd have private belongings of importance to you."

"I have little left in the way of personal belongings." Rosalind clutched her towel tighter. She had wanted to cry when two months back she'd gone to her jewelry box to fetch a pair of pearl ear bobs that once belonged to her mother, only to find them gone. And any jewelry of value. Franklin had hocked them, and when confronted, he'd simply shrugged and said he'd needed the coin.

"But I do have a silver brush and comb that belonged to my mother, and I would like to keep them in my possession."

"Did you sleep well?"

Armond had changed the subject so quickly his question took her off guard. "Y-yes," she stammered. "Armond, do you mind?" She glanced down at her nearly naked state.

"No, I don't mind," he answered, and a half smile shaped his sensual lips.

"Well, I do," she said. "I know I'm your wife now, but I hope that doesn't mean I am no longer to have my privacy."

He walked toward her. "Hawkins is upset that we don't have a personal maid in residence for you. I thought I might suffice until I can hire someone . . . if I can hire a woman who'll work for me in this house."

The thought of Armond helping her dress made her blush. It also brought thoughts of him helping her undress. She turned her back to him. "I can manage on my own."

She felt him behind her, so close his body heat penetrated her chilled skin. He pushed her hair over one shoulder. His lips touched the sensitive place where her shoulder and neck met. "Do you know how beautiful you are? How seemingly perfect in every way? Do you know how badly I want you?"

Rosalind fought the urge to close her eyes and lean back against him. The way his voice lowered an octave when he was impassioned affected her strangely, almost as if he could put her under a spell. She recalled her decision that what she wanted, in fact needed, from Armond was more than physical pleasure.

"You said that the choice of intimacy would be mine," she reminded him, although she was embarrassed by the husky sound of her voice, the slight shaking of her legs. "It seems like a long time has passed since I've had choices of my own. I want more than what you want to give me, Armond." She felt his sudden withdrawal from her in more than a physical way when he stepped away from her.

"I cannot give you more," he said. "I did not lie to you, Rosalind. I did not try to deceive you. The pleasure we can give each other might be a sorry substitute for love in your eyes, but it is all that we can have together. I told you that before we made our vows to one another."

His honesty was admirable. And heartbreaking. Rosalind's future still loomed bleak before her. "Then the vows we made were false," she said. "Everything about our marriage is false. I would have done just as well to have married Lord Penmore."

She wasn't prepared when he reached out and turned her to face him. His expression was stricken. "Do you truly believe that?"

Guilt immediately rushed up to claim her. The future was not as bleak as it had once been. "No," she admitted. She sighed. "I'm sorry for saying that to you, Armond.

Too much has happened too quickly. I need time to adjust. I relish the idea of making my own decisions again."

What she didn't tell him was that for the first time in a long time she might feel safe again, but she wanted to feel loved again. Rosalind could face anything the future might bring her, if only she had a deep connection to another human being again. One that was returned.

"And so you shall make your own decisions," Armond said, although he didn't look that happy about the one she'd already made. He moved toward the door. "Meet me downstairs in the dining room when you're dressed. You didn't eat much last night. I've had Hawkins instruct Cook to make us a big breakfast. Gabriel will be present."

His last statement sounded like a warning.

Still clutching her towel, she nodded.

He made one last lazy sweep of her and left the room. Once he'd left, Rosalind let out a sigh. This was awkward. Being Armond's wife, yet being denied a suitable amount of time to have been courted by him, to get to know him better. Suddenly she felt like they were polite strangers dancing around each other. She supposed that it was when the music stopped that she should worry about.

She recalled that she had much more to worry about at present and decided to focus her attention on that. Perhaps she should ask Armond if he had a pistol and if he knew how to use it. The conversation she'd had with Armond at supper last night came back to her. Was her stepbrother a murderer? She didn't want to believe he was capable of that atrocity, but she wasn't certain. Any man who held women in such low esteem as to hit them might hold women in low enough esteem to kill them as well.

Her stomach growled, reminding her that breakfast waited downstairs. Breakfast and Armond's brother, who did not look at all happy last night upon learning of his older brother's recent nuptials. Rosalind went about the business of making herself presentable. She put her hair up and struggled into the same clothing she'd worn the previous day. Her undergarments were another must that she would fetch from the house next door.

Once she'd dressed, Rosalind left the room and went downstairs. She heard the clank of dishes and walked into the dining room. Armond and his brother sat at the table. Neither spoke to the other. As if he felt her presence, Armond glanced up at her.

"Come, sit next to me, Rosalind," he instructed.

He stood, gave his brother a dark look that also had the man rising as she entered, although she could tell Gabriel didn't want to. In the light of day Gabriel was even more handsome but, she thought, not so handsome as Armond, or perhaps it was only her preference that made that distinction between them. Gabriel wore his hair shorter, just to the point where it curled around his collar. His eyes were a vivid green, and again, she was struck by his commanding presence.

"Good morning, Lord Gabriel," she said as she joined Armond. Her husband pulled out her chair and she noted that he'd also had a plate filled for her.

"Morning," Gabriel muttered, then seated himself and immediately focused his attention on his breakfast.

Awkward silence stretched. Rosalind picked up her fork and toyed with her breakfast. Conversation over a meal was obviously not a necessity among the Wulf brothers. She felt it important to bridge the gap between her and Gabriel, at least for Armond's sake. But what to discuss with the brooding man? Armond had said the estate was his one true love.

"What is Wulfglen like, Lord Gabriel?" she asked. "I love my father's country estate. I was quite happy there until . . . until I came to London." It suddenly occurred to her that Armond would now be responsible for Montrose, though he could not inherit her father's title. That would pass to her son . . . but Armond had said there would be no children.

"It's beautiful," Gabriel rather reluctantly admitted. "The land is good for farming, if we don't do much of that. But there is good grazing for the horses, and plenty of room for them to run."

"I love horses," Rosalind said. "The Arabian mare is my favorite in Armond's stable. Did you raise her from a foal?"

Gabriel set his fork aside. "Yes, I did, and she's still a filly. She hasn't been bred. Armond and I in fact argued over her. I wanted to keep her to raise colts, but he thought she was too delicately built and would fare better as a lady's pleasure horse."

"She *is* delicate," Rosalind admitted. "But she has such good lines. Very distinctive Arabian traits, with her flared nostrils and perfectly arched neck. Maybe if you bred her with a stallion just a bit larger than her, you could drop foals with her distinctive traits, yet of a sturdier stature."

"That is exactly what I suggested to Armond," Gabriel said, and Rosalind finally saw signs of life from him. "See, even Lady Wulf thinks so," he said to his brother.

She glanced at Armond and found a slightly bemused expression on his face. Rosalind felt a rush of pleasure, for she could tell her tactics for drawing Gabriel out pleased him.

"Rosalind likes the filly so much I have decided to make a gift of the horse to her," Armond said. "I suppose it's up to her if she wants the horse bred or not in the future. That can be a project between the two of you."

Rosalind shook her head. "A gift? No, Armond, she's worth too much. I couldn't—"

"Of course you can," Armond interrupted. "You are my wife. There's nothing wrong with a husband giving his wife a gift that pleases her."

Even though her spirits soared with the thought of owning the beautiful white filly, Rosalind saw by Gabriel's sudden frown that the reminder of her being his brother's wife had spoiled the conversation. She turned her attention to her breakfast. The rest of the meal passed in chilly silence.

Hawkins arrived with two men she assumed were kitchen help to clear away the dishes. If suddenly having a woman amid an obviously male-dominated domain ruffled him, she couldn't tell it. Armond rose and pulled her chair out for her.

"It's time to fetch your things, Rosalind."

Her stomach twisted into a knot. "Do you have a pistol, Armond? I have no idea what my stepbrother might do. I fear if he doesn't try to shoot you, at least he'll threaten you to a duel of fisticuffs."

"I'll lend my fists," Gabriel suddenly came back to life. "We Wulfs take care of our own."

"I wouldn't mind having you at my back," Armond said to his brother.

Gabriel rose and the three of them left the dining room. The closer they drew to the foyer of the house, the greater distress Rosalind felt. Armond, she noted, didn't look in the least nervous but simply determined. She glanced over her shoulder at Gabriel. He looked almost pleased by the possibility of a fight.

Hawkins held the door for them. The day outside had dawned sunny, though she did not feel sunny on the inside. They hadn't stepped two feet outside of the house when a carriage pulled up and Franklin and Penmore got out. When Franklin saw her with Armond, his face turned purple. He marched toward them.

"You will release my stepsister this instant!" he shouted. "You had no right to take her from me!"

Rather than speaking, Armond marched straight up to Franklin and delivered him a sound blow to the jaw. Her stepbrother stumbled back and had barely righted himself when Armond lunged forward and delivered a second blow.

"I should kill you," she heard Armond say. "And I will, if you ever touch her again!"

"I say, Wulf," Penmore sputtered, taking a step forward.

Gabriel left Rosalind's side and went to stand beside his brother. "You say what?" he inquired of the man, his voice very low.

Penmore's round face flushed and he quickly took a step back.

"Coward," Franklin sneered at the viscount.

"He's as a big as tree. Chapman, you take him on." Penmore hurried back to the coach, climbed inside, and slammed the door closed.

Further enraged by his companion's cowardice, Franklin reached inside of his coat and withdrew a nasty-looking pistol. Rosalind nearly screamed.

Behind her, she heard the sound of a pistol being cocked. She turned to see Hawkins holding a weapon trained on her stepbrother.

"I don't believe you are welcome here, sir," the man said formally, but his usually bored expression had hardened into a mask of resolve. Rosalind had no doubt that Hawkins would shoot her stepbrother if it became necessary.

Franklin lowered his weapon; his cold eyes were alive with hate when he turned them upon Rosalind. "You've ruined everything," he bit out. "But don't think you've won. The man you have married is a murderer. He'll kill again; I feel certain of it. Next time, it might be you, little sister."

"You are not to speak to my wife again," Armond said. "You are not to so much as glance in her direction. I am not a murderer, but you tempt me to become one. Don't push me too far, Chapman."

The glove had been tossed. Franklin backed toward the carriage—Penmore's, she recognized, because the matched set of grays was pulling it—then turned and climbed inside. Penmore shouted to his driver and the coach lumbered off. Rosalind breathed a sigh of relief. The first confrontation was over, and the coach did not take the direction of the house next door. She was free now to fetch her things and make a visit to her stepmother.

Armond still stood staring after the coach, his stance rigid. She moved forward and touched his arm. "He's gone," she said softly.

"For now," Armond agreed, still staring after the retreating coach. "But I don't think that's the end of it, Rosalind. Will you hate me if I end up killing him?"

He was perfectly serious, she realized. "I hope matters won't come to that," she answered. "Maybe you've frightened him away."

"His kind doesn't scare easily," Armond commented. "He's not used to being thwarted. Don't ever lower your guard where he is concerned, Rosalind. Maybe where I am concerned, as well," he added, turning to look at her.

This was yet another side to Armond she had not yet seen. A dangerous side, for she felt his barely pent-up anger. She felt his desire to go after Franklin, to finish what the two of them had started. And she had little doubt that they would clash again and perhaps again until one of them was dead.

"Is that the house?" Gabriel drew their attention. He nodded toward her stepmother's townhome.

"Yes," Rosalind answered. "Let's go now while he's gone."

Armond turned toward Hawkins. "Send a coach next door to collect Lady Wulf's trunks." He turned back to Rosalind. "Will you walk with me? I have a need to burn off some of my energy."

She nodded. Rosalind seemed to suddenly have an abundance of energy as well.

"I'll come along," Gabriel decided. "You'll need a man at the door, watching."

The three of them set off toward the house next door. Gabriel hung back behind them. Rosalind had trouble keeping up with Armond's long strides. He noticed and slowed his pace. She glanced sideways at him as they walked. His features were hard, his jaw muscle flexed. Danger radiated from his every pore, and to her surprise, she found that it excited her. He excited her. Not a coward, after all. Not by any means.

It had given her a great deal of satisfaction to see her stepbrother on the receiving end of Armond's fists. Franklin had terrorized her for three months and she'd been helpless against him. Now she had a protector. Rosalind didn't know why she felt moved to do what she did, but she slid her hand into Armond's as they walked. He glanced at her, and she felt the anger seeping from him, rising up to the sky to evaporate into the sunny air. He glanced away from her. But he did not remove his hand from hers, and as they neared the house next door he even gave her fingers a comforting squeeze.

Rosalind suspected were she to turn and look at Gabriel, she would find him frowning. Why did he dislike her? Why couldn't he be happy that Armond had married? Was it the curse? Now she recalled that all the brothers had vowed to remain unmarried.

She needed more information about this curse that

hung over the Wulf family. Had Armond's parents shown signs of madness long before the affliction had struck them both down? She would find out. If she and Armond eventually fell in love—and she hoped, since they had married, they would, despite Armond's claim to her—she wanted children. Blond little boys as handsome as their father.

The picture that formed in her mind made her smile. Another thought chased her smile away. She'd almost forgotten that when she'd asked Armond about the curse, he'd said it was not what society believed it to be.

What was it then? He'd told her to pray she never found out. But she would find out. She was his wife, and if they were ever going to be happy with each other, she must know his fears, his doubts, his secrets. And she would discover them all, she silently vowed. And she hoped once she had, she could make him love her.

Chapter Thirteen

Once Rosalind and Mary packed her few belongings in trunks—for Rosalind refused to take any of the gowns Franklin had ordered made for her—she went downstairs to tell Armond to have the coachman come up and carry them down. She would go to her marriage with seemingly little, thanks to Franklin and his greed. She supposed it was in fact her own money that had paid for the gowns her stepbrother had ordered for her, but it was also his bad tastes that had dictated the styles and fabrics.

"I need to speak with the duchess before I go," she told Armond, then headed back upstairs to meet Mary in the drab room on the third floor.

The duchess looked neither better nor worse. Rosalind bent before her, taking the lady's cold hands in hers. "I've married," she told her stepmother. The news drew no response. "I won't be living here anymore, but I promise to visit you as often as I can." Again no response. Rosalind sighed. She rose and turned toward Mary. "Mary, I would ask a favor of you."

The housekeeper stood a short distance away, dabbing at her eyes with a handkerchief. "So sorry it's come to this," the woman sniffed. "You forced into being that dark man's wife. No telling what will happen to you, my Lady."

"I'll be fine," she tried to assure the housekeeper. "But

I must continue my visits with Her Grace. She was once very kind to me. I know this is perhaps asking too much, but each day, could you let me know when Franklin leaves the house so that I may visit my stepmother?"

Mary took to wringing the handkerchief. "Do you mean come next door, my Lady? To the Wulfs' lair?"

Rosalind wasn't in the mood for Mary's nonsense. "You'll be perfectly safe. In fact, I'll tell my husband's man, Hawkins, to expect you. All you need do is instruct him to give me the message that your employer is out."

"I don't know," Mary fretted. "If Mr. Chapman finds out I'm going behind his back—"

"I have another idea," Rosalind decided. "When Franklin is gone from the house, hang a sheet from the balcony of my former room. That will serve as a signal to me, and if my stepbrother should ever happen to spy it, you can simply say that you're airing the bedding."

"I suppose I can do that," Mary agreed. "I think the lady knows you're here, even if she doesn't show it by her expressions. I think you give her comfort."

Rosalind walked back over and placed a hand upon her stepmother's shoulder. "I hope she knows I care for her," she said. "Does Franklin ever visit her, Mary?"

"Rarely," the woman answered. "Has me fix up her tea the way she likes it every day though, so I guess that's at least something."

"I suppose," Rosalind responded. "Lord knows she's given up enough for him. Her marriage to my father. Once he demanded that Franklin be sent away, she stood by her son and left the country house. I know it was a difficult decision for her. I hope my stepbrother realizes how devoted she is to him."

Mary made a snorting noise. "Begging your pardon for saying so, but Mr. Chapman doesn't care about anyone but himself. But I guess you know that."

A response wasn't necessary. Rosalind suspected Mary knew about Franklin's abuse of her. There was little that went on beneath a family's roof the servants did not know about. Of course sleeping in a room that adjoined the duchess's had no doubt spared Mary from knowing all that went on when night fell. Rosalind suddenly thought about Armond's suspicions regarding Bess O'Conner and Franklin.

"Mary, have you ever known suspicious events to take place in the house? Has Franklin ever brought women here?"

"He used to entertain more," she confessed. "Before you came. He didn't like me here when he had his friends over. He'd send me off to spend the night with my daughter. I went, too, because that was back before the duchess fell ill."

"When exactly did my stepmother first start to show signs of illness?"

Mary puckered her wrinkled brow. "Been a while now. She seemed odd before the sickness struck her. Nervous and upset about something. I remember she and her son argued a lot back then. I don't think she liked his friends, or his parties. But then, they never got on well."

"Rosalind? Your trunks are loaded."

Armond's voice drifted up the stairs. Fearing another confrontation with Franklin should they dally much longer, Rosalind reached down and took her stepmother's hand in hers again. She gave the woman's fingers a gentle squeeze.

"I won't abandon you, Your Grace. I'll come as often as I can. If I thought for one moment that Franklin would allow it, I'd have you moved from this house, from this room." She glanced around at the shabby decor of her stepmother's prison. For that's what the room had become, she realized.

She couldn't be certain, but she thought for a brief

moment that, before she released the lady's hand, the woman had given her a weak squeeze in return. It gave Rosalind hope to believe so.

"You'd best be going before Mr. Chapman returns," Mary warned.

Rosalind hugged the housekeeper before she left. She walked down the stairs to the second-floor landing and passed her former room without even a glance inside. She would miss nothing about this house except her visits with the duchess and Mary's kindness to her. It was as if she'd finally awoken from a nightmare. Armond stood waiting for her at the next landing leading downstairs.

He was so handsome he took her breath away. Was she insane to balk at what he could offer her and demand more? Certainly there were many marriages of convenience that took place yearly in London. Countless wives had gone to marriage beds with only duty in mind. But of course part of their duty was to provide their husbands with heirs. Rosalind had been given no such duty. She'd been given instead a choice.

A choice she had no doubt would weigh heavy upon her in the days to come beneath Armond Wulf's roof, sleeping in a room separated from his only by an unlocked door.

Chapter Fourteen

Once Armond escorted Rosalind home, knew that she would spend the afternoon unpacking her trunks, and had left strict instructions for Hawkins to keep a close eye on the lady, Armond and Gabriel set out in search of Jackson.

"Where do we begin to look?" Gabriel asked, saddling his horse.

"I'm surprised you ask," Armond commented drily.

"I meant, which of the many brothels that litter London," Gabriel specified.

Saddling the chestnut stallion for himself, Armond answered, "We both know that Jackson was once quite fond of Queenie's on the outskirts of the city. We'll begin there."

"He's quite fond of several places," Gabriel reminded his brother. "I don't understand him."

Armond lifted a brow. "There's nothing wrong with tumbling a willing woman once in a while, Gabriel. I suppose there's nothing wrong with having an occasional drink, or playing an occasional game of cards."

"But," Gabriel said before Armond finished, "all things in moderation. Something Jackson can't seem to get the gist of."

"Exactly," Armond agreed.

Both men swung up onto their mounts and rode from the stable. Armond tried not to look at the place where a woman had recently been found dead. Although he hadn't known the woman, had barely glanced at her lifeless body, he felt a sense of outrage on her behalf and upon his own. The first woman, she might have been an accident, might have wandered into his stable trying to escape her attacker, but this last one, she was deliberately placed there to implicate him in her murder.

Chapman would have a reason to do such a thing. Just for spite, Armond supposed. But why would he do something so obvious, and upon the heels of the maid dying in his very home? He had to know such a thing would also draw attention to him. It didn't make sense.

"Your wife is nice," Gabriel suddenly commented. "I would like her if not for the circumstances."

"I would love her if not for the circumstances," Armond commented in return.

Gabriel lifted a brow before he said, "The stepbrother, though, needs a sound thrashing, or better, a bullet between the eyes."

Gabriel wore a perfectly serious expression. He liked to fight. He always had. He liked to fight and he liked to work, but he did not share Jackson's enthusiasm for whores. At least not to Armond's knowledge.

The brothers rode in silence. They soon entered the teeming streets of London.

"We're causing the usual stir," Gabriel pointed out. "What do they expect? That we'll sprout fangs and claws and come after them?"

Armond glanced around the crowded streets. People stopped in their strolling, in their wagon-loading, in their onion-selling, to gape at them as they rode past. His gaze happened to land upon a young woman he'd seen Rosalind conversing with at the LeGrandes' soiree. Lady Amelia Sinclair, he thought was her name. One of the titled's daughters. The young woman stared boldly at the two of them as they passed and received a cuff on the head from either her chaperone or her mother, Armond wasn't certain which.

"Who was that?"

"Who?" Armond inquired of Gabriel.

"The pretty blonde with the bold eyes."

"A friend, I believe, of Rosalind's. I saw them speaking to one another when I entered the ballroom at a recent social affair."

Gabriel's mouth dropped open. "Good God, you're even making the social rounds these days? What has gotten into you, Armond? You know the more we keep to ourselves, the better off all of us will be."

He was in no mood for another interrogation, and from his own brother. "I was lonely," he admitted. "Don't you ever get lonely, Gabriel?"

"No," he answered. "I don't get lonely because I don't allow myself to get lonely. I don't become involved with women because I don't allow them to get that close to me. You would have done well to follow my example, Armond. Being the oldest doesn't necessarily make you the wisest."

Armond was glad to see the end of town ahead. They'd soon be at Queenie's. The last thing he wanted to hear at the moment was a lecture from Gabriel. He had enough worries on his mind, enough to deal with now that he'd married Rosalind. How in the hell would he keep her at a distance when he wanted to get so very close to her?

Queenie herself answered the door when Armond and Gabriel arrived. It had been a few years since Armond had visited the establishment. The woman looked old

without the help of face paint and dim lighting. Judging
by the dark circles beneath her eyes, midafternoon was
early for her to be up and about.

"Aw, come back tonight," she grumbled upon seeing
them standing before her door. "The girls have to sleep
sometime, you know."

The woman started to close the door, but Armond
stuck his boot inside. "We're looking for our brother. We
thought he might be here."

Squinting, she ran her red-rimmed gaze the length of
Armond and Gabriel. "I haven't seen you boys in some
time, but your brother is upstairs."

"Might we have a word with him?" Armond asked.

She sighed. "Come in then, but be quiet. The house is
asleep."

They followed the woman into a parlor where red velvet ran amok. "You know the way," she said, indicating
the direction of the stairs. "First door on the left. He's got
stamina, your brother. The girls all like him. Fear they
wouldn't collect from him at all unless I made sure of it."

"That sounds like Jackson," both Armond and Gabriel
echoed.

"Let yourselves out," Queenie instructed, scratching
her broad rump. "I'm going back to bed."

The woman ambled off in the direction of the back of
the house. Armond headed for the stairs. "No need for
both of us to intrude on what I'm certain is a delicate situation," he said to Gabriel. "Wait for me here."

Gabriel nodded. "Be quick about it. This place smells
of sour liquor and, well, you know what it smells like."

He was right. Their special gifts made the smells seem
even stronger. Armond walked to the stairs and up them.
The room where Queenie said he could find Jackson was
dark when he entered. He'd knocked quietly, but the snoring in the room was so loud that he'd heard it from the

hallway, and he doubted the room's occupants would hear his knock over the god-awful racket.

He spied his brother in the bed, golden hair tousled, looking ironically innocent given his location and the fact that there was a woman sleeping beside him. A woman snoring so loudly Armond didn't see how Jackson could possibly manage to sleep . . . until he spotted the other two women also crammed into the bed. Only a man exhausted could sleep through the noise.

None of the women looked any worse for wear for having spent the night with his brother, Armond noted. He walked to the edge of the bed and nudged his brother.

"Jackson, wake up."

Sleepy dark eyes looked up at him. "Armond? What are you doing here?"

"I might ask you the same, but it's rather obvious." He indicated the sleeping women with a nod. "I know now where we get our reputation. From you."

Jackson smiled, his boyish dimples doing nothing to dismiss his air of innocence. "I like women. Where's the sin in that?"

"I think the sin, Brother, is liking three at once in the same bed on the same night. Get dressed. I need to talk to you."

"How did you know I'd be here?" Jackson asked, careful when he rose not to wake his companions.

"Gabriel is downstairs. Hawkins called the two of you to London over some business we will discuss when we reach the house. When Gabriel learned you weren't at the townhome, that I in fact had not seen you, we figured we could find you here, or at a place very much like it."

Jackson stretched. "I was bored," he explained. "And I have been thinking about a quest. I wanted to make certain I had my fill of women and spirits before I left."

Armond could barely hear Jackson's remarks over the

snoring woman. "Get dressed and meet us downstairs," Armond instructed, then quietly let himself out of the room.

It took longer than he anticipated for Jackson to arrive downstairs. Armond supposed by the sound of the squeaking bed upstairs that at least one woman had awoken before his brother could make a clean break of it. Finally, Jackson joined them, pulling himself together as he descended the stairs.

"About time," Gabriel growled at him. "I don't suppose you considered we're stuck down here smelling all manner of foul deeds that took place here last night while you're up there trying to impress a whore, for Christ's sake."

To irritate Gabriel, Jackson flashed one of his dimpled smiles. "Duty called. What could I do but answer? And I wasn't trying to impress the lady, but merely pleasuring her."

"What for?" Gabriel snorted. "That's her job, I'm thinking."

"Let's go," Armond ordered his brothers before an argument broke out between them. He knew they were close, perhaps too close, since both were confined at the estate most of the time, at least until Jackson took it in his head to rebel.

Jackson spent a good portion of the ride home complaining of his swollen head. He gleefully admitted to getting so foxed the previous evening that he thought he was with the same woman and merely seeing triple and wondered why she was so insatiable. Armond might have found his brother amusing—he usually did—but darker thoughts kept him from enjoying the ride. He did not discuss recent events with Jackson. Better that conversation take place at the townhome in his study.

Hawkins had the door for them before they reached it, the grooms rushing out to take their horses when they'd first ridden up. "Is Lady Rosalind all right?" Armond asked the steward.

"Napping, I believe," the man answered. "There's been no trouble so far, Lord Wulf."

Jackson drew up short, his brow furrowed. "Who the bloody hell is Lady Rosalind?" he asked.

"To the study," Armond instructed.

"I'll have a bath drawn for you immediately, Lord Jackson," Hawkins said, wrinkling his nose.

Once the brothers gathered in the study, Armond closed the door and moved to his desk. Jackson immediately went to the liquor cabinet. "Now, who is this Lady Rosalind, and what's she doing here?"

Armond steeled himself. "Rosalind is my wife."

The glass Jackson held slipped from his fingers. It bounced against the thick carpet without breaking. "Your wife?"

Rarely did Armond see Jackson at a loss for words. Jackson stared at his brother as if he'd suddenly sprouted another head. Before the usual questions could begin, Armond launched into the same explanation he'd given Gabriel the previous evening and also told Jackson about Rosalind's stepbrother and his suspicions regarding the man.

Jackson turned up another glass and poured himself a drink. "And I thought I was the one who attracted trouble. Good Lord, Armond, even I am smart enough to stand by our vow to never marry. You haven't given your heart to this woman, have you? You aren't suffering the effects?"

"No," Armond assured his younger brother. "She left me no choice. I will protect her, give her my name, but that is all I will give her."

Jackson studied the amber liquid in his glass before he drained the contents. "I hope so, Armond. I hope for your sake that you can resist any deep feelings for this woman.

You're much too responsible to be cursed. I don't think you'd fare well at the mercy of the moon."

Since Jackson had raised the subject, Armond asked, "And what about you, Jackson? Gabriel has expressed concerns about your behavior since your return from abroad. Did something happen while you were in Paris?"

The younger brother cast Gabriel a dirty look before addressing Armond. "Only the usual. Gaming, whoring, hunting, and not necessarily in that order."

Armond wouldn't be easily put off. "Did you meet someone? Someone who became special to you?"

"Did I fall in love?" Jackson lifted a cocky brow. "Hell, I fall in love every night. I wouldn't worry about me, Armond. I'm not the one who has gone and gotten himself married."

His brothers were not taking his marriage well, but then, Armond hadn't expected them to.

His expression serious, Jackson asked, "When do I meet your bride? I could use a nap as well. Maybe I should go upstairs, climb into bed with her, and introduce myself." He smiled broadly at Armond.

Armond leveled a look upon his younger brother that would send bigger men scrambling for cover.

Jackson merely shrugged. "I see that marriage has caused you to lose your sense of humor," he said. "I hope that is all you lose, big brother."

Gabriel, silent through much of the conversation, now spoke up. "What are we going to do about that nasty stepbrother of your wife's? I say we all go over there tonight and put an end to his threats."

"Will it take all of us?" Jackson wanted to know. "Fighting is not my strong suit, I'm more of a lover, but of course if my services are needed in that area, I will rise to the occasion."

"You spend too much of your time rising to the occasion,

Jackson," Gabriel grumbled. "Maybe better that Armond and I handle this business."

Suddenly Armond was given a glimpse of why his younger brother suffered from irresponsibility. Armond realized he and Gabriel had spent much of their adult lives taking care of anything that needed to be taken care of. Jackson, to the opposite, had been given nothing of importance to do.

"I can fight," Jackson assured his brothers.

Armond made a decision in that moment, perhaps not the wisest one but one that went hand in hand with his position of leadership in the family. "This is my business," he said. "I will handle it alone. I want both of you to return to the estate tomorrow and stay out of harm's way."

Both brothers immediately put up a protest. Armond raised his hand to stop them. "I have a strong feeling now that the murders have started up again, they will continue. At least until I catch the man responsible. I will be suspect. If both of you are in London, you will be suspect as well. I'll think better if I don't have to worry about the two of you."

"If you don't have to worry about me, you mean," Jackson said. "Contrary to what you both believe, I can be responsible if need be, Armond."

He saw that private counsel was needed with his younger brother. "Gabriel, will you excuse me and Jackson for a moment? I wish to speak to him privately."

Gabriel wanted to grumble, Armond could tell, but in the end, the next in line to inherit should anything happen to Armond bowed to his older brother's authority. He left the study. Armond strode to his desk and leaned against it, indicating that Jackson take the chair before him. His brother slumped down into the chair.

"What lecture now, Armond? Do I drink too much? Yes, I suppose I do, but what of it? There's little in my life to look forward to. Women, do I overindulge in them as well? Yes, but I do take precautions to keep myself from disease, and of course to see that not one drop of our cursed seed is spilled inside a woman's fertile womb. So you see I can be responsible, at least over what I can control."

For a moment Armond was tempted to reach out and touch his brother's blond head. Jackson had been barely out of short pants when the curse took their father. When they also lost their mother as a result of the curse. Now Jackson was a man and Armond realized that he and Gabriel treated him for the most part as if he were still a boy.

"I must ask you a serious question, Jackson." Armond didn't want to ask, didn't want to believe for one moment that Jackson could have anything to do with Bess O'Conner's murder or with that of the woman found recently in his stable, but he had to know for certain. "It's about the murders."

Jackson, slumped in his chair, sat up straight. "Do you believe I might have come in contact with this person because of the company I've been keeping of late? That I might have seen something and not realized that it was of importance?"

Armond couldn't meet his brother's gaze. "No. I must ask you if you are in any way responsible."

When Jackson didn't answer, Armond glanced at him. His brow was knit as if he was trying to understand the question. Suddenly his dark eyes focused on Armond. "You think I killed those women?"

"You were here when the first murder took place. Now, you are here again. And Gabriel is worried that you aren't acting normally. Do I think you would kill a woman? No, not you as I know you. Not as I love you," he felt moved to add. "But if you aren't telling us the truth, and—"

"A drunkard, a womanizer, why not a murderer as well, is that it?" Jackson rose from his chair. His face had lost any appearance of youthful innocence his dimples might falsely provide him. "This is what I have to say to your accusations. To hell with you, Armond, and to hell with Gabriel as well."

"Jackson," Armond called after him when he stormed to the door and wrenched it open. The door slammed shut a moment later. Armond rubbed his forehead. He hadn't handled that well. Jackson had every right to be angry. He should trust his brother. Trust him regardless of what might appear suspicious to either him or Gabriel. That was not a mistake Armond would make again.

A rap on the door and Hawkins stuck his head inside. "I take it Lord Jackson will not be staying for the bath I was to prepare," he remarked. "He's left the house."

"I'll take the bath in his stead," Armond said. He would send Gabriel after Jackson. If he was lucky, his younger brother was headed back to the estate. With Jackson and Gabriel out of the way, he could concentrate on other matters. Like his wife. And all the problems marriage to her had brought to his door.

Chapter Fifteen

Rosalind was asleep when he checked on her. She'd changed her gown. Her dark hair fanned out like a dark river upon the white linen of the sheets. Her lashes made soot-colored shadows against her pale cheeks. She was the picture of innocence and of temptation.

Her lips were parted and called to him even if she didn't make a sound. He wanted to bend down and kiss her, to unbutton the modest row of buttons at her neck and taste her skin. He wanted to crawl into bed with her and spend the rest of the afternoon making love.

While he watched her sleep, he loosened his stock and unbuttoned his shirt. Before temptation got the better of him or his growing adoration became too painful, he walked across her room and entered his own through the open door. A bath sat steaming in the middle of his room. He would let the water ease his tensions, though he'd rather ease them between Rosalind's long legs. He couldn't get the picture of them from his mind since he'd come across her nearly naked earlier that morning.

What would it feel like to have those long, slender legs wrapped around him? To plunge into her womanly softness and lose himself to the worries that plagued him? Gabriel had packed his meager belongings and set off in search of Jackson, who Armond hoped had heeded his instructions to return to the estate. Armond now had the house to himself again . . . well, almost.

He stared through the open doorway at Rosalind. She hadn't moved, seemed to be sleeping deeply and probably peacefully for the first time in months. A surge of protectiveness rose up inside of him. No man would ever hurt her again . . . he hoped. Ironic that she might have more to fear from him than she did from her cruel stepbrother. But that would not happen, he tried to assure himself. Control was something he did well. He could control his feelings for Rosalind, make certain they become nothing beyond physical desire. He must. The consequences were too unthinkable to face if he did not.

She wasn't asleep. Rosalind stared through the open doorway at Armond from beneath heavy lashes. He'd stripped off his shirt and stood only in snug-fitting trousers and knee-high boots. She'd never seen a man as beautiful as he was. True, her experience in seeing half-dressed men was limited, but still, she sensed what she saw was not the ordinary.

She'd likened him to a great hunting cat the night she first saw him: sleek and built for speed, but he had muscles beneath his fine clothes. Lots of muscles. And glorious tawny-colored skin wrapped around them. His visage rode easy on a woman's eyes—made her want to sigh with appreciation that such a man existed. That, in fact, such a man was hers.

But he wasn't hers, Rosalind had to remind herself, before she lost all ability to reason. He had quite clearly indicated that he would share the outer part of himself with her but not the inner. Not his heart. His heart became less important when he pulled off his boots and went for the fastenings of his trousers. Rosalind knew she should close her eyes, but he held her spellbound.

He slid the trousers from his slim hips, exposing smooth flanks, also a golden cast, which meant either he allowed the sun to beat down upon him when he was naked or it was the natural color of his skin. Skin. Lots of skin. She swallowed the lump in her throat. His legs were long and muscular, dusted with light-colored hair, and indeed, she imagined they would propel him to victory in a footrace with relative ease.

Slowly, her eyes traveled up his legs toward a place she had avoided looking at, a place that would label him male, although there was nothing about him in the least feminine, except maybe those long golden locks that brushed the tops of his broad shoulders. He turned from her before she reached her objective and instead gave her a stunning view of his backside.

And it was stunning. From the muscles in his back that rippled slightly when he reached for a glass he'd set upon his mantel, down to where his hips narrowed and flowed into his tight, firm buttocks. That was where her gaze was focused when he turned from the hearth and faced her full-on. She might have gasped. If she didn't make the sound physically, she certainly made it mentally.

"There's nothing short about me, Lady Rosalind." The words he'd said to her at the Greenleys' ball came back to her instantly, and with good reason. His male member stood out straight from his body. It was long and thick and actually rather intimidating but, at the same time, fascinating to behold.

And oddly enough, the longer she stared at it, the harder it seemed to grow.

"Have you looked your fill, Rosalind?"

Her gaze snapped up to his face to discover he was watching her. Watching her watch him. Her face flooded with heat. Heat not nearly as hot as the moist warmth she felt between her legs. Her nipples had hardened to painful

peaks, poking out, she suspected, from the worn cotton of
her day gown. She'd chosen the older gown because she
had spent the afternoon working in her new quarters,
dusting out the empty wardrobe and arranging what items
she'd brought with her.

"No."

Had she said no? She'd been thinking she should say
yes and turn away from him, but deep inside she enjoyed
looking at his body, had found she wasn't ready to stop
the visual exploration.

"I can stand here longer while you continue to eat me
alive with your eyes, but there is one part of me that obviously cannot remain unaffected by your curiosity."

She knew which part and had trouble keeping her gaze
trained upon his handsome face. Curiosity, yes, she was
curious and saw no reason not to be truthful about the
matter.

"I've never seen a naked man before," she explained.

"Nor will you ever see another one," he countered, and
she wasn't certain but thought possessiveness had flavored
his voice. He seemed to realize his mistake and glanced
away from her.

"If you're finished looking, I'll climb into my bath before it grows cold. Unless there is something more I can
do for you."

She couldn't think of what something more might entail, but then, she was being an idiot. She felt a blush stain
her cheeks. "No, that will be all." She wanted to groan.
She'd dismissed him as if he were a servant. "I mean, thank
you very much."

His lips quirked. "You're quite welcome," he said, then
moved from her line of vision.

Rosalind flung herself on her back and looked up at
the ceiling. Had she thanked him? Lord, her mind turned
to mush when he was in close proximity and especially, it

would seem, when he was extremely naked. She heard the sound of splashing as he climbed into his bath. Why hadn't he closed the door? After lying there for a moment, she realized a bed was not the best place to be while her very attractive, very well endowed, or so she assumed, husband bathed in the next room.

It brought visions to mind. All that tawny wet skin sliding against her on the fresh linen sheets. Rosalind rose, went to the mirror over her bureau, and fussed with her hair. It took her only a quick comb-through with her fingers to realize she could see Armond's reflection in the mirror. She quickly glanced away. Then she realized he had his back to her. He wouldn't know that she watched him again.

Water ran in rivulets down his muscled back. His tawny-colored skin gleamed with moisture, and steam hung heavy in the air around him. His knees were slightly drawn up due to the shortness of the tub. It was the same tub she'd bathed in earlier that morning. Her naked. Him naked. Both of them in the same tub. She suddenly took to fanning her face.

"Since you still find me curious, would you mind soaping my back, Rosalind?"

She jumped. Did he have eyes in the back of his head? "Beg your pardon?" she called. "I was just arranging a few personal belongings here on the bureau."

"I can see you."

She left her place before the mirror and walked to the doorway, sticking her head inside. That's when she noticed that a mirror in his room was placed in such a way that he could see into her mirror. She refused to blush and ramble about this time. Instead, she bravely entered his room, walked to the tub, and knelt behind him.

"The soap please," she said in a clipped voice.

He didn't turn and look at her, simply handed her the same bar she'd been forced to use earlier that morning. The one that smelled like him. Rosalind took a deep breath and began to lather the soap onto his back. The texture of his skin was smooth, hot to the touch. She liked it, touching him.

"What else are you curious about, Rosalind?"

His voice had lowered and it penetrated her senses and sent her heart speeding a measure. "Curious about in general?" she asked.

"Regarding my body," he specified.

"Nothing," she lied. His shoulders sloped in an intriguing way, flowing into well-muscled arms. Arms he rested on each side of the tub. A woman would think he'd have his hands more strategically placed for modesty's sake. Armond obviously had no modesty.

"Liar," he said softly. "It would be more unnatural if you weren't curious. Feel free to explore any areas you would like to better acquaint yourself with."

She wouldn't fall for that trick. "As I'm sure you would then feel justified in doing likewise with my body."

"Not if you didn't wish me to," he said. "I told you the choice was yours. It still is, regardless of what you do to me."

Rosalind didn't believe him. She wanted to believe him, because she did, in fact, want to do further exploring. "It would be wrong," she decided.

He shrugged and muscles rippled beneath wet skin. "We are married. Nothing we choose to do together in these bedchambers from this point on is wrong."

She'd almost forgotten she was his wife. Moral issues, at least to a degree, no longer applied to her. But it was the physical she was trying to avoid until Armond was ready to give her more than that. "I don't think it would be fair," she said. "I'm not ready to . . . to consummate our marriage, and touching you in an intimate way might lead you to believe that I am. It would be like . . . like—"

"Teasing," he provided. "Love play."

"Love play? What does that mean?"

She heard him laugh softly. "Come around and face me and I'll show you."

Did she dare? She recalled that she'd already dared much with him. She'd dared to leave with him at the Greenleys' ball. She'd dared to take a coach ride with him that led to far more intimacies together than they had shared since. She'd dared to marry him. And she'd dared to make a silent vow that he would one day love her. Love her with his heart and not simply his body.

"Do you swear that I can do whatever I wish to you and you won't wish to do anything to me in turn?"

"No," he answered. "I'm certain I'll want to make love to you, I want to make love to you now, but yes, I swear to refrain from following the desires of my body until you are ready for me to follow them. I have excellent control. If I didn't, you'd already be mine. You would have been mine that first night at the Greenleys' ball."

Rather a slap in the face to remind her that she'd been willing and he'd been the one to walk away from her. But she hadn't even known him then, had merely meant to use him to further her plans of escape from Franklin. And he'd helped her to escape, after all. But escape to what? A loveless marriage? One where their future together would be based solely upon a physical attraction toward each other? And his smugness over the issue of control grated upon her very sensitive nerves. She, to the opposite, felt out of control when confronted with the feelings he stirred in her.

He'd given her a reason to do exactly what she wanted to do and to test his trustworthiness. Rosalind rose from her position behind him and walked around to face him. Their gazes met, locked, and although he tried to hide it, she could tell her decision surprised him. She bent beside the tub, their eyes never breaking contact.

Rosalind still had the soap in hand and she reached out and rubbed it against his bare chest, creating lather before her hands followed to draw patterns in the suds against his skin. The steam made her hair curl around her face, but she couldn't seem to break eye contact with him long enough to brush it away.

Her fingertips grazed his nipples and she heard his sudden intake of breath, but still he held her gaze with his. She wanted to look at his chest, but she'd seen it earlier. The muscles, the flat, round copper-colored nipples. His chest was smooth except for a darker trail that started below his breastbone and traveled downward. Downward past his stomach, which reminded her of a washboard, to a place where his hair was darker around his jutting member. She didn't realize her hand had followed her thoughts . . . followed that thin trail of darker hair, until his eyes became more intense as they stared into hers.

Her hand had disappeared below the water's surface, was poised just above the indention of his navel. Did she dare touch him there? She wanted to, she realized. Wanted to feel the texture and weight of the part of him that made him male. Her fingers slid down and closed around him. He drew in a ragged breath and his eyes took on a glow.

Her fingers could not close the width around him, and she marveled at the soft skin covering his steel-hard rod. The tip was larger, the skin there the texture of smooth velvet. She ran her hand down the length of him and back up. His body jerked involuntarily, but still, he did not break eye contact with her.

"Does it hurt you for me to do this?" she whispered,

because his jaw muscle had clenched and he no longer looked slightly amused by her curiosity.

"It drives me mad," he answered. "You drive me mad. The sight of you alone. The scent of you."

No man could stare so intently into her eyes and lie. Rosalind leaned in closer to him, close enough for their breaths to mingle. His hand suddenly cupped the back of her head. He kissed her.

There amid the steam and the heat from the water, he tasted her mouth, thrust his tongue inside to tease and dance and plunder. She didn't realize that her hand wrapped around his sex followed the movements of his thrusting tongue. She didn't realize he'd reached up and unfastened the buttons at the neck of her gown, all the way to her waist, until she felt his hand inside her bodice.

Her aching breast swelled into the fit of his palm. Her nipple hardened with anticipation. He rubbed his callused palm against it, beading it into a tight ball of sensation. Then his mouth was on her neck, forging a trail of hot kisses and soft nips at her skin all the way down her body until he pushed her gown aside and pulled her chemise down to expose her breasts.

"Lovely," she heard his muffled comment before his mouth fastened greedily upon her nipple.

She arched her neck back, squeezed him with her hand, and heard his deep moan against her breasts. Suddenly his other hand closed over hers beneath the water. He ceased her up-and-down motion against his water-slick member.

"What are you doing to me?" He pulled back to look at her. "What have you already done?"

She didn't understand what he asked. "I don't know."

"You know enough," he assured her. "Enough to shake my control. You have to stop now, Rosalind. Stop before you see me shatter beneath your innocent explorations."

Shatter? What did he mean? And she still ached for him. Not only her breasts, hungry for more of his attention, but also between her legs. She'd thought by having control she could control her own emotions as well. She was wrong. It was a trick after all. How could she have known that by his allowing her to touch him she would end up wanting his touch in return?

Rosalind removed her hand from his swollen member and stumbled back from him. She splashed water on her gown when she quickly jerked the gaping garment closed.

"I'm sorry," she whispered. "I-I can't." That was all she managed before she scrambled up off the floor, ran to her room, and slammed the door.

She leaned against the door, fighting the temptation to open it and go back in, to demand that he "shatter," whatever that meant. She halfway feared, halfway anticipated, that he'd test the door, possibly put his weight against it and send her stumbling toward the center of the room.

She'd acted brazenly with him, regardless that he'd invited her to do just that. Regardless that she was his wife and, she supposed, entitled to be forward if she chose to be. What could she expect? Nothing but for him to storm into her room now and do his worst . . . or perhaps his best.

Chapter Sixteen

Armond had resisted the urge to burst into Rosalind's room and finish what they had started. Instead he had dressed and gone out for the evening. He'd watched Chapman's carriage house, and when the man left driving his phaeton buggy, Armond had followed him. The hour was late, and it didn't surprise Armond that Chapman would be drawn to Covent Garden. The area was known as a gathering place for prostitutes.

Bess O'Conner had once frequented this area, Armond had learned eight months prior. He suspected the woman found recently in his stable was also a streetwalker. He was surprised that Chapman didn't have more expensive tastes when it came to female companionship. But then again, these women might serve his purposes better if he did indeed beat his women either before or after having relations with them.

Ahead of Armond, the phaeton slowed near a corner where four women stood. One of the women broke from the group and sauntered toward Chapman. Her gown revealed a good portion of her leg, as was customary dress for a woman of her profession. Armond closed his eyes and concentrated on hearing the conversation. It was an odd talent, but one that he now counted as an asset.

"Looking for company, love?" the woman asked Chapman.

"I am," Chapman answered. "But not your company. Send the dark-haired woman in the red dress over. She's slimmer and more to my tastes."

"She's skinny," the woman argued. "I have a nice plump shape, more to a man's liking, I'd think, than her scarecrow bones. You'll want something more to hold on to, love."

"Here's a coin to do my bidding," Chapman snapped. "Now send over the dark-haired one and be quick about it."

There was silence for a moment. Armond opened his eyes, squinting through the darkness to see the woman who'd approached Chapman speaking to another prostitute—a slim brunette wearing a gaudy red dress. The brunette joined Chapman.

"Molly says you have an interest in me," she said. The woman glanced over her shoulder and muttered, "Fat cow. I have crib—"

"No cribs," Chapman interrupted the woman. "I have a place where we can conduct business."

The brunette placed a hand on her hip. "And how will I be getting back? I'm not walking all over the city—"

"I'll see that you find your way back," Chapman assured her. "Now climb in."

The brunette didn't hesitate. She walked around and climbed into the phaeton. Chapman had found a breeding ground for women who would accompany him without question, and without the good sense to know they shouldn't, Armond thought.

He supposed it was the opinion of many in London, the authorities included, that women like the brunette took their chances and usually got what they deserved for selling their bodies on the street. That also worked to Chapman's advantage, if he indeed had murdered Bess O'Conner and the woman recently found in Armond's stable.

Chapman set the phaeton into motion and Armond followed, keeping enough distance behind the man to, he hoped, go unnoticed. Wherever Chapman was taking the woman, it wasn't in the direction of his residence. In fact, the neighborhoods grew progressively worse as they traveled. Had Armond's attention not been riveted upon the phaeton Chapman drove and keeping up with him, he might have noticed the danger that dogged him. He saw them too late.

Five men broke from the shadows and rushed him. His horse shied, and while Armond was in the process of trying to control the animal, one man managed to grab his leg and pull him off of the horse's back. Armond landed hard against the cobblestone street, knocking his head soundly against the stones in the process.

"Find his coin purse," he heard a man say. "No sense in going to all this trouble not to make a little extra in the bargain."

Hands rifled through Armond's pockets. He allowed the fondling until his senses cleared. The men's faces looming over him were still somewhat blurry due to the knock to his head, but he reached up and grabbed one man by the collar. Armond pulled back his fist and punched the man squarely in the nose. Blood gushed, splattering Armond's clothing.

The man stumbled back. "Bloody hell! He broke my nose!"

Something about the blood, the scent of it, roused him, gave him the strength to push four men off of him and gain his feet. Armond had been trained in gentlemen's boxing when he was only a boy. That wouldn't do tonight. Not with these men. All were burly, street-hardened-looking chaps. They circled him, like a pack of hungry wolves.

"Take him from behind!" one man yelled to another.

Armond turned, kicked, and landed a solid blow to the man's head behind him. The thief went down. Armond quickly turned back to the men in front of him, raised his fists, and waited.

"See him move?" one man asked the others. "Never seen a man move like that before."

"Get him!" someone yelled, and two men stormed Armond from the front, while one jumped on his back and tried to lock his muscular arms around him. He took a blow to the jaw, but he threw his head back and smashed into the man holding him, connecting with his face. The man howled in pain and released Armond.

Free from his restraints, Armond threw his fist into one man's stomach. The air left his attacker's lungs in a loud *whoosh*. Another man came at Armond and he swept the man's feet with his legs, tripping him. Armond's blood sang in his veins and he realized he fought as he had never fought before. His senses were so heightened that he almost felt as if he could read the men's intentions before they could carry them out.

He knew the man in front of him would rush him again before he did it. But Armond didn't expect the man to suddenly draw up, or his face to pale in the darkness.

"Good God, look at his eyes. Never seen eyes like that."

Nor did Armond expect, while he was focused on the man and wondering what it was about him that had frightened the thief, that a man behind him would suddenly smash something against his skull. The pain sent Armond to his knees. The shapes of the men standing around him blurred; then he saw only darkness.

• • •

Rosalind was in the process of trying to sweep her hair on top of her head when she noticed the marks. She leaned closer to her mirror. Pulling her hair over one shoulder, she turned her neck so that it was better visible to her. Odd, she thought. Two red marks stood out against her pale skin. Teeth marks perhaps, only she didn't think normal teeth could make the two small red indentions. They looked more like, well, like bite marks. Like marks canine teeth might make.

She remembered Armond kissing and biting at her neck yesterday while she had so boldly attended him in his bath. The memory brought a blush to her cheeks. She had expected Armond to come shoving his way into her room and to demand his husbandly rights, but he had not. In fact, she had not seen her husband since the incident between them took place.

Her gaze strayed to the still closed door that adjoined their rooms—or separated them, however a person wanted to look at it. She hadn't heard him stirring about in there. She walked to the door, pressed her ear against it, and listened. Nothing. Rosalind placed her hand on the knob. She tried to turn it slowly so it wouldn't make noise. The door squeaked slightly when she pushed it open. She walked into the room. Her husband wasn't there.

The bath from the previous day had been removed. The room was tidy, the bed made. She sat upon the bed. This was where Armond slept. Where, when she felt the time was right, which she supposed would be when she thought Armond cared more for her than in a physical way, they would consummate their marriage. A vision of him naked came to mind. She fanned her face with her hand, suddenly too warm.

She hoped it wasn't a sin to think about a man and wonder how it would feel to have the whole naked length of him pressed against her. Then she remembered the man was her husband, so she supposed it wasn't a sin. Rosalind rose from the bed and smoothed out a wrinkle that evidenced her presence in Armond's room. She walked around, stopping to study his brush, his shaving items, several of his personal belongings.

A soft rap sounded upon the door before it opened and she saw Hawkins standing outside. "Good morning, Lady Wulf," he said formally, looking unsurprised to see her in his Lordship's bedchamber. He glanced past her. "I wanted to tell Lord Wulf that breakfast is served."

"He isn't here," Rosalind said. "Isn't he downstairs?"

The man frowned. "No, my Lady. I haven't seen him since he left the house last night."

Rosalind glanced toward the bed. "Is Armond, Lord Wulf, in the habit of making his own bed?"

"Hardly," the man answered.

The implication hung in the air between them. Armond had not slept in his bed last night. Rosalind didn't know how to react. She didn't know Armond well enough to know if this was his usual behavior or if she should be worried about his whereabouts. It occurred to her that, being his wife, she should be worried about the fact that he hadn't spent the night in his bed regardless. If not in his bed, then whose?

"Breakfast is ready, you say?" she asked, because the moment grew awkward.

"Yes, my Lady. Will you be coming down, or should I bring a tray up to you?"

"I'll come down," Rosalind decided. She followed Hawkins out, regardless that she hadn't dressed her hair as she'd intended to do. Putting it up would only call attention to the strange marks on her neck.

She found herself hoping as she entered the dining room that Armond would suddenly appear. His place remained empty. She seated herself and made a go of having breakfast. After a while, she realized she was only playing with the food, not eating it. Hawkins strode past.

"Hawkins," she called. The man retraced his steps. He lifted a brow. "Has Lord Wulf returned?" she asked.

Hawkins glanced away from her. "No, Lady Wulf."

"Thank you," she dismissed him, a little embarrassed that she had to inquire about her husband's whereabouts only two days into her marriage with him. Rosalind gave up on eating her breakfast. The longer Armond remained missing, the more her stomach churned. Her thoughts strayed to the house next door. She hoped Franklin was not somehow responsible for her missing husband. If Armond didn't arrive home soon, she might have the nerve to march across the lawn and ask Franklin.

Fidgety, Rosalind left the dining room and returned upstairs. She fetched her sewing basket, hoping work on her sampler might pass the time. She missed several stitches due to a lack of concentration. A soft rap sounded upon her door. "Yes?" she called.

Hawkins opened the door and she held her breath, hoping he would tell her that Armond had finally arrived home. His message surprised her.

"You have a guest downstairs, Lady Wulf." He walked into the room and handed her a calling card. You could have knocked Rosalind over with a feather.

"I'll be right down," she told Hawkins. Before he quit the room, she said, "Tea in the parlor would be nice, Hawkins, if it's not too much trouble."

He inclined his head and closed her door. Rosalind gave her reflection a once-over in the mirror before she went downstairs. She entered the parlor to see a cloaked figure standing before the Wulf family portrait that hung over the large fireplace.

"Lady Amelia?"

The young woman turned, pushing back the hood of her cloak. She smiled at Rosalind. "I couldn't believe the rumors that you had married Lord Wulf were true. I had to come and see for myself."

Rosalind glanced around, looking for the young lady's chaperone and wondering why one would allow Lady Amelia to visit Rosalind or, more precisely, Rosalind in Armond Wulf's home.

"I snuck away," the young woman said, as if reading her thoughts. She came forward and took Rosalind's hands in hers. "I must be honest and tell you that you are quite shunned for your daring to marry Armond Wulf and for the rumors that you were his lover before the nuptials took place, but I for one applaud your courage." Her pretty blue eyes sparkled. "I knew more happened between you and Lord Wulf the night of the Greenleys' ball than you were telling me. Then, at the LeGrandes', the way he kept staring across the room at you . . ." She stopped to sigh dramatically. "He has such passion for you."

Rosalind might have smiled at Lady Amelia's dramatics if her heart hadn't suddenly felt as if it were breaking. Passion, yes; love, no. Hawkins entered carrying the tea service, wearing a bored expression even in light of a normally all-male household suddenly being invaded by women. "Shall I serve for you, Lady Wulf?"

"No, I'll serve," Rosalind said. "Thank you, Hawkins." The man nodded and took his leave.

Lady Amelia giggled. "If his spine were any straighter, I suspect it might break." The pretty blonde glanced around the parlor. "Your husband isn't here, is he?"

The reminder that Armond was missing took the joy out of Lady Amelia's visit. "No, not at the moment," Rosalind answered. She poured tea. The silence stretched. Finally Lady Amelia bounded to her feet and walked to the fireplace, where a small fire burned.

"I must confess that I have more reason for coming to visit you than to reaffirm our friendship."

Disappointed, Rosalind sighed. She had hoped for a friend but suspected Lady Amelia simply wanted gossip to spread among the rest of her social group. "What can I do for you, Lady Amelia?" she asked, her tone now cool.

The young lady didn't turn to face her. "First, please call me Amelia. No need for formal titles among friends. Next, you can tell me about him," she said, pointing to the Wulf portrait.

Rosalind was pleased that Amelia had reaffirmed their friendship, but she was also confused. "Lord Gabriel?" she asked.

Amelia turned to face her. The young lady's cheeks were flushed. "I saw him with your husband in town. He's so handsome I could scarcely catch my breath. I haven't been able to stop thinking about him, which is very improper, considering I can't even stop thinking of him when I'm with Lord Collingsworth, who I know plans to offer for me."

Her dilemma might have wrung more sympathy from Rosalind, but there was also a man she couldn't stop thinking about. Her husband. Where was Armond?

Chapter Seventeen

Armond came awake slowly, his head pounding and his senses dazed. He had trouble remembering where he was or how he'd come to be in his bed. He didn't remember coming home last night. For a moment, he didn't remember anything about last night. He turned and saw Rosalind sleeping beside him. Her back was turned to him, her dark hair a tangled mess.

What was she doing in his bed? He reached for her, touched her bare shoulder, and tried to rouse her. "Rosalind?"

She didn't respond, and that's when he noticed her skin was cold. Armond rose to a half-sitting position. He leaned over Rosalind to look at her. Her eyes were open, staring straight ahead. A trickle of blood ran a path from the corner of her mouth to her chin. A bruise covered the whole of her lower jaw.

"Christ!" Armond scrambled back from her. The woman was not Rosalind. The woman was dead. His gaze frantically searched the unfamiliar room. It was empty save for a mattress thrown on the floor—the one he'd obviously spent the night sleeping on—with a dead woman. Armond scrambled up. The pounding in his head grew worse.

He glanced around the empty room again, trying to remember how he'd come to be here, wherever here was,

and how the woman had come to be here as well. His gaze
strayed to her lifeless form. She was naked, but a thin
blanket had been thrown over her. Armond drew in a deep
breath and walked around the mattress, bending down before the woman.

He closed her sightless eyes. Last night's events came
rushing back to him. He'd followed Chapman to Covent
Garden. He'd seen Chapman leave with a prostitute . . . a
brunette, like this woman. Armond felt the back of his
head, where a good-sized knot made him wince. He'd
been set upon by thieves. He felt his pockets for his money
pouch. It was missing.

One of the men had hit him on the back of the head with
something, probably a rock. But how had he ended up
here? Why had he ended up here? A commotion outside
drew his attention. Armond walked to a dirty, streaked window and looked outside. He was on the second story of
what appeared to be a deserted residence. Below him in the
yard he saw a man walking with a young couple. They
were headed for the door to the house. Armond tried to
ease the window open, but it was stuck shut by dirt and
grime.

He closed his eyes and tried to catch the conversation
taking place below him.

"The house is in sad repair, but of course that is why
the rent is cheap. I'd think a nice young couple such as
yourselves could do well here. Just a bit of cleaning and
fixing up and you'd have yourselves a nice home."

"The neighborhood is not so nice," the woman commented quietly. "I had hoped for a home where I wouldn't
be afraid to go to sleep at night for fear someone would
break in and slit my throat."

"It's not that bad, Emma," the younger man said. "It's
got more room than anything else we've looked at for the
cost."

Armond heard a set of keys jingle below.

"Fancy that; it's not even locked," the older man said, laughing nervously. "I must have forgotten to lock it up last time I showed the house."

"See, Emma," the younger man said. "Not even locked and not a broken window to be seen. The neighborhood is not so bad."

Armond realized he was in trouble. He also understood that he'd been deliberately placed in this circumstance. He heard the people downstairs walking about. It would only be a matter of time before they came upstairs—came upstairs to discover him in a room with a dead woman. He tried the window again. He was unusually strong, but he couldn't budge the blasted thing. Glancing outside, he saw that the roof slanted away from the window. Even if he did manage to get it open and climb outside, he'd have a good drop to the ground below.

"There are two rooms upstairs. One, I'm thinking, would make a nice nursery."

The people were coming up the stairs. If there were only two rooms, there wouldn't be much of a landing. No possible place for Armond to hide and try to sneak out once the couple and the older gentleman had gone into one of the rooms. He didn't like sneaking about at all, but he'd been placed in this position to implicate him in yet another murder. He couldn't be caught here.

Armond couldn't be identified. He in truth had no one to vouch for what had happened to him last night this time. It would be his word, which the inspectors had little faith in, against very damning evidence against him.

He tried the window again. It wouldn't give.

"Where is my stepbrother?"

Mary looked surprised to see Rosalind standing at the

door. "In his study, Lady Wulf, but I thought you weren't to come here if he was at home."

"I need to speak to him." Rosalind walked into the house and moved toward the back where Franklin had a small study. She was frightened at the prospect of seeing him again and seeing him when she was alone, but she was more worried about Armond. He had not come home and it was now afternoon. Even Hawkins seemed worried, though he did a good job of hiding it.

She had a terrible feeling something had happened to Armond. And she had just cause to suspect that Franklin had something to do with her husband's disappearance.

The study door was open. Franklin sat at his desk, looking over papers. Rosalind straightened her spine and walked inside.

"What have you done with my husband?" she demanded.

Franklin glanced up. "Rosalind," he said. "So good to see you again."

"Where is he?" she demanded, not in the least fooled by her stepbrother's cordial manner toward her. "I know you've done something to him."

Rising from behind his desk, he walked toward her. "I haven't seen your husband since our last encounter the morning after you ran off and wed the bastard. Leaving me in a very awkward position, I might add, Rosalind. But then, you don't care about my feelings, do you?"

"No," she said honestly. "The same as you don't care about mine. Armond didn't come home last night, and I feel you are in some way responsible."

Franklin lifted a brow. "Troubles already, Rosalind? I have no idea where your husband is, and I don't give a damn. You barely know the man. Perhaps he often spends the night prowling around. Perhaps he prefers sport with more experienced women than you, Rosalind. Did you stop to consider that before you barged in here accusing me of having done something to him? Not that I wouldn't like to," he added. "He's taken something from me. Something that belongs to me."

Rosalind lifted her chin. "I don't belong to you, Franklin. I've never belonged to you." She saw that Franklin wasn't going to give her any information regarding Armond. She'd been a fool to think that he might. Still, Rosalind had been so worried about Armond she hadn't been thinking clearly. She turned to leave the study. Franklin was there an instant later blocking her way.

"Do you have any idea how furious I am with you?"

Unfortunately, she did. She felt his anger radiating from him. The pulse in his forehead throbbed. "Let me pass," she said. "I'm no longer under your thumb. You'll have to get yourself out of trouble on your own, Franklin. You no longer have me to use."

"Little whore," he growled. He lifted his hand to strike her. Rosalind immediately tensed for the blow. It did not fall. Franklin was looking behind her, his hand poised to strike, his eyes wide.

"If you hit her, it will be the last thing you ever do, Chapman."

"Armond," Rosalind breathed, and whirled around to see her husband standing behind her. She was so relieved, her knees nearly buckled. His clothes were rumpled and he had a nasty-looking place on his temple, but she was never so happy to see anyone in her life. "I was worried about you. I—"

"Go home, Rosalind," Armond interrupted. His steely gaze never left Franklin. "Go home now."

Franklin had recovered from his earlier surprise. "You are not welcome here, Wulf. Get out."

"And you are not welcome to abuse my wife," he

countered. "Not ever again. If you so much as breathe on her, I'll kill you."

Her stepbrother retreated to his desk. He seated himself as if he hadn't just been threatened with his life. "Sleep well last night, Wulf?" he asked.

Rosalind had no idea what Franklin had implied, but she felt Armond's anger. "You killed that woman," he accused.

Her stepbrother merely smiled. "Prove it."

"I will," Armond assured him. "Come, Rosalind."

Armond took her hand and led her from the study. Questions whirled in her mind, but she waited until Mary had held the door for them and they'd marched outside, headed toward the property next door, before she spoke.

"What happened, Armond? Where were you last night, and what woman were you talking about?"

"Not now," Armond said in a clipped tone. "When we get home."

Home. Armond's home didn't feel like her home, at least not yet. She hoped it someday would. Her ordeal of living with Franklin had made Rosalind realize how lonely for a real family she was, how much she wanted to love and be loved again. She knew deep inside that was the reason she'd so readily agreed to accompany Franklin to see his mother. The duchess was the only person Rosalind had left in the world who she thought might truly care about her.

Hawkins got the door for them once they reached the house. Although he tried to remain unmoved by the sight of his employer returning home, she could tell that he was relieved.

"I'll need a fresh basin of water to clean up," Armond said to the man. "Bring it to my chambers."

"Right away," Hawkins responded.

Rosalind followed Armond upstairs. They had no sooner entered his room when he shut the door and glared at her. "Did I not tell you to never go next door without me, or without knowing for certain that Chapman wasn't home?"

She was stunned by his anger. "Well, yes," she admitted. "But I was worried about you. I thought that Franklin—"

"I don't care why you felt moved to go over there," he interrupted her. "You put yourself in danger, Rosalind. It was a foolish thing to do."

Her morning spent in worry, then Franklin's near attack on Rosalind, left her emotions raw. Her eyes stung with tears. "Excuse me for caring what happens to you," she said, and then she marched to the adjoining door, walked through it, and slammed it shut.

Armond opened the door a second later and came storming into her room. "I will not excuse you. If I hadn't gone to confront Chapman immediately upon my return home, he would have hit you, Rosalind. He might have done worse to you. Don't you realize you're not just dealing with a bully? You're dealing with a murderer?"

Rosalind's heart thudded against her chest. "How do you know? I mean for certain? What happened last night?"

"My Lord?" Hawkins called from the next room. "I've brought the basin. Shall I attend you?"

Without answering her, Armond left and returned to his room. Rosalind followed him, pausing at the adjoining door as Armond stripped off his wrinkled coat and soiled shirt. She gasped when she realized he had several small bleeding cuts on his neck and hands. What had happened to him? She couldn't stand not knowing, but Hawkins had dipped a cloth in the washbasin and looked as if he would tend to Armond's cuts.

She doubted that Armond would discuss what happened last night with her in front of Hawkins. Rosalind decided to take matters into her own hands. She approached the steward.

"Please allow me to see to my husband," she said to the man.

Hawkins turned an inquisitive look toward Armond.

"It's all right, Hawkins," Armond said. "Rosalind can clean me up."

"Very well."

As soon as Hawkins handed Rosalind the damp cloth and left the room, she turned to Armond. "How did you get cut? And where were you all night? How do you know that Franklin is in fact responsible for killing women?"

Armond was still trying to bring his emotions under control. He was good at that, but he'd never been faced with the challenges he'd been given since Rosalind came into his life. Control was easy, he realized, responsibility was easy, when a man didn't care. Suddenly he cared.

"I was forced to hurl myself through an upstairs window earlier, then had to jump to the ground below."

Rosalind blinked up at him. "I'm surprised you didn't kill yourself, or at least cause yourself serious injury."

That bothered Armond as well. He'd had no choice but to hurl himself through the window sealed shut by years of cleaning neglect, but once he had, he'd rolled off the roof and landed on the ground with his knees bent, in a crouching position that should have broken his legs. It had seemed natural, the jumping. The landing was . . . unnatural. Noting that Rosalind waited for him to elaborate on last night's events and that she had to stand on her tiptoes in order to reach the cuts on his neck, he steered them toward the bed, where they could both sit.

"Why did you have to hurl yourself through a window, Armond? Please tell me what happened."

The cloth stung against his cuts. His mind raced with

everything that had occurred the previous evening, and this morning when he'd awakened in a strange place with a dead woman. Where to begin? He began at the beginning. But later, he wondered how much to tell Rosalind.

Did he tell her that he thought Chapman had chosen a woman who resembled Rosalind as some sort of warped symbolism? Did he tell her that he thought her step-brother planned to kill her and implicate him in the murder, as he'd done with the prostitute? Or was he wrong about that? Chapman had planned for him to be discovered this morning.

"My God," Rosalind whispered. "I can hardly believe— I mean, he could have just as easily killed you, Armond. You were unconscious; why didn't he?"

Armond suddenly realized something that hadn't occurred to him. "It was a trap," he said. "He knew I would start to follow him. The thieves were hired men. I remember now one of them saying they would rob me because they might as well get more in the bargain."

He felt for the knot on the back of his head, maybe just to assure himself he was on the right track. He had a suspicion about something else as well.

"It's become a game to him," he explained to Rosalind. "He's turned murder into a game."

She shivered and in her deep violet eyes he saw her terror. Armond was so angry at Rosalind for confronting Chapman about his whereabouts and placing herself in danger that he hadn't stopped to think about how much courage it had taken her to go next door. She'd faced a man she was terrified of, for him.

His gaze moved over her beautiful features. She could have been the woman lying next to him this morning. Dead. He reached out to touch her lips, trace the shape of them, touch her cheek, just to feel the heat beneath her skin that told him she was alive. He brushed her long hair back over her shoulder. Then he saw it.

"What is that on your neck?"

Her hand immediately went to the spot. She rubbed it for a moment. "I'm not sure. It appears to be a bite."

He brushed her hand aside and looked closer. "A bite from what?"

When she didn't answer and he pulled back to look at her, pink crept into her cheeks. "I believe from you."

Chapter Eighteen

It was just beginning to grow dark when Armond found himself at Covent Garden again. Chapman had taunted him with proving that he'd killed the woman last night, and Armond thought he knew a way to do so. Since it was earlier than it had been last night when he'd been at this exact location, there were more women walking the area. He was searching for one in particular. Molly had been her name.

He spotted her a ways down the street, moving slowly in his direction, her hips swaying and, again, her leg on display. Armond urged his mount toward her. When he drew up beside her, she stopped and eyed him boldly.

"Couldn't be my luck that you're looking for companionship, love," she said. "Not a fine-looking man like yourself."

Armond dismounted, holding the reins of his horse while the woman sauntered closer to him. "Molly? Is that your name?"

The woman drew up. "How'd you know that?" Her gaze narrowed, and she looked him up and down again. "Haven't had dealings with you before. I'd remember you, love."

"I want to ask you some questions."

The woman made a snorting noise. "Don't have time for questions. I'm a working woman."

"I'll pay you for your time," Armond offered, then reached beneath his coat and removed his new money purse, since his had been stolen the night before.

The woman shrugged. "Suppose talking is easier than lying on my back, although wouldn't mind lying on my back for you. Might even pay you to let me run my fingers through those gorgeous blond locks of yours."

The woman's offer didn't tempt him. Not even a little. "Last night, there was a woman standing with you on this corner. A brunette wearing a red dress. Thin."

Molly rolled her eyes. "Why men are interested in that bag of bones when I've got nice plump curves, I don't understand."

"The woman has been murdered."

He expected a reaction from Molly. Just not the one he got. She laughed. "Then I suppose it's her corpse coming up the street there."

Armond turned in the direction Molly had looked. A woman strolled toward them. A brunette wearing the same red dress she'd worn the previous night.

"Hey, Lily, you're supposed to be dead. What you doing walking my corner?" Molly called to the woman.

The woman, Lily, sauntered up to them. She looked Armond up and down as Molly had done. "Who says I'm supposed to be dead?"

Armond was thrown off guard by the development. "I saw you leave last night with a man driving a phaeton."

"Bastard," Lily muttered. "Drove me around in his buggy is all he did, brought me back here, and made me get out. Didn't even pay me for my time."

Another trick? If Chapman had known Armond had been following him, he'd also known that he could have elicited the whore, Molly, to tell the inspectors that

Chapman was the last man the dead prostitute had been seen with. Chapman had lured him into a trap, had brought this woman back and chosen another to kill and put into bed beside him. It seemed like a lot of work for one man, one man playing a deadly game.

"I am obviously mistaken," Armond said to the ladies. "Sorry to bother you." He removed a few coins and gave them to each woman.

"Sure you're not up for some sport, love?" Molly asked him. "Wouldn't mind earning the coin you just gave me."

"Thank you, but no, maybe another time," he added, just to spare her feelings. He was thinking of Rosalind now, and how he wanted to hurry home to her. He'd told Hawkins to fetch his pistol and have it handy while he was gone. He'd told the steward to shoot any man who stepped foot in the house, except Armond, of course. Hawkins had replied, "It would be my pleasure, my Lord."

The ride home gave Armond time to think. Chapman had gone to a lot of trouble to frame him for murder. Besides marrying Rosalind, what did the man have against him? Marrying off his stepsister to Penmore for a high bride's price and the release of his debts against the man was no longer an option . . . unless Rosalind was a widow.

Tomorrow Armond would see his lawyers and make certain that Rosalind was protected, at least financially, in the event of his death. His brothers, he hoped, would see to her physical protection should anything happen to him. While he was about business, he'd check on something else. He'd see how hard it would be to find out which properties around London were for rent or purchase.

What Armond wouldn't think about was the way he had leaped from a second-floor window earlier and how he'd landed upon his feet . . . like an animal. What he wouldn't think about was the way the men who had attacked him last night had become frightened right before the one behind him had clobbered him over the head. What he wouldn't think about were the strange bite marks on his wife's lovely neck.

Rosalind was in the parlor, trying to read a book, when she heard the front door open, saw Hawkins, who'd stationed himself at the parlor door, pull a pistol from beneath his coat, then relax.

"Good evening, Your Lordship." Hawkins tucked the pistol back beneath his coat. "Lady Wulf is here in the parlor. Shall I bring you something?"

Armond walked into the parlor. "A brandy would be nice. Would you care for one, Rosalind?"

Besides champagne on a few occasions, Rosalind had never tasted spirits. She'd had an eventful day, the same as Armond, who now wore the strains of the day upon his handsome face.

"I believe I will have one," she said to Hawkins. The man nodded and went on his way.

Armond slumped into a velvet chair across from her. He scrubbed a hand over his face. "Chapman covered his tracks from last night well."

Rosalind laid her book aside. A cozy fire burned in the hearth, and she'd kicked off her slippers, tucking her feet beneath her on the settee. "What happened when you went to Covent Garden? Did you see the woman Franklin first approached last night?"

He nodded. "Yes, and I also spoke with the dead woman."

"What?"

Armond sighed wearily. "At some point, Chapman took the woman back to Covent Garden, dropped her off, and went somewhere else, where he solicited another brunette, murdered her, then took her to a deserted house and left her on a dirty mattress beside me."

Rosalind straightened on the settee. His story was extraordinary. "It sounds like a lot of trouble for one man," she said.

Armond ran a hand through his hair. "My thoughts exactly," he agreed.

Hawkins arrived with two glasses of amber liquid on a serving tray. He set the tray on the table closest to Rosalind and left the room again.

Armond rose, lifted a glass, handed it to Rosalind, and took his own glass. He glanced at the book she'd put aside.

"I hope you don't mind," she said. "I visited your study. Hawkins said you had a nice collection of books and I wanted something to help me pass the time."

Her husband shrugged. "You have free run of the house, Rosalind."

"So, what do you do now?" She took a sip of the warm brandy and nearly choked. Armond smiled at her. "It burns," she said once she managed to catch her breath again.

"It warms," he corrected her, seating himself beside her on the settee. "I have a couple of things I plan to do tomorrow. I don't like leaving you here alone. Not with Chapman only next door."

"Oh." Rosalind suddenly remembered something. She reached for the invitation she'd stuck in her book. "The dowager has invited me to tea tomorrow. Lady Amelia was here and said she'd also received an invitation, which of course was sent out weeks ago."

"Lady Amelia?"

"Lady Amelia Sinclair," Rosalind explained. "The Duke of Ravenhill's daughter. She's my friend." Either the

brandy warmed her or just simply being able to say she
had a friend did.

"The pretty blonde with the big blue eyes," Armond
commented. "Yes, I know who she is."

Something very close to the color of green reared its
ugly head. "You do?"

"I noticed her at the LeGrandes' soiree and asked the
dowager who she was."

"You noticed her?" Rosalind unclenched her hand from
around the stem of her glass and took another sip of
brandy.

He smiled. "Only because she was talking to you," he
answered. "At the time, I wanted to know who it was you
were trying to impress the night of the Greenleys' ball,
but of course now I know that you weren't trying to impress anyone."

"Oh." Rosalind felt a warm flush of pleasure. She
swirled the liquor around in her glass. She decided she
liked brandy.

Armond suddenly leaned close to her. "Have I told you
that I want you today?"

She had just taken another drink and nearly choked
again. Now that she supposed they had matters of murder
and society out of the way, he was back to seduction. And
he was very good at it.

"Shall I go to the tea tomorrow?" she tried to change
the subject.

He stuck his tongue in her ear. "Yes. You'll be safe
there."

Rosalind nearly jumped from her skin. When he nibbled on her earlobe, she asked, "Did I tell you that Amelia
is quite taken with Gabriel? She said she saw him on the
street, riding with you."

His tongue traced a hot path down the side of her neck.
"She is wasting her time," he commented. "Gabriel's only

interested in the running of our estate. I've sent him back there, and hope when he arrives he'll find my younger brother Jackson also in residence."

Trying not to shiver with delight, she said, "I suppose it's just as well that Gabriel is gone. Amelia's going to marry a young man named Lord Collingsworth anyway."

Armond's hand slid up her side, coming to rest just below her breast. "I know him. In fact, Collingsworth Manor borders Wulfglen. We played together as boys, although I don't remember him keeping up with us well. He was always rather sickly."

Trying to control her breathing, Rosalind asked, "You are friends?"

"Were." His hand slid up and cupped her breast. "Not anymore."

She turned her head to look at him. "Why not anymore?"

His thumb brushed across her nipple, making her gasp softly. "Because of what happened with my parents. Those who once fully embraced us among society soon turned their backs on us. Society doesn't like scandal, you know."

Her nipple hardened and she had trouble ignoring the steady brush of his thumb across it through her gown. "Then you have no friends?"

His hand moved up and around to the buttons at the back of her neck. "No."

Her heart ached for him, and lower, she ached somewhere else for him. "Well, I haven't had many, either," she admitted. "But now I have Amelia and the dowager if she'll allow me to be her friend. I could be your friend."

While he unbuttoned the row of buttons at her back, and with only one hand, no less, he stared into her eyes. She thought they softened for a moment. He leaned toward her. "Do friends do this?"

He kissed her. The warm taste of brandy on his lips added to the burn in her belly. The kiss was pleasurable, as cozy as the fire and the homey setting. He slanted his mouth against hers to afford him deeper access, and everything changed. The cozy fire might as well have suddenly erupted into a burning inferno.

He was a master at it: kissing. He pulled her bottom lip between his teeth and then sucked it into his mouth. He released her lip, teased her with his tongue, and, when she met his challenge, sucked her tongue into his mouth, too. Deep into his mouth. She liked it, and so when he finally released her and his tongue stole into her mouth again, she did the same to him. He made a low sound in his throat.

He'd distracted her so much with the kissing, she hadn't realized he'd managed to get the fastenings down her back open. Not until he pulled the material away from her skin and her sleeves fell off her shoulders. He planted a warm kiss against her shoulder.

"Armond," she whispered. "The door is open. Hawkins—"

"Hawkins!" Armond suddenly yelled. "The lady and I are not to be disturbed!"

From somewhere in the house she heard Hawkins shout back, "Very well, my lord!"

Armond went back to kissing her shoulder. Suddenly he paused again. "Hawkins, be sure you keep your ears to the doors!"

"Very well, my lord!"

"All the doors but this one!" he added.

"Very well, my lord!"

Rosalind giggled. Armond rose and pulled the parlor doors closed. He smiled at her as he sauntered back toward her like a lazy cat, but then his eyes took on their strange glow when he settled back beside her.

"Where were we?" he asked. "Oh yes, I remember. We were here."

He leaned over and kissed her exposed shoulder again. The feel of his mouth against her skin made her shiver. The few sips of brandy she'd taken helped to relax her, but the liquor had not gone to her head. Armond went to her head. His intoxicating scent, the warmth that radiated from him, even the soft glow in his eyes.

"You taste good," he said. "I'd like to taste all of you."

Armond pulled her gown down farther and kissed a path to her breasts. He suckled her through the fabric of her chemise, the sensation almost more erotic than had he pushed the undergarment down around her waist along with her gown. The wet circles against her chemise left by his mouth made her nipples all the harder.

"I want to see you naked."

His comment reminded her that she'd seen him naked. And she very much recalled that he was glorious. Would her body please him the way that his had pleased her? As if he knew she was thinking too much, he kissed her again. She had trouble thinking when he kissed her, but she had no trouble feeling.

While his mouth stole her ability to reason, he pulled her chemise down and his hands cupped her breasts, his thumbs working torturous magic against her now exposed nipples. She moaned softly and pressed against him. He lifted her, bringing her down on his lap facing him. The position forced her knees on either side of his muscular thighs, which was highly indecent.

She started to tell him so, but he lifted her again, his mouth even with her breasts. He feasted there, ending her protest with the first hard pull of his mouth against her nipple. Her hands twisted in his thick hair and she held him to her. He nipped, teased, and sucked her nipples until she couldn't catch a normal breath, could only twist her fingers deeper into his hair and hold on.

He sat her down on top of him, now tasting and teasing her lips. She realized he'd gathered her gown in a way that left little between them below the waist. Drawers to trousers, and his trousers were sporting definite proof that he was aroused. Very aroused. He pressed against her, and she was surprised by an immediate response between her legs. A tingling that wasn't unpleasant but only a little frustrating. Like an itch that needed scratching.

When he pressed against her again, she pressed back. His breath hitched and he put a hand on either side of her face, holding her while he kissed her. She couldn't control her lower half, it seemed. The harder she pressed against him, the more friction she felt—a friction that could easily drive her insane.

"What is it that I want?" she whispered breathlessly against his mouth.

"This," he said, and he released his grip on her face, one hand moving down between them, sliding into the top of her drawers and to the very source of her frustration. The stroke of his fingers in a place where no man had dared travel before jolted her for a moment. She might have protested, certainly tried to twist away, but his fingers were magic.

He touched her in a place where all her sensation seemed centered, and that, combined with the flow and ebb of him pressing his hardened member against her soft woman's place, was heaven and hell combined. She rode his hand, rode his lap, and the pressure inside of her built and built. He continued to kiss her, although it was no easy task to keep their lips joined when neither of them could catch a normal breath.

"Let go, Rosalind," he whispered, his voice so low and velvet-soft that it sent her over the edge into madness.

The pressure that had been building broke free. A feeling like she had never experienced washed over her, and still below, she bucked and convulsed against him. Her fingers dug into his shoulders, her teeth into his neck, and the bottom dropped out of life as she had known it. She couldn't stop the soft moans and unintelligible words that tumbled from her lips. She couldn't stop shaking.

She clung to him as if he were the only solid thing holding her sanity intact. He smoothed her hair and his hand slid out of her drawers, up her stomach, and caressed her breast.

"What just happened?" she managed to whisper.

"You shattered," he answered. "Came damn close to making me do the same thing, which would have been embarrassing, considering I haven't gone off without being inside a woman since I was still in short pants."

How had they gone from talking and sipping brandy to her sprawled on his lap, bare to the waist and still convulsing between her legs? And what would happen now, since he was still hard and throbbing beneath her? Would he consummate their marriage with or without her permission? Part of her felt as if, no matter how wonderful what had just happened to her was, something was missing.

Love, she tried to tell herself. That was what was missing.

He pulled her gown and chemise back into place, lifted her, and managed to rise with her in his arms.

"What are you doing?" she asked warily.

"I'm taking you to bed," he answered.

Chapter Nineteen

Her heart thudded inside of her chest as Armond carried her up the stairs. He would surely take her now, whether she wanted to fully consummate their marriage or not. She had pushed him too far, allowed him too many liberties, to cry foul, even if she did in fact feel like crying. Armond had already made her realize that the taking and giving between a man and a woman could be a wondrous thing. But how much more wonderful could it be when the man and woman loved each other? She might never know.

Both of their doors were open. Hawkins had obviously been in to light night fires and turn down beds. Armond carried her to her own bed, rather than his. He laid her gently down, then bent to kiss her. She only half-responded to him, wondering when he would strip off his clothes and pounce upon her.

"Good night, Wife," he said, moving toward his room.

Rosalind balanced herself on her elbows. "Good night? You're leaving me?"

He turned, lifting a brow. "You want me to stay?"

"Well, no," she stuttered. "I mean, yes, well, I don't know."

His mouth curved into a sensuous smile. "When you do know, I'll be in the next room."

He closed the door behind him. She stared at it for a good long while. Then she began to seethe inside. She was half-tempted to storm into his room and demand he make love to her—consummate their marriage—never mind that she wasn't mentally ready to take that step with him. She was almost out of bed before she realized he'd gotten to her. He'd said he wouldn't play fairly, and he hadn't. Rather than become the aggressor with her, he'd backed off, probably suspecting she'd have this very reaction to a rejection by him.

"Smart," she said to the closed door. "But not smart enough."

Rosalind climbed back into bed, feeling rather smug that she hadn't fallen for his trick. She lay there for a moment before she realized she was dressed and would have to get up and change into her nightclothes. She could do that, she mentally encouraged herself. She could do that and not even be tempted to open the door separating their rooms. After a few more moments of assuring herself, she climbed from the bed. She marched straight to his door and opened it.

Armond turned from his washbasin. He'd removed his shirt, and droplets of water ran down his chest. He took a short towel from around his neck and wiped his face.

"Did you want something?"

Her eyes traveled over his tawny-colored skin. She swallowed loudly. "I forgot to tell you good night. Good night . . . Husband."

She shut the door, then leaned against it, calling herself five kinds of a fool. He hadn't looked as if he might be lying in wait for her. As if he'd anticipated her visit upon the heels of rejecting her. Maybe he really did possess the control he claimed. As she stood there, she felt the knob of the door that pressed into her back turn

slowly. She held her breath. Then it stopped. She thought
she heard him swear softly on the other side.

Armond was not in a good mood. He'd slept very little
last night, and the pounding in his head today only aggra-
vated his foul mood. Rosalind was driving him insane.
He wanted her as he'd never wanted anyone or anything
before. Her soft moans of pleasure when he'd given her
release battered his control and made him wonder what
had ever possessed him to give her a choice regarding
their sleeping arrangements.

He'd been so desperate to have her last night, he'd almost shattered the small trust she had in him. Temptation
had almost gotten the better of him, his promise to her be
damned. If he couldn't open his feelings to her, couldn't
love her as she deserved to be loved, he had decided a
physical relationship between them would be enough. But
even that was denied him. Denied him by his own cursed
words to her.

Armond entered the office of a property broker. It was
the fifth such establishment he'd visited today. He'd earlier come from his lawyer and made arrangements for
Rosalind to be taken care of financially should anything
happen to him. A thin man with spectacles perched on the
end of his nose and a rather large ring of keys dangling
from his belt greeted him.

"Good afternoon, sir. How may I help you?"

He recognized the man's voice. He was the same man
who had been showing the young couple the house Armond had been trapped in yesterday.

"I'm interested in purchasing several properties," Armond said. "What do you have available?"

Behind his spectacles, the man's eyes suddenly shone
with greed. "Do sit down, sir." He indicated a chair
across from a scratched desk that should have been used

for firewood long ago. Armond took a seat. The man hurried behind the desk, pulled open a drawer, and removed a large ledger.

"I have several properties for sale, as you can see." He indicated the list. "We simply have to narrow down what you're interested in. Neighborhood, cost of the property, that sort of thing."

Armond had a good idea where he'd been last night. His escape from the house hadn't left him time to be exact, but he'd been forced to walk the neighborhood until he'd come to a section of the city where he could hire a hack to take him home. He had no idea what had happened to his horse but assumed he was now a possession of the hired men who'd attacked Armond.

"Something on the east end," he specified. "I don't want to pay much, but the rent I could collect must be sufficient to make such a purchase profitable."

"Of course," the man agreed. He began looking down his list. "I have several properties in the area you're interested in," he commented. "Those properties are mostly rented to factory workers and the like. Some in rather sad repair," he said with a frown.

"Anything that has had the purchase price recently lowered?" he asked casually. Armond was fairly certain the young couple who'd been looking at the house yesterday had gone screaming from the place. The authorities would have been called in; the talk would have spread quickly through the neighborhood that a dead woman had been found in the house. Not good for the owner of the property.

The man brushed a lock of greasy hair from his forehead. His hand visibly trembled. "As a matter of fact, I do have a property that a seller is now rather anxious to part with, and he just lowered his price this morning. A rather unfortunate incident took place there yesterday."

Armond lifted a brow to prod the man.

"Murder," he whispered. "A whore was found dead inside. I was showing the property to prospective renters at the time. The young couple were most distressed by the sight. The killer escaped through a window upstairs." The man shuddered. "Imagine, I was in the very same house with him."

"Did you see the man?" Armond asked.

"No," the broker answered. "I was too shocked by what was taking place to rush to the window and try to get a look at him running away. The poor woman I was showing the house to fainted dead away."

"Pity," Armond said sympathetically. "Have you had other interested buyers concerning this particular property?"

The man shook his head. "Nothing serious. An inquiry or two. I had an appointment actually today to show the house, would have shown it to the interested party yesterday, but I told him I already had some renters interested in looking at the property and our appointment would have to take place either after that one or today. My client didn't keep the appointment. I assumed he'd already heard about the unfortunate incident at the house and was no longer interested."

Armond realized how easy it had been for Chapman to pick a location, inquire about it, and find out when people would be coming to view the house. Now the tricky part.

"The party interested in the property wouldn't be a man by the name of Franklin Chapman, would it?"

The man's eyes registered no recognition of the name, Armond noted, before he flushed. "That would not be information I can divulge," he said. "I have several clients who deal with the buying and selling of property, and all my dealings with them are kept confidential."

"Of course," Armond said in a clipped tone. "He's a neighbor of mine and I know that he deals in such an enterprise. I didn't want to be possibly bidding against him if he changed his mind about the property. Being neighbors and all," he explained.

"Then you are interested in the property?" The man's eyes sparkled with interest again.

"Perhaps." Armond rose. "I will think about it and if I am, I'll be back to visit again."

"And you are, sir . . . ?"

Armond didn't answer. He walked from the man's office and strolled down the street toward his waiting carriage. He'd escorted Rosalind to the dowager's tea a good hour ago. She'd been nervous, fussing with her gown and claiming it was outdated and that she hoped no one would notice. He would stop by a shop on Bond Street and solicit a seamstress for Rosalind before he went to collect her from the dowager's.

It wasn't anything Armond had dealings with before, but he wouldn't have Rosalind embarrassed to go out in public due to an outdated wardrobe. She was his responsibility now, and if he couldn't give her his heart, he'd give her what he could. He suddenly wondered how she was faring at her first social event as his wife.

The tea was a disaster. Rosalind wished she had declined the dowager's invitation. She now understood how Armond felt any time he chose to attend a social gathering. Women whispered behind their hands while they cut sly glances in her direction. She sat alone in a corner of the dowager's large parlor, sipping her tea and wishing Armond would arrive to collect her.

Franklin, as much as she despised him, had been right. Her wardrobe was terribly outdated, and she felt like a milkmaid among royalty. Amelia had cast her imploring glances a couple of times. Imploring for forgiveness because the young lady's mother was present and Amelia didn't have the nerve to openly acknowledge their friendship. Rosalind was trying to understand and be forgiving, but it was difficult for her when she was so obviously an outcast among the women present.

"How is Armond?" The dowager had made her way to Rosalind and settled in a seat beside her. "I knew he was smitten with you the first night he saw you at the Greenleys' ball. I'd never seen him at a loss for words before. I told him that the two of you would be a good match."

Curious, Rosalind asked, "And what was his reply?"

The woman frowned. "Something vulgar, as I recall. He does like to make me blush, and at my age that is quite an accomplishment."

Rosalind could well imagine what sort of suggestive reply Armond might have made to the dowager's matchmaking. "How did you and Armond become friends?" she also wanted to know. "You seem an odd pair."

"I was a very good friend of his mother's," she answered. "I liked his father, too. They were a handsome couple, as you might imagine given the outcome of their union together. Four sons, and all of them so devilishly good-looking. Pity things turned out as they did."

Rosalind knew she was being rude by monopolizing the dowager's time, especially since the lady was the hostess, but she had so many questions about Armond and his family. Questions she had not yet felt comfortable enough to ask Armond. "Was his mother really mad?"

The dowager sighed. "Quite insane in the end. Driven to it by grief, though, in my opinion. Neither of Armond's parents was mad by nature, or any inherited fault,

I don't believe. They simply weren't strong enough to weather the storm blown their way. It ended up destroying them."

Fascinated, Rosalind leaned closer to the dowager. "What sort of trouble was it?" And indeed, what could make a man take his own life and drive his poor wife insane?

"That is a tale better left for Armond to relay to you," she said. "Oh, I've forgotten. Lady Amelia asked me to tell you to meet her in the front guest room upstairs. I believe she told her mother she needed to refresh herself." The woman frowned. "I had hoped she'd grow some spine, Amelia Sinclair. She has the potential to become quite shocking, and therefore, quite intriguing, but she lacks the nerve. Pity."

"I shouldn't have kept you from your other guests for so long," Rosalind apologized. She set her teacup aside and rose. "I'll go in search of Lady Amelia."

"You're the only guest I was interested in, today," the dowager admitted. "I wanted to make certain Armond was faring well, and of course to show society that I as readily embrace you as I do him, whether they approve of it or not."

"I am grateful to you," Rosalind said. "You are a rare find among society. I thank you for your devotion to Armond. He doesn't deserve the bad hand he's been dealt. He's honorable, and he's kind, although I don't think he knows that about himself."

The dowager smiled at her. "You love him," she said softly. "I can see it in your lovely eyes when you speak of him. He deserves to be loved, but I fear, like his father, he might not realize that true love is unconditional. Maybe he will learn that with your help."

Flustered by the dowager's comments, Rosalind couldn't

think of a response. Did she love Armond? Could she love him in such a short space of time? And what hidden messages had the dowager been trying to send her? Rosalind mumbled a parting remark and left the room. She'd barely gotten up the stairs when Amelia stuck her head from the first room and frantically motioned to her to join her.

Rosalind entered the guest room. Amelia closed the door behind her. "Please say you don't hate me," her friend begged. "Mother forbade me to even acknowledge you today. I tried to stand up to her and told her you were my friend. She said being your friend would hurt my chances of marrying Lord Collingsworth. What could I do but follow her orders?"

Rosalind wasn't in the mood to deal with yet another of Amelia's dilemmas. She had a suspicion that Amelia thrived on drama. But because of her own upbringing, neither could she crucify Amelia for simply being born into high society. There were rules, and had either Rosalind's mother or father still been alive, she'd be forced to follow them as well.

"I forgive you," she told Amelia. "You mustn't get sideways with your family over our friendship, Amelia. You'll never know how important they are to you, and how much you love them, until one day when you no longer have them."

Amelia's big blue eyes filled with sudden tears. "You have the kindest heart, Rosalind, and the bravest nature. I don't deserve you as a friend."

The meeting had become much too emotional, and Rosalind was still reeling from the possibility that she could be in love with her husband. "Of course we'll remain friends," Rosalind said to the young woman. She took her hand and squeezed. "Even if you have to sneak over to my home to see me."

"I felt quite wicked doing that," Amelia admitted, the sparkle of mischief back in her eyes. "I like feeling wicked, in fact." She walked to the mirror and made a pretense of arranging her already perfect blond curls back in order. "Is Gabriel Wulf still staying with you?" she asked casually.

Rosalind smiled. Amelia was a horrible actress. "No, I'm afraid he's gone back to the country estate. Which reminds me, did you know that Collingsworth Manor borders Wulfglen? The Wulf country estate?"

Amelia turned from the mirror. "No, I did not know that. Robert has never mentioned that fact to me."

"If you marry Lord Collingsworth, you'll be Lord Gabriel Wulf's neighbor. Won't that be quaint?"

Amelia frowned at her. "You're being sarcastic. And it seems as if I *will* be marrying Lord Collingsworth. He pressed his suit with my father just last eve. My parents are both ecstatic."

Rosalind sensed the parents were more excited by the proposal than Amelia. "You don't love him?"

"I hardly know him," Amelia answered. "He's very stuffy for a young man. He's never even tried to kiss me. Am I not kissable, Rosalind? Am I not pretty?"

"Of course you're pretty," Rosalind assured her. "Lord Collingsworth is obviously a gentleman of the highest order. He must respect you tremendously to have never once gotten out of line in your company."

Amelia frowned again. "Respect? What a cold word." Her eyes suddenly danced with devilishness. "I imagine Gabriel Wulf is not so gentlemanly. I imagine he'd kiss a woman if he wanted to and wouldn't give a fig about the impropriety of doing so."

Should she warn Amelia that Gabriel Wulf cared more about running the estate than kissing women? Or so Armond had insinuated to her. Perhaps not, Rosalind decided. Let Amelia have her dark dreams about Gabriel Wulf and marry as her parents wished her to marry. Her life would end up far less complicated than Rosalind's.

A soft rap sounded upon the door. "Rosalind, dear, Armond has arrived and is outside pacing up and down my lawn waiting for you. My guests have all suddenly become in need of the sunshine streaming through my open windows. The man is a distraction. I thought you might be ready to take your leave."

Rosalind walked to the door, cracked it open, and smiled fondly at the dowager. "Thank you so much for inviting me today. I hope we will become as good friends as you are with my husband."

"Please visit me whenever you wish," the woman said. "You are always welcome in my home."

"And you in mine," Rosalind countered, feeling odd with the statement. The dowager turned and walked back down the stairs. Rosalind glanced at Amelia. "Will you come for another visit soon?"

"I promise," Amelia answered. "I'll send a note around so you'll know when to expect me."

"I look forward to it," Rosalind said, then left the room and walked downstairs, past the parlor, where conversation still buzzed and women had gathered suspiciously close to the windows affording a view of the front lawn, and through the door the dowager's manservant held open for her. Sunlight glinted off of Armond's blond head as he paced. He seemed lost in thought, and she wondered what business he had attended to while she had tea with the dowager.

He glanced up as if he felt Rosalind's presence before she reached him. The dowager was right. He was a distraction. The slight smile he gave her was unconsciously sensual. Everything about him was sensual. She supposed the ladies gathered around the windows were snapping open fans and creating quite a breeze in the dowager's parlor. Feeling a little wicked herself over their hypocrisy, Rosalind stood on her tiptoes and kissed Armond full on the mouth when she reached him.

Armond's eyes filled with heat when she pulled away and he looked down at her. "Have I told you that I want you today?" he asked.

Chapter Twenty

Now Rosalind needed a fan. "Let's go home," she said, and for the first time saying it didn't sound so odd to her. He took her arm and walked her to his waiting carriage. A fine matched set of bays pulled the carriage, their shiny coats glimmering in the sunshine. "We should ride sometime," she thought to suggest. "Does my filly have a name?"

"Gabriel calls her Sahara after her proud heritage," he answered. "If you'd like, when we get home we can ride in Hyde Park. Rotten Row is a nice path."

The thought excited her. It had been months since she'd been able to ride. "Montrose has a decent stable," she told him. "It's a lovely estate. You know you'll inherit the rents and such from the property now . . . I suppose the property itself if we have no sons. You should speak to my stepmother's lawyers concerning the matter."

"I will," he said, then helped Rosalind into his carriage. Once inside, Armond sat next to her. "How was the tea social?"

Although he posed the question casually, she sensed her answer was important to him. She wouldn't tell him the truth, she decided. It wasn't Armond's fault that she was his wife. All he'd done, even going against a vow he made to himself, he'd done for her. She wouldn't make him feel bad that his shunning had now become hers as well.

"I had a lovely time," she lied. "The dowager and I get along well together, and Amelia was there with her mother. We had a nice chat."

"I'm glad that you enjoyed yourself," he said. "While I was out this morning, I stopped into an outrageously expensive shop on Bond Street and made an appointment with the seamstress for you to be fitted. I thought you might wish to have some gowns made. Whatever you would like."

If Armond was selfish with his feelings toward her, he wasn't selfish in any other way. First the fine horse, now a new wardrobe, which Rosalind was sadly in need of. She placed her hand over his.

"Thank you, Armond. I didn't realize how shabby my wardrobe had become. I didn't need fancy clothes in the country, and the few gowns Franklin had made for me were not to my taste. I didn't bring them with me when I moved my things."

"I want you to be happy, Rosalind," Armond said, taking her hand and entwining their fingers. "Redecorate the house if you wish. I know the furnishings are all outdated, but bachelors care little about such things."

He would give her anything her heart desired, it seemed. Anything but his heart. She thought it was a rather sorry trade but said nothing about it. Rosalind was still trying to sort out her own feelings for Armond. Did she love him? She knew she'd been worried sick about him the night he hadn't come home. She knew jealousy could easily consume her where he was concerned. She knew that she desired him. But did those emotions add up to love?

The coach passed her stepmother's house and Rosalind glanced away from looking outside. The house now gave her a cold feeling inside, as if evil lived there. Evil intent upon harming her husband and, she supposed, herself as well. She resented having so much to deal with at once. Her marriage was enough of a trial. She wished all she had to worry about was making Armond fall in love with her. But finding a happy life with him would have to wait until Franklin had been dealt with and her stepmother either improved or passed on.

Recalling her instructions to Mary, Rosalind glanced outside again once the coach took the curve that would deliver her and Armond to the front door. She could see the back of the house next door, and a white sheet had been hung over the railing of the balcony to her former room.

"Mary's given me the signal," she said to Armond. "Franklin isn't home and it's safe for me to visit the duchess. Could we postpone our ride in the park until after I've checked on my stepmother?"

"I'll ready the horses while you visit her," Armond said. "I'll keep my eye on the place, too. If Chapman returns and you're still in the house, I'll be there in the blink of an eye to collect you."

The coach lumbered up before the house. Rosalind decided to hurry and change into her riding habit before she visited her stepmother. She wanted to be ready for her ride once she finished the visit. Armond waited downstairs for her. He was saying something to Hawkins, but upon seeing her, came forward and escorted her outside and across the lawn.

"I won't be long," Rosalind assured him. "The duchess isn't well enough to speak to me. She for the most part sleeps or stares off as if her mind has gone somewhere else. It's very sad, but I hope she knows that I come to visit, and that I care about her. She was once very kind to me."

"It surprises me that such a kind lady could have produced such a cruel son," Armond remarked. "But then, I suppose even the most normal-seeming couple can spawn the devil's own."

The way he said it bothered her. "I hope you aren't referring to yourself," she halfway teased. "You are hardly the beast society has made you out to be. You've proven that to me time and time again."

"I've only done my duty by you," he countered. "Beware the house pet you cuddle in your lap and feed from your fingers. It may one day bite you."

He could be depressingly dark if the mood suited him. The mood didn't suit Rosalind. But the closer she came to the house next door, the more she felt the darkness closing in around her. They reached the back door and Rosalind rang the bell that delivery persons and servants used. Mary opened the door, spied her, and smiled.

"Was beginning to wonder if you'd seen my signal," she said. The woman noticed Armond and sobered. "I hope he's not coming in."

"I'll leave you then and prepare for our outing," Armond said to Rosalind. "Don't be long. I don't like you being here at all."

Rosalind nodded and walked into the house. She cast Mary a dark glance. "Mary, I will not tolerate you being rude to my husband. He isn't at all like the dark rumors that float around him suggest. He's a good man."

Mary blushed with guilt. "Sorry, milady, it's just been the way of it for a while now."

"Well, it's time that way ended," she said. "How is the duchess?"

"The same," the woman answered. "I was just getting ready to take her up some tea."

"I'll take her tray," Rosalind offered. "No sense in the both of us walking up to the third floor."

"Bless you for a saint," Mary said. "These old legs are about worn-out from going up and down those stairs. I keep hoping Mr. Chapman will get around to hiring some more help for me, but now that you're gone, I suspect he thinks I can do everything on my own."

Cheap and cruel and, if Armond was right, a murderer. Rosalind lifted the tray sporting a small pot of tea and a cup and saucer.

"Mind that she drinks it," Mary called to her back. "Mr. Chapman said it's about the only thing keeping her alive, and I tend to agree. Can hardly get even broth down her these days."

"I'll do my best," Rosalind said in parting. She carried the tray up to the third floor, thankful her stepmother's door was open since her hands were full. The duchess sat in her usual chair by the window, staring at nothing.

"Good afternoon, Your Grace," Rosalind called cheerfully. "I've brought your tea." The lady did not respond, but then, Rosalind hadn't really expected her to. She sat the tray on a nearby table and poured tea.

Steam didn't rise from the cup, so Rosalind knew it wasn't so hot that it would burn her stepmother's mouth, but she wanted to make certain it was at least a comfortable temperature. Short of sticking her finger in the cup, she had no choice but to take a few sips. The tea had a definite clove taste, but she couldn't say she fancied the flavor. She took another sip, but it remained rather bland and even a tad bitter.

Walking carefully, she went to her stepmother's side. She placed the cup to the lady's lips. "I want you to drink, Your Grace. You need some type of nourishment. You're rail-thin."

To her surprise, the lady drank from the cup, almost greedily, in fact. Rosalind patiently handled the chore of seeing that her stepmother drank the whole cup. She tried to think of something light to chatter on about, but the woman's deteriorating health made the task difficult. Rosalind was still in a whirl from having tea with the dowager. More precisely, from what the dowager had said to her.

"I wish you were well, Your Grace. I wish you could talk to me. I'm so confused. I miss not having a mother. I miss the advice you might offer me, and an arm around my shoulders telling me all will be all right."

The duchess had closed her eyes. The woman had no doubt already drifted off to sleep. Rosalind walked to the table and replaced the lady's empty cup.

"I might be in love," Rosalind said softly. "I am married and so it would seem I should be in love, but of course not all marriages are the result of such tender emotions. I wish you could tell me what you think love is. Or I could tell you how I feel, and then you could give me your opinion. I feel so alone at times."

Rosalind rubbed the chill from her arms. She remembered that Armond waited for her. The thought lifted her suddenly low spirits. She picked up the tray, walked to where the duchess sat sleeping, and regarded the poor woman fondly.

"I must go, but I'll be back. Please try to get better. I need you."

She was certain her stepmother was oblivious to her plea. Rosalind started to turn away, then suddenly turned back and looked at the woman. A single tear traced a path down the lady's sunken cheek.

Armond was just to the point of going to fetch Rosalind when he saw her walking across the lawn toward the stable. She noticed him and waved. Having her in the house next door made him uncomfortable, even when he knew for a fact that Chapman was not at home. After Rosalind had gone inside the house, he'd snuck around Chapman's carriage house and had a look inside. His carriage and driver were gone.

Rosalind stumbled and Armond immediately moved forward, but she righted herself and soon joined him. The horses were saddled, and he held a basket Hawkins had prepared for them draped over one arm.

"What do you have there?" Rosalind asked.

"Hawkins packed us a nice lunch. I thought we'd picnic. It's a lovely day."

Her beautiful face lit up. "I love picnics. I haven't been on one in such a long time. Not since I was a little girl."

"Are you ready?"

She nodded, came forward, and he set the basket down to help her mount. Rosalind had only gotten her foot in the stirrup when she almost fell backward. Armond caught her. She placed a hand to her head. "Oh dear. There it is again."

"What's wrong, Rosalind?"

She looked a little dazed when she glanced up at him. "The dizziness. I felt it a moment ago when I stumbled, but it seemed to pass quickly."

Her paleness alarmed him. Armond quickly discarded their plans. "You must go into the house," he said. "You need to lie down."

"No," Rosalind protested. "I don't want to ruin our outing. I am so looking forward to it. I'll be fine."

Armond wouldn't take chances with her health. "We'll go another day," he assured her. "Riding a horse while your head is spinning around is dangerous. You might take a tumble and hurt yourself."

"But I—" Rosalind swayed again before she could finish the argument. She sighed. "I suppose I do need to lie down for a while."

Henry, one of the grooms, held the horses. Armond walked to the lad and handed him the basket Hawkins had prepared for their picnic. "Put the horses away and you and the other stable help can have a nice lunch."

He walked to Rosalind, swept her up in his arms, and started for the house.

"I can walk, Armond," Rosalind fussed. "I don't know what's come over me. I'm usually as healthy as a horse."

"The path to the house is somewhat rocky, as you know," he said. "I don't want you to fall because your head is spinning again. You're probably exhausted, Rosalind. You've been through a lot during the past few days."

"I suppose," she agreed. "I am suddenly tired, and a good long nap sounds enticing."

She weighed little and he easily carried her to the house and inside. Besides his brothers, Armond had never been responsible for another person. The responsibility was new to him; so were the feelings of worry that went with it. Hawkins hurried after them as Armond approached the stairs to take Rosalind to her room.

"Does the lady need anything?" he asked. "Should I send for a doctor?"

"I'll be fine, Hawkins," Rosalind said over Armond's shoulder. "I just need to rest for a while. Please go about your duties."

"My Lord?"

"I believe Lady Wulf will be fine after she's rested for a bit. If I need you, I'll call you, Hawkins."

"Very well, Lord Wulf," the man responded.

Armond proceeded up the stairs and into Rosalind's room. He gently sat her down upon the bed. Her riding habit was not only outdated but a bit too snug in certain areas as well. Armond was hardly complaining, but he knew the outfit would not be comfortable to nap in. He sat beside her, turned her to face him and went to work on the buttons.

"May I ask what you're doing, my lord?" Her voice seemed slightly slurred.

"I'm readying you for bed, my lady," he answered.

When she made no further comment, he continued with the buttons. Armond shoved the garment off her shoulders; then he loosened the laces at the front of her corset.

"You seem skilled at undressing women," she commented.

He smiled. "I'm not a saint. You knew that about me when you married me."

She frowned. "One of the few things I know about you. Was this your mother's room?"

"Yes," he answered. "Sometimes, when I close my eyes and concentrate, I can still smell her perfume."

It was the closest he'd come to telling Rosalind he wasn't like normal men. He had gifts. Gifts that seemed to be strengthening. But Armond didn't want to think about that. Not now.

"How nice for you," she commented. "I remember nothing about my mother. She died giving birth to me. The duchess is the closest I've had to a mother in my life, and her stay at the country estate was rather short."

Armond rose, knelt before her, and removed her dainty kid boots. He leaned forward and pulled her riding habit down her body and off her legs. She sat before him in chemise, corset, and one thin petticoat. He reached up and removed the pins in her hair. She'd worn it fashioned up with rows of dainty ringlets hanging down her back. Now it came tumbling down around her shoulders. Black silk. He wanted to bury his face in it, feel it sweep across his bare skin.

"You are so beautiful."

He knew now was not the time for compliments, but he

couldn't help but say what he felt. She smiled, raised her hand to his cheek, and ran her fingers down the side of his face.

"So are you."

Her hand fell limply to her side. She swayed and Armond eased her down to the bed. He thought she might have been asleep before he managed to get the covers tucked up around her. He sat staring at her for a time, watching the rise and fall of her chest, assuring himself that she seemed to be all right. Just to be certain, he took her wrist and felt for her pulse. It beat strong and he relaxed. Before he could release her, she drew her hand into his.

Their hands were different. Hers were soft, white, and smooth. His were large, brown, and used to hard work despite his titles and wealth. His vision blurred while he stared at their contrast, and for a moment his hand looked different: covered in coarse blond hair, claws jutting from his fingertips. Armond quickly snatched his hand away and lifted it before his face. His heart pounded. His vision cleared and his hand looked normal again.

What was happening to him? The leap from an upstairs window, the fall to the ground below where he had landed on his feet without injury? The way his already heightened senses seemed to sharpen during the fight with the thieves, and the men's faces as they backed from him in terror? He sensed what was taking place inside him, preparation to become someone or, rather, something else. But why was it happening? He glanced down at Rosalind, deep into sleep, innocent yet seductive, and although he knew why the curse now threatened him, he would not admit the truth. He could not. The consequences were too bleak.

Chapter Twenty-One

The noise woke her. Rosalind startled up from sleep. Flashes of light filled her bedchamber, then loud rumbles and an explosion of sound that made her jump. For a moment she felt disoriented. She glanced around her darkened bedchamber, trying to figure out where she was and why. Her gaze snagged on the shape of a man standing next to her window, staring outside. Flashes of light illuminated him. The quick succession of lightning distorted his features and gave him a sinister look. She knew him, didn't she?

"Armond?"

"Are you feeling better?" He walked into the shadows and approached the bed. "You've been sleeping for a long time."

Slowly, the day's events came back to her. The dizziness that plagued her before they were to enjoy an afternoon ride and a picnic. Armond carrying her up to her room. Armond helping her undress.

"Is it late?" she asked.

"Close to midnight." He stood at the side of her bed now. "I thought you might sleep until morning."

"The storm woke me." She shivered when the thunder crashed again. "I don't like storms. They frighten me."

Armond left her side, moved to the low fire burning in her grate, and added logs to build the flame higher. The yellow glow helped chase the shadows from the room, and Rosalind immediately felt better. Now bathed in a soft light, Armond again looked like the handsome man she had married.

"Are you hungry? You haven't eaten since breakfast."

Her stomach grumbled with the reminder. "I'm starved," she admitted.

"I have just the thing," he said, then walked into his bedchamber, returning a moment later with another picnic basket. She laughed with delight when he brought the basket to the bed. "I didn't want to disappoint you today, so here is your picnic," he said.

It felt slightly wicked to eat in bed and even more wicked to want a man to join her for the feast. But she must remember that Armond wasn't just any man. He was her husband.

"You will join me, won't you?" she asked. "That is a big basket and I'm sure more than I can eat."

He sat on her bed and removed his boots. "I won't bring the stable into your bed," he teased. "But a picnic for one is hardly jolly good fun, is it?"

She laughed again. Rosalind sat up and shoved her hair behind her ears. "No. Now, what have you brought me?"

Armond dug into the basket. "I have two meat pies, cheese, bread, wine, and sliced apples."

Her stomach grumbled louder.

"Was that thunder?" Armond continued to tease. "What will you have first, my lady?"

"The pie," she answered. "And some wine. My mouth is as dry as a bone."

"It doesn't look dry," he countered, lifting a glass from the basket and a decanter of wine, which he unstopped, pouring some into her glass. He glanced up before handing it to her. "Your lips always remind me of ripe berries glistening with dewdrops. They taste just as sweet, too."

She felt a flush of pleasure crawl up her neck. "You lied to me at Lady Pratt's tea that day," she accused softly. "You are a poet. Or simply a seducer of innocent young women," she added, teasing him back.

"The latter more likely," he said in a dry tone, handing her the pie with a dainty fork.

Rosalind quickly dug into the meal. Armond didn't join her. He poured a glass of wine and stretched out on her bed, watching her. He reminded her of a large cat with the glow from the fire casting him in golden hues.

"Did you go out this evening?" she thought to ask.

"No, the storm came in at dusk. I doubted that many women were walking the streets during the downpour. Besides, my first duty is to you, Rosalind. I wanted to make certain you were all right."

The word *duty* could sound as cold as *respect,* she decided. "I seem to be fine, now," she assured him. "I probably had overtaxed myself, although I've never felt quite that way before. Well, unless I've had a glass of brandy," she added, smiling slightly at him.

"Nothing wrong with a woman having brandy," he countered. "I enjoyed very much giving you brandy last eve."

The subject of brandy wasn't a wise decision, Rosalind realized. She didn't think brandy was what Armond thought a woman should have more of. "You're not eating," she pointed out.

"No, but I am feasting," he said, his eyes traveling over her. "Feasting on the sight of you."

It occurred to her that she sat before him in nothing but her underclothes, her hair wild around her shoulders. It also occurred to her that after what they'd done together last night, a sudden bout of modesty would seem ridiculous to him.

"Do you often try to seduce sick women, Armond?"

He stretched like a lazy cat. "You said you were feeling better."

She hid her smile by taking another sip of wine. The silence stretched between them while she finished her pie and nibbled on an apple slice. She couldn't forget last night or the way his fingers had skillfully stroked her, had brought her to heights of pleasure she never dreamed existed. She also couldn't forget the battle he had waged with himself when she felt the knob of her door turning.

"Why do you not simply take what you want?" she found the courage to ask him.

He took a sip of wine before answering. "Is that an invitation?"

"No," she said firmly, finished with teasing games. "But you are my husband. If you were to demand your marital rights, no one would blame you."

"No one except you," he said, staring at her over the rim of his wineglass. "I made you a promise. I will not break it. No matter how tempted I am," he added, and the now familiar glow of passion danced in his eyes. "You seem vexed that I can resist you. Is that what you're suddenly angry about?"

Was she angry? It seemed silly to be upset over him keeping a promise to her. Perhaps it was simply the control he seemed to easily exercise over himself when common sense deserted her in his arms. Maybe it was because she suspected she loved him, and he had vowed to never love her in return.

Rosalind set her wineglass on a small table next to her bed. "Why did you say that you would never love me?"

she asked, wishing she could have kept silent. Asking revealed too much about her own wants, her own desires and dreams.

He glanced away from her. "I told you why."

"You made an excuse," she countered. "Then said something about the curse, and praying I never found out what it really was."

"Leave the matter alone," he instructed quietly. "Take what I can give and don't ask for more."

"What can you give me?" she demanded. "Protection? Duty? Fine gowns and a tastefully decorated home? Why not children, Armond? Why not love? All the rest seems like a cold exchange—"

"Cold?" he interrupted. No longer resembling a lazy cat, he was suddenly beside her, placing his wineglass next to hers on the table. He pulled off his shirt and took her hand, flattening it against his chest. "Do I feel cold? I burn for you. You burn for me. There has been nothing but heat between us since the first night we met. Why can't that be enough for you?"

His skin nearly singed her fingers. His scent rose up to seduce her. He leaned forward and captured her mouth as if to prove to her that whatever they shared, it was not cold. He tasted like wine, his lips every bit as potent. He shoved the food off the bed with one sweep of his arm; then he was on top of her—pressed against her, sharing his warmth.

He nuzzled her neck, cupping her breasts in his hands as he continued the assault upon her senses. If he thought to teach her a lesson, she became a willing pupil. Her hands roamed his broad back, feeling the muscles flex as she touched him. His skin was velvet-smooth. Then something odd happened. Running her fingers the length of his back, she felt his spine move. Felt it expand and then snap back into place.

Before she could think too much about the strange occurrence, he moved down, pulling her chemise away from her breasts to feast upon her. She tangled her fingers in his hair, holding him to her. The teasing circles his tongue traced around her nipples nearly drove her mad. She arched against him, rather wanton in her desire to feel the friction of their bodies moving against each other.

He'd somehow removed her corset, was in the process of slipping her chemise off her shoulders, when she realized he'd soon have her naked. Naked and willing, just as he wanted. Maybe just as she wanted, as well. Was he right? Was love so important when they shared this heat, this passion, this madness for each other?

"No," she whispered. "It is not enough."

His fingers tightened on the straps of her chemise for a moment, and she thought he would rip it away from her skin. He looked up at her, and his eyes were not merely aglow; they were on fire. She was suddenly frightened. Afraid of the fire burning in his eyes, of the look of raw savageness stamped across his features. He struggled for breath, and between his parted lips she saw a flash . . . saw what appeared to be fangs. He closed his eyes, took a ragged breath, then rolled off of her.

"Forgive me," he said softly. "Whatever demon ruled me just then, it was not me. I would never hurt you, Rosalind. I would never take what you would not willingly give."

She lay beside him with her heart pounding, her mind in denial that she'd seen anything unnatural. The Armond she knew might not love her, but she had nothing to fear from him. She forced herself to turn on her side and look at him.

The fire had banked, and in the soft glow he looked as he had always looked to her. Handsome. Sensual. Irresistible.

"Look at me," she instructed softly.

He did as she asked, and there was no fire burning in his eyes now, only a soft glow of reflected light from the fire dancing in her grate.

"Say something to me," she further instructed.

"What would you have me say?"

His teeth were straight and white and quite normal looking.

"Do you hate me?"

He laughed, reached over, and took her hand, placing it upon the bulge in the front of his trousers. "Does it feel like I hate you?"

"But you don't love me?"

"This loves you," he assured her.

She could have removed her hand from him, but she found that she didn't want to. The afternoon she'd touched him, naked in his bath, she had marveled at the feel and texture of him. He'd said then that her innocent explorations would make him shatter. Shatter in the way he'd made her come apart beneath his fingers just last night?

"Can I touch you?" she asked bravely.

He groaned. "Why must you torture me?"

"I'm asking if I can do for you what you did for me last night."

He turned on his side to face her. "Only if you want to. I would not force you to do anything you're not willing to do, Rosalind. I've told you that. You don't owe me anything. I started this business between us."

"I'm curious," she admitted. And she was. Curious about his body and curious to know if she could give him the same kind of pleasure he had given to her. It wasn't consummation. Although she wasn't so innocent to tell herself that it was harmless, either.

"Tell me what to do," she said.

• • •

If Armond had one ounce of common sense, he'd rise from her bed, go into his room, and shut the door. No, even that wouldn't be wise enough. He'd leave the house altogether, despite the storm that raged outside. It was nothing compared to the storm that raged inside of him. A moment earlier, something had come over him. Lust. Animal lust. Unthinking and uncaring lust. He'd been tempted, no, driven to take Rosalind whether she was willing or not. Driven to mate.

He'd barely been able to pull himself back from the brink of his consuming desire for her. For a moment, she hadn't been a woman with a face and a heart, and feelings that he could easily crush. She'd simply been available. That frightened him. The loss of control frightened him. And now Rosalind had offered him another chance to lose control. He was almost afraid to take it.

"I've been too bold," she said, and when she started to remove her hand, he placed his on top of hers.

"I am your husband. You can't be too bold with me."

He allowed her to loosen the fastenings of his trousers. He allowed her to slip her hand inside and free him. The feel of her slim, delicate fingers wrapped around him nearly made him lose control before he was ready.

"You're so large," she said. "If we, when we, will it kill me?"

He laughed, although he wasn't much in a humorous mood. "No, I promise not to kill you with it," he teased. "You were fashioned to accommodate me," he tried to assure her. "You'll see when the time is right."

"How do I please you?" she asked, and she ran her hand up and down his shaft like she'd innocently done while he had bathed. He jerked. When he caught his breath again, he said, "Just keep doing what you're doing."

And she did.

• • •

The feel of him in her hand, hard as steel, long and thick, excited Rosalind. She continued as he had instructed her to do, all the time watching him, as he watched her. Fueled by her sudden bravery, she leaned toward him and kissed him, teased him with her tongue until he opened to her. He allowed her the heady power of being the seducer rather than the seduced. She stole a groan from him, a deep throaty sound that awakened her own desires.

Through his guidance, she understood the rhythm of her hand moving up and down his shaft. Understood, as well, her own body's response to pleasuring him. She grew hot and wet, her breathing labored as she watched him. The intensity of his eyes while he stared at her added to the flames licking at her body, the sight of his firm, full lips, slightly parted as he struggled to breathe.

The firelight cast a golden glow over his tawny skin and he'd never looked more handsome to her. Primitive, male, powerful. Hers. At least at this moment in time.

Instinctively, she increased the pressure and the pace of her hand. He closed his eyes, his long lashes sweeping down to create sooty crescent moons against his cheeks. His jaw tensed and she knew he fought her, fought her power over him. She squeezed harder, pumped him faster. A groan broke from his lips. His fingers tangled in her hair, and he drew her mouth back to his.

His kiss was savage, bruising, but the pain didn't last long before he broke from her, turned his body away from her, and clutched handfuls of her crisp white sheets in his large bronzed hands. "Don't stop," he managed to grind out, and she didn't stop.

He seemed to swell even more in her hand, grow harder, if that were possible; then he made a low sound in his throat . . . an animalistic sound, before she felt him tense, then shudder violently. She held him, in her hand as well as his back cradled against the front of her body. He continued to pulse and she knew he spilled his seed there, against her virgin sheets.

They lay that way for a time, she wrapped around him as if protectively, while he lay spent and vulnerable. Her cheek rested against his smooth back. She heard the hard thud of his heart beating.

Outside, the storm still raged, but inside, she felt warm and oddly contented. She'd stolen a piece of him tonight. She felt it with her woman's instinct, knew it in her heart. He would fall in love with her. It was only a matter of time.

Chapter Twenty-Two

It was only a matter of time. Time Armond felt that was running out for him. He had fallen asleep in Rosalind's arms last night. He had awoken sometime before dawn and crept from her bed like a coward. If he'd felt a moment of concern over a loss of control last night, he felt more concerned over the feelings that had first stirred to life in him when he'd awakened with her wrapped around him. It had felt right. God, she had felt so right being there next to him.

And the feelings she stirred were not sexual. They were emotions buried deep within his heart. A heart he could not give her. A heart she might take whether he was willing to part with it or not. Besides his instructions to Hawkins to guard his wife during his absence this morning, he'd told the man to put a lock on the door that separated their rooms. Armond had thought he could love her with his body without getting his heart involved. He suspected he'd made a grave mistake with his thinking.

He'd never thought himself a coward, but this morning he'd left the house rather than face her over breakfast. He'd left because he feared she would look into his eyes and see his true feelings for her or, worse, look into his eyes and see a monster staring back at her.

Armond strolled Bond Street with no particular destination in mind. The papers had not relayed any news of

prostitutes being murdered last eve. Tonight he would
trail Chapman again, but this time he'd be more careful of
any traps that might be set for him. In fact, he had an idea
of setting his own trap for the man.

A coach pulled alongside him. "Armond, my boy, come
speak to me," the dowager called.

He smiled upon seeing the lady. Armond strolled to her
coach. The footman bounded down and opened the door.

"Come inside," she instructed.

"But your reputation," he cautioned, keeping a straight
face. "I see that you have no chaperone along with you."

She reached out and swatted him, not with a fan but
with her age-spotted hand. "Stop teasing an old lady, Armond, and climb inside."

He acknowledged her request with a formal bow before he climbed inside. "And how are you this fine day,
madam?"

"Is it fine?" she grumbled. "I'm trying to prepare for
my upcoming ball and have realized I'm too damn old to
give balls. It takes too much work."

"Your affairs are always splendid," he assured her.

"You did get my invitation weeks ago, correct?"

He thought he'd tossed it somewhere in his study.
"Yes, thank you for inviting me. Rosalind will probably
enjoy attending."

"Oh, good," the lady breathed. "I was afraid what happened at my tea might sour her on the idea of venturing
out into society again."

Confused, he asked, "What do you mean?"

"The way the ladies all shunned her, of course," the lady
provided. "But she held up well. She's made of sturdy
stuff, your new wife. She even gave that little snot Lady
Amelia Sinclair the time of day when the young woman
wouldn't speak to her unless it was behind closed doors.
She has a heart of gold, your Rosalind."

She did, he had to mentally admit. She hadn't told him the truth. She hadn't wanted to upset him or shame him. She had faced Chapman for him; she had faced ruin for him. Good God, she deserved so much more than he could ever give her.

"Yes, she is quite a lady," he said to the dowager. "Would you do me a favor?"

"Anything but sleep with you," she commented blandly. "You are a married man, now," she explained. "Oh, to hell with it; I'll sleep with you regardless."

He laughed. The dowager smiled and he got to the point. "Rosalind needs new gowns. I would spare her from having to visit the shops to be fitted, being the object of whispers and skirts brushed aside lest she sully some proper woman. Could I have the seamstress attend to her at your residence? I doubt that I could get one to readily agree to come to mine, regardless of how much I'm willing to pay."

The dowager's eyes softened upon him. "Of course, Armond. I will see to it that your wife is outfitted like a queen."

"I once thought she looked like a princess," he commented, thinking back.

The dowager suddenly took his hand and squeezed. "I'm so happy for you to have found her, Armond. She loves you. Love her in return."

His heart stopped beating for a second. "How do you know she loves me?" he asked quietly.

The woman rolled her gaze heavenward. "Any fool can see that. And any fool can see that you are in love with her as well. Don't take too long to tell her."

Panic nearly seized him. He felt as if his throat had closed and he couldn't catch a breath. "I can't tell her," he rasped. "I can't love her."

"Of course you can," the dowager argued. "Your father was weak. You are not."

Her eyes had taken on a steely glint. Armond felt the hackles at the back of his neck rise. "You know."

"I was your mother's closest friend," she said. "I was the one who sat with her while she died of a broken heart. Your father did not give her a choice. He assumed the worst about himself, and about her. Don't make the same mistake."

The choking sensation grew worse. Armond clawed at his cravat; then he opened the door and bounded outside. He said nothing to the dowager in parting. He had to escape. He had to think. He had to run.

Rosalind feared she might go mad. Her husband was missing again. To make matters worse, Hawkins had one of the stable hands working upstairs, putting a lock on the door that adjoined her room to Armond's. A lock that was positioned on his side, not on hers. She might well understand if he feared he'd lose control and slip into her room again, into her bed, but to insinuate that he needed protection from her, well, it was insulting.

She was in the parlor, trying to read, but the words meant nothing to her. All she could think about was last night and if her boldness with Armond had somehow sickened him toward her. What was he thinking? What should she be thinking? The man was driving her insane.

"Lady Wulf, Lady Amelia is here to see you."

Thank God for the distraction. "Send her in, Hawkins."

"Shall I serve tea again?"

Rosalind started to reply in the affirmative, then had another thought. "No, we'd like brandy."

He never raised a brow. "Very good, Lady Wulf."

Amelia bustled in a moment later, draped in her cape. She looked rather like the grim reaper. "I'm sorry I didn't send a note around," she said. "I wasn't sure I could sneak away without either my mother or my chaperone dogging my heels. I told Mother I had a horrible headache and wished to retire for the rest of the afternoon. Do you know that I climbed down a tree to see you?"

Impressed, Rosalind lifted a brow.

"All right, it was a rather small tree, a bush actually— my room is on the first floor of the mansion—but still, I nearly broke a sweat."

Rosalind laughed. Amelia was one of a kind, even if she didn't have the spine the dowager wished her to have. "Come in and sit down, Amelia. I have missed your company."

After removing the cape that cloaked her from head to toe, Amelia joined her on the settee. "And I have missed you." She took Rosalind's hands in hers and squeezed. "Besides, I need your advice."

Hawkins entered with a tray sporting two glasses of warm brandy. He set it next to Rosalind and exited the parlor.

"What is that?" Amelia immediately demanded.

"Brandy," Rosalind answered.

"For us?"

Rosalind lifted a glass and handed it to the young woman. "I've had a trying day," Rosalind explained.

Amelia sniffed the liquor, wrinkling her nose. "I've never been allowed to drink anything but an occasional glass of wine, champagne at special events, but only half a glass."

"I warn you to drink it slowly," Rosalind said. "It burns."

Amelia tipped the glass up and drank the contents in a few very unladylike gulps. She sat the glass aside without so much as a cough or a wince. Rosalind simply blinked at her.

"Now, about the advice I need," she said. "It's of a personal nature. Being that you are now a married woman, I thought I could come to you with my dilemma."

Taking a sip of her brandy, Rosalind knew a response was unnecessary. Amelia would more than likely forge on ahead. The young woman didn't do anything different.

"Last night, I was alone for a few moments with Lord Collingsworth. We are to announce our engagement before the season ends. I thought now that we are to be engaged, he would surely try to kiss me. He did nothing, so I took matters into my own hands, and I kissed him. He seemed very shocked. Even more so when I stuck my tongue in his mouth. It's something the French do," she explained to Rosalind, as if she might not know about it. "He called me brazen. He said a proper wife does not go around kissing her husband any time the urge comes upon her. Is that true, Rosalind? Do you not kiss Lord Wulf whenever the mood suits you? Must you ask his permission first?"

The irony of the situation nearly sent Rosalind into hysterical fits of laughter. She tried to tamp down her own confused emotions. "I would think a wife should be able to kiss her husband if the mood suits her, and of course vice versa. Lord Wulf says that nothing two people do together is wrong if they are married." He'd obviously lied, because she'd obviously done something wrong, but she wouldn't go into the matter with Amelia.

"I would think so, too," Amelia agreed. "I have passions, Rosalind. I thought a husband might enjoy that about me, but it seems I am to marry a man who doesn't. What should I do?"

Rosalind fortified herself with another sip of brandy. "Maybe you shouldn't marry him," she suggested.

Amelia thought on the matter for a good two seconds. "I must marry him. I've already agreed. My parents are finally happy with me. It would cause the worst kind of talk were I to suddenly bow out of the engagement. Do you think Robert might become more passionate after we are married?"

Rosalind had not met the young man in question. Amelia was a beautiful young woman, however. Her figure was the type to please a man. Rosalind couldn't see Amelia's intended resisting her charms for long . . . which brought her back around to Armond and the lock on his door.

"I'm certain you have nothing to worry about," she assured her friend. "Lord Collingsworth is obviously shy. I have no doubts he'll be kissing you silly in no time after you're married."

Her friend sighed. "I hope you're right, Rosalind." They sat in silence for a moment before Amelia said, "Could I have another brandy? It was quite nice. Gives me a warm feeling in my stomach the same as thinking about Gabriel Wulf does."

Again, Rosalind had to wonder if Amelia should marry at all. And she had to ask herself the same questions Amelia seemed to be asking herself. What had she done wrong last night to send Armond running off this morning? To make him decide to lock her out? One minute, he was trying to seduce her; the next, he acted as if he were the one in jeopardy of losing his virtue.

Or was it his virtue he was afraid of losing at all? Maybe, just maybe, it was his heart he was trying to protect from her. The possibility warmed her far more than the brandy ever could.

"When you marry, Amelia," she suddenly decided to ask, "will you find it odd to share a marriage bed with a man you hardly know?"

Amelia took Rosalind's glass from her, taking a sip of brandy before she answered. "I would assume that would be one of the pleasures of marriage," she said. "Oh, I know, Mother has given me the speech about duty and simply lying there while my husband takes his need of me, but I have needs as well, and am quite looking forward to finally having them met."

"Then you won't ask him for more time?" Rosalind wanted clarification. "Time to get to know him better?"

"What for?" Amelia asked. "I'll have the rest of my life to get to know him better. I want to enjoy him while he's young and handsome and virile. I'll get to know him better when he no longer has his teeth and has developed a paunch."

Rosalind giggled. She didn't know if it was because of Amelia's sometimes shocking straightforwardness, or because the brandy had gone to her head. Amelia smiled at her, then sobered, a thoughtful expression drawing her perfectly arched brows together.

"Don't tell me that you and your very handsome husband have not consummated your marriage?"

No, she wouldn't tell her, but she was afraid by the blush she felt warming her cheeks her reaction might give her away. She was correct to assume so. Amelia sighed dramatically.

"I thought because of the rumors you were lovers before you married. Whatever are you waiting for, Rosalind?"

"Love," she provided weakly.

Amelia drained the contents of Rosalind's glass. "Love? Good Lord, I don't even believe in it. Passion, yes, desire, physical attraction, all of those things are real enough, but I don't believe in love."

Rosalind was shocked. She supposed a woman led so by her emotions would fall in love easily, perhaps on a daily basis. "Aren't your parents in love?"

"Hardly," Amelia snorted, very unladylike. "They married because they were a good social match. They have a mutual respect for each other, but they are hardly in love. My mother assures me that love is but a fleeting emotion and one that has nothing to do with happiness. She says instead to even believe in love can bring a person the worst kind of pain. She would see me spared of that."

Although Rosalind felt sorry that Amelia's mother had developed her attitude about love, the woman did have a point. Perhaps Rosalind was in love, for she felt miserable.

"I must go," Amelia suddenly announced. "I've used all of my monthly allowance to bribe our coachman into bringing me here in secret. I'm sure my mother will rap on my door at some point and decide to check on me."

"Thank you for coming, Amelia. Our visit has been most enlightening."

She rose and walked with Amelia to the front door. The two young women hugged each other before Amelia threw on her cape and rushed to her waiting coach. The day was sunny and the air smelled fresh due to last night's storm. Rosalind didn't want to go back inside and twiddle her thumbs until Armond decided to return and she could confront him about the lock he'd put on his door.

Instead she walked to the side of the house, stopping to admire the view of the stable. She glanced across the lawn at the house next door. A white sheet hung across the railing of the balcony. Mary's signal.

Chapter Twenty-Three

The duchess had not improved. Rosalind hadn't really expected to find her in any other state than the listless one she'd found her in when she first arrived in London. But she supposed somewhere deep inside she'd held out hope that she would walk into this room and find the lady up and about, spry and willing to renew the relationship they had begun so many years ago.

That was obviously not going to happen. Rosalind had shared tea with the lady, trying to clear her head from the effects of the brandy she'd had earlier with Amelia. The tea had not served to clear Rosalind's mind, but instead, she felt even more lethargic. Since there was no lively conversation to keep her awake, she found herself nodding off several times while her stepmother snored softly in her chair by the window.

"You best be going, Lady Wulf." Mary gently nudged Rosalind. "The hour grows late and I have no idea when Mr. Chapman might return."

Rosalind's eyelids felt stuck together. She pried them open, glancing outside to see that indeed the sunshine was gone and evening fast approached.

"I must have dozed off," she said sleepily. Her bones felt like liquid when she tried to rise. She managed to make it to her feet, stumbling toward the door.

"Are you all right?" Mary asked, her wrinkled brow creased in worry.

"I'm fine," Rosalind tried to assure her. "My legs have gone to sleep is all."

"Mary!"

Both she and the housekeeper froze.

"Mary! I want my supper prepared immediately! I have plans this evening!"

"Good God, he's home," Rosalind croaked.

"He mustn't know I've been signaling you when he's gone," Mary fretted.

"He mustn't find me in the house," Rosalind voiced her own concern.

"But how are you going to get out?" Mary asked. "He's downstairs and unless he comes up and goes into his room, he might easily spy you trying to leave."

Rosalind could think of only one escape. "The trellis next to my balcony," she said. "I've climbed down it before; I can do it again."

"Oh dear," Mary continued to fret. "I shouldn't have allowed you to stay so long. You looked so tired. I figured that brute of a husband of yours had been keeping you up late at night, demanding more of you than your delicate strength will allow. I thought you needed the rest."

"Lord Wulf is not a brute," she chastised Mary. He was a man who'd locked his door against her, but she couldn't think about that now. She had to escape. "Mary, go and stand at the stairs on the second-floor landing to make certain Franklin is not coming up."

The housekeeper nodded and hurried out of the room. Rosalind glanced at the duchess, still fast asleep and snoring in her chair. "Good-bye, Your Grace," she whispered, then walked down to the second-floor landing. It was no easy task. Her eyes were acting strangely and sometimes the stairs beneath her feet seemed to move. Her progress was sluggish, but she made the landing, glancing down the hall to see Mary positioned at the stairs leading down to the first floor.

The woman motioned her forward. Rosalind tried again to move quickly, but her feet refused to cooperate.

"Hurry," Mary hissed at her.

"Mary? Did you not hear me calling you?"

The housekeeper's head snapped around to stare down the stairway. "Sorry, Mr. Chapman, I was up in your mother's room."

"Well, come down and make me dinner. I have plans for tonight and wish to dine before I go."

"Yes, Mr. Chapman," Mary said. The housekeeper started down. "Are you coming up, sir?" she asked, her voice overly loud.

"Of course I'm coming up," Franklin snapped. "I wish to change my clothes before dinner."

"Very well, sir."

Rosalind forced herself to move quicker. Franklin was coming upstairs, and if she didn't make her room and the balcony before he reached the first-floor landing, he would see her. Her head felt dizzy again and she had to run her hand along the wall to keep her balance. Mary started down the stairs. Rosalind heard the housekeeper ask what he'd like for supper, she supposed hoping to buy Rosalind more time to escape.

She managed to reach her room, open the door, and go inside. The only fond memories she had of the room were of Armond's late night visits. She reached the balcony doors, left open by Mary when she'd draped the sheet over the railing. Rosalind moved onto the balcony and to the side, where there was just enough room to flatten herself against the side of the house next to the trellis.

She waited for a moment, trying to slow her pounding heart and clear her spinning head. She glanced over the railing next to the trellis. It looked like a long way down. Suddenly she heard footsteps. Oh God, she'd left the door open. Franklin might have been drawn inside simply because she had usually kept her door closed and she supposed now that she was gone Mary did the same.

She heard him moving about the room, opening drawers and shutting them. Rosalind pressed herself closer to the wall, hoping he could not see her standing there on the balcony, frozen in fear. A few moments later, she heard his footsteps again, moving away, she thought. She stayed still for a while longer, barely daring to breathe. When she didn't hear him moving about, she reached for the trellis. Any time she looked down, her head started spinning again.

It was dangerous to attempt the climb, her head spinning as it was, but it was more dangerous to stay. The two petticoats she wore beneath her gown, she knew from experience, would only make the climb more difficult. Rosalind reached beneath her gown and removed them, leaving them in a puddle at her feet before she reached out and latched hold of the trellis.

She eased her leg over the railing and tried to find solid footing. Once she had, she held on and pulled herself up so that she could swing her other leg over. One foot slipped and for a moment she dangled there, her feet kicking in an effort to find solid footing again. She glanced down. Her head spun. She would fall and break her neck.

Mustering her strength, she held tight to the trellis until her feet were once again wedged between the vine-covered boards of the trellis. Slowly, she inched her way down. The vines were still damp from last night's storm and her feet slipped away from the boards easily.

Her head continued to spin and she thought she might become ill, which would only further complicate her climb. She was nearly down when her foot slipped again. The dizziness became so bad that her grip loosened and suddenly she was falling.

Strong arms caught her. "What in the hell are you doing, Rosalind?"

"Armond." She struggled from his arms, took his hand, and drew him up against the side of the house.

"Rosalind, I asked—"

"Be quiet," she cautioned. "Franklin is home," she whispered. "I had to escape without him seeing me."

"I don't give a damn if he sees me," Armond informed her, and started away from the wall.

Rosalind pulled him back. "But I do. If he knows I come here, I can't come back. Then I can't visit the duchess anymore. It would be too dangerous."

"It's dangerous enough already," he pointed out. "You nearly caused my heart to stop beating when I saw you dangling from the trellis a moment ago. I thought I couldn't run fast enough to reach you before you fell and broke your pretty neck."

"You're speaking too loudly," Rosalind cautioned him. "We can discuss this later."

"You're damned right we will," Armond assured her.

They waited there in the shadows of the house until Rosalind felt it was safe to make their escape. Their mad dash across the lawn was more her stumbling and Armond having to stop and help her than a quick retreat. He ended up carrying her, as he'd done the day they were supposed to ride.

Once in the house, he headed toward the upstairs bedrooms. Hawkins hurried to inquire about the situation, took one look at his employer's face, and retreated.

Armond entered through her open door and went to the bed, gently placing her upon the soft mattress, though his expression was less than tender.

"Hawkins had no idea where you'd gotten off to," he immediately started to chastise her. "He'd thought you'd possibly left with your friend. I was on my way back to the stable to saddle a horse when I saw the housekeeper's signal to you. Then I saw you dangling from the trellis."

"I fell asleep," Rosalind explained. "I didn't tell Hawkins where I was going because I only meant to stay for a few moments. Then Franklin came home and I had no choice but to escape by way of the trellis. My head was spinning again and I lost my balance."

A little of the tenseness left his features. "I'm going to call for a doctor, Rosalind. These dizzy spells are happening too frequently."

"It's only happened twice," Rosalind argued. She realized something odd. "Both times after I visited my stepmother." Her mind searched for a connection. She could think of none . . . except one. "The tea," she whispered.

Armond sat beside her. "The tea? What are you talking about?"

Her dizzy spells were now starting to make sense, and if what she thought might be happening truly was, the duchess might not be ill at all. "He's drugging her," she said. "There's something in the tea he has Mary make for her daily."

"Explain," Armond said.

Another dizzy spell hit her and Rosalind put a hand to her head. Armond eased her down onto the bed. "Maybe you should rest."

"No," she insisted. "I want to tell you what I think has happened to the duchess."

"All right."

"I think the tea leaves that he instructs Mary to brew for his mother have something in them that is strong enough to keep her in a lethargic state. The day we were going to ride, I had sipped her tea to make certain it wasn't too hot. Today, I tried to drink a cup because Amelia visited and we drank brandy. I thought it would help clear my head, but it only made me worse. That's why I fell asleep and stayed much longer than I intended. The tea has a bitter taste to it that I couldn't tolerate, so I drank only half a cup. My stepmother has two or three cups of it a day."

"But why would Chapman drug his mother?" Armond asked.

Rosalind thought about it for a moment. "Maybe in order to gain my guardianship," she suggested.

"I suppose," he agreed. "Either that, or she knows something."

"You mean, about the murders?"

"About Bess O'Conner." He glanced down at her. "If your stepmother knew her son had killed a woman, what would she do?"

Rosalind wasn't certain. "She's always doted on Franklin, no matter how mean-spirited he was to everyone else. I know she has principles. I'm not sure what she would do," she finally concluded.

"Maybe he wasn't, either," Armond commented.

Her eyelids grew heavy. It seemed there was something else she wanted to tell Armond. Now she remembered. "Franklin is going out tonight," she slurred. "I heard him tell Mary."

"Then I'm going out as well," Armond said. "I want you to sleep off the effects of whatever drug Chapman is using to keep his mother sedated."

"Why drug her?" she wondered. "If he feared she would report his actions, why not kill her?"

Armond smoothed her hair back from her face. "Maybe because she's his mother. Maybe because killing her so soon on the heels of Bess O'Conner's murder would throw suspicion in his direction. It would be smarter to keep her drugged, tell all that she is dying, and when the time is right, kill her. No one would question her death if she'd been ill for some time."

Rosalind shuddered and Armond draped a quilt over her. "I must save her," she whispered.

"Go to sleep, Rosalind."

Darkness rushed up to claim her, but still, there was something she wanted to ask him. Her mind had trouble grasping what it was. Then she remembered.

"Why have you locked me out, Armond? Why have you locked me out of your bedchamber, and your heart?"

She couldn't open her eyes to see his expression. She couldn't stay awake long enough to hear his response. The darkness called to her.

Chapter Twenty-Four

Perhaps he was insane, like everyone believed. Armond gritted his teeth and held on to the underside of Chapman's phaeton. It was the only way he could think of that Chapman wouldn't see him trailing him. The only way to make certain the man hadn't set another trap for him. His muscles bulged with the strain of holding on, but somehow he managed. That no mortal man could possibly do what he was now doing, he chose to disregard.

He couldn't as easily disregard the questions Rosalind had whispered to him before she'd fallen into a drugged sleep. What answer could he give her that wouldn't turn her against him? Wouldn't repulse her? He had locked her out of his room, but he could not lock her out of his heart. She'd stolen inside of it the night he met her. He was doomed, and if she did love him, she was doomed as well. The sudden jar of the buggy brought him back to the present.

The phaeton had already stopped once to collect a passenger. Armond knew by the scent of the woman and her cockney accent that she was a prostitute. Now they pulled up and stopped on a darkened street. A street where Armond heard only silence.

"You want me to go in there?" he heard the woman ask. "It looks deserted."

"It will suit our purpose," Chapman said in a clipped tone. "Does it really matter where you spread your legs as long as you get the coin I've promised you?"

"Don't have to be crass," the woman said. "But no, I don't guess it matters."

The phaeton's springs bounced when Chapman and the woman exited the buggy. Armond would wait until they were inside of the house before he crept from his hiding place. He didn't want to frighten Chapman away, not when he might finally trap him. Armond planned to use the woman as a witness against Chapman. He might not be able to pin all the murders that had taken place on the man, but could prove that he intended to murder this woman.

Staring out from beneath the buggy, Armond saw that a glow now filled the window of a downstairs back room in the deserted house. He let go and rolled out from beneath the phaeton. He flexed his arms to relax the muscles that had been strained while he held on beneath the buggy.

The street was deserted. Most of the houses looked vacant like this one. He'd made mental notes of their journey, gauging how far they traveled and in what direction. Silently he crept up to the house, then moved around the side where he saw the soft glow from the window. He closed his eyes and concentrated.

"You want me to wear this?" the woman asked. "What for?"

"The gentleman who will be joining us wishes for you to look the part of a lady."

"What gentleman? You said nothing about a gentleman joining us."

"Didn't I?" Chapman sounded sarcastically innocent. "Well, yes, there will be a gentleman joining us."

"Wait a minute," the woman said. "Didn't agree to

pleasure two of you at once. I don't do those kinds of things."

"You will tonight," Chapman assured her. "And it won't be the both of us at the same time. The gentleman likes to watch first, and then take his turn."

"To hell he will," the woman snorted. "I'm leaving."

A sharp slap sounded a moment later. Armond clenched his fists at his sides. It took all of his control not to storm inside and beat Chapman for striking a woman. Knowing he'd done the same to Rosalind made Armond's blood boil.

"Now, put the damn dress on!" Chapman growled. "Or do I have to convince you further?"

"No," the woman rasped. "I'll do what you want, just don't hit me again."

"That's better," Chapman crooned. "I find disobedient women a trial to my temper. Just do as you're told to do and you won't get hurt."

Silence. Armond assumed the woman was putting on whatever dress it was that Chapman had wanted her to change into. He wondered when the "other" gentleman would arrive. He'd always felt there were two men involved and now he'd soon have proof.

"Take the pins from your hair and wear it down," Chapman commanded. "In fact, the more it hangs in your face, the more likely he will be able to pretend that you are someone else."

"Who is this gentleman we're waiting for?"

The woman received another loud slap for asking. "You are not to speak, not unless you are asked to speak, understand? You haven't the cultured voice of a lady, and that's what he wants. To do his dirty deeds with a lady, only of course he cannot. At least not unless he is married to her."

"I understand," the woman said, and Armond heard the fear in her voice.

"Lift up your gown and expose yourself to me," Chapman further instructed. "I want to make certain you don't have the pox."

"I told you I didn't," the woman said.

She received another slap.

"Do it!" Chapman thundered.

Chapman humiliated the woman. He pushed Armond to act before he was ready. He needed to know the other man's identity, but swore if Chapman hit the woman one more time, he wouldn't be able to wait.

"You think I like this?" Chapman asked the woman. "Performing for him? Dancing to his tune? I'd just as soon slit his fat throat."

"Why don't the two of us just—"

"Did I give you permission to speak?" Chapman interrupted.

The woman whimpered in response. Her scream a moment later made Armond jump.

"Come back here, you bitch!"

Sounds of a struggle came from inside of the house. The woman screamed again, and the sound of a fist smashing into soft flesh reached Armond's oversensitive ears. He cursed and bounded around the house, kicking in the front door.

"Chapman!" he thundered. "Get your hands off of her!"

A pistol discharged in the dark, splintering the wall beside Armond's head. He dived to the floor.

"Come on in, Wulf," Chapman taunted. "I'd like nothing better than to put a bullet in your head."

Armond had a pistol stuck inside the waistband of his trousers as well, but as tempted as he was to use it, he still had no solid proof that Chapman had killed the two women he'd found on his property, that he, in fact, intended to kill the woman he'd brought here tonight. Armond had never heard Franklin say he intended to kill her. He could only give his word, which wouldn't count for much with the inspectors or among society.

"Let the woman go, Chapman!" he called. "Let her go or I'll shoot you down."

Chapman didn't answer, but Armond's unusual night vision allowed him to see Chapman's shape, and the fact that he now held the terrified woman before him, using her as a shield.

"Go ahead and shoot, Wulf!" he challenged.

He'd like that. He didn't know that Armond could see him. Didn't know that Armond knew if he fired, he'd kill the woman and not Chapman, and then be accountable for her murder.

Armond clenched his jaw and waited for Chapman to make his next move. The man forced the woman toward the open door. When he'd almost reached the door, he suddenly shoved her away. The woman stumbled forward and fell on top of Armond. Her hands flailed and she started screaming. Armond struggled to push her off of him, and by the time he'd gained his feet he heard a whip crack and the sway of the phaeton as it pulled away from the house.

Racing outside, Armond saw the buggy ahead on the street, moving at a pace he would have never believed Chapman could inspire from his sorry horses. Armond went after him, his boots pounding on the cobbled streets. Part of him knew that it was pointless to chase a man careening down the street in a buggy, pulled by two whip-crazed horses; another part of him suspected that if he pushed himself, he could catch them.

He willed his legs to move faster, drew air deep into his lungs, and lunged forward, the dark shapes of abandoned houses and stinking alleyways rushing past him at an impossible speed. His vision shifted and instead of shapes he saw colors. The horse racing ahead of him became bright red blurs against the night. He saw their blood through their skin.

A glance to his left and he made out the red shapes of rats as they scavenged the alleyways. Faster he pushed himself, harder, and in his mind he no longer saw himself as a man. He had four legs, not two. Long fangs in place of his teeth. Claws in place of his fingernails. Fur in place of skin. He became one with the night, one with the loud beating of his heart and the blood that rushed through his veins.

He had almost caught the phaeton, was prepared to leap forward and hold tight. He was equally prepared to pounce upon Franklin Chapman and tear his throat out. Something came at him from the left. He couldn't stop in time to avoid the man and ran right into him, sending them both sprawling to the ground.

Armond rolled several times, scraping his flesh against the rough cobbled streets. He lay there for a moment, trying to catch his breath.

"Bloody idiot!" The man he'd run into rolled off the ground and stumbled once he'd found his stance. "Watch where you're going! You hit me so hard I feel like I'm going to spout up all this cheap gin I've had tonight."

The man did exactly that, dropping to his knees and retching into the gutter. Armond tried to slow the wild beating of his heart. He was a man, not the beast that had taken shape in his mind. Once he caught the breath that hitting the man had knocked from his lungs, he rose.

"Are you all right?" he asked the man.

"No bloody thanks to you," the man muttered, then went back to his retching.

Armond returned to the deserted house. He needed to check on the woman. The house was empty. She had fled and he couldn't blame her. He walked to the back room where two candles still sputtered. A gown lay wadded up in one corner. The woman had obviously discarded it, perhaps not wanting Chapman to have any reason to come after her.

Armond picked up the gown. His senses immediately stirred. He knew that scent. He shook the gown out and looked at it by the candlelight. It was the gown Rosalind had worn the first night he met her at the Greenleys' ball.

Chapter Twenty-Five

Rosalind opened her eyes to see a man standing over her. The fire's glow cast a golden halo around his head, and her first thought was that Armond had come to check on her. As his features moved into focus, she realized the man was not her husband. She gasped and tried to sit.

"Don't be alarmed," the man said softly. "Don't be afraid. I am Lord Jackson, your brother-in-law."

It was easy to take him at his word. Now that she could see him, she also saw the resemblance to Armond and Gabriel and the dimples that belonged to the young boy in the Wulf portrait downstairs.

"What are you doing here?" she felt was a sane enough question.

"This is my family home," he reminded her.

"I mean in my bedchamber," Rosalind specified, pulling the covers up closer around her, although she realized by the sleeves on her arms that she wasn't in her bedclothes but still dressed from her day.

Every bit as bold as his oldest brother, Jackson seated himself upon her bed. "I didn't get to meet you last time I was here. You were in bed then, too. I think you might spend a lot of time in bed, I know if you were mine you would, so what could I do but join you here in order to introduce myself?"

"Does Armond know you're here?"

He smiled, and his dimples cut deep slashes in the sides of his cheeks. "Here at the house or here in your bedchamber?"

"Either?" she answered.

"Neither," he assured her. "I don't imagine he would like for me to be here, in your bedchamber, I mean. The last time I suggested that I come up, crawl into bed with you, and introduce myself, he growled at me."

She nearly smiled. "He did?"

"Never was one to share," Jackson confided in her. "I thought I should meet you before I set out on my quest."

"I believe Armond is under the impression that you have returned to the country estate."

"He's often wrong," Jackson informed her. "Has he told you much about me?"

Rosalind shook her head.

"Figures," he muttered. He pinned her with the deepest, darkest eyes she had ever seen. "I'm the black sheep," he informed her. He frowned. "Well, since everyone thinks we are all black sheep, I suppose I am simply the blackest of the flock. I drink, I gamble, I'm lazy, and I am a womanizer. Oh, and now Armond believes that I am also a murderer."

She couldn't help but like Jackson. She supposed most women couldn't help but love him. He was almost too blatantly sensual—only the dimples saved him from being illegal, but then again, the dimples were quite nice.

"I don't believe that Armond thinks you are a murderer for one moment," she informed him. "It is my stepbrother who is under suspicion from him."

"He asked me if I had anything to do with the murdered women found on our property. You see, I was in London both times. I suppose that automatically makes me suspect in my brother's eyes."

"What a cad," Rosalind said.

He flashed his dimples. "He *is* a cad," he agreed. "Definitely not good enough for you. You should have met me first."

Rosalind sat up and smoothed her hair. "I daresay that it is probably much better that I didn't." She suspected that she would have never escaped the carriage with her virtue the night of the Greenleys' ball if it had been Jackson she'd approached instead of Armond.

"For the both of us, I'm thinking," he said, his features now serious. "I suspect he fell in love with you on sight."

Her cheeks flamed. Should she correct him? Somehow, she immediately felt as if she could trust Jackson Wulf. Maybe if he was a skilled womanizer, it was that trait about him that made women easy prey to his attentions.

"I'm sure he told you the reason he married me. That I had ruined my reputation by providing him with an alibi the morning they found another dead woman in the stable."

"Yes, he did tell me that," Jackson said. "And I might have believed him, before I saw you."

She flushed again. "Do you never cease trying to seduce a woman, even if she is your brother's wife?"

He seemed to consider. "You are the first wife in our family, so I can only assume 'no' would be my answer."

She giggled.

He flashed his dimples again. "Do you love Armond?"

He was back to being serious. Rosalind stared into his dark eyes, and again she felt she could be honest with him. "Yes. But he holds his heart from me. Now, he locks his door. I thought I could make him love me, but—"

He placed a finger against her lips. "Sometimes love is not a spoken word, but in the way a man looks into your eyes, in the things he does for you. Look harder, Rosalind."

She had the strangest urge to hug him. She was smart enough to realize women didn't hug Jackson Wulf unless they wanted much more in the bargain.

"I like you," she said.

He smiled. "Of course you do. You're a woman." He bent forward and kissed her on the forehead. "I like you, too, Rosalind. You deserve to be happy. So does Armond, even if I am currently put out with him. Now, more than ever, I am determined to make my quest to save our family. Armond has always been the responsible one; Gabriel, the hard worker; and me, nothing. I've been given nothing of importance to do, until now."

"What is it you think you must save your brothers from?" Rosalind wondered.

Jackson stared deep into her eyes before answering, "Hopefully, you will never know." He rose from the bed. He was tall, like all Wulfs, but he wasn't built like a tree, as Gabriel was, and was thinner than Armond. Still, he was quite something to look at. "Tell Armond I came around. Tell him I've gone on a quest to kill a witch."

She blinked up at him. "To kill a witch? Do such things exist?"

He suddenly bent back down, his face coming within inches of hers. "You'd be surprised what sorts of things exist out there in the darkness, Rosalind. If I have my way, you will never be any the wiser."

Jackson came close to kissing her, she thought. And she realized with some degree of panic that she might have allowed him the liberty. It was as if he held some spell over her, and it didn't weaken until he walked out her door and disappeared.

Armond brushed Rosalind's smooth cheek. She still slept in the clothes she'd worn yesterday. Her eyelashes fluttered open and she seemed to try to focus on him.

"Jackson?"

His hand froze against her cheek. "Did you just call me Jackson?"

She shook her head as if to clear it. "Is it morning?"

"Did you just call me Jackson?" he repeated.

Rosalind struggled up on her elbows and glanced toward the window, where sunlight filtered in. "I had the strangest dream last night. I dreamed that your brother Jackson was here, in my room, speaking to me."

"That is odd, especially considering that you haven't met Jackson yet."

Rosalind ran a hand through her hair. "At least I think I was dreaming. Did you question Jackson about the murders?"

Armond felt a stab of guilt. "Yes, and it angered him. That's why he left before you could be introduced to him."

"Then it wasn't a dream, or I wouldn't know that," she said. "He told me to tell you that he was leaving on a quest. A quest to kill a witch and save the family." She looked up at him with her deep violet eyes. "That makes no sense, Armond. That's why I thought I must be dreaming."

Jackson's revelations might not make sense to Rosalind, but Armond understood what Jackson was thinking. It was a fool's errand, he was also thinking. And his younger brother's decision couldn't have come at a worse time.

"I was hoping to send you to the estate," Armond told her. "I have decided you would be safer there with Gabriel and Jackson, only obviously, Jackson is not there, and if Gabriel arrived home to find he hadn't returned, I wouldn't be surprised if he isn't on his way back here to look for him again."

"The estate?" Rosalind pushed her covers aside and

sat. "But I can't leave, Armond. Not yet. I have to help the duchess."

"You're in danger, Rosalind!" Armond hadn't meant to snap the words at her, but he was worried about her. He had begun to put pieces together regarding Chapman and his thus far unknown accomplice. The dress, the women all chosen because they somehow favored Rosalind, it was clear either her stepbrother or his accomplice had an obsession about her. Then there were the strange things happening to him. Maybe Rosalind wasn't safe in the same house with him. Maybe she wasn't safe in London.

"What happened when you went out last night?" she asked.

He didn't want to tell her. Especially not about the dress. Especially not about himself and the way he had chased a racing buggy down a deserted street and almost managed to catch it, would have if the drunk hadn't stumbled out of an alley and into his path.

"I didn't catch him," was all he said.

Her soft touch against his cheek startled him and made him glance up at her. "You looked ragged, Armond. Have you slept at all?"

"No," he admitted, and thought she looked lovely with her clothes wrinkled and her hair wild around her shoulders.

"You should," she insisted. "I'll have Hawkins prepare you a hot bath and then you should spend the day in bed."

He lifted a brow. "Will you attend me in my bath again?"

She didn't smile at his teasing. Instead, her violet eyes met his straight on. "Will you lock me out?"

His decision had hurt her, he realized. She didn't know that it was for her own protection that the lock had been placed on his door. He couldn't very well explain to her that it might have been wiser to put the lock on her side without telling her more than he was prepared to tell her.

"At times, I prefer to be a private person," he said.

Her gaze remained steady, but her eyes watered for a moment. "Did my boldness toward you the other night sicken you? Do I disgust you now?"

His heart nearly broke in that moment. She mustn't think his decision to resist her was any fault of her own. "You could never disgust me," he said, running his fingers through her tangled hair. "You are the most desirable woman I have ever known. And the bravest."

The lovely arch of her dark brows furrowed. "Then why?"

He could at least be honest about his decision. "Because you deserve more than I can give you," he answered. "And because I won't ask you to settle for less. You offered to be my friend. Maybe that would be best."

She turned her head away from him, but not before a single tear traced a path down her cheek. It ate at his soul, that tear. That tear that he had caused her to shed.

"Damn my cursed life," he whispered, and because he couldn't stand the sight of her tears, he rose, walked through the door that adjoined their suites, closed it, and locked it.

Chapter Twenty-Six

She assumed Armond was sleeping. He'd locked her out, so Rosalind had no way of knowing for certain. There was also the matter of her stepmother that needed attention immediately and the fact that Armond would be livid with Rosalind if she acted on her own. Still, the sooner she instructed Mary to stop serving the duchess the special blend of tea Franklin insisted she drink, the sooner Rosalind hoped to find the lady on the mend.

Settling the matter in her mind, she went in search of Hawkins. He was a servant and hadn't the authority to stop her, but she would leave notice this time about her whereabouts. He wanted to argue with her, she could tell, but he knew his place and simply said that if she wasn't back in short order, he would wake Lord Wulf.

It was still early and Rosalind assumed Franklin would not be up at such an early hour. All she planned to do was go to the back entrance, hope to find Mary in the kitchen, and give her the instructions about her stepmother's tea. Rosalind kept to the hedge that separated the properties as much as possible, but there came a time when she had to bravely walk across the lawn in full view of both properties. She hurried.

Her heart was pounding by the time she reached the back entrance of the house next door. She only had to ring the delivery bell once before Mary opened the door. The woman frowned.

"What are you doing here, milady?" she whispered. "I've not hung the sheet. Mr. Chapman is upstairs abed."

"I must speak with you," Rosalind whispered back. She stepped into the kitchen. Glancing around, Rosalind spied the tin of tea leaves Mary used to brew the duchess's tea. She went to the counter where it rested and opened the lid. It had a pungent odor.

"What are you doing, milady?" Mary repeated.

"The tea," Rosalind whispered. "I suspect it has something in it that is responsible for Her Grace's lethargic state. I think Franklin has drugged her."

Mary's eyes widened. "Why ever would he do such a thing?"

Rosalind couldn't launch into a detailed account of her suspicions regarding Franklin, and she wondered if Mary would even believe all she and Armond suspected of her stepbrother.

"I want you to empty this tin and fill it with normal tea leaves. Let us just see if I'm right and the duchess improves without the tea her son has instructed you make her, and then I will explain. I haven't time now."

"I don't know, milady," Mary said, wringing her hands. "To go against my employer's wishes . . ."

Rosalind stood firm. "Please, Mary. If what I suspect is not the case, it won't harm the lady. And if what I suspect is the case, she will soon be much improved."

Mary bit her lip. "All right," she agreed. "But if Mr. Chapman finds out I went against his wishes, he'll be letting me go, and then who's to look after the poor woman?"

"I'm praying that soon the duchess will able to look after herself." And Rosalind also hoped if her stepmother did indeed know of her son's foul deeds, she would see that he paid for his crimes. Then Rosalind wouldn't have to worry what he might do to Armond if he got the chance, or to her, either.

"Mary! I've rung for you twice! Where the bloody hell are you?"

Rosalind gasped. Mary's face paled. Franklin was moving toward the kitchen. They heard him banging around.

"Go," Mary urged her.

"He will see me on the lawn and know I've been here," she frantically whispered back.

Mary shoved her toward a door leading to the basement and a small set of servants' quarters. There were only two rooms, one of them having been occupied by Lydia when she'd been employed at the house.

"Stay down there until I've seen what he wants," Mary ordered.

Rosalind slipped inside the door just as she heard Franklin enter the kitchen.

"There you are," he bellowed. "My head is pounding so that I can't sleep. I'm thinking a cup of tea, the special blend I purchase for my mother, might help. Brew me a cup and bring it upstairs."

"Very well, Mr. Chapman, right away," Mary readily agreed. "I was just getting ready to brew a pot for your dear mother and take it up."

There was silence for a moment. Rosalind pressed her ear to the door.

"Where is the tin? It's not there where you usually keep it."

In horror, Rosalind glanced down to see that she still held the tin in her hands.

"Must have misplaced it, is all," Mary muttered. "I'll find it, sir, don't you worry. I'll have your tea up to you in no time."

"See that you do find it," Franklin warned. "That blend is very expensive and I'll take it out of your hide if you've somehow managed to lose it."

"It's not lost," Mary assured him. "Just misplaced like I said. You go on back up to bed, Mr. Chapman."

Rosalind held her breath until she heard footsteps moving away. She glanced down the darkened stairs. At one time Mary had also stayed down here, or so the housekeeper had told her. After the duchess became ill, Mary had moved to a small room adjoining the lady's. There were already cobwebs from lack of use on the stairs, and Rosalind felt drawn to the room downstairs where Lydia once slept.

Rosalind wanted to make certain Franklin had plenty of time to make it back upstairs before she emerged from her hiding place. She moved down the stairs and opened the door to Lydia's room. There was only a small window, and very little light filtered into the drab little room. A scarred wardrobe took up space along one wall. A small table stood in one corner. Little more than a cot served for a bed. The bed was unmade. The covers were tossed about in a strange manner.

Rosalind moved to the wardrobe and opened it. Inside were Lydia's clothes. Rosalind nearly dropped the tin of tea leaves. The sight of Lydia's things unnerved her. Why hadn't she taken them with her when Franklin had dismissed her?

Perhaps because Lydia had never left the house. Or if she had, not by her own free will. Chills raced up Rosalind's back. She tried to remember that night she'd awoken to the sounds of screaming. But Franklin couldn't have hung Lydia from the rafters. He'd been with Rosalind that night at the LeGrandes' soiree.

"Lady Wulf," Mary whispered down the stairs. "Hurry out now; he's gone. I need that tin!"

Rosalind swept from the room. She walked up the stairs and into the kitchen, handing Mary the tea tin when she reentered the kitchen. "Have you been in Lydia's room since she left?"

"No," Mary admitted, and a guilty flush stained her cheeks. "I'm sure it needs a good scrubbing, but until the master hires someone to take her place, I didn't see the point, not with all I have to do around here."

"Of course," Rosalind agreed. "Brew my stepbrother a cup from the leaves, but remember, don't use them for his mother's tea."

The housekeeper nodded and Rosalind slipped out of the house. As she hurried across the lawn, more than Lydia leaving all her things behind bothered her. Franklin thought a cup of the tea would help him sleep. She knew she was on the right path about suspecting her stepmother was being drugged.

She would tell Armond when he woke. Her spirits sagged as she approached the house. He wanted to send her away. He wanted to keep the door locked between them. He wanted to be her friend. Their future together did not look bright. And if Franklin had his way, they would have no future together at all.

Rosalind felt as if her life had spiraled out of her control again. And she felt helpless to put it back on the right path. Her memory of Jackson's late night visit was hazy, she supposed because she'd still been suffering the effects of the doctored tea. Had she told him that she loved Armond? She feared she had, which made her all the more miserable, admitting her feelings and, she suspected, admitting her sorrow that Armond did not return them.

But then she recalled what Jackson had said to her. He'd said that sometimes a man's love for a woman was not reflected in his words but in his eyes and in his deeds.

She thought about that. She thought about Armond's worry over her, about his determination to protect her, and about the very words he had said to her concerning the lock on his door.

She'd focused on his last words to her, his suggestion that they become friends, and because she had, she'd dismissed the importance of the true reason he'd placed a lock between them.

Armond thought she deserved more than he could give her, and he'd said that he wouldn't ask her to settle for less. He'd sacrificed the physical relationship he'd wanted between them out of respect for her wants, her desires, her dreams. What sort of man would do such a thing for a woman? There seemed to be only one answer, and it was an answer that suddenly filled her with such joy and such tenderness for him that she wanted to weep.

Armond loved her. He might not wish to love her, but he did. But how to tear down the barriers he'd constructed between them? How to make him realize there was nothing wrong in her loving him and him loving her in return? No silly curse that could rob them of a happy future together. No reason they could not be friends and partners, and lovers.

Amelia's shocked remark regarding Rosalind's unconsummated marriage suddenly sounded in her head. "Whatever are you waiting for, Rosalind?" She'd answered that she was waiting for love, and now love had found her. She would wait no longer. Tonight, she would tear down the walls Armond Wulf had constructed around his heart. Tonight, she would claim him.

Armond had spent the day in restless slumber. He kept having dark dreams about Rosalind in a deserted house, wearing the gown she'd worn the night of the Greenleys' ball and lying dead on a dirty mattress thrown on the floor. At times, the dreams would shift from her to him, and he'd see his reflection in a mirror. See that he had fangs and fur and a bright blue glow to his eyes.

His world had changed since the first night he met Rosalind, and he couldn't help but feel as if he was careening down a path of self-destruction, no reins in his hands to slow his flight, no control to stop the inevitable. He had to stop Chapman. He had to stop him if it meant killing him without proof that Rosalind's stepbrother was a murderer. Armond would save Rosalind even if it meant his total destruction. The witching hour was upon him. Denying the truth would not save him.

He knew that now.

A soft rap sounded from Rosalind's suite. "Armond? Are you awake? I must speak to you."

He thought it best to ignore her.

"Armond?" she called again. "I've discovered something at the house next door that you should know about."

What the hell had she been doing next door? He'd planned to tell her that she was not to venture there again, regardless if Chapman wasn't at home. Armond didn't want to think about her in that house. Now might be a good time to make his wishes in that regard known to her.

Although he was naked, Armond gathered the sheet around his waist and moved to the door he'd locked earlier. He unlocked the door and cracked it open. Rosalind pushed her way inside.

"I went next door today to instruct Mary to stop using the tea Franklin insists his mother drink daily," she informed him. "I—" She stopped in midsentence, her gaze roaming over him. "Why are you naked?"

He smiled at her, waiting for a blush to explode in her cheeks and a little surprised when the reaction didn't happen. "I sleep naked," he explained. "I've been asleep all day."

"Oh," she breathed. "Good. Now, as I said, I went next door and I discovered something about Lydia."

Had she said "good"? Armond moved from the door and returned to his bed, where he sat. "I want to talk to you about going next door. I know that you are concerned for your stepmother, but I won't allow you to keep putting yourself in danger on her behalf."

"Don't you want to know what I discovered about Lydia?"

She'd questioned his form of attire; now he was distracted with mentally questioning hers. She wore some sort of cloak, and her usually expressive hands now clutched the garment together in a death grip that left her knuckles white.

"Armond," she said to get his attention. "Lydia's things were still in her room. I don't think she ever left. I think she might have been dragged away against her will. I heard screaming that night and thought I was having nightmares."

He glanced away from her hands clutching the cloak. "I've suspected all along that Chapman was the man who beat her," he said. "I just couldn't see how he could be responsible for her hanging when he'd been with you all evening at the LeGrandes' affair."

Rosalind frowned. "That's true. But don't you suspect that Franklin might have a partner in his dark deeds?"

He more than suspected; he now knew it for fact. "Yes, I'm certain now," he told her. "But why would someone involved with him do something like faking a woman's hanging beneath Chapman's very roof?"

She shrugged, and in doing so, the cape slid off of one shoulder, exposing her pale, creamy skin. A lump formed in Armond's throat. He swallowed it down in order to ask, "Rosalind, what are you wearing?"

She chewed on her full bottom lip rather than answer.

Then she approached him. She stood before him and he noticed that her feet were bare, the same as his.

"The night we married, you told me that you would not force me to consummate our marriage. You said the decision of when would be up to me." She drew a shaky breath and released her death grip on the cape. It slid down her body to the floor. "I have made my decision. Tonight, Armond."

Her words barely registered. How could they? She stood before him as bare as he was beneath his sheet. His eyes drank in her beauty. From her small, delicate feet, her long, slender legs, her woman's mound covered by a small nest of dark curls to her slim hips, small waist, and round, firm breasts. She was a work of art. She was what all men dreamed of, and she was his for the taking. But could he take what she offered, when she was still ignorant about what kind of man she would give herself to?

"You said you wanted more," he reminded her. "Why the sudden change of heart?"

She lifted her chin. "I know what's in my heart. And I believe I know what's in yours. Would you refuse me, Armond?"

He had to look away from her. His willpower as a man was in jeopardy, but that wasn't the worst. He felt the beast prowling beneath his skin. The beast that smelled her attraction to him. The beast that knew only of lust and nothing of love.

"Go back to your room," he ordered softly. "Whatever is in your heart, it is wasted on me."

She didn't respond for a moment, and he was afraid to look at her. Afraid her eyes would be filled with tears again and he would pull her into his arms. If he touched her, he was lost.

She touched him instead. Rosalind reached for his

hand and placed it against her breast, as he had done to her the other night. "Are you certain?"

His hand molded to the soft mound, the taunt nipple teasing his palm. His blood burned for her. His cock had grown hard the moment she swept into his room. She was a siren; and he, the sailor lulled by her song.

"You don't know all there is to know about me," he warned her, but didn't remove his hand from her breast. "I am damned, Rosalind."

Her eyes softened upon him. "Then I am damned along with you. Surrender to me, Armond. I love you. I give myself willingly."

Hearing the words from her lips was bittersweet. Part of him rejoiced; another part wept. Wept for the injustice of life and the pain of love where a future would be dark and bleak. He would release her, he decided. Once it happened, and it would . . . soon, he would disappear. She might love the man she so softly looked upon now, but she would not love what he would soon become. No woman could. His mother included.

His hand moved slowly from her breast to her waist. He pulled her down on the bed beside him, quickly tumbling her on her back.

"I thought you learned upon our first meeting to be careful what you ask for," he said. "You might just get it."

Chapter Twenty-Seven

"So you keep telling me," she taunted him. "Tonight we play no games, we worry of no consequences. Tonight is for us, and us alone."

His body slid on top of hers, the sheet he'd wrapped around him tangled between them. His skin was smooth and firm, hot beneath her fingers when she ran them along the length of his back. Her breasts were pushed flush against his chest, and she felt the thudding of their hearts. He kissed her then, slowly, deliberately, his patience in stark contrast to the wild beating of his heart.

The kiss was gentle and possessive at the same time. He lulled her with his mouth, lulled her into relaxation until he deepened his claim, until he forced her to feel more than simple pleasant sensation. His tongue stroked hers until she answered, joined him in the dance. Then the gates of passion were thrown wide.

She moaned into his open mouth; her nails bit into the smooth skin of his shoulders. Her body registered the complete feel of him against her, the sheet that was once wrapped around his waist having mysteriously disappeared. His hard, impressive member pressed against her stomach, and some instinct given to her without her knowledge made her press back, made her move against him.

"Not yet," he whispered. "I want to make you ready for me."

He kissed her neck, his teeth nipping softly at her skin, then moved lower, his hands closing around her aching breasts before he took each nipple in turn into his mouth and suckled her. He teased her mercilessly, his tongue drawing lazy circles around her nipples before he took one inside again, the hot suction of his mouth a link to the pressure she felt building lower. Her nails dug deeper, and again she couldn't control the need to arch upward against him.

His hand slid between them and he touched her where he had once touched her before, stroked her in the same manner that had made her shatter beneath his skillful fingers. She understood the rhythm now and what she strove to find, more than willing to move with him, against him, whatever it took to increase the pressure and end the ache that built and built. He slipped a finger inside of her and she momentarily froze.

"I won't hurt you," Armond said close to her ear. "I need to stretch you a little, prepare you for me."

Gradually her trepidation eased, and Armond continued to stroke the bud of her sensation with his thumb as his finger moved deeper inside of her. The combination only heightened her sensation, brought her closer to the edge of madness, and soon she found herself moving against him again, welcoming the added substance of two fingers inside of her instead of one.

Her back arched and she tried to take his fingers deeper inside of her. She knew she was wet there, hot to the point of feverish, swollen against the palm of his hand, aching, aching with a need to be filled.

"Armond," she breathed. "I need . . ." She wasn't sure what she needed. "I want . . ."

"I know," he said, his voice low and husky. He gently

slid his fingers from her, leaving a void; then he raised himself above her, parted her legs wider with his knees, and she felt his rigid manhood poised at her entrance.

She felt the resistance of her tight passage the moment the large head of his member tried to penetrate. She scooted away, an unconscious action, she supposed, survival instincts. He would not let her escape. His hands closed around her waist and he held her still.

"Do not tense against me," he instructed. "Relax; allow my invasion. It will only hurt for a moment."

Hurt? He planned to hurt her? Being raised without a mother, Rosalind was sorely lacking in information regarding intimacy between a man and a woman. She knew the basics. She did not know about pain.

"Pain?" she asked. "You're going to hurt me?"

He stared down at her, and she noticed that his eyes were aglow. "I am going to claim you," he answered, and he did.

Before she could comprehend all that his claiming might entail, he thrust inside of her, thrust deep to the very core of her. The pain came, knife-sharp, wrenching a cry from her lips. Lips he soothed with kisses a moment later, even though he could barely fuse their mouths without having to break away to gasp. He pressed his forehead against hers, as if he, too, grappled with the shock of invasion.

Tears welled up in Rosalind's eyes. The sting had been jarring, stealing her passion, blunting the pleasure she'd found in his arms up until the point of his claiming. She was glad it was over, and said so to him.

His lips found her ear; he bit gently upon the lobe. "It is far from over, Rosalind," he said. "It has just begun."

He moved and she steeled herself for more pain. But the pain did not come. He filled her completely, filled her to overflowing. His size and strength forced the air from her lungs in little gasps every time he withdrew slightly only to thrust again. But it was not painful, what he did. Not any kind of pain she could understand or had felt before. Her wetness made him slick inside of her and he maneuvered with relative ease, which surprised her, given his size.

Once she realized there would be no stabbing pain again, she was able to concentrate on him and her—the sensation that he created with his movements, the tingling where their bodies joined, the pressure building once more when he withdrew and filled her with slow, steady strokes.

His sex teased the swollen bud of her sensation, and she found if she moved just so, the contact was greater, the sensation more pronounced. It was to that end that she gave herself up completely to him.

Inhibitions fled. Something primal in her took over. Something primal in him as well, she realized. There were no soft whispered words of love from him. He seemed focused on one objective and one objective only. Her pleasure and his own. Completion of what they had begun together. His breathing became more labored, his body slick with sweat as he continued the slow, steady rhythm that brought her quickly to a place of only need, only desire, only him and her, in his room, hidden away from the world.

Her nails raked his back, her hands gliding to the tight muscles of his buttocks. She held him to her, wrapped her legs around him, as if she'd performed this act with him a thousand times, as if she knew what she wanted and what he wanted as well.

He whispered her name; no, he growled her name. A low, throaty sound in the back of his throat that brought her to dizzying heights of ecstasy. His teeth clamped down against her throat, not painful but possessive, like something she'd seen the toms in the barn at the estate do to the females during mating season. A show of his dominance. A show of his complete possession of her. And he did possess her. Heart, body, and soul, all wrapped together, all fighting for dominance inside of her.

Body won. His steady strokes stimulated her to the point of near pain, of certain obsession. She could think of nothing but the way their bodies moved together, nothing except the perfect way they seemed to fit, although at one time she would have sworn he would never fit at all. But he did, and in a way she could not find lacking.

He filled her completely, filled her to bursting, and when she arched her hips to increase the tempo, she found he had not even given all of himself to her. He did so now, thrusting so deep she thought he might break through clear to her womb, but still, it was a different kind of pain. A pleasing kind of pain. A pain that left her little choice but to cross the thin boundaries of sanity into madness.

She clung to him, her body now slick against him with her own sweat. She angled and arched until the building sensation once again grew and grew and could not be contained.

Suddenly she burst apart, shattered beneath him, the waves of ecstasy breaking over her only intensified by the continued thrust of him deep inside of her. Her nails dug deep, drew blood, and she called his name, convulsed and thrashed, and even bit into his shoulder.

"Unwrap your legs from around me."

His voice came to her from far away. She could not move but only hold on to him as if he were the only thing solid in the world. She was afraid to let go, afraid she'd slip away to somewhere form whence there was no return.

"Rosalind," he growled again, his thrust deeper, faster,

harder. He fought to untangle himself, she realized, too late to register that he wanted release from her grip on him.

Then he tensed, buried so deep inside of her she wondered if he could possibly find his way back out again. He cursed in her ear. A very bad curse word. The worst, in fact, she had ever heard. He shuddered and she felt him deep inside of her, releasing his seed.

Again too late, she realized that was why he'd wanted to be free. To spill his seed somewhere else. Somewhere harmless. It was as if she felt her womb open to him. Invite him inside to plant, as was his purpose in life, and hers to receive him.

He withdrew by degrees, until finally he lay back against the sheets, one arm flung over his eyes, his chest still rising and falling with obvious effort.

"God, what have I done?" he finally muttered.

Even in her very limited experience, Rosalind sensed it was not a thing a woman wanted to hear a man say after making love to her. Since boldness seemed to rule her emotions this evening, she replied, "I believe you did what I asked you to do. And even in my ignorance over such matters, I believe you did it remarkably well."

He was silent for a moment. Finally, he said, "When I take you again, you must not allow me to come inside of you, Rosalind. My seed is tainted and I would not see it take root."

Once more, hardly words a woman wanted to hear from her husband after making love. Then something he said registered. "Will there be a next time?" She rose on her elbows to look at him. "I mean, tonight?"

He removed his arm from over his eyes. They still had a faint glow. The longer she stared at him, the brighter they shone in the darkness around them. "I plan to have you again," he said. "And again after that, and maybe once more before morning. I told you to be careful what you asked for."

She sighed dreamily and lay back down beside him. "I suppose if you must."

He was suddenly leaning over her again. "I must," he assured her.

Chapter Twenty-Eight

He'd had her twice again before the first pain took him. Armond now sat huddled in a corner of the bedchamber, coated in sweat, shaking uncontrollably, while his wife slept the sleep of the exhausted in his bed. Even suffering the pain that twisted his body into knots, he wanted her again. Was it the man who couldn't get enough of her, or was it the beast that refused to be sated?

He loved her. He knew before tonight, before they came together as one. He knew the moment he saw her at the Greenleys' first ball of the season. He'd believed that denying what he felt would save him from the curse. It was upon him now. He glanced toward his window, the slight breeze moving the curtains around as if they were dancing in the dark. He could see the moon, see that it was nearly full. How long did he have? One night? Two? Three at the most.

Rosalind stirred and mumbled his name in her sleep. He could not go to her, not as he was, not fighting what he would soon become. He thought about his father then. He understood now his despair. How he had feared that he might hurt his wife, his children. The pistol had been his only friend in the end. Then Armond thought about what the dowager had said to him regarding his mother.

She'd died of a broken heart. His father hadn't given

her a choice the day he took his life. Just as Armond wouldn't give Rosalind one once he was forced to disappear from her life. But before he went, there was one thing he had to do. He had to kill Chapman. And his accomplice as well.

He'd been thinking about that. He strongly suspected he knew who aided Chapman in his dark deeds against women. It was obvious, really. Tomorrow, provided that his pain subsided and he could present a normal facade, he would find out for certain.

"Armond?" Rosalind sat up in bed. He watched her glance around the darkened room. Beneath her skin, he saw the blood pumping through her veins. He squeezed his eyes shut. Forcing the air in and out of his lungs, he tried to stop the shaking, tried to ignore the pain that twisted his insides.

A gentle hand touched his brow. "What are you doing here on the floor?"

What could he tell her? The truth? She wouldn't be able to comprehend the truth. Most people couldn't. It was selfish, but he wanted to leave her knowing she still loved him. "Trying to refrain from making love to you again," he answered. "You'll think I'm some kind of beast."

"If you are one, then you've made me one as well," she said softly. She leaned forward to kiss him. He had her on her back before she could make contact.

Good Lord. Rosalind felt as if she'd been beaten. There wasn't a place on her body that didn't ache. At some point during the night, Armond had taken her to her own bed, she supposed in consideration of her sleeping upon his bloodstained sheets, or maybe just in consideration of her person. Were all men so . . . so virile? When he'd taken her on the floor, he'd been insatiable. He'd been primitive, almost wild, and he had stirred something in her that was the same.

He'd done something else that confused her. He'd done what he told her he mustn't do again. Buried deep inside of her, he'd given her his seed again. Why if he didn't want children? Maybe he had changed his mind about that, she hoped. Could one night of lovemaking change everything? If so, perhaps she should have instigated consummating their marriage before last night.

A discreet knock sounded upon her door. Hawkins called, "Lord Wulf has ordered you a bath and I've set it up in his suite, since he said you were not to be disturbed at an early hour."

Rosalind could use a nice long soak. Set up in Armond's room? Would he be joining her then? She rose, put on her wrapper, and opened the door adjoining their suites. Just as Hawkins had said, a tub of steaming water sat in the middle of the room. The bed had been made, she imagined the sheets stripped, which made her blush. Hawkins would have little doubt about what she and Armond had done in this room the night prior and well into the morning hours. Everything in the room looked in order, everything in its place, except for one thing . . . her husband.

Disappointment chased away her happy thoughts. She had hoped Armond would at least have breakfast with her before he took himself off to do whatever it was that he did when he took himself off. She moved to the tub and stripped off her wrapper, easing her sore body into the steaming water. Her soaps had been set out, and the smell of lavender soon worked to help soothe her. She lay back and closed her eyes. Memories of making love with Armond brought a soft smile to her lips.

She had claimed him, and he, her. Simply because her day hadn't started as she had wished didn't mean their

relationship would not move forward as she had hoped it
would. She tried to keep her spirits up. She tried not to
think about the house next door and the dark stain that
also marred her happiness. If only she had irrefutable
proof of Franklin's guilt, she and Armond could go to the
authorities and let them deal with her stepbrother.

Rosalind wondered then how her stepmother was doing without her daily ration of doctored tea. Had the effects had time to wear off? Would the lady soon be on the
mend and able to speak to Rosalind? Would the duchess's
confessions against Franklin be enough to convince the
authorities of his guilt? And would the lady confess
against her own son at all?

The tumble of thoughts running through Rosalind's
head made relaxing in her bath impossible. She soaped
herself, washed and rinsed her hair, then climbed out,
drying herself on a fluffy towel Hawkins had left. She replaced her wrapper and walked into her room to dress.
Once she finished, she returned to Armond's room. Again
she walked around the room, touching his personal belongings, though they were a sorry substitute for having
Armond there with her this morning.

She came across a book pushed back on a shelf of his
bureau. It looked very old, and curious, she picked it up
and considered whether she wanted to borrow it. The one
she'd taken from Armond's study did not hold her interest. As she flipped through the worn pages, a faded, yellow piece of paper fluttered to the floor. Rosalind bent and
picked it up.

It was written in Latin, but her father had indulged her
with tutors over the years she spent in the country and she
had no trouble deciphering the handwritten scrawl. It appeared to be a poem.

Hawkins knocked softly upon the door again. "Are you
dressed, Lady Wulf?"

Rosalind quickly stuffed the paper back into the book and replaced it on Armond's shelf. "Yes, Hawkins, you may come in."

The steward entered. "Lord Wulf told me to inform you that this morning, the Dowager Duchess of Brayberry will send her coach around to collect you. I believe you are to have a fitting at her residence. His Lordship thought you might enjoy having another woman's opinion on the gowns you wish to have made."

"Thank you, Hawkins," Rosalind mumbled. "How very thoughtful of him." But not as thoughtful as it would have been for Armond to stay and have breakfast with her. "Would you bring a tray up to me, Hawkins? Now that I know I shall pay a visit this morning, I should take more care with my appearance."

"Very well, Lady Wulf," Hawkins answered.

Once Armond's man left, Rosalind glanced toward the book again. Armond had said she had free run of the house. Would he mind if she took the book? She snatched it up and carried it with her into her room. Once there, she laid it on the table next to her bed, but the poem folded inside seemed to call to her.

Again she flipped through the pages and found the old piece of parchment. She'd only been able to translate the first line when Hawkins rapped on her door again.

"Your breakfast, Lady Wulf," he called from the other side. "May I enter?"

Rosalind stuffed the poem back inside the book and went to get the door for Hawkins.

"The coach will collect you in a half hour's time, milady," he said. "I hope that will be sufficient."

The way he eyed her undressed hair, Rosalind supposed it was a hint from Hawkins that she needed to take greater care with her appearance. She nodded. Rosalind would be hard-pressed to get breakfast down and dress her hair. There was no time to go back to the poem, although she would as soon as she returned. The first line had intrigued her.

Damn the witch who cursed me.

The line kept running over and over in her head while she nibbled on toast and marmalade, then drank her hot chocolate as she dressed her hair. A witch. It was odd that Jackson said he was off on a quest to kill a witch. A curse. The Wulfs were supposedly cursed, by insanity, she had thought, but Armond said that wasn't true. Even the dowager had claimed she didn't believe the madness that had taken Armond's parents was inherent but brought about by the storm they were forced to weather.

What sort of storm? What sort of curse then? Her curiosity piqued, she more than ever wanted to hurry to the dowager's and have her fitting, then hurry back and read more of the poem. Perhaps it would enlighten her regarding Armond's secrecy about the curse. Of course she had no way of knowing if the faded parchment had anything to do with Armond or his brothers at all.

"Her Grace's coach has arrived," Hawkins called to Rosalind through the door.

Rosalind went to her wardrobe and removed a shawl she hoped would disguise her outdated gown. She walked across the room toward the door, but she couldn't keep her eyes from straying toward the book. She opened the door and followed Hawkins downstairs. He saw her out, but as soon as the footman alighted and held the coach door for her, Hawkins bade her to have a good day and returned to his duties.

Rosalind accepted the footman's offer to help her inside, thinking the dowager's coach was nice indeed. Something made her glance over her shoulder toward the house next door, and there fluttering in the wind was the sheet draped over her former balcony.

"Oh dear," she whispered.

"Milady?" the footman addressed her.

Conflicting emotions warred within her. Armond had said she was not to go next door alone again. But the silly man never stayed home long enough to see that she didn't find herself in this very predicament. What if Mary needed help with the duchess? What if the lady had come out of her lethargic state and could now converse with her? Rosalind refused the footman's offer of assistance.

"I've just recalled a former engagement," Rosalind said to the man. "Please relay my apologies to Her Grace."

As it was not his place to question her about the matter, the footman nodded formally to her, shut the door, and went around to tell the driver to return home.

Once the coach rumbled away, Rosalind was again torn. She had a suspicion Armond had probably told Hawkins that Rosalind was not to venture next door again. The steward might take it as his place to forbid her to go. She would go, she decided. Go and tell Mary not to hang the sheet anymore unless it was a dire emergency. When Rosalind needed to see her stepmother, she'd simply have to make arrangements with Armond to leave room in his busy schedule to accompany her.

Not that Franklin would gladly welcome them into his home. The matter left her mulling over possibilities as she walked down the rocky path past the stable, along the hedge, then across the lawn.

Mary had left the back door standing open. Rosalind entered the house through the kitchen. Even though the sheet had been hung, she took precautions, making her way quietly through the house and up the stairs. Franklin's door stood open. The room was empty. She hurried up the next flight of stairs and into her stepmother's room to see Mary wrestling with the woman.

"Now, calm down, Your Grace!" the housekeeper huffed. "You'll hurt yourself thrashing about so!"

"My word," Rosalind whispered, then hurried forward to give Mary a hand. "What is happening?"

"I didn't know what else to do but signal you," Mary huffed out. "I withheld the tea all of yesterday and this morning like you told me, and the lady has gone quite mad! I dare not tell Mr. Chapman about her condition for fear he'll find out I went against his instructions."

Rosalind managed to pin the duchess's thin shoulders to the bed. She sat beside her. "Your Grace, you must lie still. You'll hurt yourself."

"The tea," she whispered, her voice raspy for lack of use. "I must have my tea."

As upset as Rosalind was to find the duchess in her current condition, her heart leaped with joy at finally hearing the lady speak. "You mustn't have the tea, Your Grace," she explained. "You have been drugged for months."

The lady's brow was coated in a thin layer of sweat. In spite of that, she shook. "He's gotten me addicted," she said through chattering teeth. "I feel as if I'll go mad without it."

When Rosalind had ordered Mary to stop the tea, she had not taken into consideration that the lady's body would suffer serious withdrawal symptoms. She should have ordered Mary to weaken the tea with each serving, she realized. She turned to the housekeeper. "Mary, do you still have the leaves my stepbrother brought for you to prepare his mother's tea?"

The woman nodded. "Afraid to throw them out in case he asked for another cup himself and realized it wasn't the same."

"Good," Rosalind said. "Run downstairs and make the duchess a cup, very weak," she instructed. "We were wrong to take it away from her so abruptly. It has caused her to have a reaction."

"I'll have it in a hurry," Mary assured her. "The stove is still warm from breakfast, so it shouldn't take long to brew."

While Mary left to prepare tea, Rosalind smoothed the lady's hair and tried to say soothing things to her. Despite her stepmother's symptoms, it was the first time Rosalind had seen any real signs of life from the duchess since she'd come to London. The situation gave her hope, but it also brought worry. What if her decision ended up injuring the lady worse than the doctored tea?

"I'm so sorry," she whispered to the duchess, on the brink of tears. "I only meant to help you."

To her surprise, the woman grabbed her hand and squeezed. "I've known you were here with me," she rasped. "You have been a comfort."

Lifting the lady's frail hand, Rosalind rubbed it against her cheek. "He's not going to get away with this," she assured her stepmother. "I'll see to that."

Violent shaking wracked the lady's thin body. "You are in danger," she whispered. "He's a monster. My boy. I thought I could change him, but I have failed."

"Don't try to talk now," Rosalind said. "Save your strength."

Mary bustled back in with a cup of tea. "I've got it, milady," she said.

Together, Rosalind and Mary helped the duchess drink, and soon after she finished the cup, she settled down and fell back to sleep.

"I think she'll rest easier now," Rosalind said to the housekeeper. "Give her more later, but keep making each cup weaker than the last until her body can tolerate being without the drug."

"She's talking again at least," Mary said. "Moving around like I haven't seen her do in months."

Rosalind hated to leave the lady but had already stayed too long. "Mary, only put the sheet out unless it is urgent that you see me. Otherwise, I can only come if Armond is with me. My stepbrother is dangerous," she said to the housekeeper. "You must watch your back with him and you mustn't let him know what you and I are about with his mother."

"Never thought he was right in the head," Mary confided to Rosalind. "I've only stayed for the lady's sake."

"I must go for now." Rosalind rose from her stepmother's bed. "If she worsens, hang the sheet. I'll come as quickly as I can."

The housekeeper nodded. Rosalind hurried out of the room and down the stairs. She didn't breathe easy until she'd reached the hedge that separated the two properties and was once again on the rocky path leading to the house. She hoped to find Armond at home when she entered the house. By the quiet, she knew that was not the case. Hawkins looked surprised to see her.

"Back already, Lady Wulf?"

She only muttered a guilty "yes" and hurried up to her room. Once inside, she began to pace. Where was Armond? She needed to talk to him. She'd decided they might need to go behind Franklin's back and move the duchess. Rosalind needed to monitor her condition and be at leave to call for a doctor if necessary. She couldn't do that as the situation stood.

The day wore on and still Armond did not come home. What was he doing?

Chapter Twenty-Nine

Armond sat in his coach watching the broker's office. Men had come and gone, but not the man Armond was looking for. The pain that had twisted his insides late last night had subsided, and he'd been able to carry on a normal day. He wondered when the pain would come again. When he wouldn't be able to stave off the effects of the curse that threatened to take him. He felt as if time was running out and he had to settle the matter of Chapman and his accomplice quickly and efficiently.

Reaching down to grab a small duffel, he emerged from his coach and approached the office. The man glanced up when Armond entered, recognition immediately dawning in his eyes behind the spectacles.

"So, you've come back?"

Armond strode to the man's desk and took a seat across from him. He decided to be blunt. "Is Viscount Harry Penmore one of your clients?"

The man blinked at him before he sputtered, "I've told you that I cannot give you information about the clients I serve."

Too late, Armond had read the man's recognition of Penmore's name before he responded. "What property is he currently interested in?" Armond pressed.

"I cannot tell you," the man insisted. "Who are you? And what right do you have—"

"I am Lord Wulf, the Marquess of Wulfglen, Earl of Bumont," he interrupted the man, then he reached down and opened the duffel. He withdrew several stacks of money and laid them on the man's desk. "I wish to purchase the property Penmore has inquired about most recently."

The man's eyes widened. "But you haven't even asked the price."

"I'm certain this is more than enough, correct?"

Licking his lips, the man reached for a stack of money. "Yes," he agreed.

"I want the location, and the key, and I want them now."

"Of course." The man's stringy hair bobbed around his shoulders when he nodded.

Armond slapped his hand down on top of the man's. "And you are to tell no one, especially Viscount Penmore, that the property has been sold."

"Never buys anything anyway," the man complained. "Just wants to know what is standing empty."

And Armond knew why Penmore wanted that information. He would set a trap for Chapman and Penmore. This time, Armond would be hiding in the house they planned to use for their dark deeds. This time, they would not get away. He left the broker's office with the deed to the property and the key. He'd make a sweep past the house he now owned before he went to the dowager's to see how Rosalind progressed with her fitting.

Rosalind. Just the thought of her sent his blood racing through him. He felt a stab of guilt for the way he'd mistreated her last night. Her virginal body was not used to the demands he'd placed upon her. He'd had to force

himself from the house this morning lest he fall upon
her again. Now that she had given herself to him, he
could not resist her. He could not get enough of her. He
wondered if he ever would. But then, that option would
soon be taken from him. Rosalind would soon be taken
from him. His life as he had known it would soon be
taken from him.

It wasn't so much of a life, he realized, until Rosalind
had entered it. As soon as he fell, he would leave her.
He'd take refuge at the country estate, hoping his brothers
would hide the fact that they knew anything about his
whereabouts. Gabriel would take his place in the world,
and Armond would suffer through whatever was left of
his life. Rosalind could remarry, provided she could find a
man willing to overlook her less than acceptable first
marriage.

The thought of Rosalind married to another man made
his hand twist tightly around the duffel he still held. He
wanted no other man to touch her, yet his wants were selfish. She should have all that she deserved in life. A happy
marriage, children. The latter thought caused him to twist
his hand around the duffel again. What had possessed him
to spill his seed inside of her a second time last night? He
knew what had possessed him. He had only now to wait
for it to possess him fully.

Rosalind held the poem again. She'd almost forgotten
about it in her worry over the duchess. Rosalind had more
trouble than she thought she would with the translation.
Evening approached, and the light outside had begun to
fade. She moved closer to the window. Some lines were
less faded than others and drew her eye. She read them
aloud to herself.

" 'Betrayed by love, my own false tongue, / she bade

the moon transform me. / The family name, once my pride, / becomes the beast that haunts me.' "

What family name? Her gaze scrolled down the crinkled parchment to the signature. She'd ignored the author's name at first because it was the most faded part of the poem, and therefore, the most difficult part to decipher. Rosalind squinted until finally she was able to make out the signature. "Wulf," she whispered.

Chill bumps rose on her arms. The hair on the back of her neck stood on end, and her eyes watered. She blinked and stared outside of the window, waiting to refocus before she read further. When her eyes cleared, something outside caught her attention. It was the house next door and the sheet hung over the balcony that beckoned her.

If Mary had hung the sheet again, something had happened. Maybe the duchess had taken a turn for the worse. The lady could be dying, and Mary would not know what to do. Rosalind hurried to her night table and placed the poem on top of the book. Worry now chased away the haunting words she'd read, and she ran down the stairs and flew through the house and out the front doors, down the rocky path past the stable, along the hedges, and across the lawn.

She was panting by the time she reached the house. The back entrance stood open, as Mary would have left it if she'd signaled her, then had to be by her stepmother's side. Rosalind entered and raced through the kitchen, through the dining hall, past the front parlor, and up the stairs. She was almost across the second-story landing and to the stairs leading to the third floor when a voice stopped her.

"Hello, Rosalind."

She gasped and turned around. Franklin stood in the hallway, blocking her exit back down to the first floor.

"Where is Mary?" she panted, trying to regain her breath and disguise her sudden terror.

"I insisted she visit her daughter," he answered. "I told her I would tend to my poor mother this evening."

Rosalind's gaze moved toward the stairs leading up to the duchess's room.

"She's sleeping, as always," he said. "I wanted to see you, Rosalind. I know about the sheet, and you shouldn't leave your petticoats in a puddle on the balcony. I saw them later that day on my way out. This morning I pretended to leave, but waited to see if Mary would hang the sheet again. When she did, and shortly thereafter I saw you hurrying across the lawn, I realized you had been paying my mother visits whenever I left the house."

"You tricked me," she whispered.

He smiled, but as always, the expression never reached his eyes. "You left me little choice. Penmore grows tired of substitutes. He wants you."

"Penmore?" Was the repulsive man Franklin's partner in murder? It made sense that he was, she realized. The man had more than her stepbrother's gambling debts to dangle over Franklin's head. No wonder Franklin was under the viscount's thumb. "He's just as guilty as you are," she said.

He shrugged. "But his title and his wealth make his word worth more than mine. He likes to play games. Lydia he left as a reminder that I should deny him nothing, not even you. He forced me to go out later and leave another dead woman in Wulf's stable to take suspicion off of having a dead one show up in my very home. He's ruthless when it comes to getting what he wants, Rosalind. A pity he had to want you."

"Why did you bring me to London?" Now Franklin's motives didn't make sense. If he'd only wanted to fetch a high bride's price for her to pay off his gambling debts,

Penmore would still have the murder of Bess O'Conner to hold over his head.

"I had a plan to escape him," he admitted. "I thought if I could sell you for a high bride's price, sell the house, and collect my mother's inheritance from your father once I had given her sufficient time to die of her long-standing illness, I could escape. I could go abroad with enough money to buy myself a title and live the life your father denied me. I hadn't counted on Penmore seeing you and deciding he had to have you."

His confessions made her livid. He would use anyone for his own gain. He had no heart. "If you would kill your own mother for simple monetary gain, you are as much of a monster as he is."

"I know," he admitted, then shrugged. "The world is full of monsters, Rosalind. My father was one. You didn't know that, though, did you? He beat my mother, he beat me, and what a pity that day he took me hunting at the tender age of ten and I turned the rifle on him and shot him dead. My mother thought I had a chance then, I suppose, but she was wrong. It was too late. I had already learned the only way to feel good was to have control over people, to prey on the weak, the way that he did."

Franklin considered her the weak. He always had, Rosalind realized. Women, she supposed, in general. She wasn't weak, although he had bullied her to the point of nearly losing her spirit before Armond had rescued her from him. She couldn't recall if the duchess's room had a lock on the door. It was worth a try, even if she could only hold him off for a time. Perhaps she could find something in the room to use as a weapon against him. She bolted for the stairs.

Franklin was upon her before she made it halfway up. He twisted his hand in her hair and dragged her backward. She screamed and he clamped a cruel hand against her mouth. Struggling, he pulled her back down to the first-floor landing.

She fought him with all of her strength, clawing at the hand he had clamped across her mouth. She bit into the flesh of his palm and he swore loudly and released her. She only made it a few steps before he grabbed her by the hair again. He whirled her around and then he hit her. Hit her so hard, spots danced before her eyes before darkness descended upon her.

Chapter Thirty

Armond arrived home in a nasty mood. He'd gone to collect Rosalind at the dowager's home, only to find out she had never arrived. The dowager's footman had told him that his wife said she had a previous engagement she had forgotten. What engagement? Hawkins greeted him at the door.

"Is Lady Wulf home?"

The man blinked. "I believe so, my lord. I haven't seen her since I went up earlier to inform her when dinner would be served."

Armond marched past the steward and headed upstairs. The scent of lavender lingered in his room from Rosalind's morning bath. He inhaled deeply for a moment, then walked into her room. She wasn't there. He glanced around and spied a book on her night table; on top, a faded scrap of paper. His heart started to pound. He sucked in a deep breath and approached the night table. He knew what it was before he picked it up and made certain. The poem. One written long ago by the first Wulf cursed.

She knew. Surely she had read the poem and made the realization that it was connected to him, to his brothers, to the family curse. His hand trembled as he laid the faded piece of parchment back on top of the book. He must

speak to her about it, explain what he knew, warn her of
what was to come, beg her to forgive him for not telling
her sooner. Pray that she wouldn't hate him or, worse,
fear him. But where was she? Had she run away in terror?
And if so, where would she seek sanctuary?

First, he would search the house, he decided. If
Hawkins hadn't heard her leave, she could simply be hiding. That thought made him feel physically ill. That she
would hide somewhere from him, as if she thought he
might hurt her. And he did not know for a fact that
he wouldn't, once the beast claimed him. Armond began
a meticulous search of the house, trying to keep his growing concern hidden from Hawkins. He didn't find his
wife, he didn't smell her in any of the rooms that were not
in use, or the rooms his brothers chose to use when they
were in residence.

He ended up in her room again, searching for clues to
where she might have gone. He moved around the room,
catching her scent, stronger in certain areas where she
must have last been. One of those places was next to
the window. He stood, staring out, his thoughts in turmoil.
He had hoped to have at least another night with her, another day when she would look at him and see only a
man. If she ran, how did she go?

The stable seemed his next logical choice to visit. She
might have taken her horse. He started to turn away when
something caught his eye. A sheet draped over the balcony of the house next door. The housekeeper's signal to
Rosalind to visit when Chapman had left the house.

He turned from the window and moved quickly from
her room to the stairs. He found himself nearly running.
He did run once he left the house and started down the
rocky path and past the stable. The rear door was closed
and locked. He ran around to the front entrance, finding it
the same. Armond used the heavy knocker to announce

his presence. No one answered the door. He ran around to the carriage house and glanced inside. The coach was there, the phaeton missing. There were no servants inside roaming about.

Armond glanced toward the balcony where the sheet still ruffled with the breeze. He approached the trellis and began his climb. The balcony doors were not locked. He moved through Rosalind's former room and out onto the landing. The house was deathly quiet. No one was home. But someone had to be home. The duchess, Rosalind's stepmother. He moved to the landing and up the stairs to the third floor. Her door was open, the room dimly lit and the lady asleep on the bed. He approached the bed and stared down at her.

Something inside of him told him Rosalind was in danger. Her scent was in the house. . . . So was Chapman's. He gently shook the woman. She opened her eyes and stared up at him.

"Rosalind, Your Grace? Do you know where she is?" he asked.

The lady closed her eyes again. Armond turned away. He would search the house.

"He took her," came a raspy voice from the bed. "I heard her scream. I could do nothing to help her. You must save her from him. He is a monster."

Armond's blood turned to ice. Chapman had Rosalind? He walked back to the bed. "Where is your housekeeper? I cannot leave you here alone."

"Sent her off for the evening, I imagine," came her hoarse reply. "Sent her off so he could do his dirty deeds. You must stop him. He's mad. As mad as his father was. I kept hoping he would change. I kept trying to save his soul, but I could not. I realized that when he beat that poor woman so in my very home. I heard her screams. One of his parties that got out of hand. He wanted to blame someone else. I told him he couldn't. I told him he must confess to his crimes and take responsibility for them. Then he turned on me."

"I can carry you next door, Your Grace," Armond offered.

"No," she insisted. "My life is over. Rosalind's has just begun. She is in love. I heard her tell me so, although she didn't know that I could understand what she said to me. You must go now, find her, save her from him."

The lady was right. There was no time to spare. Thank God he knew where Chapman would take Rosalind. Thank God he had the key. He would kill Chapman tonight. Kill him for daring to touch Rosalind again. Kill him so that he would threaten her no more.

Rosalind opened her eyes to the sight of Franklin slouching against a wall, staring at her. Candles flickered inside an empty room. She lay on the floor, resting upon a dirty mattress. Her jaw ached. She imagined it was bruised and tried to lift her hand to rub the throbbing pain, but her hands were tied behind her back. She tried to move her feet. Her ankles were tied as well.

"What are you going to do to me?" she asked, and hated the quiver in her voice. It made Franklin smile.

"I'm not so sure you want to know," he informed her. "But then, I want to tell you so I will. Remember when I told you that Penmore had a problem with his manly parts?"

She nodded.

"Well, I didn't tell you everything." He shrugged away from the crumbling wall behind him and paced back and forth in front of the mattress. "Penmore does have a problem to be sure, but quite by accident the night I was entertaining him, along with Bess O'Conner, he realized something helped him tremendously with his problem."

Rosalind tried to move her hands. She was lying on them and had nearly lost circulation. Franklin stuck his boot in her ribs and nudged her.

"Pay attention. You can't get away," he assured her. "Now, where was I? Oh yes. We were drinking and playing cards, and I decided I wanted to have Bess O'Conner, so I took her right there in the parlor. Seems Penmore got excited watching me have her, but when he wanted a turn, Bess did not wish to comply. I slapped her around a little to convince her to service Penmore, but the bitch started screaming and fighting back.

"My mother was asleep upstairs, so I couldn't let her keep screaming. I hit her some more." He sighed. "I hit her a lot. I strangled her, too. Penmore was more stimulated by me beating the woman than he had been by me humping her. I thought I killed her. Penmore had her while he thought she lay there dead. My mother called to me from the stairs. I had to keep her from coming into the parlor and seeing the dead woman, so I spoke to her for a time upstairs. Penmore, the idiot, fixed himself a strong drink and turned his back on Bess O'Conner's bloody and beaten corpse."

"Only she wasn't dead," Rosalind already knew.

Franklin suddenly bent and put his hands around her throat. "I'm telling the story! Shut up!"

Rosalind gasped for breath. Franklin seemed to realize he was killing her and let go of her throat. He rose, straightened his collar, and continued with his pacing.

"The whore escaped through the back entrance and managed to drag herself next door and into your husband's stable. I went after her, but then I saw the bastard come home. Then I realized what a stroke of luck I had

had. Everyone knows the Wulfs are dangerous, are cursed with insanity. Lord Wulf would look more suspicious than I ever would if he had the bad sense to call in the authorities, which of course he did. So, that was the end of it, I thought."

Penmore wanted more, she wanted to say, but didn't dare speak again. Not with her hands tied behind her back and her helpless.

"Penmore enjoyed it so much, he said if we didn't do it again, he'd see me hanged for murder. I was, after all, the one who beat Bess O'Conner, the one who was responsible for her death. So, he had me, not only with the money I owed him in gambling debts, but with the murder."

Franklin paused to wipe sweat from his brow with his sleeve. "We tried for a time just to repeat that night without killing the whores. It wasn't enough for Penmore. His member grew limp again, and we had to play new games to keep him amused. He liked to dress the women up like ladies. He liked to pretend he was having his way with an innocent society miss, which of course he could never do without serious repercussions . . . at least until you came along.

"I should have seen it coming," he admitted, as if what he spoke of was simply an offense that required a slap on the wrist. "He knew you had no family except me and my mother, whom, by the way, I had to drug to keep silent. When she heard the news about the dead woman found next door, she knew I was responsible. She tried to get me to go to the authorities with the truth, to take responsibility for what I had done. I pretended to consider it, but only long enough to get her addicted to a special blend of tea I had made up for her. Tea laced with opium. You know the rest."

"Why was Penmore willing to marry me?" she wanted to know.

"So he could have his cake and eat it, too, dear sister. A society miss he could treat like a whore, and who would come to your defense? Your mother and father are dead. You had no one, except me. I would have been the one to, no doubt, father your children, Rosalind. Penmore doesn't think even if he does manage the deed, his seed is strong enough to take root."

She shivered with more than fear; she shivered with disgust. Rosalind was tempted to taunt Franklin with her knowledge of the doctored tea he served his mother, but then it would only endanger the duchess. "What are you going to do to me?" she repeated the question.

He bent beside her again. "Whatever we wish."

She suddenly heard footsteps coming close to the room. Penmore stepped inside a moment later. He grinned broadly at her. "Lady Rosalind, oh," he corrected, "Lady Wulf, so nice to see you this evening."

"You can't get away with this," Rosalind informed both men. "My husband knows what you're about. He knows about you being involved, too, Penmore." She didn't know that for a fact, but she suspected Armond had figured out the truth.

"Your husband is quite a pest," Penmore pouted. "And I will not forgive him for taking what by right belonged to me. He spoiled everything."

"He'll kill you if either of you lay a hand on me," she assured them.

The two men looked at each other and merely smiled. "The joke," Penmore explained, "is that we plan to make it very obvious that he killed you. That he, in fact, killed all the women recently found murdered. You could have lived," Penmore continued, his fishlike lips forming into another unattractive pout. "Had you just not married Wulf. Then you could have been my wife and simply been forced to entertain your stepbrother and me until we grew tired of the game. Of course I don't expect we would have grown tired of it for a good long while. You're very beautiful, Rosalind."

"And you're insane," she bit out. "The both of you."

"Get to it, Chapman," Penmore suddenly ordered. "I grow weary of talk. I want to sample the lady's charms and need added stimulation."

Franklin bent beside her. He stared into her eyes and she tried to appeal to him. "Franklin, please don't do this," she whispered. "I am your stepsister. I am your kin."

He looked saddened for a moment; then his dead eyes moved over her body. "I've been waiting for this for a good long while," he confessed. "Do you remember that day when you were playing in the barn and I asked if you'd like to play a special game with me?"

She tried to remember. "No," she answered.

"Well, your father would remember if he was still alive. I would have taken you then, but a stupid groom overheard our conversation and went racing to get your father. That is when he ordered me off of his estate and said he wished never to set eyes on me again."

The admission sickened her. "I was a child, Franklin."

"A very beautiful child," he defended himself. "And an even lovelier woman. I'm going to enjoy this."

He reached forward and ripped the bodice of her gown open. Rosalind gasped. She tried to struggle, but being tied thwarted her efforts. He pulled the torn edges of her gown aside, then removed a knife from his belt. She thought he meant to slit her throat and welcomed it over what he and Penmore had claimed they would do to her. Instead, Franklin began cutting the laces of her corset away; then he slid the knife through the thin straps of her chemise and cut them loose. She was bared to the waist in a matter of moments.

"Let me see her," Penmore breathed. "I want to look at her."

Humiliated, Rosalind saw Franklin move back so that Penmore could loom over her. Drool had pooled in the corner of his mouth, and his beady eyes roamed her nakedness. "Perfect," he croaked. "Just as I knew she would be."

Franklin reached out and cupped her breast. His painful squeeze made her gasp. He then took his knife and moved down, cutting the thin rope that tied her ankles together. Once free, she immediately kicked out at him. She managed to land a blow to his arm and the knife skittered out of his hand. He cursed and grasped her flailing legs, forcing them apart before he lunged on top of her.

His weight forced the breath from her. He didn't try to kiss her. He didn't try to fondle her breasts or behave in any way as if there were emotions tied to his desires other than a lust to demean her, to rape her and exercise his power over her. He lifted his weight only long enough to shove her gown up around her waist; then he tore at the tapes of her drawers. Her arms ached with his added weight pressing her down against them. The pain became less important when he managed to get her tapes free and tried to pull her drawers down her hips. She bucked against him.

"Be still, damn you!" he shouted down at her.

"Hit her," Penmore encouraged from his position above them. "Punish her like all good little society whores deserve to be punished."

Franklin drew back his fists. She squeezed her eyes closed.

"Hit her and I'll only make you suffer more before I kill you."

Rosalind felt Franklin freeze. She opened her eyes to see Penmore also standing above them as if frozen in place. Her heart lurched inside of her chest. Armond had come. Armond would save her. She nearly fainted with the relief of hearing his voice.

"Get off of my wife, Chapman," Armond ordered. "I'd hate for the pistol I have aimed at your head to go off and splatter blood all over her."

Franklin eased his weight off of her.

"Penmore, you and Chapman move over there to the corner and stand still," Armond instructed.

"There's a knife somewhere on the floor," Rosalind warned her husband. "I kicked it out of Franklin's hand."

"And I'm sure either one or both of you have a pistol concealed on your person somewhere," Armond drawled. "Open your coats."

Both men did as instructed. Penmore had a pistol. Her husband ordered him to remove it from his waistband and lay it on the floor, then kick it toward Armond. He soon had the weapon; then Armond walked over, never taking his pistol off the two men, and bent to the floor. He came up with the knife. Only then did he glance at Rosalind. Rage flared in his eyes when he saw her lying on the floor, her breasts exposed and her gown up around her waist.

He moved beside her and bent, his gaze still trained on the two men in the corner. Armond flipped her gown down over her knees. He laid the knife beside her, then carefully removed his coat, draping it against her nakedness before he pulled her up to a sitting position.

"How did you find me?" she wondered.

"I bought this house today. It wasn't so difficult to convince the broker to tell me what property Penmore was most recently interested in. It took buying the house for two times what it was worth."

Franklin glanced accusingly at Penmore, obviously for

not foreseeing this possible development, then took a brave step toward them. Armond lifted his pistol.

"I'd love for either of you to try something while I cut the rope off of my wife's wrists," he said. "It's all I can do to keep from killing you now, but I won't force Rosalind to witness your deaths."

"Allow me to fetch a constable, Armond," Rosalind said. "I won't have their blood on your hands."

He gazed into her eyes for a moment, and she noticed the sweat on his brow, noticed also that the hand he used to cut the ropes wound around her wrists trembled. He looked ill.

"I could allow you to do that," he agreed before he turned his gaze back on Franklin and Penmore. "Your mother is feeling much better, Chapman. Rosalind realized that you were drugging her and has had the housekeeper stop her rations of tea. She told me that you had my wife."

Rosalind felt a moment of deep satisfaction when Franklin's face paled and his jaw muscle began to jump inside his cheek.

"Franklin told me about Bess O'Conner," Rosalind said to Armond, feeling the blood rush to her hands when he finally got the ropes off of her wrists. She turned her back to the two men while she shrugged into Armond's coat. "He told me about Penmore's involvement, too. They killed Lydia." Her voice broke.

"I want you to get out of here," Armond said. "Take my horse and go."

"To find the authorities?" she wanted to confirm.

"No," he said softly. "Go to your stepmother's home and watch over her. She's there alone. I'll join you shortly."

He was going to kill Franklin and Penmore. He was going to kill them because of her. Could she have their deaths on her conscience? Could she have their blood on her husband's hands? She hated them, Franklin much more so than Penmore. But to kill them . . .

"Armond," she whispered, placing a hand on his arm. "This will follow us the rest of our lives. Let the courts decide their punishment."

"I will decide their punishment!" he snapped at her. He turned to look at her and she gasped. His eyes now held a blue glow. When he had spoken, she saw that his eyeteeth were longer and more pointed.

"Armond," she whispered. "What's wrong with you?"

He suddenly doubled over in pain. He gasped and tried to straighten. He shoved both pistols into her hands, picked up the knife, and flung it across the room.

"Go now!"

Franklin made a move toward them. Rosalind saw him from the corner of her eye and jerked around to face him, both pistols pointed at Penmore and her stepbrother. She knew about pistols because her father had taught her to use them. She cocked first one and then the other. "Stay back," she warned.

"Go, Rosalind!" Armond ordered, but then he doubled over again, obviously in great pain.

"I will not go," she said, her gaze darting back and forth between her husband and the two men who would kill them both if they got a chance. "I will not leave you here while you're ill!"

He gasped in pain, but he managed to glance up at her. For a moment his eyes cleared. "I love you, Rosalind. I always have. The curse has found me now. Please go."

Chapter Thirty-One

Tears burned her eyes, but she blinked them back in order to keep Franklin and Penmore in her line of vision. The curse? She remembered the few lines she'd read of the poem. Something about the moon transforming him, and a beast. Did she believe in such things?

Rosalind felt as if they were both too vulnerable, she sitting on the mattress and Armond hunkered down close to the floor. She scooted off the mattress and stood, her pistols still trained on Penmore and Franklin, who both watched her husband like vultures waiting to pounce upon a dying animal.

Suddenly Armond's body convulsed. He moaned, closed his eyes, and began ripping at his clothing. Only then did she see his hands—see that his fingernails now jutted from his fingertips like claws. She gasped and moved to the corner but still held the pistols trained on her would-be killers.

"What the hell is happening to him?" Penmore asked.

Franklin was obviously too stunned to answer. Rosalind watched in horror as something took hold of her husband. He writhed upon the floor. His body seemed to change shape. His hair grew longer before her very eyes—grew until it covered his body. He had gone to the floor a man, but when he rose on all fours, he was a wolf.

A wolf with glowing blue eyes and long fangs that it displayed by growling at Franklin and Penmore.

"Shoot it, Rosalind!" Franklin yelled.

The pistol in one hand swung toward the growling beast. The wolf stopped long enough to swing its head toward her. She stared deep into the wolf's eyes, and somewhere in the body of the beast she knew that Armond still lived. Trapped. Cursed. Good Lord, she feared she might faint. But she couldn't faint. She swung the pistol back toward Franklin.

"No," she whispered. "I won't kill him."

Penmore made a run for the doorway. The beast leaped, pouncing upon him. His screams echoed in the empty house. Franklin was suddenly upon Rosalind, trying to wrestle one of the pistols from her hand. She knew if he managed, he'd shoot the wolf, kill it, and Armond along with it. Her strength surprised her. Adrenaline raced through her and she tried to bring the other pistol around and shoot Franklin. He knocked the pistol from her hand, she feared breaking her wrist in the process. She moaned with the pain but kicked out at him.

He slapped her and knocked her back against the wall. The other pistol fell from her hand. Franklin started to bend to get it, but suddenly the wolf was there, growling low in its throat, the iridescent blue of its eyes focused upon Franklin.

Instead of reaching for the pistol, Franklin reached for Rosalind and pulled her in front of him. She came face-to-face with the beast. The growling immediately stopped. She stared into the wolf's eyes. "Armond," she whispered. "Don't kill me."

Her gaze was drawn to Penmore, struggling to crawl along the floor. The man had his hand clutched to his throat; blood gushed from a wound there. Bile rose in her

throat, and her gaze returned to the wolf. It looked past
her at Franklin, curling back its lips to expose its deadly
fangs.

Franklin used Rosalind as a shield, keeping her between himself and the beast as he inched their way toward
the doorway leading out of the room. The wolf growled
low in its throat, following but not attacking. The animal
would have to get past Rosalind to reach Franklin, and as
terrified as she was, she realized it was not going to attack
her. Penmore made strangling sounds and tried to crawl
toward them.

"Don't leave me here," he said, his voice merely a gur-
gling noise.

Once Penmore had drawn the wolf's attention again,
the animal pounced upon the man. Franklin used Penmore's demise to his own advantage and quickly pulled
Rosalind through the doorway, shoving her away and
pulling the door closed before the wolf could react. She
heard the loud thud of the animal hurling itself against
the door.

Franklin turned, grabbed her arm, and pulled her with
him through the house. The front door stood open and they
were suddenly outside, headed toward the phaeton he'd
left at the side of the house. Another buggy sat there as
well. Penmore's, she was guessing, and one of Armond's
horses, his reins dragging on the ground.

Franklin steered her to the buggy and pulled her up
and inside. He took the reins and slapped them against the
horses' rumps and the animals took off. They were careening down a deserted street when it occurred to Rosalind that she had gone with a man who planned to
murder her tonight. She was in shock, she realized. The
buggy was moving too fast for her to jump. Although she
supposed if she was going to end up dead, better at her

own hands than Franklin's. She had mentally prepared herself to make the jump, but she physically hesitated, which cost her.

As if her stepbrother knew her intentions, he struck out and knocked her silly. She swayed, thought she might plummet over the side of the phaeton to her death after all, before she lost consciousness.

When she awoke, Rosalind was lying in a bed, in a room she recognized. The one in Franklin's home. She struggled up, wincing with both the pain in her wrist and the pain in her face where Franklin had struck her, not once but several times, since he'd tricked her into visiting the duchess. The reason for Rosalind's pain sat in a chair before the cold hearth, staring at her.

"What in the hell did you marry?" he asked. "A monster?"

Her mind would just as soon dismiss all that she had seen earlier. Whatever Armond was, and she wasn't certain even herself, he was not as much of a monster as the man who sat across from her. Armond had known her, had not attacked her, had tried to protect her, even when the beast took him.

"It's his curse," she suddenly understood. The one he had tried to keep secret from her. The one his forefather had written about in a poem. She wished she had taken the time to read the entire poem. She had no idea what she was dealing with, what Armond was dealing with.

"I thought he was cursed with insanity. What I saw was impossible," Franklin said, and she noticed that the strain of what he had witnessed had managed to penetrate even his evil soul. His hands visibly shook when he ran them through his hair. "If anyone knew the truth, they would hunt him down like the animal he is and kill him," he further deliberated. "This will all work to my advantage."

It hadn't taken her stepbrother long to return his attention to his greatest concern . . . himself. "How do you plan to turn this to your advantage, Franklin?" she snapped. "You are a murderer. I can attest to that. Your mother can, as well."

He waved a hand. "Neither of you is of consequence. I've already forced her to drink more tea. She's asleep now. When Mary arrived earlier, I sent her away. There is only the problem of you left for me to deal with, Rosalind."

Rosalind wondered if Franklin had realized the tea in the tin was no longer his special blend. She glanced toward her balcony windows, surprised to see that dawn streaked the sky. She must have been unconscious for hours.

"I'm quite certain Penmore is no longer among the living," Franklin said. "His body will be found in a house owned by none other than your husband. Lord Wulf is now an animal. He will stay that way, won't he?"

Oh God, she hadn't thought of that. Would he? But no, his ancestor who had written the poem had been cursed. An animal couldn't write a poem. Armond's father had also been cursed. He'd killed himself. An animal couldn't put a pistol to its head and pull the trigger. She had no idea what Armond might be at this very moment. A man or still a wolf.

She did know with certainty that, if he possibly could, he would come for her in either form. But how to stay alive until he did?

"No one knew you had any affiliation with Penmore other than a shared love of gaming," she said. "But if you kill me and your mother, suspicion will naturally turn to you."

"My mother will continue to linger at death's door for a while longer," he said. He turned his cold eyes upon her.

"But if you are found dead, and Penmore's body is discovered in a house recently purchased by your husband, all will assume you have simply become two more of Wulf's victims."

And Franklin would get away with murder. She needed to buy herself time. "What makes you think I want to stay with a man . . . with a man who is no longer a man?" she asked, so many emotions churning inside of her. Fear, shock, and, worse, worry over Armond and what had become of him, what would become of him in the future. "Perhaps we can make an arrangement."

Franklin lifted a brow. "Good try, Rosalind," he said. "You wouldn't shoot it, even though your own life might have been in danger. You're in love with a monster."

She thought about what Franklin said. Her emotions were raw, scraped and bruised like her face. She had to look deep into her heart; she had to judge Armond on what she knew of him before last night. He hadn't told her the truth, but would she have believed him unless she'd seen what he'd become with her own eyes? He had protected her, taken care of her, made love to her. He had vowed to never love her, but in her heart, she'd known he had, and last night he had told her. He'd done what needed to be done when Franklin and Penmore had threatened her life, first in the form of a man and then in the form of a wolf.

"He may be a monster," she admitted. "But not nearly as much of one as you are."

"It didn't have to end this way." Franklin stood and approached the bed upon which she sat. "You should have never left me, Rosalind. At least beneath my roof, you could have lived."

She met his gaze straight on. "I don't consider being under your thumb, being abused and used for whatever benefit you might think to be gained on my behalf, living."

He smiled a bit sadly at her. "Then you won't mind dying so much."

He came awake naked and shivering, lying next to a dead man. Armond rolled away from Penmore, sickened by the man's sightless eyes and the gaping wound at his throat. He glanced around the empty room where the candles had burned down to melted wax and a dirty mattress and a blanket lay on the floor. Then he remembered. Rosalind. Chapman. And the curse that had come upon him while he was trying to rescue his wife from being murdered.

Armond snatched the blanket off the mattress and wrapped it around his shivering body. Worry twisted his gut and added to the sick feeling churning his stomach. He glanced toward the closed door. What would he find on the other side? He was afraid to look. He couldn't remember what had happened once the curse had transformed him. Had Rosalind died of shock alone at seeing him become a monster?

The door had deep scratches in the wood, and he glanced at his hands. His fingertips were bloody, his short nails torn and jagged. He did remember the last thing he had said to Rosalind. He had told her he loved her, but then had he killed her? Slowly, he rose and approached the closed door.

He swung it open and looked down the short hallway to the front door that stood open. The morning light tried to penetrate the dark shadows in the house. A glance outside showed a buggy and horse alongside of the house, and his horse still stood, head bent, reins dragging the ground. The phaeton that had been there when he'd ridden up last night was missing.

Franklin had escaped . . . and Armond had a feeling, a very strong feeling, that he'd taken Rosalind along with him. She was in danger, if Chapman hadn't already killed her, but no, Armond couldn't accept that. She must be alive; he wouldn't allow her to be dead. And he must save her, even though all he wanted to do at the moment was slink away and hide from the world. To drown in the self-pity that threatened to overwhelm him. But he could not. Not yet. Rosalind needed him.

He turned and walked back down the hallway and entered the room where Penmore's body lay. Armond's clothes were shredded on the floor. He had no choice but to strip Penmore of his bloody clothing. Armond did so quickly, trying not to look at the man. He wouldn't feel guilty. One animal killing another. It was only natural. Penmore's trousers were too large and too short, but he made a quick makeshift belt out of the ropes that had tied Rosalind's ankles and hands. He stripped Penmore of his coat, not bothering to remove the man's bloody shirt. Armond pulled on his boots, then rolled Penmore up in the blanket. He hefted the man's deadweight over his shoulder, carried him outside, threw the body in his buggy, and approached the man's horses, luckily not the grays he had sold him, but a set of not nearly as nice blacks.

The horses snorted and startled at his approach. Even his own horse, the fine chestnut he'd taken because it was the fastest, shied away. Armond's scent was different now, he realized. The horses were frightened of him. And Rosalind—when he found her and rescued her, would she fear him now as well? He couldn't think about that. He could only think about finding her, making certain that she was safe.

Chapman would have taken her to his home, Armond suspected. The man would have probably been as scattered and shocked as Rosalind and Penmore had been to see him turn into a beast. Franklin wouldn't have been thinking clearly enough to take Rosalind anywhere else.

Armond shied the buggy horses and they took off down the street, carrying the dead body of their owner, he hoped back to Penmore's home, where the horses would automatically try to return. He approached the frightened chestnut, using soothing tones so that the animal would recognize him. He held out his hand and the chestnut sniffed him. The horse was still skittish, but Armond didn't have time to calm him further.

Armond jumped upon the chestnut's back; then they were racing through the streets. He had to get to Rosalind. It was the only thought he allowed himself. That thought and a prayer that when he did find her, it wouldn't be too late.

Chapter Thirty-Two

"I won't go quietly," Rosalind assured Franklin. "I will not cower from the pain of your fists, or give you the power of my fear. You will get no satisfaction from killing me, Franklin. I won't allow it."

His smile faded. "Brave words for a woman," he sneered. "I'll see how brave you are when I throw you down upon that bed and take you."

Brave words indeed. The thought of Franklin defiling her sent repulsion flooding through her. Despite the reaction, she raised her chin. "I have been loved and given love to a man of my choosing, a man who has won my heart. Nothing you can do to me will foul the memory of what we shared together."

Her stepbrother's face turned an angry shade of red. How frustrating his life must have become since she'd married Armond. To have her so close but beyond his cruel reach. She would pay the price for his pent-up rage. Of that she had little doubt. Rosalind steeled herself for the pain to come. For the humiliation he would force her to experience. She would search the deepest core of her strength and regain the pride in herself he had once stolen from her. Pride that Armond had given back to her.

She steadied her gaze upon Franklin as he approached her. She curled her fingers in claws, hoping her nails would rake and tear, wishing, in that instant, that she had been cursed as Armond had been cursed. For his curse had been a gift last night. A gift that had saved her from being defiled by two men, instead of only one.

"You will not touch her, Franklin."

The command surprised her. Surprised Franklin as well. He wheeled around. The duchess stood in the doorway, allowing the frame to support her frail body.

"You should not be here," Franklin growled.

His mother seemed to will herself to stand straighter. "I should have been able to come to Rosalind's aid sooner," she argued, her voice still raspy. "For months you have keep me a prisoner of the addiction you forced upon me. I knew she was here. I knew when she visited me that her heart was heavy, that you were cruel to her, but I could not escape the bonds of my addiction to help her, to even tell her that I understood her suffering."

Rosalind's eyes watered. She had hoped that her stepmother realized she was with her and that she cared deeply for the lady. How awful for her to have been trapped in her unresponsive body while her mind was still able to understand the injustices taking place around her. The injustices even being done to her by her own son.

"I should have killed you long ago, Mother," Franklin said. "Stilled your voice of goodness and responsibility so that I wouldn't have to listen to you ever again. You are weak. Just as you would not stand up to my father when he beat you, even when he beat me, you will not stand up to me today. Go back to your room. I'll deal with you later."

"No," the duchess said, and her voice sounded stronger. "Not this time, Franklin. I thought I could help you, but you are beyond help. You are your father's son, and all you hated about him you now possess within you. Rosalind has always been a dear child. The innocent one in all the darkness we have brought to her life. I could not save you, but I will save her."

So saying, the lady lifted a pistol. Where the duchess had gotten the weapon Rosalind didn't know, nor did she care. Relief flowed over her. Rosalind was just about to rise from the bed and go to her stepmother when Franklin struck. He moved with lightning speed, was upon his mother before she could cock the pistol and fire it. He knocked her to the floor. Rosalind screamed and lunged from the bed. She jumped on Franklin's back, pelting him with her fists to keep him from further injuring his mother.

With a roar of outrage from being threatened by two women, Franklin reached behind him, managed to get a grasp on Rosalind's hair, and pulled her off of him. She landed hard against the floor, her scalp stinging from where Franklin had yanked at her hair. Suddenly he loomed over her and the rage in his eyes told her he would not defile her. He was past the patience of prolonging her death. He bent and put his hands around her neck, closing off her air.

Rosalind clawed at his hands. She gasped, but no air would fill her lungs. The sound of breaking glass turned Franklin's head toward her balcony doors. He loosened his grip, and Rosalind gulped in deep gasps of air. Through her watering eyes she saw a man rise from the floor. A tall man, his blond hair wild around his shoulders. He wore an open coat that was too small for him, his broad chest bare beneath. He looked like a pirate. He looked half-crazed, and she was never happier to see him in her life.

"Wulf," Franklin breathed. He scrambled up off of Rosalind, facing Armond.

"I told you if you ever touched her again, I would kill you," Armond said. "Consider yourself dead."

"Y-you were a wolf," Franklin stammered. "I saw it with my own eyes."

"And now I am a man." Armond stalked toward her stepbrother. "A man who is going to make certain you never threaten Rosalind again."

Franklin tried to run. Armond was on him in a heartbeat. Her husband might be a man this morning rather than a beast, but he showed no mercy. He punched Franklin so hard the man crumpled to the ground; then Armond reached down, hauled him up, and hit him again. Rosalind had no doubts as to Franklin's fate. She scrambled on her hands and knees toward the duchess, who still lay upon the floor.

"Your Grace," she sobbed, cradling her stepmother's head in her lap. "Are you all right?"

The lady opened her eyes. "Forgive me, Rosalind," she begged. "Forgive me for being the instrument Franklin used to trap you in this house. My heart broke when I left your father, and when I left you. I still foolishly believed I could help my son—that I could shape his character—but it was twisted long ago by violence."

"Shush," Rosalind whispered. "You mustn't blame yourself. You were kind to me once, loving and, for as long as I had you, the mother I had longed for all of my life. I would never hold you to blame for Franklin's cruelty toward me. I will take you away from this house."

The lady closed her eyes as if in pain. She gripped Rosalind's hand. "My time is over. Your time has just begun."

Tears ran down Rosalind's cheeks. She feared the duchess was dying. Judging from the sounds of Armond's fists smashing into Franklin, he would soon be dead as well. She had to get her stepmother help.

"Armond! We must fetch a doctor for Her Grace!"

Her husband seemed oblivious to her pleas, so focused

he was on killing Franklin, on beating him to death. Her stepbrother looked unconscious. Rosalind rose from the floor and ran to Armond. She grabbed the fist he pulled back to deliver another blow.

"Armond!" she shouted to penetrate the fog of rage obviously clouding his brain. "My stepmother! She's dying. We must get her help!"

For a moment, Armond merely looked at Rosalind, as if his focus could not shift long enough for him to understand what she said to him. Finally, his fist fell to his side. He let Franklin slide to the floor. She pulled Armond to where the lady lay. He bent before her, Rosalind alongside him.

"Franklin dealt her a deadly blow," she explained to her husband. "I fear she will not survive it."

"Your Grace?" Armond asked gently. "Can you hear me? You must stay with us."

The woman opened her eyes again and looked at Armond. "I know you," she whispered. "You're from next door. I've heard things about you, but if Rosalind loves you, you must have a good heart. Take care of her."

"No!" Rosalind's voice broke. "Don't leave me, Your Grace! Everyone I have ever loved has left me."

"You must both go." Her stepmother suddenly struggled with a frail attempt to rouse herself. "I didn't want this business to follow Rosalind. I've set the upstairs on fire."

Rosalind had been too involved with what was taking place to notice the smell of smoke. She noticed it now. "We must get her out," she said frantically to Armond.

He nodded and quickly moved around to lift the duchess's shoulders. Rosalind wondered why the lady stared past her. Why her eyes suddenly widened. She turned to see Franklin, bloody and beaten, looming over her, the poker from her hearth raised above her back.

"No!" Armond shouted, but before he could release the duchess and lunge at the man, a shot rang out. A small hole appeared in Franklin's forehead; then he fell backward. Rosalind jerked her head around to look at Armond. He didn't hold the pistol. The duchess had managed to lift it and kill her son. Pain flashed across her face; then her eyes focused upon Rosalind, and she saw the light of life fading from them.

"Be happy," she whispered before she went limp in Armond's arms, her eyes sightlessly staring ahead.

"Your Grace!" Rosalind covered her face with her hands. She felt Armond's hands on her shoulders a second later.

"She's gone, Rosalind. We have to get out. Now!"

The smoke began to choke her. She coughed. The next thing she knew, Armond gathered her in his arms and he was racing down the hallway toward the stairs leading down to the first-floor landing. She clung to him, her lungs stinging as smoke started to drift down to the first floor. He set her down in front of the door, hurrying with the locks. He flung the door wide, took her hand, and pulled her outside. He picked her up in his arms and raced across the lawn.

At the stable, he paused to shout for his grooms to gather the horses and move them. He carried her up the rocky path and cursed when Hawkins didn't get the door, having to put her down in order to do the task himself. Rosalind rushed in ahead of him.

"Hawkins!" Armond shouted.

The man came running.

"The house next door is ablaze. Keep your eyes peeled. The fire may spread."

"Very well, my lord," Hawkins said, then hurried outside.

Taking her hand, Armond led Rosalind upstairs. Once

in his room, he began stripping off his ill-fitting clothes. Rosalind realized why. They were Penmore's clothes. Once Armond had stripped and thrown the clothes in a pile, he said, "Burn them, Rosalind."

He started dragging clothes from his wardrobe. Rosalind realized she was still in shock, for she could do nothing but stand and watch him as he hurriedly dressed.

"I'll have my coachman take you to the dowager's," he said, pulling a shirt over his head. "You are to tell everyone that once I saw you to safety, I went back, hoping to rescue your stepbrother and your stepmother. You never saw me again, understand?"

She blinked at him. "What? No, I do not understand."

He wouldn't come close to her. "It is best this way, Rosalind. Now you know why I could not love you, why I could not give you children. The curse is passed from seed to seed. I would not bring that upon my sons. I would not bring that upon you."

With all that happened, all she'd been forced to witness and forced to endure, she still did not understand what he was saying to her. Then suddenly she did understand. "You are leaving me."

"I am sparing you," he corrected. "Gather what you need to take with you to the dowager's home. I have provided for you, Rosalind. You are free now. Penmore and Chapman can never threaten you again. You can have a life."

"But not one with you," she further understood.

He glanced away from her. She thought for a moment that she saw the moisture of tears in his eyes. "No. Not with me. Good-bye, Rosalind. Remember me as a man, and not the monster I have become."

He turned away from her and left the room. Rosalind stood frozen. She had yet to fathom all that had happened since last night. Her mind had yet to accept things she'd seen, the terror of being at Penmore's and Franklin's mercy, what had happened to Armond when he'd come to save her, the death of her stepmother. Still, there was one thing that Rosalind knew for certain. It could not end this way. She raced out of Armond's room to the top of the stairs.

"Armond!" she shouted, her voice raw with emotion.

He was gone.

Chapter Thirty-Three

"I am sorry, Rosalind, my dear," the dowager said, patting her hand. "I met the duchess on several occasions years ago, and I quite liked her."

Rosalind took a sip of tea the dowager had ordered prepared as soon as she'd arrived. "She was a lovely lady," she responded as if automatically. Her emotions had gone from being raw to being numb.

"Your stepbrother, now I didn't know him well," the dowager said cautiously.

"I do not grieve for him." Rosalind took another sip of tea, grateful for the warmth spreading down her throat and into her stomach. "We shall not talk of him."

A moment of silence followed. "Where is Armond, Rosalind?" the dowager asked. "Taking care of matters for you?"

She glanced down into her teacup, as if a suitable answer would appear there. "He says I am to tell everyone that he is dead."

The dowager's cup rattled against her saucer when she set it aside. "What is going on, Rosalind?"

Slowly, Rosalind lifted her gaze. "Armond is . . . he is not himself."

"Oh dear," the dowager said softly. "So it has happened. Just as he feared it would."

Still cautious in what she said, Rosalind asked, "You know about him? About his family?"

The woman nodded her balding head. "Only what his mother told me in those dark days as she wasted away. A shocking tale. One would have had to believe her mad to say such things."

"Only you knew that she wasn't mad," Rosalind said. "Did she still love her husband?"

"Do you mean after the curse took him, or after he killed himself because of it?"

"After it took him," Rosalind specified.

The dowager's sad smile touched Rosalind. "Oh yes. But he didn't give her time to tell him that it made no difference to her. He assumed the worst. And I think he feared that he might hurt her, and his children. He chose the simplest solution to his problem, as men often do."

As Armond had obviously done as well. Rosalind had learned something during the past few months in London. Life was not so simple, and neither, it seemed, was love. She hadn't had time to fully absorb what had happened to Armond, and if it had changed her feelings toward him. It seemed ludicrous that it would not, and yet her heart ached far more than her bruised body. Her heart ached for Armond and the future that fate kept stealing away from them.

"You look ragged, dear," the dowager said. "And bruised. And you smell of smoke. Allow me to have a nice bath prepared for you; then you must rest. I've had a guest room prepared for you."

"I am tired," Rosalind admitted. "And I appreciate your hospitality, Your Grace."

"Armond was right to send you to me. Come along, dear."

Rosalind set her teacup aside and rose. She wearily followed the dowager to a room upstairs. The bed beckoned her, but she waited patiently while the dowager sent her servants scurrying to prepare Rosalind's bath and make her as comfortable as possible. A young maid attended her. It had been a long time, it seemed, since Rosalind had the luxury. Not since poor Lydia had died or, rather, been murdered by Rosalind's stepbrother.

She allowed herself to be pampered, to be undressed and helped into her bath. She'd changed her ruined gown and underclothes before she'd allowed Armond's coach to deliver her to the dowager. Now Rosalind stepped into a tub of soothing hot water and let the maid wash her from head to toe. Afterward, Rosalind climbed between the cool sheets of the bed. Exhaustion quickly claimed her.

She slept soundly as afternoon faded into evening. When she woke, she thought of Armond. What was he thinking? What was he doing? What should she think and do? Should she do as he had asked and tell everyone he had perished in the fire? Even though she knew it would be best if she could lie, at least best for her, Rosalind didn't know if she could forever sever the tie between her and Armond Wulf.

She had to see him again. If she saw him, her heart would speak for her. She had told her stepmother that everyone Rosalind loved left her. Now her husband wanted to leave her. Could she allow him to turn his back on her and the love he claimed to hold in his heart for her? Could she turn her back on him? Even with him cursed, could she walk away and never look back?

These were all questions she must answer. Questions Armond must answer as well. Rosalind rose and found her clothing laid out neatly at the end of the bed. She dressed quickly, then went downstairs to thank the dowager for her hospitality and ask for the use of her carriage.

"I forgot to tell you," the dowager said as she walked her

out. "Yesterday when you missed your fitting appointment, I went ahead and chose a few styles and fabrics for you. I am a good guess at sizes and I hope you don't mind, but I thought you needed some things right away. They should be delivered in the next few days and I'll have them sent over to you as soon as possible."

Nice gowns seemed less important to Rosalind now. She'd only wanted to look good for Armond. "Thank you, ma'am."

"Are you sure you won't stay a while longer, maybe even just for the night?"

Rosalind shook her head. "I feel as if I should be home."

The dowager touched Rosalind's arm. Her brow creased. "Are you certain you'll be safe there, Rosalind?"

Her first instinct was to say no, she wasn't certain, but deep in her heart, Rosalind knew that Armond, regardless of who or what he was, would never hurt her. "I'll be fine," she tried to assure the dowager. "I'll call on you soon."

Rosalind's trepidation grew as the carriage drove her through the London streets toward home. Night had almost fallen. Would Armond become the beast again tonight? Would he become one every night now? She needed to ask him about the curse. She needed to read the poem.

The house her father had bought for her stepmother now lay in ruin. Smoke still rose from the black ash that covered the ground. Rosalind noted that the fire had not seemed to spread. Armond's stable looked untouched, as well as the home they shared or, at least, had once shared.

Hawkins held the door for her as she walked toward the house. His stiff presence was a comfort to her. "Is Lord Wulf at home?"

"He's been upstairs since you left earlier," Hawkins informed her. "He said he was not to be disturbed for the remainder of the evening. I was told to take myself off for the night. . . . Should I change my plans, Lady Wulf?"

"That won't be necessary, Hawkins," she said. "I am not to be disturbed, either."

"Very well then, my lady. I've left a cold supper out should either of you decide you are hungry."

"Thank you, Hawkins. Good night," she called as he moved up the stairs.

Armond's door was locked. Both of them, she soon discovered. Rosalind walked to her night table. The poem still lay there on top of the book she'd taken from Armond's room. She lifted it and read:

> *Damn the witch who cursed me.*
> *I thought her heart was pure.*
> *Alas, no woman understands duty,*
> *be it to family, name, or war.*
> *I found no way to break it,*
> *no potion, chant, or deed.*
> *From the day she cast the spell,*
> *it will pass from seed to seed.*
>
> *Betrayed by love, my own false tongue,*
> *she bade the moon transform me.*
> *The family name, once my pride,*
> *becomes the beast that haunts me.*
> *And in the witch's passing hour*
> *she called me to her side.*
> *Forgiveness lost, of mercy none,*
> *she spoke before she died:*
>
> *"Seek you and find your worst enemy,*
> *stand brave and do not flee.*
> *Love is the curse that binds you,*
> *but 'tis also the key to set you free."*

> *Her curse and riddle my bane,*
> *this witch I loved yet could not wed.*
> *Battles I have fought and won,*
> *and still defeat I leave in my stead.*
> *To the Wulfs who suffer my sins,*
> *the sons who are neither man nor beast,*
> *solve the conundrum I could not*
> *and be from this curse released.*

Rosalind blinked at the last line. Be from this curse released? Then there was hope? Why had Armond not told her that he could break the curse? That all was not dark and doom, as he would lead her to believe? She would ask him, Rosalind decided.

She turned toward the door that separated them, surprised to see him standing in the doorway, watching her.

"You should have stayed with the dowager," he said. "It's almost dark. You won't be safe with me."

"Why didn't you tell me that the curse could be broken?" she demanded, ignoring his warning.

"Because we haven't exactly figured how to break it."

Rosalind walked toward him, the poem in hand. "The poem points the way. It says to seek you your worst enemy, be brave and do not flee."

He ran a hand through his disheveled hair. "I have sought my worst enemy. I have faced Penmore and Chapman, and I did not flee. Anyone who hurts you is my worst enemy, Rosalind."

"But that was last night that you faced them. Maybe tonight it won't happen again."

He stared down at her, his expression stern. "I don't want you in the house," he said. "I don't want you anywhere near me."

His words hurt her, because she feared he might mean them for more than tonight. She feared that he might mean them for forever. "Why won't you fight?" she asked. "Why won't you fight for us?"

Suddenly he grabbed her shoulders, pulling her close to him. "Breaking the curse cannot be that simple. Did you read all of it? Did you read the part where he says: 'Battles I have fought and won, / and still defeat I leave in my stead'? If that does not sway you, look at me. Look very closely, Rosalind."

She stared up at him. His teeth were longer. She glanced at the hands he had pressed to her shoulders. His nails were clawlike. "No," she whispered, her heart breaking.

"Yes," he hissed. "It begins to take me even now. You are not safe with me. I would rather take my own life than ever hurt you. I know now why my father made his decision."

"He gave your mother no choice," she said. "Just as you want to take my choice from me. You say your worst enemy is whoever would hurt me, Armond. Then you are my worst enemy. Your willingness to forsake the love we have for one another hurts me far worse than a man's fist, or his knife, could ever do. If you let your fear defeat you, if you let it rip your life from you and mine along with it, then you are your own worst enemy."

He released her and walked back into his room. "Go now, Rosalind. Return to the dowager's home and stay there until I am able to locate my brothers and tell them what has happened." He turned back to her and his eyes were filled with blue light. "You deserve more than this." He indicated his face with a sweep of his hand.

She gasped slightly and took a step back at the sight of him. Her fear hurt him. She realized her mistake too late. He grasped the door and started to close it on her. Rosalind hurried forward. "What do you fear most, Armond?"

He paused, his eyes glowing brightly in the coming dark. "I fear I will hurt you. I saw what I did to Penmore.

I don't remember what I do when the beast takes me, Rosalind. If he takes my mind, how am I to control him? How will I ever know if I might pounce upon you and rip your throat out?"

"You could have hurt me last night," she told him. She remembered now how Franklin had used her as a shield because the wolf would not attack her. "You would never hurt me, Armond. It doesn't matter what form you take."

"I don't know that!" he thundered at her; then suddenly he gasped and doubled over. He staggered farther into his room and fell to the floor.

Rosalind remembered last night when the pain had come for him. She realized when the pain came, the wolf was not far behind. She had asked him to have faith in himself; now she must find the strength to do the same. She had to trust in Armond when he would not trust in himself. Rosalind took a deep breath, stepped into his room, closed the door, and shut them in together.

Chapter Thirty-Four

The pain stole Armond's breath and fogged his mind. He pulled his knees in toward his chest. Beneath his skin, he felt his bones moving, reshaping themselves. He had assumed that, since he could not escape the room Chapman had closed him in with Penmore, he could not escape his own room with the doors closed. Despite his pain, he managed to pull his shirt over his head; then, with misshapen fingers, he unfastened his trousers and kicked them off.

The pain allowed him little in the way of rational thought, and soon his thoughts would not be his own. Still, for a moment, Rosalind's scent penetrated his tortured senses and he realized she was in the room with him. The thought struck terror in him. It would destroy him to ever hurt her. For years he had guarded his heart, and she had come into his life and stolen it within a bat of a lash the first night he met her at the Greenleys' ball. He loved her more than life itself. He had to fight off the pain and make certain she left . . . while she still could.

He forced his throat to work, the words to leave his mouth, when the pain wanted to demand all of his attention. "Leave me, Rosalind! Escape while you still can!"

From far away, her voice drifted to him. "I trust in you, Armond. I know you will not harm me."

Damn her! The agony of knowing she would stay with him, regardless of what he became, meshed with the joy of knowing her love for him was deep. Once, his life had been a dark, cold place. People had whispered about him and scattered to avoid contact with him. Rosalind had changed everything, and yet she had changed nothing. She couldn't stop the curse that now took him. He couldn't stop it, although he fought it now with all the strength he could muster.

He forced his eyes open, his gaze scanning the room while his body convulsed and contorted in preparation for the change. What he saw was not her but only the outline of her body, the red haze of her blood pumping through her veins. Visions of Penmore's lifeless body flashed through Armond's mind. The gaping wound at the man's throat. He tried to shout at Rosalind to run from him, to save herself, but all that emerged from his throat was a strangled howl of frustration.

She had seen him turn last night, but Rosalind had been in shock and the memory seemed hazy to her. Now the proof of what he was seemed all too real. She couldn't imagine the pain he suffered while his bones shifted and shaped themselves into a form far from human. While hair sprouted from his skin and became fur and his tall frame shortened and shifted into the shape of a wolf. But when it rose on all fours, the man now gone, she couldn't deny that even in this form, Armond was beautiful.

The hair rose on the back of her neck when the beast peeled back its lips and growled at her. She hoped the response was nothing more than the fading remnants of Armond's anger toward her for not fleeing as he'd wanted her to do. Rosalind swallowed down the lump in her throat and stared deep into the glowing eyes of the beast.

Somewhere inside the animal was Armond, and she must remember that.

The door was at her back, her hand behind her on the knob. It took almost more willpower than she possessed to keep from turning the knob and opening the door, slipping into her room, and closing the wolf off from her. That was not her objective. Her objective was to prove to Armond that he would never hurt her. She prayed she wouldn't pay for her own trust in him with her life.

Gradually, the wolf's low growls ceased. The animal simply stared at her. She stared back until the game became tiresome. Even though her heart pounded inside of her chest and a thin sweat had broken out on her brow, she twisted the knob behind her and opened the door leading into her room. Rosalind stepped backward into her room but did not close the door. Slowly, she backed away, putting distance between herself and the wolf. She left the door open. The animal did not venture inside. Instead it stayed in Armond's darkened room, its glowing eyes watching her from a distance.

She tried to do normal things, although she was sane enough to realize her life now was far from normal. Her sampler sat in her sewing basket, and she tried to stitch. Her hands shook so badly, her efforts were futile. Rosalind put the sampler aside and picked up the book on her night table. She tried to read, but her gaze kept straying to the room next door and the glowing eyes watching her.

It would be a long night.

Armond came awake upon his cold floor. He was curled into a ball, his knees against his chest, naked and shivering, just as he had been yesterday morning when he awakened next to Penmore's lifeless body. With sickening clarity, he recalled last night and Rosalind being in his room with him when the change had started to take him.

He was up off of the floor so fast the blood rushed to his head and he staggered.

He glanced around his room but didn't see Rosalind anywhere. Then he noticed that her door was open. He walked into the room, the morning cold causing his body to spasm with chills. Rosalind lay on the bed. His heart slammed against his chest as he approached her. He stared down at her pale beauty, her dark hair spread out against the whiteness of her bed linens. Her lashes fluttered and she opened her eyes.

His knees nearly buckled with relief to see her alive and, as much as he could tell, uninjured. His teeth chattered so badly he couldn't speak. Armond supposed the transition from fur to skin was what had caused the reaction. That and the fact that with Hawkins out last night, no night fires had been lit to warm either Armond's room or Rosalind's. She didn't speak to him, but her actions said more than words ever could. She threw back the covers and welcomed him into her bed.

He went willingly, but only because he needed her warmth to stop his uncontrollable spasms. He needed to be able to yell at her for going against his instructions to leave. She still wore her clothing . . . a wise decision in case she'd decided to flee into the night in order to escape him. Her body heat remained trapped beneath her clothing, and with shaking hands he tried to undress her.

Rosalind seemed to understand what he needed, and brushed his hands aside, quickly rising long enough to strip down to her undergarments and slide back beside him. She pulled him to her and wrapped her arms around him, sharing the warmth of her body. His head rested against the swell of her breasts. She smelled of lavender, and beneath his ear he heard the steady beat of her heart. Gradually, her warmth penetrated his skin. He realized the sacrifice she had made last night for him. She had trusted him with her life. Trusted him when he could not even trust himself.

His heart swelled with love for her, and lower, he responded to her being pressed against him as any warm-blooded man would do. With his head nestled against her breasts, it seemed natural to turn his face and capture her nipple through the thin fabric of her shift. She sucked in her breath sharply, but she did not push him away.

Her nipples were small and rose-colored. They beaded beneath his tongue. Hungry for more, he pulled the fabric of her shift down lower to expose her breasts. He suckled and teased at first one breast and then the other. Rosalind's fingers twisted into his hair and she arched against him, her soft moans of pleasure firing the blood rushing through his veins.

Slowly, he inched his way down her body, pulling her underclothes away as he went. He pressed hot kisses against her stomach; then lower, he inhaled her intoxicating woman's scent. She tried to clamp her knees together against him, but he held them open, bending to taste her, to seek out her most sensitive place and give her pleasure.

Her slight intake of breath turned into a soft moan of pleasure. He stroked her with his tongue, sucked gently upon her sensitive nub, and felt the first tremors of release take her. She called his name, convulsing beneath his mouth until her fingers, still twisted in his hair, pulled him away and up to her waiting lips.

He kissed her while his body invaded hers. She was warm, wet, and tight, and the feel of her wrapped around him was heaven on earth. He thrust slowly inside of her, back and forth until she regained her senses and her body answered the call of his own. In the cold light of dawn, he rolled over and brought her on top of him.

Her lovely eyes rounded with surprise and she gasped at

having him so deeply embedded within her. He showed her how to move, how to ride him, how to bring him pleasure, and how to seek her own. Though he still considered her an innocent, she caught on quickly.

Rosalind felt empowered by her position atop him. He allowed her to set the pace of their lovemaking, to experiment with what movements most stimulated her, and he suffered her inexperience with great patience. She rocked her hips, slowly at first, then faster when she saw the effect she had on him. His eyes flared with heat and his jaw clenched as if he battled to maintain his control.

He let her have her way with him for a time, then his hands settled upon her hips, and he guided her, slowed her so that the pressure she felt building had time to simmer before it became a raging boil. She found release before he did, arching her back as the spasms of deep pleasure washed over her. A moment later he suddenly thrust deep, then lifted her off of him. She collapsed on top of him, felt his pulsing erection against the lower half of her stomach as he spilled his seed harmlessly outside of her womb.

As she lay there, feeling the wild beating of her heart and his, it occurred to her that they had not spoken one word to each other. It also occurred to her that to allow him to make love to her this morning, after a night when she had tested her faith in him and her faith in herself, told her the truth of her heart. She loved him. She would always love him. She would not allow his curse to stand between them, to rob them of the happy future she had once dreamed they might find together. But could she convince him to feel the same?

"That should not have happened."

She sighed and glanced up at him. "Although you are

quite skilled at lovemaking, your choice of words after the deed is done so far leaves much to be desired. Why must you always make me feel as if I am a regret, Armond?"

He lifted a lock of her hair and twisted it around his finger. "Maybe because I am humbled by the force of our lovemaking. Maybe because I feel as if I am unworthy of you, and all the joy you bring me."

"Well, that is better," she admitted. She sobered. "We must talk, Armond."

Using the lock of hair curled around his finger, he drew her face closer to his. "Later," he said, then he kissed her.

Chapter Thirty-Five

Later they did speak. But they spoke of matters that needed attending to rather than of their future together. The house next door had burned to the ground. There were no bodies to lay to rest, but Rosalind wanted a stone erected on her stepmother's behalf.

"You will have one erected for Chapman as well," Armond surprised her by saying. "There is no need for the world to know that he was not a loving son."

Armond's gesture surprised her and made her love him more for the sacrifice he made. He might dispel the rumors about his family being murderers if they both told the inspectors what they knew, but instead, her husband had decided to honor her stepmother's memory.

"You don't have to do that," Rosalind said softly to him.

"When I leave, I don't want more than the stain of being my wife to mar your future, Rosalind."

He might as well have punched her in the stomach. The soft feelings she had for him were quickly replaced by anger. "You make love to me, then tell me you are still planning to abandon me? It is all right if I am your whore, but not all right if I am your wife?"

His intense gaze caught hers as he stared at her across

the table where they were dining on a cold supper. "I told you that was a mistake."

His response only infuriated her more. She rose from the table. "And was it a mistake the second time you made love to me today, or the third?"

Armond glanced away from her and ran a hand through his hair. "I wanted to feel like a man, and only a man."

"*You* wanted?" she echoed, growing more furious by the moment. "What about what I want, Armond? What about our future together? What about the children I want to hold in my arms? What about—"

"What about the curse?" he suddenly shouted. "Dammit, Rosalind, I won't ask you to suffer my sins, or my shame, with me! I love you too much."

Although her heart should soar over his confessions of love, it could not take flight. "If you truly love me, you will understand that nothing could be worse to me than losing you. Didn't I prove to you last night that you would not hurt me, Armond? You cannot hurt me because you share a heart with the beast."

"And you want to share a life with it?" he asked. "You want the curse to rest upon the heads of our sons? How could you want that, when you could have so much more? When you could have a normal man, and a normal life?"

She walked around the table to look down at him. "Is that what you truly want? For me to be with someone else? To give him all that I want to give you? Your father made this mistake with your mother. He did not give her a choice. His decision destroyed her."

"The curse destroyed her," Armond argued. "What she had to witness, what she realized would someday befall her own children. That is what destroyed my mother."

Rosalind shook her head. "No. He broke her heart, just as you want to break mine. He made a decision for both of them. It was the wrong decision. I pray that you don't make the same mistake." Rosalind walked away from him.

"Where are you going?" he called to her back.

Rosalind had said her piece. Armond knew that she loved him, that she loved him in spite of the curse that loving her had brought down upon his handsome head. She could not force him into the light. Her dark one. He had to fight for his own happiness. He had to fight for his future and hers. He had to face his worst enemy. Himself.

"I'll be at the dowager's. She can help me with the arrangements for my stepmother's stone. Now the decision is up to you, Armond. You can leave, slink away in the dark of night, or you can walk in the sunlight, with me by your side. This curse upon you is an inconvenience to be certain, but together, we might find a way to break it. Apart, we can do nothing."

Armond watched her walk away. Letting her go was the most difficult thing he'd ever done in his life. But it was for her that he would sacrifice his own happiness. Two nights of having to suffer the sight of the beast taking him didn't seem perhaps that daunting to her. What about a lifetime of it?

What was he supposed to do? Be selfish? Take what he wanted above all else, and to hell with what that meant for Rosalind? He had sworn to protect her. Didn't that mean to protect her from all that might harm her? A spoken word could rip and tear as easily as a knife. He knew that all too well. To deny her children would hurt her, but wouldn't the hurt be worse for her to bear his sons and know they were damned from birth?

His decision seemed best for her. In time, she would find someone else. Even that thought brought him no peace. He rose from the table and began to pace. He couldn't stand the thought of another man holding her, touching her, making love to her. She was his, dammit! His love. His life. But her happiness smote out his anger. He wanted her to be happy. In order for her to live the life he would wish for her, he must let her go.

"Lord Wulf?" Hawkins stood stiffly in the hallway.

"What is it, Hawkins?"

"Lady Wulf has asked me to have the carriage brought around. She's packing some things—"

"Yes," Armond said in a clipped tone. "She's going to spend time with the dowager."

"And that is all right with you, Lord Wulf?"

Hawkins had been with him for nearly ten years, and the man never made it his business to meddle in Armond's affairs. "Why shouldn't it be all right, Hawkins?" he snapped.

"I simply thought . . . I thought with all the lady has suffered, she would wish to be with you, my lord. The house seems odd without her."

And it would become odder yet. "For the next few nights, I wish to be left alone after supper. You are not to come upstairs . . . regardless of what you might hear."

"Very well, my lord," Hawkins regained his formality. He turned away, paused, then turned back. "You are quite certain you wish to let her go?"

No, he did not wish to let her go. But her going was for the best, for her leastwise. "Yes," he answered quietly.

It was the first time he'd ever seen Hawkins slump. The man walked away.

Armond stayed in the dining room until he heard Rosalind leave. The house was eerily quiet, but then, he supposed it had always been before Rosalind came to live with him. He'd sent a note off to Gabriel to come, but he'd had no answer from him and he had yet to put in an appearance. Armond had sent him after Jackson. If Gabriel had given chase, no telling where that journey might lead him.

Armond hadn't been seen outside of the house since the fire next door. Only Hawkins knew he was home, and Armond supposed when the time came, even Hawkins could be bought off with a nice bundle to see him comfortably into retirement. Then what? Life at the estate, hiding. The thought held little appeal to Armond. Gabriel liked the solitary life of the country, but Armond had always needed to feel life teeming around him, even if he had been more of a bystander than a participant.

Well, he corrected, he'd been a bystander until Rosalind came into his life and forced him to participate. He smiled at the memory of her daring approach the night of the Greenleys' first ball. What if she had never approached him? Would he have noticed her there among the crowd? Would he have lost his heart to her even if she'd never spoken a word to him? Yes, somehow he knew that he would have. Somehow he knew that fate would have brought them together, if not that night, on another.

And now fate had ripped them apart. He walked to a window and looked out upon the side of the house, toward the stable. Rosalind had yet to ride her prized white Arabian. They had yet to picnic in the park or attend a social function as husband and wife. He felt robbed. But then again, he felt blessed in knowing her, in loving her, even for a short time.

She had asked him to walk in the sunshine with her. Could there be sunshine for him? For a man cursed? He had never thought so—had never dared to dream or hope that his life could be any more than what it had been before he met her. And that was what she asked of him. To let go of the bitterness that had kept him a prisoner of his own fears.

He had rescued her from her dark world, and she had rescued him from his. Could he let go? Could he accept the gift she offered him? To love him regardless? To love him unconditionally? These were questions he would ask himself and questions he would try to answer in the next few days, while the moon waxed and he was at the mercy of the beast.

Rumors abounded in London. During her stay with the dowager, Rosalind had learned that Viscount Penmore had been murdered. The man's body had arrived at his home in a buggy pulled by two frightened horses. He had been stripped, his throat cut, and was obviously the victim of thieves. No one made much of a fuss, it seemed, about the viscount's death. He was wealthy, but he was not popular.

The dowager had helped Rosalind to pick out a stone for her stepmother and stepbrother. Knowing what she knew of the duchess's past now, Rosalind instructed the stone to be placed at Montrose beside that of her mother and father. Franklin, she'd decided, could have his stone erected next to the father he hated. The father from whom he had inherited his cruelty.

The packages had arrived bearing her new gowns, even new underwear, capes, mittens; the dowager had evidently spared no expense when it came to spending Armond's funds. The lady had also made a good guess as to Rosalind's size, and a seamstress who arrived with the packages had found only a few alterations necessary.

Now Rosalind stood in one of those very gowns, an apple green muslin frock that fit her perfectly and complemented her complexion. She was enjoying the sunshine in the dowager's garden. The blooms reminded Rosalind of hope. The sight of flowers, delicate but vibrant, lifted her spirits when they threatened to plummet. It had been a week, and she'd not heard a word from Armond.

Nor had she gone out among society. She had asked the dowager to remain silent as to Armond's fate. Rosalind supposed if she must, she would do what he asked and let it be known that he had perished in the fire that had taken the life of her stepmother and Franklin Chapman. Armond's death would mean her freedom from their marriage, but it was freedom she did not wish to have. Her monthly menses were late. She suspected the first night she had made love with Armond had produced results. Regardless of the curse that haunted his family, she could not find it in her heart to be sad that she might carry his child. She would pray for a daughter, but she would love and cherish a son no less.

Stopping to admire a perfect round rose, Rosalind bent to inhale the flower's subtle scent. She felt a presence before she glanced up and scanned the garden. A man stood in the shadows, watching her. The beat of her heart sped a measure. He was tall, and when he stepped from the shadows into the sunlight, sunbeams danced in his blond hair. God, how she had missed him. But Rosalind would not allow her spirits to lift just yet. Why had he come?

As he walked toward her, he still reminded her of a great tawny-colored cat, graceful and dangerous. His stormy blue eyes were locked with hers, and his expression gave nothing away of what he might be thinking. He suddenly stood before her, his intense gaze still locked with hers.

"I've decided to come into the sunshine, Rosalind."

She threw herself into his arms. Tears of happiness streamed down her cheeks and she clung to him, wanting never to be denied again the feel of being in his arms, his scent, the low, rich texture of his voice.

"What changed your mind?" she whispered brokenly.

"What you said to me." He stroked her hair, then pulled her back so that he could look down at her. "You were right, Rosalind. I am my own worst enemy. For years I have guarded my heart and wallowed in my self-pity. I did nothing until I was forced to act. It's no way to live, and it took all that you have taught me to finally see that. My father made the wrong decision. He should have stayed and fought. His surrender to the dark defeated us all before we could grow to understand that staying takes more courage. Your bravery inspires my own, Rosalind. I will not surrender my life to the beast, but I will fully surrender my heart to you."

Her own heart soared. He had saved her, and now she would save him. "Whatever the future brings us, Armond, we will face it together. Two hearts are always stronger than one."

He bent to kiss her. His lips had barely brushed hers when he sucked in his breath and staggered back from her. He went to his knees, clutching his stomach.

"Armond!" Rosalind shouted, rushing to bend beside him. "What is it?"

"I thought it had gone for now," he gasped. "For two nights I have gone to bed a man and arisen a man. But the pain . . ." He paused to gasp. "It is the same."

"How can it be?" Rosalind glanced up at the clear, sunny sky. "It is broad daylight!"

Armond didn't answer. His body contorted. Even so, he tried to rise. Suddenly he flew backward, landing hard against a tall column made of stone that thick ivy grew up and around.

Rosalind blinked in surprise. The last time she'd seen him change, he had not done that. Armond groaned in pain; then his body flew forward, smashing him hard against the brick walkway that wound through the dowager's garden. It was as if some invisible force had taken ahold of Armond and battled against him.

Again Rosalind rushed to his side. He rolled over onto his back, gasping for the wind the fall had knocked from him. As she watched him, feeling helpless, his mouth opened wider, wider, she noted, than was humanly possible. His chest heaved, his body arched, and a bright light spilled from his mouth.

Rosalind screamed and stumbled back from him. The light streaming from his open mouth took form, took shape, though the form was not solid, for Rosalind could see through it. The shape was that of a wolf. It stood on all fours, staring at her. She stared back, mesmerized, hypnotized by its glowing eyes, brighter than the hazy light of its body. Brighter even than the light of day. She did not know why it stood staring at her, but she knew she must somehow banish it from them.

"Begone," she whispered. "Begone from here."

The spirit, for it had to be a spirit, turned its head to look at Armond, who lay frighteningly still on the ground; then it slunk away, through the flowers, the bushes and shrubs, and over the wall that enclosed the dowager's private garden. Rosalind sat shocked for a moment; then she regained her senses and scrambled toward Armond.

"Armond," she cried. She tried to shake him. "Armond!"

He wasn't breathing.

Rosalind pounded upon his chest. "Armond!"

Suddenly he gasped, drew in a long, deep breath of air, and his eyes opened. "What happened?"

She nearly sobbed in relief that he had spoken, that he was breathing. "I don't know," she whispered. "But thank God you are alive."

He reached up and gently touched her cheek. He lay still for a moment; then he said, "It is gone, Rosalind. I don't feel it anymore. All of my life, it has been inside of me, waiting to get out, and now it has."

Tears streaming down her cheeks, she said, "The curse has been broken. You broke it, Armond."

He shook his head. "No. You broke it. My love for you broke it. Love is the curse, but it is also the key. You forced me to face my worst enemy. To put aside my doubts, my fears, my self-pity, for one chance to love, and to be loved."

"I do love you," she whispered.

He pulled her down to finish the kiss they had started earlier.

Epilogue

It was her fist ball as Lady Rosalind Wulf. The dowager's affair was quite grand indeed, and Rosalind knew that she and Armond were only invited because the woman doted upon them. Their presence caused whispers, to be certain, but Rosalind didn't care. There wasn't a man in all of London as handsome as her husband.

"Can you hear what they're saying about us?" she asked Armond. He had told her about the strange gifts he'd had since boyhood.

He paused to listen. Then he smiled at her. "Not a word."

"Perhaps that is just as well," she said. "Besides, I don't care what they are saying. I am the happiest woman alive tonight, and the luckiest."

"You look beautiful," Armond said, staring down into her eyes. "The dowager spent my money well."

He looked beautiful too, although when she'd told him that earlier, he'd said men were not beautiful. He was wrong.

"I'm excited to see Wulfglen," she said. "A nice quiet honeymoon in the country sounds nice."

Armond frowned. "I still have no word from Gabriel, but if he has gone in search of Jackson, I know he'll return to the estate first. It is his one true love."

Speaking of Gabriel made her naturally search the room for Lady Amelia Sinclair. Rosalind spied her friend across the room, standing next to a rather thin, pale young man. As if she felt Rosalind's regard, Amelia glanced in her direction. The pretty blonde blushed, then looked away.

That Amelia would still not publicly acknowledge Rosalind stung, but she refused to let anything spoil her evening. "I want to ride my horse," she said to Armond. "And I want you to ride along beside me. I want to have a picnic."

He smiled. "I would like another picnic as well. In your bed."

Her blood heated with the sensual look he cast her. They spent a good deal of time abed together. She wasn't complaining. Her monthly menses had not visited her. Instinctively, she knew a child grew inside of her. She wasn't ready to tell Armond yet. She wanted to be certain.

"Rosalind?"

She turned, surprised to see Amelia standing before her. The pretty blonde took a deep breath and stepped forward, taking Rosalind's hand in hers. "I am so sorry to hear of your loss. I should have come around to visit you before now, but I have been fraught with the bother of making wedding plans."

Rosalind lifted a brow. "You will marry Lord Collingsworth, then?"

Amelia sighed. "Yes, I will please my parents and society in that, but tonight, I rebel." She turned to Armond. "I once told your wife that if I ever encountered you at another social event, I would ask you to dance."

Armond smiled down at Amelia. "You are brave."

"Yes," she agreed. "The dowager has great faith in me to become the most shocking woman in London. I will not disappoint her."

Reaching for Rosalind's hand, Armond said, "I would

love to dance with you, Lady Amelia, but first, I must dance with my lovely wife."

"Of course," Amelia said. "I shall wait right here for your return."

Rosalind giggled as Armond led her toward the dance floor. He swept her up into the dance, and like the night she met him, it was magic between them. They moved in perfect accord, staring into each other's eyes. She glanced away long enough to see that several young ladies had joined Amelia, and Rosalind had a feeling that her husband would dance more than she did tonight. Society might come around after all.

She glanced back up at Armond and found him staring deep into her eyes. He bent close to her ear and whispered, "Have I told you that I love you today?"